Mere**···** Webber **··**···· Queensland, Australia, but takes regular trips west into the Outback, fossicking for gold or opal. These breaks in the beautiful and sometimes cruel red earth country provide her with an escape from the writing desk and a chance for her mind to roam free—not to mention getting some much needed exercise. They also supply the kernels of so many stories that it's hard for her to stop writing!

Alison Roberts is a New Zealander, currently lucky enough to be living in the south of France. She is also lucky enough to write for the Mills & Boon Medical Romance line. A primary school teacher in a former life, she is now a qualified paramedic. She loves to travel and dance, drink champagne, and spend time with her daughter and her friends.

Bondi Bay Heroes collection

The Shy Nurse's Rebel Doc by Alison Roberts
Finding His Wife, Finding a Son by Marion Lennox
Healed by Her Army Doc by Meredith Webber
Rescued by Her Mr Right by Alison Roberts
All available now

Also by Meredith Webber

The Halliday Family miniseries

A Forever Family for the Army Doc
Engaged to the Doctor Sheikh
A Miracle for the Baby Doctor
From Bachelor to Daddy

Also by Alison Roberts

Sleigh Ride with the Single Dad

Rescued Hearts miniseries

The Doctor's Wife for Keeps
Twin Surprise for the Italian Doc

Discover more at millsandboon.co.uk.

HEALED BY HER ARMY DOC

MEREDITH WEBBER

RESCUED BY HER MR RIGHT

ALISON ROBERTS

MILLS & BOON

First Published in Great Britain 2018
by Mills & Boon, an imprint of HarperCollins*Publishers*
1 London Bridge Street, London, SE1 9GF

Healed by Her Army Doc © 2018 by Meredith Webber

Rescued by Her Mr Right © 2018 by Alison Roberts

ISBN: 978-0-263-93369-7

MIX
Paper from
responsible sources
FSC® C007454

This book is produced from independently certified FSC™ paper
to ensure responsible forest management.
For more information visit www.harpercollins.co.uk/green.

Printed and bound in Spain
by CPI, Barcelona

HEALED BY
HER ARMY DOC

MEREDITH WEBBER

MILLS & BOON

CHAPTER ONE

SHE MIGHT BE Kate's favourite relative and most stalwart support, but Aunt Alice was adept at catching Kate in unguarded moments and tonight was no exception.

'You've only worked a half-shift today, and you're off duty tomorrow, so it couldn't be better, *and* you've got the excuse of that team meeting you had this afternoon,' Alice pointed out.

The team meeting that afternoon was the reason Kate was unguarded, though flummoxed would have been a better word. Arriving late from Theatre, still pulling off her theatre cap and running her fingers through her chaotic, needing-a-cut hair, she'd rushed into the SDR meeting room, and the first person Kate had seen had been Angus.

Not surprising, the seeing part. Men who stood just over six feet tall and had the shoulders that went with the height weren't easy to miss.

But Angus?

Here!

Shock halted her momentarily, then, as her bones had turned to jelly, she'd subsided into the nearest seat, rather wishing her weight would take it straight down through the floor.

Or there'd be an earthquake, tornado, hospital on fire—any distraction...

The worst of it was that whatever had flared between them three years ago on the island was just as electrifyingly alive as it had been back then. She could feel that inexplicable awareness that had rocked both of them arcing across the room between them. Looked up to check she couldn't actually see it in the form of flashing lightning because she'd heard it in the thunder in her veins.

Angus!

'You can tell Harriet what was discussed,' Alice was persisting, bringing Kate out of the horrendous memories of the afternoon meeting of the Specialist Disaster Response team. 'She's really down about missing it, well, not the meeting so much but as being part of the team. She could have gone to the meeting, but I think that Pete was supposed to collect her and, as far as I can make out, he's been conspicuous by his absence lately.'

Not much got past Alice, who, although unconnected to the hospital, was a long-term resident of the apartment block where so many of the staff lived.

In her head Kate acknowledged her great-aunt was right, and not only about Harriet's boyfriend disappearing. Before she'd injured her leg in an accident on a training day for the SDR, Harriet had been an integral and enthusiastic part of the team but after battling operations and infections she must be wondering if she'd ever be able to join it again, while she and Pete had been one of the glamour couples of Bondi Bayside Hospital's social scene.

Not that Kate was part of that scene, but in any hospital there were few secrets.

'Go on,' Alice was saying. 'You've lived here two years, you work at the same hospital, belong to that team together, and you barely know Harriet. You can't shut yourself away for ever—it's just not natural. She probably thinks you're a terrible snob because you're a surgeon and she's only a nurse.'

'Hardly "only" a nurse, Alice,' Kate said. 'She's one of the top nurses in the ICU and that's probably one of the most important jobs in the whole hospital.'

Kate was glad of the conversation—anything to keep her mind off the SDR meeting.

Off Angus!

He *can't* be here!

He is!

She dragged her mind back to the subject of Alice's conversation, to Harriet Collins.

'Intensive Care is high-level nursing. It's just that with work and study and keeping up the level of fitness I need to stay on the team I don't really have time—'

'Tosh!' said Alice. 'You're hiding away from something—from life itself, in fact. I know you needed to grieve for the baby, that's why I asked you to come and live here with me. New hospital, new job, new people—but you should have moved on by now. This self-imposed isolation of yours has gone on long enough. So get over to Harriet's apartment and tell her about the meeting. Find a way to convince her she'll get back on the team before long.'

Knowing it was futile to argue, Kate had a quick shower, washed her hair, pulled on jeans and a light sweatshirt and made her way along the corridor to Harriet's apartment, her feet beating out an accompaniment to the phrase running over and over in her head.

I will not think about Angus, it went. I will *not* think about Angus. I *will* not think about Angus…

Harriet's apartment was at the front of the block so as Harriet opened the door—more than slightly startled—Kate could see straight through the living room to the ocean beyond, painted pale pink and violet as it reflected the colours of the sky at sunset.

'Kate!'

The exclamation told Kate she'd guessed right, although she now substituted 'extremely' for the 'slightly' in the startled stakes.

'I hope I'm not interrupting you but I thought you might like to know what went on at the meeting.'

Harriet stared at her and seeing the blankness in her hazel eyes, and the pale drawn skin beneath the lovely auburn hair, Kate had to set aside her own preoccupation and accept that Alice—as ever—had been right. All was not well with the usually vibrant Harriet.

'So, can I come in?'

Wordlessly, Harriet stepped back and waved her hand towards the living room.

'What a fantastic view! You take in the whole bay. It's unbelievable. You must see the beach and ocean in so many moods. Are you a photographer? You could take a thousand pictures from your balcony with not one of them the same.'

Kate knew she was blethering, but Harriet's silence was unnerving and she'd already been totally unnerved once today.

'Did Alice send you to cheer me up?'

Not exactly the conversation opener Kate had expected but it would do.

'Yes, she did. She's worried about you. We're all worried about you.'

Deep breath!

'Actually, to be honest, she's worried about me too. She thinks I work too hard, but the SDR meeting *was* interesting. Blake had brought along an army bloke who has been working on a new emergency response tent. You know, one of those ones that fold up and can be dropped into disaster zones and comes complete with all our medical needs. Apparently, he has a new prototype he wants to trial next time we have a callout to somewhere fairly isolated.'

'Not close to a local hospital or, say, in a bushfire where the hospital's been damaged or destroyed,' Harriet said, picking up on the idea immediately. 'I've seen army ones on exercises we've taken with other teams. They really are a complete package, right down to food, water and accommodation for the first responders— enough for them to be self-sufficient for a fortnight.'

Taking the words as a small spark of interest, Kate said, 'Shall I tell you about it? Will we sit down?'

Harriet was frowning slightly, but as Kate perched on the sofa, her hostess dropped into an armchair. The frown was understandable. Here was this neighbour, who'd been in the apartment block for two years yet had never ventured over the threshold, making herself at home.

And talking, talking, talking—

The doorbell shrilled, and Harriet's frown deepened.

'It must be someone from another apartment because they didn't ring at the front door.'

It shrilled again.

'Would you like me to get it?' Kate offered, her

heart going out to the woman she'd only known as lively and active, now a pale shadow of her former self.

A shadow with her injured leg still in its ungainly brace.

'No, I'll go.'

Harriet rose to her feet and limped to the door, opening it to reveal the person Kate was still telling herself not to think about.

'I'm sorry to disturb you,' came the deep growl from the doorway. 'I'm Angus Caruth, and Blake gave me Kate's address, and then Alice said she was here and that you wouldn't mind if I popped in to say hello. I barely recognised her earlier, at the meeting. I don't think I'd ever seen Kate with dry hair.'

Kate's gut had twisted more with every word he spoke, but she'd regained some control over her mind, so as Harriet ushered in her new visitor, she used anger to mask all the other reactions that had rioted inside her since the meeting.

'Blake gave you my address?' she demanded. 'Whatever happened to staff confidentiality?'

'Oh, I'd blame Sam for that,' Harriet said, obviously intrigued by this second visitor. She waved her arm towards the sofa, and invited Angus to sit. 'Ever since she and Blake got together, she's been seeing the world through a pearly haze of love.'

She turned to Kate and smiled—smiled properly!

'So what's with the wet hair?'

The smile was the first sign of the old Harriet that Kate had seen so she felt obliged to reply.

'Angus and I met in a cyclone. Everyone had wet hair.'

She kept her eyes on Harriet as she spoke, for all

the good that did her. Her body was as aware of Angus as it would have been if he had been sitting on top of her—her skin prickling with something she'd rather call discomfort than—

No, it couldn't possibly be attraction...

How could this have happened?

Why did it have to be her hospital he'd turned up at?

And why, after all this time, could he still affect her like this?

But now he was talking again, and if she closed her eyes—

She straightened in her seat.

'"Angus and I met in a cyclone" hardly covers it,' he was responding, smiling at her before turning to Harriet. 'We were stuck in the dining room of a resort hotel and a tree had crashed into one glass wall, so we had about sixty panicking people to deal with. Kate calmly organised the wait staff to tear tablecloths into bandages and once we had all the injured settled as well as we could, she started everyone singing. I think trying to manage "Come to dinner" sung in four parts certainly took their minds off the howling gale and thunderous winds outside.'

Refusing to yield to the memories, Kate tried desperately to ignore the man on the sofa beside her—to ignore all the signals that were zapping between their bodies.

She had to get away, to sort out what was happening and why, after three years, she should still feel this way about a man she barely knew.

It was the coward's way out but she turned to Harriet.

'Angus is the man I was telling you about, the one

with the new tent, and now he's here, he can tell you about it himself.'

She pushed herself to her feet, hoping her face wasn't revealing the torrent of emotions roaring inside her—hoping her legs would hold her up and, most of all, hoping Angus couldn't see the quivering mess his presence had made of her body.

'I really should go,' she added. 'It's my turn to cook dinner.'

She strode to the door, opening it and pausing briefly to waggle her fingers in farewell.

And to take in the face of the man who'd haunted her dreams for the past three years.

Angus!

Closing the door behind her, she leant against the wall in the hall, eyes shut so she could see him again on her eyelids—check him against her memories.

No, he hadn't changed. Still the same dark, almost shorn hair, black quirky eyebrows above deep-set blue eyes, slightly crooked nose, the result she knew of a youthful brawl, and lips—

She wouldn't think about his lips—not the shape of them, or the paleness, or the way they'd felt as they'd brushed across her skin…

Her heart fluttered and for a moment she was back on the island—back in his arms—lost in blissful sensation…

She pushed angrily away from the wall. How dared Blake Cooper give out her address? How dared Angus walk back into her life like this?

Angus felt her absence, which was ridiculous given he hadn't seen her for three years, for all he'd thought about her. Wondering where she was, what she was doing, thinking about contacting her, but how?

And why?

To hurt her as he'd hurt Michelle—never being there for her when she'd needed him, never considering just how hard their separations had been for her?

This new project would take him away even more. Their orders to leave would come within twenty-four hours of a disaster occurring somewhere in the world. Here today and gone tomorrow—how fair was that on any woman, let alone one he'd come to remember as special…?

Then she'd rushed into the SDR room where he had been explaining the new emergency structure, her fingers flipping her hair into a dark halo around her head.

Too far away to see the pale blue-grey of her eyes, but aware they'd widened in shock—

'I'd rather hear about the cyclone than the tent.'

Harriet's words made him realise he was still staring at the door through which Kate had vanished.

He caught the speculative gleam in Harriet's eyes and smiled at her.

'About the cyclone or about Kate Mitchell?' he asked, and Harriet blushed.

'Well, she *has* always been something of a mystery woman,' she admitted. 'I imagine the army is a bit like a hospital where everyone knows everyone else's business, but Kate…'

She shrugged.

'Perhaps we're better talking about the tent.'

Angus smiled again and agreed, although his mind was whirling with questions. Kate a bit of a mystery woman? Blake Cooper had given much the same impression. A loner, he'd said. Yet the Kate Angus remembered had been outgoing and cheerful, shrugging off the pain she must have been feeling when she'd joked about honeymooning alone on the island.

'Well, I'd booked it and paid for it, why shouldn't I enjoy it?' she'd said with a smile that had belied the cloudy sadness in her eyes.

Had he hurt her more?

Caused the change?

Surely not, but something had…

He turned his attention back to Harriet.

'You probably know all about regular emergency structures but most of them are intended for long-term use, say after an earthquake. The "tent", as Kate called it, is a smaller affair—an inflatable, easily set-up protected area that combines a trauma unit to act as the ED, a surgical theatre for life-and-limb-saving surgery, and a multifunction unit with drugs and blood products, facilities for lab tests, and sterilisation support. Some of these are "add-on" units in other emergency set-ups, but what we've tried to do is provide the best facility possible for first response units like your SDR.'

'That makes sense,' Harriet said. 'Most patients are airlifted, or taken by road transport once they're stabilised, so you wouldn't need an intensive care unit or ward beds like some I've seen. It sounds like a great idea.'

'It's only a great idea if it works,' Angus told her. 'I've been planning and organising the construction of this one for some time, but I've only recently been posted to a base on the outskirts of Sydney. I knew Blake back when I was studying medicine so when I heard about his—well, the hospital's—SDR team I hooked up with him, hoping maybe we could get to trial it.'

He paused, then added, 'Not that I'm looking for a disaster—heaven forbid—but things happen, don't they?'

Harriet gave him a weak smile and pointed to her leg.

'Don't they just,' she said, and a finality in the words finished the conversation.

Could he go? Just stand up and walk out? Say good-bye, of course—but even if he went, could he go back to Kate's—or Alice's—apartment? He doubted he'd be welcomed. Kate had been out the door here before he'd got settled on the sofa.

He stood up.

'I'd better go,' he said. 'I do hope you get back on the team before long. You might even get to try out my "tent".'

But Harriet didn't respond and he'd seen enough PTSD cases to know that even if she hadn't been di-agnosed with it, she was deeply depressed. She'd made all the right noises when he'd first come in and even shown interest in his knowing Kate, but that short stint of casual conversation had taken all her energy.

And although he wanted nothing more than to go back to Alice's apartment and see Kate, he sat down again.

'How long since you hurt your leg?' he asked, watching her face so he could read the argument going on in her head about whether or not she would answer.

Politeness won.

'Months now—I've lost count. I got a post-op infection that knocked me back, and the rehab seems to go on for ever.'

'You'll get there,' he said. 'You've got to keep believing that you will. Don't give up. Giving up's easy, it's sticking it out that's hard, but in the end, it's worth it. The inner strength you gain will make you a better nurse and better SDR team member.'

'And a better person? Did you forget that bit?' Harriet asked, but at least she was smiling again.

'Don't know about that, but seeing medicine from the other side definitely improves your understanding of patients and what they are going through.'

'Been there yourself?'

He smiled and shook his head.

'Close enough,' he told her, remembering the long bleak months after his last posting, part of a humanitarian response team to an overcrowded refugee camp in South-East Asia. Some of the things he'd seen—the stories he'd heard—had made him wonder if he'd ever feel normal again.

'And Kate?'

'Nice try,' he said, as Harriet's teasing smile told him he could leave with an easier conscience. He'd jolted her out of her dark mood, although for how long he didn't know.

He said goodbye, adding that he hoped they'd meet again, and was pleased when she roused herself enough to walk to the door with him.

As he left he realised he had an excuse to talk to Kate again—he could knock on the apartment door, mention his concern about Harriet's mental state.

It was a weak excuse and she'd see it that way, but having met up with her again he knew he—

What?

Wanted to see more of her?

Yes, there was that—definitely—but…

What he really wanted to know was what had changed her from the woman who'd smiled through the pain of the end of her relationship, who'd settled terrified guests with a warm word and a joke during the cyclone, who'd been friendly and outgoing and…

Well, fun!

Back when he'd met her, she'd have had every reason to be withdrawn. She'd discovered her best friend had been sleeping with her fiancé and had broken off the engagement, heading for the island to escape the talk.

But she'd taken one look at his pale face on the island boat and made him stay on deck, explaining it was far better to be outside than in if you felt the slightest bit queasy. So they'd clung to the rail, salt spray washing over them both, and she'd kept his mind off the journey, telling him about the little coral cay that lay ahead, and the research station on it that she'd visited each year with her great-aunt Alice, a marine biologist.

Alice!

The great-aunt!

By the time they'd reached the island he'd realised Alice probably meant more to Kate than her parents, and now here she was, living with Alice—a 'loner'!

Because?

He realised that, in spite of all they'd been through together, he didn't really know her.

He looked around the elevator lobby, and finally pressed the 'down' button.

* * *

Kate did her best to concentrate on cooking the chicken breasts in lemon and capers that was one of Alice's favourite dinners, but she'd made it so often it couldn't distract her enough.

Why wasn't Angus wearing a wedding ring?

Hadn't he gone to the island to check it out as a place for his and Michelle's honeymoon?

They'd joked on that terribly rough boat trip that they were both on pretend honeymoons, talking to take their minds off the wild seas.

And the cyclone hadn't even been close at that stage. It was only two days later it changed direction—as cyclones so often do—and headed straight for the island.

Maybe army personnel didn't wear wedding rings, she decided. Some kind of safety thing? Could a light flashing off a gold or silver ring tell a sniper where to shoot?

Kate shook her head as she turned the capers in the frying pan, crisping them nicely. Think about the capers, not have ridiculous thoughts about snipers. Angus had been based in Townsville, anyway, and she doubted he'd have been bothered by snipers there.

Angus.

'You burning those capers, Kate?'

Surely not! She looked down at the pan, forcing her mind away from the man who'd come back so unexpectedly—shockingly, really—into her life.

'No, but you like them crisp. Nearly ready!'

She put the thin slices of chicken breast back into the pan, with the lemon juice and zest, swirled it around, then served them onto the waiting plates. The bowl of salad was already on the table, and Alice joined her there as she set down the plates.

They ate in silence for a few minutes, savouring the tasty food, but Kate could hear the wheels turning in Alice's head as she decided how to phrase the question Kate knew she would ask.

Except she didn't ask a question, instead issuing a statement.

'So that was the man who caused you all the trouble!'

Kate shrugged.

'He wasn't to blame for anything,' she said quietly.

'Oh, so you got pregnant all by yourself?'

Kate pushed her plate away and looked at her aunt. Great-aunt really, but they'd never made the distinction. She'd been closer to Alice than she had to her mother, had learnt more about life and the way the world worked on those holidays on the island than she'd ever learnt at home or at school.

'The getting-pregnant part was definitely my fault,' Kate admitted. 'I'd been on the Pill so didn't give a thought to the fact that I hadn't been in my room for three days during the height of the storm, which meant I hadn't been taking it. Stupid, I know, but it had been a tense time with so little sleep, and the relief of finally getting the injured and the majority of the upset tourists off the island had overwhelmed us both.'

She paused, then looked up to meet Alice's eyes.

'It was survivor sex, if that makes sense, yet…'

'It was more than that?' Alice asked gently.

Kate nodded.

'It seemed that way,' she murmured, a little of the remembered passion sparking to life inside her. 'We'd been through so much together, it was as if we had a…bond, I suppose, is the only way to describe it. A special bond.'

'Didn't you tell him you were pregnant, get in touch with him?'

Kate shuddered as she remembered the anguish of those early days.

'How could I? I'd done exactly what my best friend had done—slept with someone else's fiancé—and that had broken up my marriage plans. Should I break up his as well?'

She sighed.

'In the end, I knew it wasn't right to *not* tell him so I kind of left it up to him. I sent him a note, care of the base in Townsville, just asking if he'd like to give me a call—gave him my number. I never heard anything after that, which, I think, given all that happened, was for the best, don't you?'

Alice shook her head.

Angus made his way back towards the hospital where he'd left his car, his left hand in his pocket, fingering the card Blake had given him.

Some impulse made him stop and look around at the dark water of the ocean disappearing into the night, at the sand, patterned in shadows by the street lights on the esplanade. He breathed deeply, drawing in the salty tang of the air that only existed this close to the beach.

He was a free agent at the moment, at the beginning of an untimed trip to talk to groups like Bondi Bay-side's SDR all over Australia. He'd started here because it was closest to his army base, intending to find a hotel in Sydney to use while he covered the other response teams and government officials he needed to see. But wasn't that a hotel? Just across the road from the apartments? Bondi wasn't so far out of Sydney city that he couldn't base himself here for the local appointments.

He pulled out Blake's card and phoned him, inordinately pleased when Blake said he was only too happy to take him on their next callout. Another reason to stay in Bondi!

'So you can see how our system works,' Blake had added, causing a small twinge of guilt in Angus's gut. 'I'll give Mabel your mobile number. We meet at the chopper on the roof of the hospital. Check in at Reception if you get a call. I'll leave instructions for them to give you a special visitor's card that will give you access to the elevator, and allow you to go up to the roof.'

It was only when this was organised that Angus realised Kate might not be on the next SDR callout, but she *was* here, in Bondi, he'd seen her, and he had no intention of leaving until he'd seen her again. Seen her properly! If he didn't catch up with her this way, he'd have to think of something else.

Why?

The question struck him as he was about to turn away from the beach, and he couldn't brush it away.

Was it simply determination to find out why, according to the little he'd heard, she'd changed from a lively, friendly, outgoing young woman to a loner? Back then, he'd seen the shadows of sadness in her eyes, but she'd talked and laughed and even joked about her solitary honeymoon—been vibrantly alive...

Or was it because she'd somehow got beneath his skin three years ago?

Because something special, quite apart from the

sex, which had been momentous, had happened between them on the island? Something had drawn them together during those terrifying hours in a way he'd never felt before?

Or since, come to that.

Until she'd walked into the SDR meeting earlier today.

Until he'd felt a surge of excitement—electrifying excitement—rush through his body...

Okay, so maybe there was more reason for him to see her again, than to find out what had changed her...

He walked back to the hospital, retrieved his vehicle from the car park and headed to the hotel, telling himself he was being foolish yet unable to persuade himself to move on. He had to see the leaders of the State Emergency Service and the Fire and Rescue Service. He'd chosen Bondi Bayside Hospital as his starting point because he'd known Blake was there, but he'd begin phoning other services in the morning, make appointments, arrange meetings. There was plenty to keep him in Sydney.

Kate was almost pleased when the phone rang in the early hours of the morning. She'd been tossing and turning all night, her sleep disturbed by memories of the island, of the fury of the cyclone, of fear...

Of Angus.

'Yes, Mabel,' she answered, knowing from the ring tone it was their SDR co-ordinator. As usual, Mabel wasted no time on pleasantries.

'RTA at a crossroads in a farming community north-west of Sydney. Road train, fortunately on its way to collect cattle, hit a car, number of passengers unknown. Blake will keep you posted as he hears more.'

Kate was pulling on her SDR overalls as she thought about the accident—road trains consisted of the huge prime mover with three double-decker trailers hooked on behind. Stopping one suddenly would be almost impossible. Although easier without the cattle…

She laced up her boots so she didn't trip as she hurried back to the hospital. Their other gear was kept in a shed on the hospital roof—helmets with headlamps and communication equipment, safety vests and the big backpacks that carried both basic first-aid and life-saving, equipment.

In a little over ten minutes she was on the hospital roof, joining the others as they snapped on protective vests, fitted their helmets and clambered on board.

Where a large man, similarly dressed, was sitting in what she thought of as 'her' seat.

Angus!

'What are you doing here?' she demanded, tasking the empty seat next to him and strapping herself in. 'We won't need your tent.'

He grinned at her, which caused a flood of unwanted reactions.

'Just wanted to see how the other half do it,' he said, and she shoved away her personal issues and shuddered as she thought of the emergencies that army medical response teams must answer. She'd seen her share of torn and damaged bodies cut from vehicle wrecks, but bodies mangled by unexpected bombs?

'Do you still do it?' she asked, as the rest of the crew settled themselves, desperate to keep things on a professional level.

He shook his head.

'Not for a while—not after the last trip.'

And something in the way he spoke told her it had been horrific. Her hand moved towards his knee then quickly retreated, although her heart ached that this was how it had to be between them.

He was obviously having no trouble with professional distance, continuing to explain his situation.

'I'm strictly home based for the moment. My last overseas posting was when I got back from the island— within a day, in fact.'

So maybe he'd never received the note she'd sent.

And why that brought a sudden blip of pleasure she didn't know.

Relief she'd have understood, but pleasure?

Because it meant he hadn't ignored it completely, you idiot, she told herself, then conversation ceased as Blake checked who was on board and the aircraft took off.

They lifted into the air, the engines settled into their customary throb, and Blake began to fill them in on what lay ahead.

'Country crossroad, no lights or signals but a stop sign for traffic in the minor road, and clear views both ways along the major road.'

'It's still dark enough for the road train to have had its lights on. It would have been hard to miss it,' Paul, one of the paramedics, remarked.

'Not our problem,' Blake reminded the speaker. 'The hows and whys are up to the police and the coroner, our job is to treat the injured. Unknown number of people in the car, which was still being extricated

from the prime mover when Mabel called, then the
driver of the big rig.'

'Do we know if he was carrying a passenger—his
wife, or a relief driver perhaps?' someone asked, and
Blake shook his head.

'The local police, fire and ambulance services will
all be at the scene by the time we get there. There's a
very small town with a district hospital nearby but it
hasn't the facilities to handle anything serious so we'll
probably be flying anyone badly injured back with us.
Paul, I want you on triage. We've got an extra doc with
us in Angus, the fellow some of you met the other day.'

Several heads turned to nod at Angus, while Blake,
briefing over, walked forward to stand behind the pilot
and air crewman so he'd see the scene from above.

'He doesn't waste words, does he?' Angus said,
twisting his mike away from his face so he could talk
to Kate.

'We all know the routine. Right now, he'll want
to check out the terrain and see where the best place
for us to set up might be. The helicopter usually puts
down some distance away so people on the ground
aren't affected by downdraught. We cart all our stuff
to the scene in the backpacks. The ambulance on site
will have its monitoring equipment already set up but
in a small country town there's likely to only be one
ambulance so they need us as well.'

Was she relaxing as she talked to him?

Angus hoped so.

If he wanted to find out what had gone on in her
life to change her so much, then he needed to get close
to her.

And was figuring out her life over the past three years the only reason he wanted to be close to her?

Honesty forced him to admit it wasn't.

Since the seemingly endless hours they'd spent together, keeping the resort guests safe and relaxed—not to mention the night in the only dry bed on the island after the cyclone had passed—Kate had regularly sneaked into his thoughts.

Try as he might to forget her, an image of her would suddenly appear in his head, and at times she'd filled his daydreams and haunted his nights.

Even on that last traumatic posting in South-East Asia, where he'd been treating refugees, men, women and children, fleeing their country, their homes blazing behind them, and their attackers shooting at them as they fled to the nearest border to escape. Even there he'd thought of Kate far more than he'd thought of Michelle.

And his fiancée had undoubtedly picked up on this to have broken off their engagement within days of his return.

Although telling her about Kate—about that one night of intimacy—had probably had something to do with it as well...

And now, even through the layers of clothing they both wore, he could feel the warmth of Kate's body at his side—feel a rightness in it—as if they belonged.

Kate...

CHAPTER TWO

THE CLUSTER OF strobing lights from the emergency vehicles told them they were close, although inside the cabin of the chopper all they could see were the blue and red flashes.

They put down outside the circle of light and, each grabbing a backpack, jogged closer to the scene.

'We're still cutting the vehicle free,' a policeman told them. 'The road train driver's been removed. He's in that ambulance over there.' He pointed, before adding, 'You might take a look at him. He's in a bad way.'

Blake nodded to Kate, who headed for the ambulance, disconcerted but somehow not surprised when Angus followed her.

An ambo was using a bag mask ventilator on the driver, while his fellow attendant stuck ECG leads to the man.

'GCS?' Kate asked, referring to the Glasgow Coma Scale that measured how responsive their patient was.

'Fourteen when we got here, but he's in and out of consciousness.'

'Coupcontrecoup injury,' Kate murmured to herself as her mind pictured the scenario. The powerful rig powering through the night, then the car right there.

The driver would have slammed on his brakes, and his body, held in place by a seat belt, would have stopped abruptly. But his head?

She knelt and spoke to the patient, glad to hear a response. She introduced herself and Angus, learning the patient's name was Mike.

All good so far.

'Can you remember what happened, Mike?' she asked.

'The car came flying towards the crossing, I tried to stop.'

Kate nodded, but wondered just how quickly he had stopped and whether the deceleration had caused his brain to jolt forward into the front of the skull then virtually bounce back to hit the rear.

The action could result in a serious brain injury but scanning it here would be a waste of time when it would have to be done more precisely at the hospital— and as soon as possible.

'Are you in any pain?'

'Gut hurts, and headache. The guys gave me something.'

Which probably explained why he was woozy.

'His blood pressure is dropping,' the paramedic said, nodding towards the monitor.

Kate checked the fluid line already feeding into a vein in the man's hand, then took in the abrasions to his neck and chest.

'Seat-belt syndrome,' she said to Angus, pointing out how deep the indentations were. 'With a shoulder-lap seat belt the shoulder strap took the brunt of the force. That could cause damage to the carotid. Could you check his distal pulse?'

She studied the monitor for a moment. Blood oximetry was fine, and when Angus felt a pulse in Mike's wrist, she was reassured that any loss of blood was not life-threatening.

Yet.

She examined his chest, and felt the ribs under the seat belt, but there was no palpable damage.

'Would the big rig slow for the crossing, do you know?' she asked the ambos.

They both shook their heads, but one said, 'I wouldn't think so. The place is usually deserted at night.'

'So a high-speed collision, rapid deceleration, possible internal injuries including damage to carotid artery.' She checked the fluid line again then poked her head outside the ambulance.

Paul was standing nearby.

'Possible internal bleeding from damage to the carotid. Can we lift him immediately?' she asked.

Blake, who was over to one side, watching as the car was extricated, came across, took in the information the monitor was now offering and hesitated.

'It's unlikely anyone in the car survived, but if they did, he or she will be seriously injured and will need immediate transport. We can work on them on the flight. Can you hold him a little longer?'

Kate nodded.

'We'll need to keep up the fluids and open up a bigger port in case he needs a rapid infusion,' she said to Angus as Blake hurried away.

'IO?' Angus suggested, but Kate already had the intraosseus pack in her hand and was holding the drill that would insert a needle into the bone marrow, while the ambo, who'd kept up with the exchange, was cutting their patient's shirt and opening it up.

'Here, let me,' Angus said, taking the drill from her as she used a sterile wipe to clean the site on the man's unaffected shoulder, at the head of the humerus. 'We use this more often than not in field situations,' Angus assured her, 'and I promise I've never once drilled right through the bone.'

Kate had to smile. It was always a worry, although the devices they used now for IO infusion were very sophisticated. With this access, they could deliver anticoagulant drugs to ward off a possible stroke and add high-volume drugs should the patient go into cardiac arrest.

Kate administered a local anaesthetic and watched as Angus drilled, then inserted a wide-bore cannula.

Working together, they set up a fluid line to keep the port open, and, while Angus watched for any change in their patient's condition, Kate continued her examination. The seat belt had left abrasions across the driver's chest and lap, and the depth and severity of them told her how violent the impact had been. Once in hospital, there'd be scans that would show the extent of the damage to the chest and abdomen.

Yet, even with possibly serious injuries, he was luckier than the people in the car. It had been dislodged from under the prime mover, and the damage told a grim story even before the firies started cutting out the bodies. Two people, driver and passenger, and neither had survived, which dampened the spirits of the SDR crew as they flew home with the rig driver.

Kate did the handover in one of the resus rooms in the ED, hoping they'd got the man to the hospital quickly enough to be saved, although she couldn't help wondering whether, if they'd flown him out earlier, his chances would have been better.

'You only do what you can,' came a voice from behind her as she left the hospital.

She knew before she turned that it was Angus.

'I'll walk you home,' he said, and because she was tired, not to mention doubtful about the outcome for her patient, she was hardly gracious.

'It's two blocks and broad daylight, I don't need to be walked home.'

'Ah, but my hotel is just across the road from your apartment building, and I might have been suggesting it because *I* needed to be walked home, only asking you to walk me home might have seemed a bit unmanly.'

Worried as she was, Kate had to smile. She turned to face him, taking in his height and breadth, and the aura of strength that hung around him, contrasting sharply with the gentleness in his dark eyes.

'Unmanly?' she echoed. 'That's not an assumption many people would make!'

He held out his arm, crooked at the elbow.

'So, shall we walk each other home?' he said, and somewhere deep inside a little bit of the Kate she used to be began to unfurl, like the petal on a tight rosebud. She slipped her hand inside his arm, telling herself it was just a friendly gesture, except that he cheated and turned his hand to grasp hers, linking them even closer together.

She should protest.

Move away!

But walking like this with Angus was warming

places that had been cold for a very long time. Was it so very wrong to be enjoying it?

Well, probably, yes, given the secret she held so tightly in her heart.

But he'd be gone tomorrow, back to his own life, and she'd be back at work in Theatre and studying after hours, with exams drawing closer, so how could this little bit of closeness hurt?

He gave her hand a squeeze and because this was just for now, she squeezed back.

She pulled away from him as they reached the apartment block, intending to say a cool goodbye, but he caught her hand again, turning so he was facing her.

'Can I see you again?'

She shook her head.

'I don't think that's a good idea.'

He looked puzzled so, although he hadn't asked why not, she added, 'You're married, aren't you? You and Michelle? After all, that *was* what you went to island for—checking it out for a honeymoon.'

He smiled.

'I'd forgotten that's why I'd gone to the island— well, I hadn't thought about it for a while. No, we didn't marry.'

She waited, not wanting to ask why but aware he had more to say.

'She broke it off. I'd been away, came back changed, she said. And she was probably right. I *felt* different, less certain of things, not only between us but about life in general.'

Because of what had happened between us? Kate wondered, guilt biting deep inside her.

But before she could say anything, Angus was speaking again.

'And it didn't help telling her about you—about what had happened on the island.'

'You told her about the island? About the night we spent together? Oh, Angus, why on earth would you do that? It was one night. We were in another world—we knew it didn't mean anything but relief, or celebration, or something. I can't—' She looked up into his face as she said it, and saw that he still disagreed.

And understood.

His integrity would have insisted he tell, while she, Kate, had held onto her own secret, although it hadn't really been a secret until Angus had reappeared in her life.

And telling now? Wouldn't he feel the pain she'd felt? Those endless, sleepless nights and empty aching arms? Did he deserve that?

She shook away the thoughts and tried to ignore the cold, hard lump inside her.

'I need some sleep,' she said, and turned away from him, although she knew sleep would be impossible.

She made her way up to the apartment in a daze, ate some cereal—soggy—and toast—cold—and tried to pretend it had been just another callout.

'I'm sorry about the breakfast but I always get it ready when I hear the helicopter land,' Alice was explaining. 'Did you have a lot to do when you got back that you were late?'

Kate shook her head. The driver of the road train would have had a battery of tests and was probably getting appropriate treatment right now.

And the two young people, their lives cut short, were being taken by road transport to the nearest hospital.

'Bad, was it?' Alice asked, guessing from her silence that things hadn't gone well.

'Just about as bad as it gets,' Kate said, and then, knowing Alice would see or hear a report on a news broadcast, she added, 'It was a road train against a small car and the two young people in the car were killed.'

'That's shocking,' Alice said. 'So dreadful for their families.'

She paused, then added, 'But surely we should always take something from these terrible things—from such waste of life. Shouldn't it make us think about our own lives?'

Kate looked at the woman who had taken her in when she'd been at her lowest ebb and had coaxed her slowly back to at least a semblance of normal life.

'Do you have regrets about your life? Wish you'd done things differently?'

Alice smiled and shook her head.

'I'm talking about you, my dear. I know you're busy with your studies but life is meant to be lived, Kate. You should get out more, meet people away from your work. Those two had their lives taken from them, you still have yours and for their sakes, if nothing more, you should make the most of it.'

'And being the best surgeon I possibly can be isn't making the most of it?' Kate retorted.

Alice just shook her head and began to clear the table.

But Alice's words, perhaps because she so rarely talked about personal things and this was twice in two days, remained with Kate as she headed to her bedroom. And a hot shower failed to wash them away, so they lingered in her head, preventing any possibility of sleep. She heard the front door of the apartment open and shut and knew Alice had gone to help out at the charity shop down the road—Animal Welfare on Fridays. Alice's life was nothing if not predictable.

Giving up on sleep, Kate pulled on shorts and a light singlet. She'd go for a run, head out along the coastal path towards Coogee. Exercise and fresh, salty air would surely make her sleepy.

She enjoyed running, and today was even more special as the sun sparkled on the ocean while a gentle breeze kept her cool, and concentrating on where she put her feet and dodging walkers on the path kept her mind off both Angus's revelation and Alice's lecture.

She'd moved to the side of the path to allow a young woman jogging with a toddler in a stroller to pass in the opposite direction when she noticed the tall, upright figure striding—marching?—along the path in front of her.

Her heart flipped, and confusion fogged her mind—secrets, he's not married, another secret, her secret, and living life before it was too late all jumbled in her head.

And if she kept running she'd have to pass him.

Just run past?

Could she do that?

Not really!

Turn around and go back?

She usually ran as far as the huge cemetery, where sloping grounds gave such a wide view of the ocean, and to turn before that—well, it was hardly a run at all...

The memory of the young lives cut short sent her forward, slowing as she reached the marching man.

'Couldn't sleep?' she said, slowing to a jog beside him. 'I couldn't either, but running always helps.'

He turned his head and looked at her for a moment, not breaking stride.

'The team should have had a debrief after an incident like that—after every incident, in fact.'

'We do, although today, because Blake went with the bodies to the nearest hospital, we'll have it later. Probably this evening. Mabel will let us know.'

'Jogging is bad for your knees and ankles,' he muttered, in an even more critical tone.

'I don't usually jog, I run,' she told him, curt to the point just short of rudeness because the man was causing so many strange reactions in her body. 'I'm jogging out of politeness to keep up with you, although you obviously don't want company, so I'll keep running.'

And she ran on, building up speed until she was running almost flat out by the time she reached her goal.

But even at full speed she couldn't outrun her awareness of Angus, stoically marching along the track behind her.

She settled on a grassy patch in the middle of the cemetery, beside a carved marble statue of a cherub that presided over the grave of a small boy who'd died back in 1892. His name had been Joshua and she'd been drawn to him although he'd lived for seven months, while her child, also a boy, had not lived at all.

And although her occasional chats with Joshua usually comforted her, today her thoughts were with her baby—Jasper she'd called him—and the way he'd felt in her arms as she'd held him that one time—

Had she been so lost in memories of that terrible day that she hadn't seen Angus approaching?

'Sorry I was grumpy,' he said, hovering above her. 'I couldn't sleep.'

He squatted down to read Joshua's memorial.

'I suppose parents in those days were aware their kids could die young,' he added, settling himself comfortably on the grass beside her as if it was the most natural thing in the world for them to be sharing this particular patch of grass.

Her patch of grass!

Hers and Jasper's...

'Do you think that would have lessened their grief?' she asked, handing him the water bottle she'd pulled from her small backpack, while certain she knew the answer to the question.

Nothing lessens grief like that...

He tipped his head back to drink and she saw the strong column of his neck, the slight bump of his Adam's apple, and added the images to others that she had of Angus, stored away safely in the back of her mind, only taken out to study on very rare occasions.

'No,' he said, startling her out of her dreams as he returned the bottle, his fingers brushing hers, confusing her body with the intimacy of a single touch.

'It could never be easy. I keep thinking of the families of those young people today. I've seen too many young people die, Kate, and the more I see, the more I think we owe them something. Owe it to them not to waste our own lives—to make the most of whatever time we have—not solely in pursuit of pleasure but both in work and play.'

Kate was silent for a moment, then admitted, 'Alice was saying much the same thing to me this morning. It was why I couldn't sleep.'

Was she saying what he thought she was? Angus hesitated, wondering if he could put it to the test.

Nothing ventured, he reminded himself.

'So, if I asked very nicely, would you come to dinner with me?'

'Is that you asking, or asking if you can ask?'

She smiled as she said it and Angus took it as a small victory.

He laughed.

'I could say pretty please, but someone my size talking like that would be making a joke of it, and I'm not joking. I'd like to see you again, see you socially, nothing heavy or complicated, just a '"getting to know you" kind of arrangement.'

He wasn't really holding his breath, but studying the cherub on the grave gave him a chance to watch Kate's face more surreptitiously than staring at it. He could almost see the argument going on in her head, read it in the shadows in her eyes—more grey today— reflecting the sea?

'Okay,' she finally said, turning to face him, 'but it will be dependent on Blake and when he wants to do a debrief.'

She didn't smile and something about the set of her face suggested she was pushing herself to accept.

Because she'd been a loner for a long time?

Because whatever had made her that way had left her scarred?

He was surprised to find that it hurt him to think of Kate hurting—scarred by something that had changed her so much.

'I'm flexible,' he said, 'and as I'd like to be part of

the debrief we can make it before or after—whatever works.'

She stood up and stretched, her long, lightly tanned legs mesmerising him, her body reminding him—

Nothing heavy or complicated, he reminded himself.

'Are you walking on to Coogee?' she asked, and he shook his head.

'Then we might as well walk back together.'

Without waiting for a reply, she reached out a hand to pull him to his feet, and as he grasped it he wondered just how hard it would be to keep things light between them. Whatever magnetic force that had taken them to that dry bed in Cabin Thirty-Two—whispered to him by one of the staff as they saw the last of the injured and shocked guests off in the helicopter three years ago—was still alive and well between them. Or it was on his part, anyway.

The debrief, held late in the afternoon, eventually came to discuss whether the train driver should have been airlifted out immediately it was discovered there could be internal bleeding. The patient's falling blood pressure had suggested that scenario, and although holding onto him until they'd known the condition of the passengers in the car hadn't made any difference to his outcome, had the bleeding been worse, it could have been fatal.

Discussing it rationally, without the pressure of the emergency situation, was one of the ways they could improve their actions in the field, and was one of the important parts of the debrief.

'I think we were right to wait,' Kate said, although she'd been the one who'd asked for immediate evacuation. 'He was relatively stable and we had the IO line open if he'd needed massive doses of drugs or blood products. The ambulance attendants had started fluid resus and he had a distal pulse. The internal bleeding could have been from a tear to his carotid from the seat belt crossing his shoulder, or damage to an internal vein or artery from the lap-band of the seatbelt. There was no palpable swelling in his abdomen to suggest a lap-band tear and his trachea showed no signs of deviation so if there *was* bleeding from the carotid it wasn't affecting his airway.'

'Yet you suggested lifting him sooner?'

Kate smiled at Blake.

'Don't we always think the patient we're tending is the most important? Besides, it made minimal difference. The car was already out from under the road train and it was only a matter of minutes before you'd have ascertained if either of the occupants was alive. By the time we had Mr Grosvenor in the chopper you were able to tell us to take off.'

'Thankfully,' Blake said, and after a short general discussion the meeting broke up with Blake's usual reminder of the availability of a counsellor should any of them want to talk.

'Does he always beat himself up over what happened?' Angus asked as they walked out of the hospital.

'That wasn't exactly beating himself up,' Kate protested. 'He's just determined that we should be the best we can, and it's only by going over the things we did—or sometimes didn't do—that we can improve.'

'But he *had* to hold the helicopter until he knew

there were no survivors in the car,' Angus said. 'Anyone would.'

Kate stopped at the always open gates into the hospital and looked out over the shops and restaurants that lined the front to the ocean beyond.

'Are we going to continue to discuss this all through dinner?" she asked, and caught the surprise on Angus's face.

He held up his hands in mock surrender.

'Sorry, I get carried away.' There was a little pause before he half smiled and admitted, 'Actually, I'm incredibly nervous about this dinner.'

Kate grinned at him.

'Snap,' she said. 'I think the last time I felt this way was when I was fifteen and a boy I liked at school asked if I'd go to the pictures with him.'

'And did you?' Angus asked as they walked on. 'Go to the pictures with him?'

'I did,' Kate said, 'and we had popcorn and a milkshake and I got such a shock when he put his arm around my shoulders, I spilled the milkshake all over my dress. He did walk me home but he never asked me out again.'

'First dates!' Angus said, a small smile flirting around his lips.

'Tell me about yours,' Kate said, as they reached the promenade and turned to walk along it.

'Fifteen, and when I tried to kiss her, Michelle slapped my face.'

'Michelle?' Kate gasped. 'The Michelle you were going to marry? You went out with her from when you were fifteen?'

Guilt that she might have caused the break-up of

such a long-standing relationship filled her chest, leaving her breathless as she waited for his reply.

'Why not?' Angus said, confirming Kate's worst fears.

'Well…'

What to say?

Did people still do that? Go out with each other exclusively from the age of fifteen?

'Did you go out with other people in between?' she asked, desperately hoping it had been an on-and-off relationship from the beginning.

'Off and on, both of us, but somehow we always ended up back together,' Angus said, sounding as unemotional as someone discussing the weather.

They'd been together fifteen years—she knew he'd been thirty when she'd met him—then had broken up after—

One night of madness…

Only it hadn't been madness, well, not to her. It had been as natural and necessary as the air she'd breathed.

The memory still felt that way.

But now the conversation, harmless as it had seemed at first, had erected a barrier between them, a wall of stupid, residual guilt as palpable as glass.

Angus wondered what she was thinking. They'd been chatting amiably enough and now even he, who wasn't always attuned to nuances in conversation or tension in the air, realised something had shifted.

Because he'd only ever seriously dated Michelle?

Surely not!

Time for a conversation change.

'Where's good to eat?' he asked, and when Kate looked blankly at him he added, 'Well, you're the local.'

'The bistro at the lifesavers' building,' she told him. 'There, on the rocks at the end of the beach.'

'The place beside the swimming pool in the rocks?'

'That's it,' she said, picking up speed as they headed towards it.

Escaping him or the conversation?

But the beauty of the night caught him, pushing away the awkwardness he'd felt. A pale half-moon had appeared just above the horizon, and its silvery light turned the unusually calm ocean into a sea of mercury.

'It's unbelievable—the beauty of the ocean,' he murmured, and she stopped and turned so they stood beside each other to admire the view.

'It is,' she said, and took his hand, squeezed his fingers. 'Thank you for reminding me. Living here, it's easy to take it for granted.'

He looked down at her, at the dark hair that curled around her head like a cap, at neat brows and long eyelashes. Had she felt his gaze that she looked up, and her lips were right there?

He touched her cheek, lightly, and sensed her hesitation, then whatever it was that had flared between them on the island sent colour to her cheeks as she lifted her lips to meet his.

The kiss was slow, exploratory really, but it loosened something deep inside him that had been tight for a long time. Her lips were soft and warm against his, and her skin smelt of the beach, and sun, and flowers he couldn't name, and of a woman he'd kissed three years ago...

They turned and walked again, closer now, her hand in his, and the silence sat more easily between them.

But it didn't stop the doubts raging in Kate's head.

This was stupid, getting closer to Angus when all the physical stuff that had thrown them together once before was obviously still there between them...

The physical stuff that had led where it had...

It was only dinner!

And if dinner led to another dinner—even a date?

Led further?

How fair would that be, getting involved with him and not telling him.

She should tell him.

And just what would that achieve? Quite apart from the pain *she* could feel just thinking about talking about it, how would it affect him?

Wouldn't it hurt him too?

And if it didn't—

No, she couldn't tell him—couldn't talk about it—not without bringing up those traumatic days and the agony of grief that had followed them.

The pain that still hit her when she saw a small child—

'—heard a word I've said?'

She turned to the man who was causing her so much confusion.

'Sorry, miles away.'

And thinking unhappy thoughts, Angus decided, seeing sadness in her eyes as she'd looked up at him.

'Well, that's okay, because it wasn't very interesting chatter anyway,' he said, but her distraction reminded him of the 'loner' tag she had at the hospital. Wasn't that why he was hanging around Bondi? To see if he could find out what had changed her?

Not that it was any of his business, but he'd liked the Kate he'd met at the island, and maybe he could find her again beneath the shell she'd built around herself.

Oh, yes? a voice in his head taunted. *You want to see more of her for purely altruistic reasons? To find out why she's changed? Nothing to do with the attraction you feel towards her? The physical attraction you felt back then, that's still there between you? The attraction you'd like to follow up on? Have a bit of a fling?*

Except instinct told him that Kate wasn't a 'just a fling' kind of woman. A woman he could enjoy and walk away from.

Yet, if he'd hurt her in some way? If his actions had somehow contributed to the change in her personality, shouldn't he make an effort to sort things out?

And a fling would do that? that voice in his head said mockingly, and he pushed all the useless thoughts away and concentrated on his guest.

'That rock pool looks fantastic. Someone was telling me there are people who swim here all year round.'

'Not me!' Kate assured him. 'I rarely go into the ocean until November when it's warmed up enough that I don't turn blue with cold.'

And just like that, things were easy between them again.

They were shown to a table by a window, far enough from other diners that they could talk freely, Kate asking him about his last posting, which he glossed over with a shrug and as few details as he could get away with.

Ordering dinner made a natural break in the conversation, so when that was done, he diverted the conversation back to her.

'And you?' he asked. 'Why surgery?'

For a moment, it seemed as if she might not answer, then she turned from the contemplation of the darkness beyond the window and looked directly at him, so he could see her face and read every expression on it.

'I liked the surgical work we did during training and then thought I'd follow up, but general surgery isn't as easy as it sounds and I'm determined to do well at it.'

'Why?' he asked again.

She frowned at him, although he was sure she knew full well what this question meant.

He leaned forward and touched one finger to her chin, a silent prompt.

'I wanted to do it for myself, to prove to myself I can be the best—or the best I can be.' She hesitated, then sighed as if she'd decided it was easier to get it all out than for him to keep prompting her. 'My parents were both high-fliers—lawyers—disappointed when I chose to study medicine instead of law. They'd wanted me to join the family firm, take it over in time. So, I felt I'd let the family down—failed.'

She looked out at the ocean again, remembering.

'I slightly redeemed myself by getting engaged to a lawyer then failed again by breaking off the engagement for what they felt was something trivial. Apparently, their marriage had survived many an affair! Other stuff happened, and I began to believe I *was* the way they saw me—a failure.'

She turned back to him, and he could read the determination in her face as she continued.

'I decided then I needed to do something for myself,

something worthwhile that I could be good at, succeed at. Not for my family—I rarely hear from them now—but for myself. To regain my self-esteem.'

Angus studied this woman he knew but didn't know. There'd been a power in her words that told him they were true, but what could possibly have hit her so hard *she'd* believed herself a failure? Her family had started it, but the 'other stuff happened' was the real clue.

Would she tell him?

He reached out and grasped her hand. Gently squeezed her fingers, knowing he wanted her to, guessing she wouldn't.

CHAPTER THREE

'WHAT ARE YOU doing here?' Kate demanded, coming across Angus at the hospital gate the evening after their dinner.

'Waiting for you,' he said, giving her a peck on the cheek. 'Alice said you started work at seven so shouldn't be much later than seven coming home. What appalling hours.'

He'd linked his arm through hers and with her heart racing and her nerves tightening right through her body, she knew she should pull away—casually, of course.

But her arm didn't move, so she concentrated on the conversation, managing, she thought, to sound quite calm when she said, 'I'm often far later than this. I'm on call to the ED, and a patient who needs stitching invariably comes in as I'm sneaking off home.'

'That wouldn't have mattered,' Angus replied. 'I had the paper to read while I waited and that was only after I'd checked out the fish and chip shops. Fancy fish and chips on the beach?'

More fizzing going on inside her, which was just plain ridiculous!

Or was it?

Surely she could just enjoy the moment, whatever the moment might bring. Wasn't that what Alice had been trying to tell her?

'Sounds great,' she said, and relaxed, letting her body rest close to his as they walked down to the front and the fish and chip shop he'd chosen.

'Why this one?' she asked, although she knew it *was* the best.

'Longest queue,' he said, grinning at her in such a way her insides turned to mush.

'I should phone Alice,' she said as they waited at the end of the queue.

'Don't worry, I've already told her I was taking you out to dinner.'

'Fish and chips on the beach—you call that dinner?' Kate teased.

She was startled when he turned to her and said quite seriously, 'Well, I don't know how long I'll be able to hang around, so I can't waste too much time on the preliminaries.'

And just in case she hadn't caught his meaning, he kissed her lightly on the lips—a kiss that came and went so quickly she was left wondering if she'd imagined it.

Except that her body knew she hadn't. It had reacted with a quiver of excitement that brought her nipples to peaks and produced an ache of longing between her legs.

They inched forward in the queue, Angus chatting to the woman in front of them, Kate's mind in a whirl.

If he wasn't going to hang around, surely she could go along wherever this led, enjoy it while it lasted? And with a clear conscience about not telling him because it wasn't a 'relationship' but just a fling. And a flingee could have as many secrets as he or she liked, surely?

The idea of a fling, of seriously considering it, sent a tremor through her body, settling deep into the pit of her stomach, while a warmth began to envelop her.

Angus's arm brushed against hers, stirring up more chaos in her body, and strangely enough making her smile.

It would be fun, she realised.

Risky but fun.

A light touch on her arm…

Worth the risk…

They sat on a seat on the promenade to eat their dinner, not wanting sand in the chips, but after eating they took off their shoes to walk on the beach, hand in hand, replete, and content, for the moment, just to be together. But in the shadows at the far end, where the rocks began, he turned her so they faced each other, drew her close with his free hand, and this time kissed her properly.

His lips were hard and firm against hers, insistent, demanding, so her lips opened to him, his tongue invading the softness of her mouth, tasting her as she tasted him, teeth clashing as he dropped his shoes and used both arms to bind her tightly to him, her body pressed to his so she felt the shape and strength and heat of him, filling her with a need—an ache—to know more, feel more, be one with him.

And somewhere, in some still functioning part of her brain, she thought, This was what it was like the first time—this feeling of being truly alive—every cell of her body somehow recognising this man, wanting him, needing him, part of him somehow.

Heat built within her, consuming all thought, and she found herself responding with a passion she'd forgotten could exist.

'We have to talk,' he said when, needing to breathe, they finally drew apart.

It took a moment for Kate to register the words, but when she did the excitement drained from her body, leaving her cold and shaken.

We have to talk usually heralded something the listener didn't want to hear. And would his talking mean she had to talk…?

Tell…?

Angus had bent to retrieve his shoes, and now he slung an arm around her shoulders and steered her back along the beach, closer to the water now so little wavelets lapped across their feet.

But the silence was killing her, stretching as tight as a bowstring between them.

'So, talk,' she finally said, and he laughed.

'If only it was that easy.'

He paused, turning her again to face him, touching her hair, her cheek, his fingers outlining her lips.

'I think we're both adult enough to acknowledge the attraction between us, and I don't know about you, but I'd like to see more of you, enjoy some time with you—some special time.'

'You sound as if you're making a speech about your tent,' she told him, bemused by the delivery of his 'talk'.

He smiled and shook his head.

'This isn't easy, you know. In fact, it's damn near

impossible. But what I'm trying to say is that whatever happens between us will be for now, can only be for now.'

His eyes grew serious.

'I don't want to make a big melodrama of it, but once I'm back on normal duty I won't know where I'll be from one day to the next. Most of my army mates have wives and families, and even though there are separations at times, it still works and works well. But now, possibly because I've been single, I've taken a different path. I've become involved with an emergency response unit and that led to designing and overseeing the manufacture of the prototype of what you rudely call "the tent" and some ancillary ones as well. But once it's past the testing time in Australia and into production, then I'll have to go where they—the tents—go. Can you see that?'

Earthquake zones, war zones, disease outbreaks in developing countries—yes, Kate could see each and every one of them, see them all in terrible, horrific detail.

'So what we have is now,' she said softly, not wanting to think beyond that, but at the same time relieved because with 'now' the past didn't matter.

Couldn't matter...

Then again, given how her body was reacting to him, wouldn't this idea of 'just for now' leave her wanting more or, worse, hurting again?

That was the risk.

But at least she'd feel alive again—and have happy memories to take into the future.

How could it hurt?

Silly question—it had hurt before, hadn't it?

And back then she'd known that all they'd have was just one night!

Except this time there'd be no consequence, and that part had hurt the worst.

So why *not* just live for the moment—for however many moments they might have?

Wasn't this just what she needed?

Something to jolt her out of the hole she'd dug for herself, to feel again—anticipation, excitement, desire, fulfilment—emotions she hadn't felt for so long...

He kissed her lightly on the lips, stopping all the arguments going on inside her head.

'The now,' he said, as they walked on. 'This isn't some great doom-laden thing, I'm pretty good at surviving anywhere, but it's the being away, the not knowing when I'll be back—it's destructive on relationships. I tried that with Michelle and it didn't work. It put too much pressure on her, far more than on me because I was always too busy to be thinking about anything but the minute, or hour, or day ahead.'

He paused as they walked up the steps, back to the promenade, then added, 'And I wouldn't like to do that to you.'

They sat again, Angus putting on his shoes, though Kate still held hers, the bottoms of her jeans so wet she was better without shoes.

'Well?' he said, when he'd tied his second lace.

Kate sighed.

'What am I supposed to say?' she asked. 'Back when I was dating—about a million years ago—we didn't have discussions like this. We went out a few times, kissed a few more, and if we both wanted to go to bed together, eventually we did. Or that's how it seems to have happened. Now it's like a timetable. If I say yes, will you tell me where to be and when so we can continue the whatever it is.'

He laughed and she added crossly, 'It's not funny!'

He leaned forward and kissed her on the lips, defusing the bit of what she'd felt was righteous anger, and bringing back all the sensations she'd been feeling... Was yearning the word?

'It's a little bit funny, you must admit, and hopefully fun,' he whispered against her lips. 'I just needed to be honest with you so you knew right from the start this wouldn't be a for ever and ever thing. I tried it once— well, more than once, but with the same woman—and it didn't work, so what do you think?'

He kissed her again before she could answer, not that she had an answer to give him, but somehow the kiss told her it would all work out, and made her admit that Alice had been right. She'd shut herself away not only from others but from her own emotions for far too long.

It was time for a change!

'I'm on call tonight so I'm going home now,' she told him with only a little quaver in her voice. 'But now you've done your honesty thing, I should warn you that I work horrendous hours, and my work is just as important to me as yours is to you, so you'll have to put up with broken dates...'

She paused, looking at him.

'Will they be dates?' she asked, and he smiled at her, mischief glinting in his eyes.

'Oh, they'll be dates all right, just you wait and see.'

He stood up and put out his hand to help her to her feet.

'Come on, I'll walk you home and kiss you good-night and you can text me your work schedule for the next few weeks or as long as you know it, and leave the rest to me.'

Kate chuckled.

'For such a good organiser you've forgotten one fairly important thing,' she told him. 'How can I text you when I don't know your number?'

He pulled her close and kissed her again, oblivious to the passers-by on the promenade.

'I'm glad you can still chuckle,' he said quietly as they drew apart, though not too far apart. 'That was something I remembered most about you.'

Angus gave her his card, pressing it into her hand, and felt her fingers close tightly over it—as if it was somehow precious—and for a moment he wondered if he was doing the right thing, seeing more of Kate while he was here. He'd made it clear to her that it was just, in her words, 'for now', but what of him?

Could he walk away so easily when this woman—and her chuckle—had not been far from his mind for the last three years?

But would it be fair not to?

In the darkened apartment entrance, he kissed her goodnight, holding her close, allowing a little of the emotion he was feeling to seep into the kiss.

Had she felt it that she responded, running her fingers up his neck to clasp his head with both her hands, and hold his lips to hers. It probably didn't go on for an aeon, but when she'd drawn away, then lightly pressed her lips to his with a whispered, 'Goodnight,' and he was walking back to his hotel, he felt as if it had lasted for ever.

Not that 'for ever' featured in his life these days.
From now on it was nothing more than 'for now'.

His mind was still in a pleasant haze, imagining what
lay ahead, as he walked along the promenade towards
the hospital late the next afternoon. His visit to the
State Emergency Service headquarters had been pro-
ductive, with positive comments about the little model
of his tent—damn it all, she had him calling it that
now! He'd taken notes of all the suggestions they'd offered, particularly in regard to some new fire-retardant
spray under development. He'd have to follow up on
that. The fabric of his tent was fire-retardant but no
one had ever tested to what degree it would withstand
fire and keep the workers safe inside it.

He'd made appointments for the next day, including one at a factory whose management had expressed
interest in manufacturing the internal fittings for the
tent—might as well stick to tent now—although the
prototype was being made in Western Australia, and
the real thing would probably be manufactured in
China.

And he'd also made a booking at a restaurant up the
hill behind the hospital that, he'd been assured, had
a magnificent view of the beach. With Kate's roster
saved on his cell-phone, he was confident that if her
shift supposedly ended at five, she should be available
for dinner by eight.

And about now, if she *did* finish on time, he'd be
able to walk her home.

'Mickey!'

The frantic scream came from behind him at the
same time as a small, tousle-headed boy flew past on

a scooter, crashing full tilt into one of the recycling bins a careful council had placed along the promenade.

He reached the boy and bent to untangle him from the now buckled scooter, and saw the blood running copiously from a split lip.

If that was the only damage, he was lucky, Angus thought, feeling in his pocket for the clean handkerchief he'd folded in there that morning.

He was pressing it against the wound when the mother arrived, and the child, getting over his initial shock, began to wail.

'He's okay, just a split lip,' he said to the mother. 'I'm Angus, I'm a doctor and I think it will need stitching. I can carry him up to the hospital—it will be faster than an ambulance.'

The mother half smiled, relief wiping some of the worry from her face.

'Are you sure?' she said, one arm around Mickey and the other hand holding the mangled scooter. 'He's got so big now I can barely lift him.'

'Quite sure,' Angus said, putting his arms around the little boy and lifting him as he stood up. 'Okay, Mickey?' he said. 'We'll get that lip of yours fixed in no time. I bet the other kids at kindy will be jealous when they see your stitches.'

Mickey stopped wailing while he thought about that, then recovered enough to say, 'School, I go to school. I'm a big boy now.'

'That's grand,' Angus told him as he strode towards the hospital, Mickey's mother trotting by his side. 'It's even better to go to school with stitches. And you'll have a great bruise to show your friends, all blue at first and maybe purple.'

'Or black?' Mickey asked hopefully. 'I like black.'

They were still discussing the colours of bruises when they reached the ED, where the first person he saw was Sam Braithwaite, Blake's fiancée, whom he'd met at the talk.

'Uh-oh,' she said, as she took him straight through to a small paediatric room. 'Looks like Kate's not getting off on time. We do minor stitches here but for a face, especially a child's face, we call for help.'

Kate felt a spurt of annoyance as her pager went off. She'd really thought she'd be leaving on time for once—secretly hoping Angus might be there to meet her. Putting on a bit of make-up and lipstick, and blushing as she did it, so out of touch with 'dating' she felt more trepidation than excitement.

She blotted off most of the lipstick, and hurried down to the ED.

Where Angus was dominating the space in the small theatre room.

'You're like a genie who pops out of a bottle, just appearing in front of me wherever I go,' she muttered at him.

Only not quietly enough, for the child—a small boy—on the table piped up. 'Genies come out of lamps, not bottles,' he told her, his voice muffled by a gauze pad he was holding to his upper lip.

'Angus rescued me and he's going to stay with me instead of Mum, 'cos Mum faints when she sees a needle, and if she's on the floor the stitching lady—is that you?—would have to walk around her all the time.'

'I see,' Kate said weakly, wondering just how Angus, Mum and the small boy had all come to be together. Apparently, they'd shared more than a few minutes because she could hear Angus in the boy's words.

'So, let's see what we've got,' she said, and lifted the pad. While Angus talked to the boy about the new scooter he'd have to get, Kate examined the wound.

'Whatever he'd hit must have had a sharp edge as it's a through and through cut, impacting on the inside of the mouth.' She smiled at the boy—Mickey Richards, she'd discovered from Angus's talk—and said, 'I'm going to have to stitch your lip, Mickey, but I'll give you something that will stop it hurting. We use what we call gas and you just breathe it in like you breathe in air and you might go into a dreamy sleep, but you won't feel a thing while I fix your lip.'

She turned to Sam, who'd followed her in to assist.

'Have you spoken to the mother? Explained we'll need to sedate him—?'

'And got her written permission,' Sam finished for her. 'And I know you like using nitrous oxide so I've got it ready. Nose mask and fifty-fifty with the oxygen?'

Kate checked the admission report with Mickey's weight and nodded.

'Now, Sam's going to put the mask over your nose and all you have to do is breathe through it for a few minutes.'

She paused.

'And no chatting to Angus while I'm stitching. I need your lip to stay still.'

But Mickey was already in a pleasant dream world and she doubted there'd be much chat.

She checked for any broken or cracked teeth. He'd been lucky as they were all intact.

Sam slid a suction device into his mouth, keeping it away from the wound. Kate flushed the tear, checking there were no tiny pieces of debris in it, then set to work.

She used absorbable sutures to fix the wound inside his mouth, knotting each stitch four times.

'Why the bigger knots?' Angus asked, peering into Mickey's mouth. Kate realised she'd been so caught up in her work she'd forgotten he was there.

Almost forgotten.

Except for little prickles on her skin.

And a slight flutter as she caught his deep voice saying something to Sam.

Concentrate on what you're doing!

But she still risked a glance at him as she answered.

'You know what it's like when there's something irritating in your mouth, a broken tooth, a tiny cut or graze?'

'You can't help poking it with your tongue,' he replied, and although she couldn't see him now as she *was* concentrating on her stitching, she knew there'd have been a smile on his face.

'Exactly!' she said, tucking the knots into the tissue under the repair to further safeguard them. 'Tying more knots stops them unravelling.'

'Do you use absorbable sutures on the outer skin as well?' Angus asked, and Kate nodded.

Medical chat made things easier.

'They're best on young kids as it saves them the added trauma of having to have them removed. The outer layer is trickier as we need to align the vermilion, that white line around the lips, or the scar will show.'

She worked quickly but carefully, smiling ruefully

to herself as she realised Angus would know as well
as she did what the vermilion was.

Angus.

She'd finished and as she wiped small spots of re-
maining blood from Mickey's face, she allowed herself
to again give in to her awareness of Angus's presence.

As a man.

Her man!

Well, her 'for now' man anyway…

Sam brought Mickey's mother into the room to be
with him as he rested, a dreamy smile on his face.

'Did I go to sleep?' he asked Angus.

'Maybe dozed, sport, and now you've got a new lip,
want to see?'

He found a mirror and held it up so Mickey could
see the repair.

'Cool!' the kid said, with a slightly lopsided smile.

'He's so good with children,' Mrs Richards said,
and Kate's heart clenched in her chest.

He *had* been good with Mickey.

She put two small strip dressings on the repaired
skin above his lip, then turned away to write a script
for antibiotics, giving it to Mrs Richards and explaining she could get them at the hospital pharmacy or
from her local chemist.

'Can I go now?' Mickey asked, obviously anxious
to be gone so he could show off his stitches to all his
friends.

'In a little while,' Kate said, touching him lightly
on the shoulder. 'I'd like you to stay here and rest for
a few minutes. See the clock on the wall? When the
big hand gets to the nine you can go. Do you know
your numbers?'

'Of course,' her patient told her in a tone of great disgust. 'I'm five.'

'And a very sleepy five,' his mother said, running her hand over his forehead as his eyes closed.

Leaving Sam to watch the child, she walked out with Mrs Richards, introducing herself properly and explaining that Mickey would probably be sleepy when he got home, and not to be concerned if he didn't want anything to eat, but some jelly or an electrolyte ice block would be good.

'See he keeps up his fluids and if he's in pain, he can have some children's paracetamol. If you're worried about anything, contact the hospital. There'll be someone who can talk to you.'

Voices from inside the room told them Mickey was ready to go.

'Can I see my scooter?' he asked as the two women returned.

'I put it in the bin,' Mrs Richards told him. 'It was all broken and we'll get you a new one just as soon as your lip's better.'

'Only you'll have to learn how to stop it,' Angus said, and Mickey laughed.

I could go now, should go now, Kate thought as Angus, Mickey and Mrs Richards chatted about scooters. One of the duty doctors will discharge him.

But she stayed until Mr Richards, apparently summoned by his wife, arrived to take his family home.

Kate followed them out the door, only too aware of Angus, who'd stopped to speak to Sam, just a few steps behind her.

Aware too of an inner unease that she'd felt since she'd first seen Angus with the child.

Unease she couldn't quite define, not sadness—or perhaps a little of that—but more what-ifs.

'You were terrific with that little boy,' she said to him as he drew up beside her. Saying something—anything—helped to hide all the physical manifestations of being near him that were now becoming common.

At least they'd chased away the unease...

'I like kids,' he said. 'I'd have liked to have some but Michelle felt, with me away so much, it might not be fair on them. I had to agree with her, but still...'

Michelle's name acted like a bucket of cold water on Kate's too-sensitised skin. Or had it been his talk of not having a child?

Practically blinded by the muddle of emotions churning inside her, Kate paused in the bustling hospital vestibule.

'I need to go back—get my things,' she said, and fled.

This was madness!

She was rushing into something because her hormones were in chaos, nothing more.

Except there *was* something more—something to do with feeling alive again, feeling at one with another human being, and wanting to share, to talk and laugh and, yes, make love.

Oh, yes, that was definitely part of it.

But she couldn't go into it—whatever it might be—with doubts or second thoughts. *Wouldn't* go into it that way!

She smiled to herself as excitement built within her once again. It might be just for now, but this was going to be a now she'd remember for the rest of her life...

Angus frowned as he watched her go. He'd been congratulating himself on being able to talk and joke with Mickey and his mother when all he'd really wanted to do was watch Kate. Not so much watch her stitch a cut lip but just watch her, wonder at the fate that had brought them back together, really look at her to see if he could understand just what it was that attracted him to her—or was it her to him—so strongly.

He tried to make sense of it as he walked out of the hospital, certain Kate would eventually exit but probably through some staff door he hadn't yet discovered.

She was smart—clever—and he liked that, and driven to succeed—a trait he shared—but that was mind stuff. What really puzzled him was the body stuff. He was sure his heart had probably skipped a beat when he's seen Michelle way back when they'd begun to go out together, but not every time he'd seem her, more when they'd been parted for a while.

With Kate, the little skip was there not only when he saw her but when he heard her voice, or thought about her agreeing to a short-term relationship.

For now, as she'd called it.

For a moment, he wondered if it had to be 'for now', the thought startling him so much he stopped midstride. No, the army was his life—well, not so much the army but definitely the tent. He wanted to see it through.

But if he *wasn't* in the army?

He pushed the thought away...

CHAPTER FOUR

KATE HAD A quick shower in the staffroom, washing
her hair, which always seemed to smell of disinfectant
after even a small procedure at the hospital. She tow-
elled it dry, pulled on the clean undies she kept in her
locker, then studied the other clean clothes stashed in
it. They weren't up to much, apart from being clean—
jeans, a T-shirt, an ancient parka in case it was cold
walking home, and…

On a hanger, right at the back, a pair of black slacks
and a dark blue cotton-knit sweater that she'd brought
along one night when the SDR team were going out
to dinner to celebrate something she could no longer
remember.

She'd been held up in Theatre so hadn't gone, but
the clothes had stayed in her locker. They'd have to do,
although a little bit of her wished she'd had something
to dress up in to go out on this 'date'.

Not that she had much that counted as dressy at
home either. Alice had been right. She'd shut herself
away for far too long.

Not any more!

Hurrying now, she dressed, applied minimal

make-up—a little mascara to her eyes and bright red lipstick—and set off to meet Angus again.

For a date!

Her heart skittered and she paused to wonder if it was normal for a woman of her age to be feeling so— so what? Nervous certainly, yet excited. Upbeat, yet worried about what she might be flinging herself into.

Then the thought of Angus brought warmth rushing through her body, and a glint to the eyes she could see in the mirror.

You only have one life, she reminded herself, thinking of Alice's words after the accident.

So go live it! she told her reflection, and all but marched out of the hospital.

'Nice transformation,' Angus said as he met her, but it was the admiration in his eyes that was her reward. She smiled at him, more at ease now.

They walked up the hill to the restaurant, a light sea breeze teasing Kate's hair, Angus's deep voice teasing other bits of her.

How far would a 'for now' relationship go?

How far did she want it to go?

A different stirring inside her now, giving her an answer, so when Angus linked his arm through hers, she let him draw her close and sensations as powerful as a kiss flooded through her.

And through him, that he drew her into the deep shadows of an overhanging tree and kissed her hard and long?

Her legs were shaking as she drew away, desire flaming through her, heating her body, sensitising her nipples.

'I can cancel our reservation,' he whispered, telling her he'd felt it too.

'I guess we have to eat,' she said, denying the new surge of emotion.

'I guess we do, but perhaps…'

They'd reached the restaurant and hesitated in the light outside it, and the matching heat of desire in Angus's eyes all but stole her breath.

'One course,' she said softly. 'And a glass of wine, not a bottle.'

He grinned, devilment dancing in his dark eyes.

'And all the time I'll be thinking what we'll do— what I'd like to do to you and like you to do to me.'

Kate felt the heat flare in her cheeks.

'Perhaps we should have cancelled,' she murmured, the huskiness of her voice a dead give-away of her feelings.

Alex took her elbow and swept her up the steps.

'Come on, I've booked a table with the best view of the beach.'

The waiter showed them through onto a small balcony, and Kate could only shake her head.

'It's beautiful! I've seen the suburb at night but never like this,' she said.

"So glad m'lady approves,' Angus said, doffing an imaginary hat and bowing low.

Blushing again, Kate sank into the chair the waiter was holding then breathed in the fresh sea air.

Things were moving far too fast for someone who'd been a loner for two—three really—years. Yet she wanted this man in a way she'd never felt before— wanted to be in bed with him, hot and hard and urgent in her need.

'What?' she demanded, turning back to see him smiling at her.

'You could never play poker,' he teased.

'Why not?' she asked, and he laughed.

'Every thought you have is written on your face, every doubt is shadowed in your eyes.' And, still smiling added, 'I won't rush you into this, Kate.'

This time any colour in her cheeks would be from embarrassment, but she didn't have the words for her unease. Perusing the menu took a bit of time, and ordering a little more, but when that was done Angus reached across the table and took her hand.

'What's bothering you?'

She smiled, partly because his holding her hand was very nice indeed but also because it was easy to talk to Angus.

'Every single thing about this whatever it is—not the actual getting together bit of it, or even the "for now" part, but I suppose it's because we don't really know each other, do we, yet later tonight we'll probably be in bed—'

This time his grin sent goose-bumps down her spine.

'Getting to know each other better,' he pointed out, and she gave up.

She'd tuck all doubts—particularly about secrets—deep down in her heart, and go with the flow, see where it led, knowing it would end when the army sent him somewhere—tomorrow, or next week, or, with any luck, maybe in a month.

Or two?

Now you're being greedy, she chided herself, removing her hand from Angus's grip as their meals arrived.

They talked of Mickey and his mother, which led to childhood accidents.

'I fell out of a tree when I was six,' Angus told her. 'Mum saw me lying on the ground and fainted, which was helpful. Fortunately, a neighbour had heard me yell and came rushing in. He called an ambulance and they thought it was for Mum, who was still lying on the ground, so no one took much notice of my broken arm until they'd made sure Mum was all right and had driven away.'

'So, what happened then?' Kate asked, mainly to divert her mind from picturing Angus as a young boy.

'Oh, the neighbour drove me to hospital. I think he fancied Mum but she never looked twice at him. Or at any man after my dad died. He'd been in the army and was killed in a helicopter crash—not shot down in anger, just a chance malfunction of some kind back at home.'

'That's terrible,' Kate said, and he shook his head.

'It was for Mum but I didn't really remember him. I was barely two so my memories are from photos of him in his army uniform.'

'And your mother?'

'Died when I was ten. The official word was cancer, but Gran, who brought me up, with a bit of help from a couple of uncles, always said it was grief.'

It was Kate's turn to reach across the table to touch Angus's hand, but although he squeezed her fingers in response, he wouldn't accept sympathy.

'Don't feel sorry for me, I had a perfectly happy childhood. Gran was fantastic. One of my uncles is a doctor and so I chose the army for my father and a doctor because of him, which got me to where I am today.'

'But losing your mother like that,' Kate murmured.

Angus shrugged, broad shoulders rising.

'Mum was sick for a long time so Gran had always been my rock—'

He paused, looking at the woman across the table—the woman he barely knew yet felt he knew.

'A bit like Alice was yours, I imagine,' he finished, and was pleased when Kate smiled.

'Only too true,' she said, pushing her empty plate away. 'Shall we go?'

As a hunger unlike any he'd ever felt before had been gnawing away at his intestines since she'd walked out of the hospital—slim and upright, the blue top thing she wore making her eyes seem bluer—he didn't argue.

He gave the waiter his card, signed the bill and, as quickly as decency allowed, led her out of the restaurant.

'Should you phone Alice?' he asked.

She leaned into him, kissed his cheek.

'Did it from the hospital—told her not to wait up. But I'll have to go home sometime, I'm on an early shift.'

'Then off for three days, is that right?'

She chuckled, a soft warm sound that sounded like small bells in his ears.

Small bells in his ears?

What was that about?

'Yes, three whole days,' she was saying when he'd pulled himself together.

'Shall we go away?'

She turned to face him, obviously puzzled.

'Go away?' she echoed.

'Yes,' he said, 'together, somewhere nice—well, different—just the two of us. To Sydney maybe.'

'We're already in Sydney,' she pointed out as he steered her back down the street.

'But right in Sydney, in the city, a big anonymous hotel, do the sights, Luna Park, the Zoo, ferry rides to Manly or up the river. Let me show you my home town. There's more to Sydney than Bondi Beach, you know.'

'Hush your mouth,' she said, laughing as she spoke. 'Don't let anyone around here hear you say that!'

So they were both laughing when they reached his hotel, and although he could feel her body, close beside his, grow tense as they walked in, she didn't falter, standing beside him while he got his key and following him to the elevator, his hand now clenched in hers.

'Hey,' he said softly, using his forefinger to tilt her head to his as the elevator rose, 'we don't *have* to do this, you know.'

The ping told them they'd arrived, and he put his arm around her shoulders and steered her down the hall to his door.

But once inside he held her lightly in the circle of his arms, face to face.

'I like you, Kate, and I'm attracted to you, and I'd like to get to know you better—both in bed and out. It's not just about the sex so if you're not comfortable with it just tell me.'

He dropped a light kiss on her lips and waited.

'I suppos—' she began. 'I don't—'

She hesitated again. 'Oh, damn it all!' she finally said. 'Just kiss me, Angus. I don't want to analyse it all.'

He did as he was told and kissed her, and she kissed him back, which led eventually to a frantic shedding of clothes before they fell on the bed, wanting each other but prolonging it, learning each other's shape and textures, teasing, heightening the pleasure until neither of them could wait any longer.

Kate must have dozed and she woke in Angus's arms, filled with a peace and contentment she hadn't felt for a long time.

Would she wake him if she moved?

Was not waking him enough of an excuse to stay?

She smiled to herself and ran her free hand along the arm that held her, up to his shoulder, warm, and hard with muscle.

Sneaked a finger further along to touch his cheek, his straight nose, his close-cut hair.

Would the ba—?

She pushed the thought away, far away, back down into the bottom of her heart.

She was with Angus here and now and the past would stay the past...

And she had to leave—had to get home, grab a couple of hours' proper sleep and get to work.

Reluctantly she eased her way out of the warm comfort of his arm, away from the treacherously tempting body that had filled her with such delight.

He slept on. An army thing, she imagined, grabbing sleep when it was available because who knew when they'd need to not only be awake but aware with every sense of the enemy around them.

She scrabbled around the room, finding her hastily shed clothes and pulling them on, raking her fingers through her hair, aware that walking out of the hotel at two in the morning was going to be highly embarrassing.

But well worth it, she decided as she crossed the road to her apartment block and crept silently into her own bed where she could close her eyes and remember— relive the sensations—as she fell asleep.

But when the alarm woke her, what seemed only minutes later, she tucked all the memories and sensations away in a new box in her mind—the 'for now' box—and concentrated on what might lie ahead of her when she reached the hospital.

She'd barely shut her handbag away in her locker when her pager summoned her back to the ED. One of the young doctors on duty apologised as he explained.

'She's not entirely sober and she fell through a glass coffee table. Eight-inch gash on her upper right arm and other minor injuries. We've flushed the arm wound. Apparently, the table broke cleanly into three pieces, rather than shattering.'

He led the way into the suture room where a large woman in tight jeans and a red bra was sitting on an examination couch, crying quietly. A nurse was holding a pad to the injured arm, and the local anaesthetic and sutures Kate would need were laid out on a tray at the side of the room.

'So silly,' the woman said to her new audience. 'I was fighting with my boyfriend—just yelling, not pushing and shoving kind of fighting, and he made me so mad I stormed across the room and, bang, there I was with the table broken all around me.'

She paused, peering over her shoulder to watch Kate take the dressing from her arm.

'Now he's going to be really angry because he loved that table. He didn't even bring me to the hospital, just

phoned for an ambulance and it took for ever and now
I'm going to have a great ugly scar down my arm—'

'We'll try to make sure it isn't a great ugly scar,'
Kate said quietly, pleased to see the wound, though
deep in parts, hadn't damaged any major blood vessels.

Her brain was racing. She understood why the staff
here had called her, rather than send the woman up to
Theatre. According to the chart, she'd eaten a full dinner at about ten the previous night and been drinking
wine and nibbling on cheese and biscuits until shortly
before she'd fallen, so she couldn't have a full anaesthetic.

Not that the wound necessitated that, but with the
alcohol in her, she needed to be sedated. A mild dose
of ketamine, easy to administer into a muscle and safe
to use on inebriated patients. She spoke to the nurse,
who hurried away to get the drug, while Kate checked
the sutures on the tray.

Some internal absorbable ones for the inner layer
of skin on the deeper part of the wound, and exactly
what she'd have chosen for the closure.

She smiled to herself, aware she shouldn't be surprised. She'd spent a lot of time in the ED, sewing up
injured patients, and most of the staff knew how she
worked. And conscious of not leaving a bad scar, she
worked carefully, although it meant she was going to be
late for assisting in a scheduled op with her supervisor.

Not that he'd need her—it was an op an intern could
assist with, but she admired the man who was guiding her career path at the moment, and loved watching him work.

Slipping late into Theatre, the nod her supervisor
gave her acknowledged that he'd known where she'd

been, but settling into her accustomed place across the table from him was—

Well, different somehow.

As if!

Surely one night of romance didn't mean everything had changed.

So why did it feel that way?

She looked around but all the faces were familiar, so she glanced up into the glassed-in gallery above the theatre—the usual bunch of students there, some in white coats, some in civvies.

Some in civvies?

She darted another look into the gallery.

No, she hadn't been mistaken, that was definitely Angus up there, talking to one of the hospital administrators, a new man she'd heard of but had rarely seen.

She forced herself to concentrate on what was happening in front of her, steeling herself against the silly flutters in her body, focussing on cauterising small bleeders, holding organs out of the surgeon's way, taking over the closing of the wound, slowly and carefully, not daring to look up but hoping he was gone.

Or that maybe he'd been an apparition!

She went straight from Theatre to the side room, where she stripped off her scrubs and tossed them into a bin before showering and changing back into clean ones. One of the gynaecology surgeons was doing a keyhole removal of an ovarian cyst, and she wanted to watch the screen as he worked through a tiny slit— well, three tiny slits.

The ever-expanding use of keyhole surgery fascinated her and although she'd only ever used it to clear infection from an injured knuckle joint—under the watchful eye of a hand surgeon—she wanted to learn as much as she could of the different uses to which it could be put.

Or was this rushing to another theatre more to do with avoiding the possibility of meeting the apparition in the corridor? It probably hadn't been him, although her skin had thought it was. But what could he possibly be doing here, and how could she concentrate on work if he was going to keep popping up all over the hospital? She didn't care whether genies came out of bottles or lamps, there was definitely something genie-like about his appearances in front of her.

Not to mention distracting!

Angus had been surprised when his uncle had suggested they look in on an operation. He'd imagined that, as an administrator, his uncle would sit in an office all day.

Waking to find Kate gone, the day had seemed to stretch endlessly in front of him. The phone call from his uncle had also surprised him as the last time he'd seen him, the man who'd been his role model as a child had been working at Royal North Shore Hospital on the other side of the city.

Apparently, increasing difficulties with the arthritis that had plagued him for years had led him to consider administration—and Bondi Bayside had needed just such a person.

'Word reached me that you were about,' he'd said, then invited Angus to meet him at the hospital. 'I've got a bit of administrative stuff to do, then we'll have lunch.'

The 'administrative stuff' had taken them to one of the theatres and it had to have been fate that Kate had walked into the tableau below the viewing balcony. Even in a blue bandana and oversized blue scrubs she had looked beautiful to him, and his body had tightened just looking at her.

Had she seen him when she'd glanced up?

He couldn't tell, although he could almost feel her concentration as she avoided looking up again…

'Are you with me or off somewhere in that busy head of yours?' his uncle asked as he led him into the admin lunch room.

It was a question his uncle had often asked the child who'd been Angus, usually in the middle of a 'little talk' about the world and its ways. Angus had invariably stopped listening, his attention caught by a butterfly alighting on a flower, or a passing bus if they'd been in the city.

'Sorry,' he said. 'I was diverted.'

'By a woman, I hope, or thoughts of one. It's time you were married.'

'Aah!'

It was an old conversation. His family had known and liked Michelle but although that was over, as far as this uncle was concerned, it was a man's duty to get married and have children.

But Angus had the perfect diversion for him.

'I was actually wondering what it would be like working in a hospital if I left the army,' he said, because this was another of his uncle's favourite topics.

'Well, I could put in a word for you at North Shore, or I'm sure there'd always be a job for you here,' he said. 'Actually, one of the doctors on our Specialist Disaster Response team has recently left, and you'd fit right in there.'

Which led to talk of his trip out with the SDR and the development of his tent and the subject of marriage was forgotten.

But the marriage idea stayed in his head, and it was only by reminding himself of the dangerous positions he'd been in in the past that he was able to banish it.

He turned his thoughts to where to stay in Sydney. Harbour views, not too far from the city centre, close to Centennial Park for walks. He'd grown up in Balmain, near enough to the city to know it well, and although the army had taken him far and wide, Sydney would always be home to him.

Somehow, Kate got through the day. The apparition hadn't helped but by the time she left work, on time for once, she'd convinced herself she'd been seeing things—memories of the night before sending false messages to her brain.

But as she was leaving the hospital, the sight of a tall, well-built man leaning into the window of a rather posh car, and the skip of a heartbeat, suggested she hadn't been mistaken.

The car was leaving the executives' car park.

And for one, probably foolish, moment she allowed herself to imagine Angus had been at the hospital enquiring about a job—thinking of leaving the army.

By the time he'd straightened and given the top of the car a tap, she'd remembered the tent and his passion for it—his determination to eventually provide the best possible facilities for teams sent into disaster areas.

And to be there to see that they got it!

Of course he wouldn't leave the army...

She sighed, remembering too that this was just for now...

He turned as the car drove away, saw her and strode towards her.

'Just found out my uncle—the doctor one—is one of your bosses. It's hard to keep up with me moving around all the time and him being so busy. Last time I heard from him he was on the other side of the harbour. He'd heard I was around and asked me to lunch.'

He'd put his arm around her and dropped a kiss on the top of her head as he spoke, causing such a riot of sensations in Kate's body she barely made sense of the words.

'Saw you in Theatre, too,' he continued, steering her onto the footpath, his arm still clamped around her waist. 'Wanted to wave but didn't want to distract you.'

Kate stopped, which pulled him up quite sharply. He looked down at her and smiled.

'Talking too much?' he asked. 'I'm just so glad to see you, and I've been thinking about the fact we'll have three whole days together.'

She saw the gleam of excitement in his dark eyes and felt a shiver of anticipation.

'You okay to leave tonight? It's not too soon? Will it be all right with Alice?'

'Tonight? We're going tonight?'

Was it too soon? Was she ready for this? Had she even said she'd go? And did she really want to spend three days with this man who, considered realistically, she barely knew?

Except she did know him—knew he was great in a crisis, knew he was kind and considerate, knew, too, that he was honest, that this would be just what it was—something for now.

And he was patient, too, she realised, for he was just standing there, waiting for her answer, not asking again or persuading her.

But just looking at him her body throbbed with excitement.

No, it wasn't too soon and, yes, she *was* ready!

So why not tonight?

'Alice will be delighted,' she told him, and they turned to walk again.

But packing proved a more difficult task than talking about it. She dithered in her bedroom while Angus chatted to Alice as if he'd known her for ever, his ease with older people no doubt coming from growing up with his grandmother.

Just stop thinking tangential thoughts and pack.

But what?

September in Sydney meant warm sunny days but cooler nights, and who knew when a westerly wind would blow in at any moment and turn the city into an ice-box.

A very windy ice-box.

She put in slacks, three summery tops, a jacket for the evenings, and would take a parka just in case the wind did come.

But, oh, why was all her underwear so practical, so predictable? White bras and knickers, black bras and knickers, not a bit of lace or pretty ribbon anywhere.

If they didn't go tonight she could make a dash to Bondi Junction and...

And tell Angus what?

That you can't go tonight because you don't have

pretty underwear? From what she was getting to know of the man, he'd insist on taking her to a lingerie shop first thing in the morning and probably make her parade in front of him for his approval.

More for his amusement as he'd know she'd be embarrassed.

She paused, cotton knickers in hand, as a thrill ran through her. Was this really happening? Was she about to take an enormous leap out of her self-imposed isolation—out of the safe little world she'd made for herself—into the arms of a man she barely knew?

Except she *did* know him in ways it might take a lifetime for other people to know each other. The fraught hours when they'd hidden their own fears to care for the terrified tourists and even staff on the island had formed a bond between them that she knew, meeting him again, was still there.

Damn it all, underwear was underwear, and she doubted she'd be standing around in it for long. He'd managed to get it off her very expertly the previous evening.

She threw in the underwear, toiletries and make-up, a squashy hat and some good walking shoes, and was done.

Quick shower and they could go, although Alice had probably already regaled him with all the mishaps of her youth and the disaster of her non-wedding!

Night had fallen by the time they'd checked in at the hotel and reached their room. As the door closed behind the porter, Angus put his arm around her shoulders and led her to the windows.

'It's breathtaking,' she whispered, awed by the spread of beauty before her. The twin trails of red and white lights as cars crossed the Harbour Bridge, the well-lit ferries carrying commuters home from work and bringing people back to play in the city, and closer, just beneath them, the city itself, neon lights pulsing and strobing, as if in time to the heartbeat of the city.

Angus had raided the mini-bar and opened a half-bottle of champagne, handing her a glass as she stared in wonder at the view.

'Just a glass now because we've a big night ahead of us,' he said, but when he put his arm around her the hunger she'd felt earlier returned and as the light kiss he dropped on her lips became hard and demanding, she knew his plans for the evening would have to be delayed.

'We can't go on like this for three days,' she said some time later, sitting up in bed, finishing her warm and flat champagne. 'I'll be too exhausted to go back to work.'

Angus was lying behind her, running one finger slowly down her spine, as if counting her vertebrae, making sure they were all there.

'Angus?' she said, thinking his finger might be moving in his sleep, but he'd reached the small of her back and flattened his hand against her skin, curling it around her waist and effortlessly easing her back down beside him so they lay face to face.

She studied him, this man who had almost literally swept her off her feet. What was it about him? What made him different? Surely it had to be more than body chemistry.

There was his kindness—she'd seen that with

Mickey. And in the way he chatted to Alice, showing a genuine interest in her charity work.

And his passion for his work—that ran deep within him.

Then—

Her brain stopped working as his finger traced her face, and the lips she'd been watching spread in a small, satisfied smile.

'Don't look so smug,' she told him. 'I'm here because I want to be, not because you're some irresistible lover.'

'Ah, but I am to you, aren't I?' he said, tracing her lips now and slowly awakening all the feelings that had led them to this position.

'Yes,' she admitted. 'It's the why that's got me puzzled.'

He leant up on one elbow and leaned over to kiss her.

'Don't overthink it, just enjoy it.' He sat up, all business now. 'So, do we go out to eat or order room service?'

'I love room service when I stay in hotels, especially at conferences and seminars,' she admitted.

'That's because you've become antisocial—I've been around the hospital and staff often enough to have picked that up—and someday you'll tell me why but I think probably a little bit of fresh air would do us both good so let's shower and get some clothes on and see what this wonderful city has to offer us in the way of a meal.'

The shower took longer than expected but eventually they were dressed and out on the street, wandering hand in hand among the bustling streams of people who never seemed to leave city streets.

'Ha!' Angus suddenly declared, halting their aimless meander. 'I wondered if it was still here. You like Moroccan food?'

'Love it,' Kate assured him. 'It's something I like to cook, so I'm sure I'll find plenty of new dishes to try.'

The restaurant was richly decorated with carpets, intricately carved panels and filmy curtains, draped to provide private spaces for the diners. Low, satin-covered sofas and huge cushions provided the seating and candles burned in ornate silver holders, sending a faint, musky scent into the air.

'Have you been there, Morocco?' Kate asked when they were seated.

'Once—a flying visit. Unfortunately, I missed all the colour and splendour of the architecture and saw a lot of desert. Famine in the Western Sahara had brought a horde of refugees flooding across the border, many of them with diseases we rarely see, like malaria, cholera and Hep A. I was in Stockholm at the time, they do a lot of disaster response work, so I went with their team to do what we could to help those who were sick, but mainly to set up water purification plants.'

Kate smiled and shook her head.

'Stockholm and Morocco,' she said. 'Both sound equally exotic to me.'

'But you could travel—you get well paid. At least you could take holidays in some of these places.'

Her smile faded as she realised just how limited her life had become.

'I've just never thought about it,' she admitted. 'I suppose it was the thought of doing it alone—not having anyone to turn to, to remark on the beauty or wonder or something in particular and no one to share the memories with afterwards.'

Angus hoped the frown he was feeling inside wasn't showing on the outside. Admittedly, back on the island, he hadn't known Kate well, but he was absolutely certain that that Kate would have at least *considered* foreign holidays. And she'd been quite happy—well, maybe not *happy* happy but content somehow—when she'd honeymooned alone...

In fact, he remembered talking to her about far-off lands during the night they'd sat out the cyclone. Travel had definitely been in her future.

So, what had happened that had made her turn in on herself, as if curling herself around some hidden hurt?

Would he eventually find out?

He couldn't ask—at least, he didn't want to ask. Deep inside he was hoping she'd trust him enough to tell him.

Eventually?

Except there wouldn't be an eventually.

Couldn't be one. Not with the lifestyle he led, and would be leading for the foreseeable future.

He shook away his thoughts, glad Kate had been diverted by the description of the dishes on the menu while he'd brooded. While he'd realised, with a definite shock, that the last thing he should be considering was an 'eventually' together!

'Listen to this,' she said, turning to him with a smile. 'It sounds like an Indian biryani, which has layers of rice and meat, only this one has couscous in place of the rice and the meat has apricots and dates through it.'

She read out the description and as he watched the animation in her face he—

What?

Forget it!

This is for the here and now, remember. Tomorrow you could be anywhere.

He ordered the dish she'd talked about, and distracted his wayward thoughts in a discussion with the wine waiter. A nice rosé should do the trick, they decided.

He turned back to Kate, caught her perusing him in much the same manner he'd been watching her with the menu earlier.

'It's kind of exciting, getting to know someone new,' she said, adding with a smile, 'Well, almost new.'

The smile made his bones melt.

Men's bones didn't melt!

Not soldiers' bones anyway.

Shouldn't have had the champagne.

'It is,' he said, smiling back. See, it's easy being normal.

Except if this was normal he was in trouble...

Angus seemed a little distracted, but Kate was so entranced by the décor and the menu she was happy to carry the conversation, pointing out carpets she particularly liked, or reading the ingredients of dishes she'd like to try at home.

'You could come for dinner one night and I'd cook it,' she said, and although Angus smiled and accepted the offer politely, she knew something had shifted between them.

Maybe not between them, but on his side anyway.

Was her inviting him to dinner a step too far from their 'here and now' relationship?

She shook away the thought. They had three days together, that was the here and now, and she was going to enjoy every minute of it.

No doubts, no regrets, no analysing their relationship, because there really wasn't one. And when it finished, at least she'd have good memories this time, memories of fun and laughter, and of simply being together.

They rode the ferry to Manly the next day—the old ferry, not the fast commuter—and Kate marvelled at the number of little bays and inlets on either side of the harbour, many with houses right down to the water's edge, others with carefully preserved bushland, while still more had massive steep sides of sandstone, with houses perched on top.

Angus stood beside her at the rail, one arm round her waist, pointing out a tree, a bird, a tiny sailing skiff, his body talking to hers in a way that added magic to the boat trip.

The tall Norfolk pine trees along the beachfront at Manly reminded her of all the pictures she'd ever seen of Manly beach—so familiar it was hard to believe she was here. Or that she'd lived in Bondi for two years and had never been to Manly. Her life really had become restricted.

She hooked her hand through the arm of the man who'd brought her back to life, squeezing his arm in a silent thank you because words would never be enough to explain how wonderful she felt.

It was an idyllic day—the sun warm, with sufficient breeze to whip up a few foaming white horses on the ocean. Hand in hand, they walked the beach, then ate hot dogs at one of the tables on the esplanade.

The problem was it felt so right, being with Angus, talking or not talking, holding hands, bodies close, doing their own communication. It felt like for ever, and she mustn't fall into the trap of thinking that way— mustn't be misled into imagining this was anything but here and now.

They made the most of the day, catching the fast ferry back to the Quay and a little one across to Luna Park, Angus having expressed disbelief that she'd never been there.

'Scared of heights?" he asked.

'Like I could rappel down to an injured victim on a cliff face if I was?' she teased.

'You do that?' he asked, so astonished she had to laugh.

'Mostly in training but once here and several times when I was in the SDR in Brisbane. We've mountains just north of the city—the Glasshouse Mountains— that idiots with no experience insist on climbing by the hardest route.'

He was leading her towards a Ferris wheel, and looking up to see the height of it she was very glad she wasn't afraid of heights. Although...

'You know, sitting in one of these swaying cradles right at the top isn't quite the same as working on cliffs with a safety harness on and ropes attached to solid objects and team members around to make sure you're safe.'

He put his arm around her, pulling her closer.

'I'll anchor you,' he whispered, and for one wild moment it sounded like a promise of forever.

They rode up into the sky with stupendous views over the harbour and the city, then wandered through the park, eating fairy floss and hot dogs because that's what you ate at fairs. They rode the big dipper, Kate shrieking as they zoomed down the steep slopes, and got lost in the mirror maze.

To Kate, it was a magical experience—nothing more than going out and having fun really—but to somewhere new, and especially with someone, well, special, her whole being seemed filled with joy and happiness.

'And just what are you contemplating so seriously?' Angus asked, as they paused under a shady umbrella, eating ice cream.

She smiled at him but hesitated about answering. To be contemplating fun?

He'd think she was crazy!

Except she had been!

Having fun, that was.

Probably best not to mention the joy and happiness...

CHAPTER FIVE

IT HAD BEEN enough of a day to justify room service back at the hotel, and as Angus fed her fresh fruit and her body shivered in delight and anticipation, she found it hard to remind herself that it was just for now.

And later, much later, as they lay, still breathless, on the bed, with Angus nuzzling the sensitive spot behind her ear and whispering that he'd have to order room service more often, the thought of it not being just for now lodged in her head, and she put her arms around him and drew him close.

To hold him forever?

No, it couldn't be but for now they were together and if what she was beginning to feel felt like for ever, that was just too bad.

'Today we do the city!' Angus announced when they finally surfaced at close to ten in the morning. He added quote marks with his fingers, and although deep down he was thinking he'd just as soon spend the day in bed with Kate, something told him that would be a bad idea.

Being together twenty-four hours a day, doing simple things like sightseeing and fun park rides seemed to have shifted something inside him.

He couldn't define it and definitely didn't want to think about it too much, but it had somehow changed from a good idea to show someone around his city, to finding huge pleasure in that someone's company, and an awareness that this had become a very special time.

For Kate too, he was sure. To him, she seemed to grow more beautiful every day as if happiness was radiating from inside her.

While in bed—well, he wouldn't think about bed or they'd never leave the room. But her body seemed to match his in its ardour and excitement, in the intensity of some of their encounters and the soft, slow lovemaking of the early morning.

He knew he had to walk away from her—his life too uncertain, too chaotic for him to offer much in the way of a husband.

Husband!

Where the hell had that come from?

'Well, I'm done in the bathroom,' the subject of his concerns said, appearing in a pair of long tailored shorts, a blue patterned top, and a silly hat with orange sunglasses at the front perched on her head. He'd bought it for her at Luna Park the previous day, more as a joke than anything else.

'Urchin!' he said, and she laughed.

'I thought you'd like the hat,' she told him. 'It kind of finishes off the outfit.'

And as she stood there, clean and ready for the day, grinning at him from under the hat, he wanted nothing more than to get up off the bed, take her in his arms and hold her.

Possibly forever.

He pushed off the bed and dodged past her into the bathroom, dodging past just in case his arms reached out—

Perhaps, he thought when he was under the shower, not quite cold but cool enough, it was just because they were with each other all the time and having fun together—that would explain things.

Practical as that explanation was, it didn't sit easily with him, so he set the matter aside and concentrated on their itinerary for the day.

Art gallery first, he decided, then...

They were halfway across the beautiful park leading eventually to the gallery when he stopped.

Kate had moved on another step but was pulled back by their joined hands.

'You do like art galleries, do you? I didn't ask. I love this one, and there's a super exhibition on at the moment.'

She smiled, came close, and kissed him lightly on the lips.

'I love them, big ones and little ones. They are the parts of Sydney I do know.'

An hour later, they were in a new exhibition of Australian aboriginal art when he felt his phone buzzing in his pocket.

Cursing inwardly, he pulled it out, praying it was something simple, an enquiry about the tent maybe—

'I've got to go!' he said, staring blankly at the message telling him to report to base ASAP and well aware his words were equally disbelieving. 'I'm so sorry, Kate. I was going to take you to the Queen Victoria Building after this, you can still go, and you can stay on at the hotel and have room service. I'll sort the bill when I pick up my car but I—'

She put her finger to his lips.

'You have to go,' she said. 'I do understand. I always understood it was just for now, and now has been tremendous fun. I'll stay on here at the gallery for a while and go to the arcade but probably go home to Alice tonight.'

He wanted to argue, but what about? This was his life.

He pulled her tight and kissed her hard, oblivious of the people around them.

Opened his mouth to say he would be in touch, then closed it again because would he?

Where was he being sent?

How long would he be away?

Would he even return?

He squeezed her hand and walked away, determined not to look back, not to check if she was as upset as he was, crying perhaps—not that he was crying.

Not on the outside anyway, and definitely not when walking through a public gallery, but he felt as if something had been wrenched out of his insides, out of his gut perhaps—couldn't be his heart...

He was halfway out the door, still battling to find a way through all the swirling emotion in his head— well, his head *and* his body—when he noticed the gift shop. Art gallery gift shops sold mostly books on art and classy posters, but they also sold top-of-the-range souvenirs.

Jewellery?

He ducked inside and was rewarded with an array of

Australian gemstones set in earrings, bracelets, necklaces and—yes, just over there—a pendant.

It was an opal, radiating brilliant red and blue and green with flashes of gold as the sun caught it. To him, it seemed to exemplify all the colours of the happiness he and Kate had shared. He bought it, wrote a quick note on a card, and left it at the hotel when he went back there to get his stuff. She'd have to return there to pack and he wanted her to have it as she left the city—have something to remember him by, something as beautiful as their time together had been.

Now he could go back to work…

Kate watched him leave, waiting for him to turn, to wave, determined not to cry in case he did turn, wanting to cry when he didn't. Then, aware of the covert glances of the few people who'd been in this part of the gallery, she continued her inspection of the paintings, a little blurry perhaps, because she knew that 'now' was over.

From there she went to the Queen Victoria Building, the beautifully restored old building that housed some of the city's most expensive jewellery stores and small boutiques.

There, tucked into a corner on the upper level, she spotted a beautiful sign, scrolled in gold, Lady Marmalade! Intrigued, she went closer, and smiled as she saw the red velvet-covered antique chair in the window, a mannequin sitting demurely on it in black lace underwear.

With the taste of Angus still on her lips after their farewell kiss, she slipped inside. The exquisiteness of the garments stole her breath, and her fingers trembled as she touched sheer silk and delicate lace. She might never see Angus again, but the last few days had changed her in ways she barely understood.

Outwardly she might look the same, and she'd return to work as dedicated as ever, but inwardly she'd been awakened to such joy and happiness that it seemed only right she should celebrate it. *And*, she decided as she slid a few more hangers off the rails, having sexy underwear under her work clothes was as good a way as any. The slither of silk against her skin would keep her memories alive.

Keep her alive?

She returned to the hotel, considerably less well-off but with the pain of loss lessened just a little by her mad, impulsive buys. As she walked through the lobby, a receptionist called to her, handing her a package.

'Your friend left this,' she said, and, although intrigued, Kate slipped it into one of the carrier bags and went up to their room before she opened it.

Inside the package was a small white box, tied with blue ribbon, and inside that—

Her legs went from under her and she dropped down onto the bed, holding the opened box in both hands, staring in wonderment at the beautiful gem inside it.

'So you'll always remember our "now",' the note said. As if she'd ever forget it!

And as she sat there, on the bed, her fingers running lightly over the words Angus had written, she felt again the terrible pain that loss could bring—the ache inside her threatening to spoil her memories of the joy, and loving, and laughter.

Had Angus guessed this was how she'd feel that he'd sent this beautiful gift?

She picked it up, clenched it in her hand and sent a promise through the ether to wherever he was that she *would* remember.

She slipped it around her neck, fastened the catch at the back and smiled at her reflection.

How could she not?

Once packed, she had the concierge call a taxi for her and headed back home—to Alice and to real life, but to a better real life, she told herself. She owed it to Angus to get back to the Kate she had once been. He'd shown her the life she'd forgotten; the way life should be lived.

Oh, she'd still work as hard, and train for the SDR, but she'd start saying yes when the team went for a drink after training, and she'd take Alice out to dinner once a week.

As the taxi pulled up outside the apartment block and she found money to pay the driver, she wondered just how long these great resolutions would last.

And, more importantly, just how would they help heal the ache she felt inside, fill the emptiness in her heart?

Those questions were answered, or at least set aside, when she returned to work, where one of their almost cyclical busy weeks had already begun. Hurrying from theatre to theatre, being seconded to orthopods and gynaes, as well as working with her supervisor, Kate had no time to brood over Angus's departure, although she did try to call in and see Harriet at least once a week, bringing her news and gossip from the hospital and encouraging her to join her occasionally for a quiet dinner uptown.

Harriet's ex-boyfriend Pete had finally manned up enough to admit the relationship was over and had taken his toothbrush and shaver and what clothes he hadn't managed to sneak out during his 'disappearing' weeks.

Kate felt Harriet was taking it well, but when her new friend said rather bitterly, 'I no longer suited his image of us as the perfect couple,' Kate knew just how upset, how hurt Harriet had been by his defection.

Although a rather complicated camera sitting on the coffee table in Harriet's room did please Kate, as did Harriet's enthusiasm for her new hobby.

'I know you're right and I could spend all my time just taking photos from my balcony of all the different moods of the sea, but it's been great for my leg as it's got me out walking and I'm going a little further each day.'

'Good for you!' she told Harriet, before heading back to Alice's apartment to see what was for dinner.

So far her 'going out for a drink with the team' hadn't happened, but she and Harriet had become closer and one day, hopefully, she'd get off work early enough to actually go out—with anyone or no one, even for a walk on the beach.

Work did ease off and if the SDR team teased her a little when she joined them for a pizza after a meeting, she just smiled and laughed with them and actually felt enjoyment in the company.

She told herself she owed it to Angus to get out more but the real upside was that working hard, chatting to Harriet or eating pizza with the team took her mind off the hollowness inside her, even if it was only temporarily.

At times, it seemed as if it was the physical side she missed so much—his closeness in the bed, the touch of his hand as they walked together, the way he slung an arm around her shoulders...

But she missed their talk as well, from work discussions, to what wine to drink with crab, to silly things about their youth. She'd been totally consumed by the man, and although she'd been left bereft, she worked on, and socialised, and tried desperately to fill this new emptiness inside her with whatever she could find.

Angus had been called not to a military or humanitarian disaster but to the far side of the country where the second of his prototypes was being manufactured. He'd incorporated various modifications into it, and the manufacturer had other projects lined up but was having difficulty with the new tent, hence the urgent summons.

So, although he spent what seemed like twenty hours a day either arguing with the project manager at the factory, or writing up changes to the specifications into the wee hours of the morning, he found himself missing Kate.

And although he wasn't in any danger—except perhaps from increasing frustration—he reminded himself that his sudden departure from Sydney had been because of his job—a job that could just as likely taken him into a war zone.

But Kate had sneaked beneath his skin. He could feel her there, feel the way she moved against him, smell the scent of her shampoo on the pillow next to him, hear her chuckle at a silly joke—this last one when he was arguing with an increasingly bad-tempered project manager.

Highly inappropriate that he had smiled at the memory...

But this particular prototype had to be just right for it was going to a big convention in the US and the army was hoping for enough orders to balance out the considerable amount of money they had already spent on it, perhaps even enough to enable them to expand the programme.

So he worked and tried hard not to think about Kate, glad in some ways for the difficulties he was encountering so he had little time to brood over their short time together.

He'd done the right thing, he knew he had, in making it 'just for now', but now could have lasted a little longer, surely.

He could contact her when he got back to Sydney, hook up again—

And when the next call came?

Probably from China where components of the tents would be manufactured once they had the prototypes right, or would the army decide he'd been dithering around with this business for long enough and send him back into mainstream army life—Special Ops awaiting him if he wanted it.

Maybe the spirit-breaking training he'd have to do would take his mind off Kate!

The next call, when it came, was a relief from the seemingly endless petty problems that had had him tied in knots. Landslide in the Snowy Mountains, several chalets affected, people trapped inside, and while he felt for all those injured or in danger, he also felt a thrill that his tent—had they brainwashed him at Bondi Bayside that he kept thinking of it that way—would finally be tested.

He figured, as he flew back to his base in an air force jet, that the mountains were probably closer to Melbourne, so disaster relief response would come from there.

He was being fed more information as they travelled. It was cold in the mountains, still too early for too much snow, although the snow blowers had been working on the slopes. Apparently, plenty of visitors had been taking advantage of the last of the cheaper off-season accommodation, so the affected lodges had been full.

Then there'd been rain in weather not quite cold enough to turn it into snow, and more rain, and more rain, and the sodden ground had shifted, just slightly at first but eventually carrying the ski lodges and the people inside them down into the river valley.

Floodwaters?

There'd be army engineers there by the time he arrived so that wouldn't be his problem.

Back at the base, helicoptered from the air force runway, he had a quick word to the commander, grabbed some clean clothes and a heavy, waterproof jacket, shoved the small pile of mail that had been just inside his door into one pocket, and headed back to where another helicopter waited, his precious tent and two add-on accommodation tents already packed inside, along with his regular support crew.

The view as they circled the mountains prior to landing was spectacular, but his attention was more on where they could set up their rescue mission. There was a relatively flat area below where the chalets had been, close to where they'd ended up, and he could see one helicopter already there.

'Enough room to land beside it?" he asked the pilot, and received a thumbs-up in reply.

The whine of the engines changed as the pilot decreased speed and within minutes they were on the ground, the crew already out, dragging the cumbersome bundles with them and carrying them to a clearing closer to the devastated buildings, unzipping and unfolding as they moved, working like a well-oiled machine.

Angus joined them and the chopper lifted away. He'd already seen the familiar SDR logo on the other helicopter, although it was probably a Victorian response unit.

Kate was crawling through a space the USAR team had shored up when she heard the helicopter.

Good, more help on the way!

She could hear the tap, tap, tap of wood on wood, the sound that had told the USAR team there was someone alive ahead of her. But although she called to the tapper, she received no reply, so it was only when she glimpsed the shoulder she alerted those up top to her find.

Because whoever it was couldn't speak? Crushed chest? The taps told her she was getting closer, although there were fewer of them and they were getting weaker.

Don't go beyond the red ribbon, the USAR fellow had said, but she could see the shoulder of someone just beyond it and there was no way she could stop now.

Very cautiously—she'd done an Urban Search and Rescue training course herself—she moved what looked like a corner of a pool table, edging it sideways so she could see further into the wreckage.

It was a woman, blood colouring her blonde hair a deep pink.

'I'm here, we'll get you out,' she told the woman, although that could well prove to be a lie. More of the pool table—thankfully not slate—had fallen on the woman's legs and one leg of the table, thick, heavy wood, lay across her chest.

There was no room for her to get past the woman to try to lift the obstacles, so she dug, slowly and carefully, one small piece of rubble at a time. She could see the table leg was jammed at both ends so it wouldn't—shouldn't—give way as she excavated.

When she felt she had sufficient space cleared beneath the woman, she slid her arms beneath her shoulders and pulled as gently as she could.

A little movement!

She tried again. The table leg stayed stable as she edged the woman from under it, but the material that had come down on her legs was coming with them.

Talking all the time, she eased the woman inches closer, until she was free enough for Kate to examine her—well, the top half!

She pulled a thick triangular bandage from the bag that she had dragged along beside her, and found a decent-sized piece of timber to wrap it around it to support the woman's head.

Felt for a carotid pulse—regular, but weak—let her fingers feel around the scalp, an open wound but no ominous grating of bone or bone indentations to hint at skull fractures with likely brain damage.

If she could find the woman's hands, she could find a viable vein and start a drip, adding a little pain relief to keep the woman comfortable until someone could get to her. It was pointless calling for more help yet, as any helper coming in would have to use the same tunnel so would have to wait until Kate crawled out.

Hands were at the end of arms, so should be easy to find, but the first arm she felt carefully along had a piece of what felt like metal protruding from it. Heart hammering, Kate's fingers continued the exploration.

Not good! The metal—a rod as thick as her thumb—was through and through, the woman was held by whatever the rod was connected to. At least while it remained in place there'd be less bleeding, but remembering she'd already shifted the woman, Kate felt carefully around the entry and exit wounds and sighed with relief when she could find no extreme blood loss.

Best she get herself out and leave it to the experts. She'd give the woman pain relief and go for help.

Easier said than done. No room for turning so she had to inch backwards on her stomach, all the while being careful not to bump against any shoring props or anything else that might bring the whole building crashing down on her.

And her patient!

When it seemed as if she'd been worming backwards for ever, she felt someone take a good grip on her ankles and haul her the rest of the way out.

Paul!

He put out a hand to help her to her feet.

'I hope you didn't go further than the red ribbon,' he

said with mock severity as she brushed dust and mud and sawdust from her clothes.

'Not much further but there's a badly injured woman in there and we need to get her help *now*!'

'I'll get some of the USAR team back here,' he said, and jogged away, while Kate wiped more dust from her eyes and finally looked around.

Looked around in disbelief!

While she'd been deep in the bowels of the destroyed building, a huge white tent had appeared. A huge white tent with a red cross on the roof and a tall, broad-shouldered, angry-looking man bustling around it, yelling orders to the crew securing guy ropes and generally getting things shipshape.

Or tent-shape in this instance.

The crew were obviously not doing it quickly enough for Angus, who was acting as if imminent disaster might befall them all if his tent wasn't ready in whatever time-frame he'd promised. Of course he'd be anxious—this was the first trial of his tent in a real emergency situation, rather than the practice sessions it would have been through.

But although her feet wanted to cross the uneven ground towards him, and she could almost feel his presence on her skin, duty took her back to Blake, where she reported on the state of the woman and asked for her next job.

'In the tent if ever Angus gets it up to his satisfaction,' Blake said, finding a smile in spite of the chaos all around them. 'We've moved about four survivors into it already and Sam's in there with a couple of paramedics.'

So she'd get to be closer to Angus anyway, Kate

thought, but after the initial flutter of excitement she'd felt at seeing him, she was now uneasy. The 'now' was over so how would he be? How should *she* be?

Casual, old friends—that would be the best way to play it, and forget excited nerve endings and little tugs low in her belly.

She headed for the tent.

CHAPTER SIX

As it happened, it wasn't until the end of a very long day spent dealing with casualties inside the tent that Kate caught up with Angus, who'd spent his entire day ironing out glitches in the setting up of the primary tent then erecting accommodation tents, army issue, for the relief workers, and a mess tent to feed the masses.

He came into the mess as she was in line to grab a hamburger, Paul behind her, telling how they'd managed to extricate the woman by opening another tunnel and coming in at a right angle to where she was trapped. She was one of the rescued who was airlifted to hospital without stabilisation in the tent, her injuries serious enough that another of the specialist doctors would stabilise her the best he could in flight.

Kate shook her head as she thought about the woman, knowing that the piece of steel would still be through her arm, no one wanting to move it in case it caused catastrophic bleeding.

'They had to put fire-retardant padding around her body because they needed a small, battery-operated angle grinder to cut through the steel to release her and it could have spat sparks.'

'The poor woman,' Kate was saying, when the hairs on the back of her neck stood to attention only a second before a deep voice said, 'Fancy meeting you here.'

Paul turned first, greeting Angus like an old friend.

'Look, Kate, it's Angus. I thought that tent was pretty special, and I wondered if it was his.'

Kate closed her eyes briefly. The way Paul spoke it was obvious the hospital gossip mill hadn't linked her and Angus.

She said thank you to the young soldier passing the hamburger and turned towards the man she'd thought she'd never see again. Not that seeing him again meant anything. She knew that! Knew the 'now' was over.

'Hi!' she said, as brightly as she could, considering that actually looking at him had sent her heart rate rocketing and she could feel blood drumming in her ears.

'Hi, yourself,' he said, his eyes moving over her as if to take in all of her, caressing her somehow.

Or perhaps it was just the smell of the hamburger making her feel weird.

'Your tent's fantastic to work in,' she told him, desperate to break what was becoming an awkward silence. Desperate to think of anything apart from touching him, feeling his skin beneath her hand, her body pressed to his...

But now Paul had been served they could both walk away.

'Just fantastic,' she added to Angus, and followed Paul to a table at the far side of the mess, hoping it looked as if she was walking normally, not fleeing from the man who, by simply being there, had thrown her body into turmoil.

* * *

Well, that went well, Angus thought to himself as she walked away. He turned to watch her until he realised he was probably drawing attention to himself, propped like a post in the middle of the mess.

And wasn't it for the best?

Didn't her brush-off—what else could you call it?—indicate that she'd realised the time they'd had together was over?

Which it was, wasn't it?

Hadn't he set up the programme that way?

Explaining that because he never knew where he'd be from one day to the next, he couldn't offer permanence?

Except seeing her at a distance when someone had pulled her feet first out of a tunnel—dusty and dishevelled—his body had tightened and a strange pain in his chest had made breathing difficult for a moment.

And he'd certainly thought, once assured she was on her feet and okay, Great, we can get together again!

But that's what he'd done to Michelle—on and off—and not only had it not worked but it had hurt her, making her feel she was little more than a casual companion. Made her feel used, she'd once told him. Convenient.

He couldn't do that to Kate.

Because Kate was different?

Because he'd wanted to find out what had changed her, and he'd been pleased to see glimpses of the old Kate re-emerging as they'd enjoyed time together?

Hmm! He was thinking of excuses now—excuses so he could make the most of this unexpected reunion.

Hardly fair on Kate, though, would it be?

He walked out of the tent, dinner-less, too confused to stay inside, too aware with every fibre of his body of the woman sitting not twenty feet away from him.

Kate watched him go. Her outward reaction to seeing him must have been the right one—cool and casual so he would know she wasn't expecting their...whatever it had been would continue.

So why was there an ache right through her body and a heavy sadness pressing down on her chest?

Why was her inner reaction so...?

Wrong?

Paul was telling her about another rescue, and about a new lot of shoring the USAR team was putting through to the second building. There'd be work to do and if there was one thing she'd learned over the past few years, it was that work was the perfect way to blot everything else from her mind.

She finished her food and while Paul lined up for more, she went back outside to where the sunset was painting the snow on the higher mountains a rosy gold.

'There's a safe passage through to the other building now,' the site manager told her, repeating Paul's news, but this man pointed the way. 'As far as we know, there are at least three families in that lodge, not sure how many kids.'

Kate slung her bag over her shoulder, checked her pockets for gloves, and headed for the new tunnel.

Blake was at the end of it, supervising the removal of a man on a stretcher, easing the rigid equipment around a bend.

'Just do what you can,' he said. 'They've set up lights but it's still gloomy in places. Check under anything that might have been a bed or a table for kids that were pushed there to shelter.'

Kate nodded, going forward now the stretcher had passed, joining other relief workers on what was, for now, the front line.

A quiet sobbing took her to the right, stepping carefully over broken timber and shattered windows, glad her boots and tough overalls were at least protecting her body. The noise was coming from down near her feet, so she knelt, very tentatively, making sure the ground was solid beneath her knees in case she sent debris raining down on someone.

'Hello. Can you hear me?'

Wait ten seconds and call again, but before she got to ten, a little voice said, 'Here.'

Great! Kate thought, but at least the child—the voice had been a child's—could speak.

It had come from a mess of bedding and broken wood, and Kate poked her arm in underneath as far as she could.

'Can you see my arm?' she asked, waving her hand about as much as she dared.

A tight grip on one finger gave her the answer, and she pulled out her torch and bent lower so she could see beneath the mass of damage.

'I'm going to shine a torch so shut your eyes for a minute,' she said, keeping hold of the little hand that had now sneaked into hers.

Lying flat again, she shone the torch and made out the face of a small girl, eyes shut tight.

Shining it away from her face but deeper into the hole where the girl was, she said, 'You can open them

now and have a look around. Can you move your legs
and arms—just a little bit?'

'Yes,' came the answer. 'I was in another place and
I couldn't find Mummy and so I crawled in here.'

'Good girl,' Kate said, bringing the torch back to
shine on her own face. 'I'm Kate. What's your name?'

'Libby.'

'Okay, Libby, I need the torch to look around to
see how we can make a hole big enough for you to get
through, then if I need some help to make it safe for
you, I'll give you the torch so you can hold it while you
wait for me to get back. Okay?'

The answering 'Okay' was so wavery and soft that
Kate looked desperately around the tangled material to
see if she could get Libby out without calling in someone to shore up a hole.

The damaged mattress she could see was good. It
was slung between two what must have been wall joists
and would form a stable roof. If she could get Libby
that far she'd be safe while Kate shifted other obstacles.

'Need help?'

It *would* be Angus and, for all she knew she
wouldn't, she could have hugged him. Although with
both of them now stretched prone on the ground that
was hardly possible anyway.

'Little girl, Libby, just through there,' she said, ignoring the totally inappropriate reactions of her body to
Angus's presence by her side. 'Libby, here's Angus and
he's going to help us. He's big, and brave, and strong,
so we'll soon get you out.'

'My daddy's big and brave and strong,' Libby told
him and Kate found herself smothering a smile.

Angus had shifted, getting carefully to his knees

so he could see over the trap in which the little girl was caught.

'I think there's a sturdy piece of timber over there that I can get without bringing anything down on top of us.'

'That would be nice, then what do we do?' Kate asked, totally focussed now on the child they had to rescue.

'I poke it in very carefully until it's beside Libby then I can use it as a lever to cautiously raise the mess in front of her and she should be able to scramble forward—'

'To under the mattress!' Kate finished for him. 'I'd worked out that bit just not how to get her that far.'

She looked at the piece of timber Angus was now holding, and pictured how far in it would have to go to work as a lever.

'I'll wiggle in a little further,' she said, 'so I can guide it past where Libby is then ease her out.'

'You stay right where you are,' Angus told her.

This time she chuckled. She knew it was probably adrenalin making her a bit silly, but to have Angus squatting there bossing her about—well, it was just too bizarre.

And as she was already wiggling forward, what was he going to do about it?

She found the end of the timber he was using and guided it, talking all the while to Libby, explaining, checking she was okay.

Though what was 'okay' in this situation?

Once they had the timber in place, Angus lifted it cautiously, and Kate was able to grasp both of Libby's hands and pull her gently with her as she, Kate, wiggled backwards.

The timber had lifted whatever had been blocking Libby's passage closer to Kate as well, so she could pull the child right through.

'There was absolutely no need for you to go that far in,' Angus was saying crossly when she was finally able to sit up and lift Libby onto her knees.

Kate looked up at him and smiled, then began to examine the little girl for any injuries, Angus crouching beside them now, his arm around them both, making it difficult for Kate to concentrate on what had to be done.

Libby was scratched and bruised in places, but shock was the most likely thing to be affecting her right now so, easing away from Angus, Kate just sat and held her, rocking her back and forth, feeling the little arms clasped around her neck and praying that Mummy and big, brave, strong daddy were still alive somewhere.

Angus watched them, sensing the child needed the reassurance of Kate's arms around her, and Kate's soft words of comfort, but something in the way Kate had bonded with the child, the way she held her so tightly—a precious bundle in her arms—bothered him slightly. As if there was something deeper going on.

Unless what was bothering him was the image of a woman and child—like a mother and child—like a family...

Or that he'd had to watch as she'd put herself in danger to get to the child.

He shook his head, trying to clear the—was it frustration? Or simply the situation itself, being with Kate yet not with her, being distracted by her presence when all his attention should be on the job at hand?

'Okay,' she finally said. 'I think I'll pass you up to Angus and he can take you out to see the helicopters and the tents and all the stuff we've got out there to rescue people like you.'

Realising it was his cue, he turned to lift the little girl and caught the glint of tears on Kate's cheeks.

He moved away, bent double for the first few yards. He had to go. There was work to be done, but not stopping to comfort Kate—or to puzzle out what had brought on those shining tears—was one of the hardest things he'd ever done.

Kate was emerging from the tunnel a little later when a dishevelled and slightly bloody woman caught her arm.

'I heard there was a child rescued,' she said, panic making her voice rise with each word.

'What's your child's name?' Kate asked her, holding the woman's arm to steady her.

'It's Libby, Libby, and she's only six.'

Kate gave the woman a quick hug.

'And she's brave as a barrow full of bears,' she told the mother. 'You'll find her in the white tent, probably with a tall guy in army fatigues.'

The woman took flight, her feet barely touching the ground beneath her, obviously not feeling the cold or anything other than relief.

Kate watched her go, praying that big, brave, strong Daddy had also been found and at least one family could be reunited. She headed back down the tunnel. The USAR team, or maybe the army equivalent of it, had made branch tunnels off the main one and every one of them would have to be investigated. The USAR would have gone through their search routine, calling out to survivors, and Kate imagined that, by now, most of the victims they found would be unconscious.

As the new tunnel diminished in height, she bent, and then crawled her way along it. There'd been two families in this building—where was the other one?

Paul had found a man, wedged in a space beneath a fallen refrigerator, and a quick glance told Kate why they wouldn't be moving it in a hurry as it was holding up a tangle of shattered building material that might once have been kitchen cupboards.

'He said his foot was bleeding before he passed out, possibly from pain, and I've managed to get a faint pulse in his neck but if he's losing blood fast—'

'We need pressure bandages and a tourniquet,' Kate finished for him.

She was studying the space beside the man. Paul had been able to get close enough to feel for the carotid, for a pulse, but she was reasonably sure she could slide down beside him. Though whether far enough for her to check his foot, she wasn't sure.

'I'll try to get in there,' she said to Paul, and the team had been together long enough to know that sometimes only a woman *could* reach into certain places, and he didn't argue.

Angus would!

The thought, coming out of the blue when she'd been totally focussed on the problem in front of her, sent a jolt of annoyance through her body.

And a bit of warmth as well, she had to admit. It was nice to have someone thinking of her safety for all they should both be concentrating one hundred per cent of their intention on their jobs.

She eased under the refrigerator, pausing to check

there was still a pulse in the man's neck, counting his
breaths—slow and steady. As the space narrowed she
was forced to turn onto her side and crab along like
that, as close to the man's body as a lover.

And she knew why that description had come to
mind—Angus again.

Focus!

Whatever had happened between her and Angus
was in the past, and that's where it would stay. She'd
reached the man's thighs and felt carefully around the
one closest to her, shoving her hand to get it underneath, feeling for obstructions.

But that one, at least, was free, although the other
was under a tangle of crockery and she didn't have
time to waste clearing it.

Just a little further, not far now, edging past knees
and on down to his feet.

Or what was left of his feet.

One seemed to be intact but the other had been par-
tially severed, possibly by a sheet of glass, right across
beneath the toes. A complete amputation might have
caused the blood vessels to shrink back and close de-
fensively, but this was bleeding profusely.

Hauling her bag up towards her, she took out gauze
padding and clamped it on the injury, holding it tightly
with her hand, applying all the pressure she could,
packing more gauze against it when it was still bleeding after what had seemed like an hour but was only
ten minutes.

'Have a man in blue tunnel,' she said into the mouth-
piece on her helmet, glad she'd noticed the colour of the
ribbons on this one. 'Bleeding profusely from a partial

amputation of his left foot. He must be trapped by his other leg as we can't move him. The injured leg is free.'

She added more gauze then bandaged the wound as tightly as she could, lying on her side in a space more suited to a rabbit.

Tourniquet?

She had a commercially produced one in her bag, but there were pros and cons.

She glanced back at the blood seeping now through the bandages, and reached for the tourniquet, slipping it out of its plastic bag and swiftly getting the strap in place around the man's lower leg, just above the ankle. She tightened the strap and buckled it then used the small rod to wind it even tighter—noted the time using a stylus on the small screen attached to her overalls above her top pocket. Waited for a minute, then removed the padding from the wounded foot. There was still blood seeping out but it would be controllable with the gauze and a new bandage.

Now she could feel around the other leg to see if she could find the obstruction that was holding him, praying that it would be something fixable and they wouldn't have to amputate the man's trapped leg in order to free him. He'd already lost half a foot.

'Hop out and let me see what I can do,' a male voice said.

The man was in USAR overalls, and although he was larger than Kate, she wasn't surprised to see him sit down beside the injured man and sinuously work his way in.

'Feet first so I can see what's above him,' he said to Kate. 'You said it's his right leg that's trapped?'

Kate agreed, while the newcomer felt all around the refrigerator, testing its stability.

'Seems solid,' he said. "I'm Charlie, by the way.'

'Kate.'

'Well, Kate, I don't think we can lift the fridge to get at him,' he said, and Kate refrained from telling him she'd already figured that out.

'The fridge is holding this partition down and it's the end of the partition or whatever it was that's landed on his leg.'

Kate had swabbed the man's hand and was inserting a cannula, preparing to start some fluid running into him, but she understood what Charlie was saying.

Not only understood, but also realised they were getting closer and closer to a nasty solution to the problem.

Satisfied she'd done what she could for the moment, she checked the fluid bag she'd left resting on the fridge and made sure the line was clear, then backed away until the tunnel was high enough for her to stand.

Not wanting the man's situation to be broadcast to everyone, she made her way to the tent in search of Blake. If the limb had to be amputated, they would have to prepare the necessary equipment.

'A team member from USAR will contact me if we need to go back in,' she told Blake, whose face already looked grey with fatigue.

'Well, you take a break,' he told her. 'Maybe in the mess. I'll call you if you're needed.'

Kate nodded. Her body told her it would rather rest on a bed, but Blake was right. If they had to amputate, he'd need her there.

CHAPTER SEVEN

SHE WAS LEAVING the tent when she realised that on shelves that had miraculously appeared along its side, and were apparently held up by air, were stacks of equipment. In fact, everything she needed to restock her bag.

She replaced all the items she'd used, ticking each one off a list on a clipboard on the shelves.

Slinging her bag back over her shoulder, she headed for the mess.

Angus had been treating a woman with crush injuries to her left arm and shoulder, splinting the arm to keep it stable as she was airlifted to hospital.

Had he sensed Kate's presence in the tent that he wasn't surprised when he looked up to see her speaking seriously to Blake?

The thought was disturbing. Hadn't he always prided himself on giving one hundred per cent of his attention to whatever he was doing?

He shook away the notion and concentrated on securing his patient to the stretcher.

But as Kate stopped near the entrance to replenish her supplies, he came abreast of her as his patient was wheeled out towards one of the helicopters, both now ferrying the injured and their families to hospitals.

'Are you taking a break?' he asked, when he'd said goodbye and good luck to his patient.

'Just until Blake needs me,' she said, explaining about the possible amputation.

'I could assist with that,' he said, thinking it might spare Kate the horrifying sight of a field amputation.

She looked up at him, a glint in her eyes.

'Think I can't take it?' she challenged, and he had to laugh.

Though when he spoke, he was serious—speaking softly, gently.

'I think you could take whatever life threw at you.'

The glance she shot him was startled, and he imagined she'd grown a little paler, but as she straightened her shoulders and colour returned to her cheeks, she said, 'I might take you up on that offer to assist Blake. I think a quick nap would do me more good than another meal or even a hot drink in the mess.'

'If that hamburger is all you've had to eat today, you need some real food. Come on, I'll pull rank and get you a decent meal then even find a bed for that nap.'

He went to sling his arm around her shoulders, but she moved away, whether deliberately or not he didn't know, although he was glad she did. Neither of them would enjoy being gossiped about if people thought they were interested in each other.

Because they weren't, were they?

Well, not now—not after the now...

Much as he wanted to, he could hardly bang his hand to his head either, but he needed to get it straightened out—concentrate on work, not emotion.

He scanned the blackboard menu as they entered the mess, and decided on the rich beef stew for himself, pleased when Kate agreed it would be just the thing for a cool night in the mountains.

Sending her to find a table, he got the meals himself, bringing them across to where she sat beside one of the 'windows' in the mess tent.

'The night is so light—bright with stars, I suppose,' she said, thanking him when he set down the meal but continuing to look out the window, colleagues, nothing more. 'We don't really see stars in the city.'

So they talked of stars, and the city, and he told her how overwhelmed he'd been by the stars in the Sahara—finding it hard to believe there could be so many of them when the night skies he was used to had so few.

'So few visible,' Kate reminded him, and he smiled at her.

'I sometimes wonder if a lot of things aren't visible in the city,' he said.

'Like homelessness,' she suggested. 'We get so used to seeing people sleeping in doorways we don't stop to think about what horror they've known in their lives to have ended up there.'

He shook his head, surprised yet not surprised at her reaction.

'Here I am thinking about emotions, how the everyday rush and hurry in the city, the need to earn enough to be able to live in the place, can overwhelm the things in which we should find joy, like looking at the stars or walking on the beach. And you come up with homelessness, which is, of course, only too true. We don't look hard enough'

She smiled at him, but he felt it was a polite smile,

nothing more, no hint of the Kate who'd been coming to life only a few weeks ago—the one who would use her fingers to stifle a chuckle at something absurd.

'The man Blake's with is in the blue tunnel,' she reminded him, in case he hadn't got the message that they were here to work, not chat about stars and life in the city. Let alone emotions. 'And the bed?'

He stood up, collecting their plates so he could drop them over at the servery, and led the way out of the mess.

'It's just a basic tent, I'm afraid,' he said. 'Shared facilities and hot beds, with someone dropping into one the moment it's vacated.'

She half smiled.

'I didn't expect five stars,' she assured him.

They found an empty bed, complete with a sleeping bag opened up to act as a duvet.

'Pull it over you,' Angus said. 'You won't realise how cold it is until your body relaxes.'

He paused, sure there was more to say—more he wanted to say—but only silence stretched between them.

Kate thanked him, and dropped her bag at the end of the bed before slumping down on it, suddenly so tired she knew she would sleep just as she was, not even bothering to remove her boots.

Not even sparing a thought for all her physical reactions generated by Angus's re-emergence in her life.

It was only temporary anyway, and the work was so important she could ignore them.

Most of the time…

She set the alarm on her watch to wake her in an

hour, and lay down, only vaguely aware that Angus was still standing there.

'Blue tunnel,' she reminded him, before she closed her eyes and slept.

'Like intern year all over again,' she muttered to herself when the alarm hauled her back to consciousness. Back then, sometimes on duty far beyond the twelve rostered hours, grabbing an hour's sleep had been the only way to keep going, but she'd forgotten how fuzzy she'd always felt when she woke up.

Like now. Her head full of cotton wool.

A quick but surprisingly hot shower partly restored her, and a coffee and pastry in the mess completed the job. The army sure knew how to live!

A new site commander was organising things from above the ruins and he directed her back to where she'd first been.

'They've shored up a lot more of the wreckage in there,' he told her, 'and they're trying to get through to a small group of survivors—talking to them and all.'

So back down to the red tunnel, trying hard to think of the survivors they might rescue, rather than the man who'd virtually put her to bed an hour ago.

But how could she not think of him?

For weeks she'd been trying to shut away the memories of their time together, trying to box them up to look at far in the future when thinking about him wouldn't be so painful.

It shouldn't have been, she knew that.

It had been a brief affair, nothing more, but those magical days in Sydney, although cut short, had made her realise—

No, she wouldn't go there!

Couldn't go there!

Red tunnel, concentrate on that.

She found the team working to get to this group of survivors—five, they told her—in an offshoot of the tunnel she knew, and joined them in lifting rubble, piece by careful piece, aware from the sounds beyond them that the little group was doing the same thing on their side. And as they moved debris on their side, a couple of soldiers shored up the new length of tunnel, making sure the rescue workers stayed safe.

They were almost through when an ominous creaking above made everyone pause.

'Don't touch anything,' one of the army rescuers shouted through to the survivors, before radioing for an engineer to get down there fast.

They were all peering upward, trying to figure out what might be shifting above them, while the silence from the other side sent an uneasiness through the rescuers.

It was probably inevitable that Angus arrived with the engineer.

'You could have slept longer,' he said to Kate, who was so busy trying to cope with all her physical reactions to his presence—the ones that wouldn't go into that damn box—she just ignored him.

Until he moved closer, stood right behind her and touched her lightly on the shoulder.

'The engineer will be a while figuring out the best way forward,' he said. 'Why don't you take another rest? I'll stay in case they need a doctor.'

Kate turned to look at him, her fingers curling into

balled fists so she didn't reach out to touch his cheek, his arm, any bit of him.

'You look worse than I do,' she told him. 'Why don't you take a break?'

'Who me? A soldier? Take a break?'

He tried to look shocked but all he looked was more tired, and Kate could feel her heart aching for him. Aching to help him, to look after him, to hold him and—

Yes, to love him!

She turned away, hoping he wouldn't see her thoughts written on her face or in her eyes.

Where had love come into it? she demanded of herself as she moved back a little way up the tunnel to let the team do their work.

And when?

Surely not right back at the island, for all her heart had lurched at the sight of him in the SDR meeting.

Maybe as they'd sat together beside wee Joshua's grave—or perhaps on the Ferris wheel high above the harbour when the world had been a magical place, she and Angus the only inhabitants.

It must have sneaked in, a subconscious knowing, just waiting for a propitious moment to firm in her head.

Not that this was anything like a propitious moment! She was trying not to think about him at all, so definitely didn't want to consider what she felt might just possibly be love.

He was working beside the engineer, his broad back towards her, and though suitably and completely covered in army fatigues, she saw it as she had in bed, the flat planes of muscle around his shoulders, the shape of his vertebrae that she'd touched with fingertips—

And the thoughts she couldn't keep away when she was studying him sneaked back into her mind. The 'would the baby' thoughts—useless comparisons—the past she thought she'd conquered finding its way into the present—

Focus!

The rescuers were now passing rubble back along the tunnel, hand to hand, others now joining the line that stretched out into the open air.

Desperate to think about anything other than Angus's back, Kate squeezed into a space, passing debris with the best of them.

'You got gloves?' the woman beside her said quietly, and she stepped back for a minute to pull her heavy gloves from a pocket down the leg of her overalls and fit them on snugly.

It became mechanical—take a bundle from the woman on one side and pass it on to the man on the other, the movement gaining a rhythm of its own, so she was surprised when she looked up to see how much further they had gone, edging little by little towards the survivors.

'Are you free?'

Blake's voice in her helmet jolted her slightly, and once again she stepped out of the line, this time making her own way to the mouth of the tunnel, already telling Blake she was on her way.

Angus, answering a call on his headphones, followed her, realising she, too, must have been contacted for something more urgent than moving rubble.

As ever when he saw her, or was in her presence,

his skin tightened with a sensory awareness that was hard to ignore, for all he knew he had to be totally focussed on the job.

Lives depended on it.

Blake Cooper was standing with the site manager and one of Angus's colleagues beside what looked like a newly opened tunnel.

Except when they got there, he hard on Kate's heels, it was more a steep shaft than a tunnel.

'From what we can make out, there's a badly injured woman down there.'

Silence greeted the remark, all of them only too aware they'd passed the thirty-hour mark since the buildings had collapsed, and the hope of finding anyone still alive was lessening by the minute.

'The USAR have done their best to make it safe but the space they've managed to shore up is too narrow for you or me to get in there, Angus.'

He turned to Kate.

'You've already done more than your share of crawling into tight spaces,' he said. 'Are you up for one more? Be honest about it. No one's going to think less of you if you say no. We don't want you going in only to find you're too exhausted to get out.'

'I can find a soldier to do it,' Angus said.

But Kate shook her head.

'If she's injured maybe there's something I can do, and if I can't make it out at least I can stay with her. I'm sure you lot would eventually dig down to us.'

She was looking at Angus as she spoke, making light of it, but his tight mouth and undoubtedly clenched teeth told her just how much he disapproved of the idea.

Someone had rigged up a rope and harness, insisting she should wear the harness even though the shaft sloped gradually at first.

'At least this way we can haul you out if we need to,' the USAR man told her.

She tightened the harness around her chest, checked that her bag was secure, and went cautiously into the sloping shaft. Easy going initially. She had to bend slightly but that was okay, then as the gradient grew steeper and the shaft walls began to close in on her, she sat and worked her way down on her backside, glad of the harness, even happier that whoever had tunnelled down here had been able to string some lights along one side.

She used her boots as brakes to slow her progress as the gradient grew steeper, not wanting to slide full tilt into the injured woman.

But now the shaft widened and levelled out slightly, and Kate realised it had been specifically dug to get to the lowest section of the ruined lodges.

Some parts were shored, but she guessed if the woman lay that way she'd have been found.

'Can you hear me?' she called, praying for an answer.

Nothing!

She shone her torch, deep into the wreckage.

'Can you hear me?'

This time a movement of some kind—over to the right—not distinct, more a slight shuffle.

The other rescuers had heard a woman!

She shone her torch to the right, asking this time, 'Can you see the light?'

The faintest of moans, but at least Kate now knew where to look.

She could see a space that seemed stable some way in. All she had to do was get there.

On hands and knees she started forward, lying down to slither under beams, pushing herself forward with her feet, crawling where she could, talking all the time, telling whoever was there that she was coming.

The woman, when she finally came to her, was sheet white and barely conscious. A trail of blood going back into the rubble told Kate she'd already made her way through a lot of debris.

Now she lay on her back, blood seeping from her body, too far gone to answer even the simplest of questions.

With space to move, Kate set up fluids before beginning any examination of her injuries, instinct telling her there was something seriously wrong. But it took a long moan from the woman and a reflex writhing motion for Kate to realise the significance of the blood.

She ran her hands over the woman's abdomen, felt it tighten as she examined it, then relax, flaccid—empty!

And between the woman's legs, the placenta she'd just delivered, the cord that should have connected it to a baby now severed.

The baby! Where was the baby? She had to find the baby.

But the woman was bleeding more heavily now, too much blood added to what she'd already lost.

Post-partum haemorrhage.

Kate pressed down hard on her patient's belly, hoping to seal off the offending blood vessel, but the blood kept coming.

And somewhere in the wreckage there was a baby—a newborn.

She breathed deeply, closing her eyes and willing herself back under control, thinking, thinking, thinking.

Then a remembered picture from some book she'd studied flashed into her mind. Lacking medical help, post-partum bleeding could be handled manually.

First, pressure on the abdomen, pressing downwards, holding it—hopeful the damaged vessel would close of its own accord.

No luck—the bleeding continued.

Back to the remembered picture.

Twisting her mike so she could speak into it, she knelt between the woman's legs and carefully inserted one gloved hand into her body, using her other hand on the woman's belly, pressing down against her own hand as hard as she could.

Now she could speak.

'I need a collapsible stretcher sent down on a rope. Woman with post-partum haemorrhage and no sign of the baby. Once I have her free of the debris and ready for you to lift, you'll have to pull me too because the only way I've been able to stem the bleeding is manually.'

Someone up there would get the picture, she told herself, and hopefully have blood products and anticoagulants on hand for the woman as soon as they reached the top.

There's a baby somewhere…

She had to fight the thought, fight even harder the urge to go and look.

Rattling noises, dirt coming down the shaft and Kate was glad she and her patient were clear of it.

But someone *had* understood—understood enough to send down a slightly built soldier with the stretcher.

'Reckoned you'd need help,' the new arrival—a young woman soldier—said, and Kate smiled with relief.

'Can you slide the stretcher through that opening?' she asked, shining her torch along the hole she'd crawled through.

'No worries,' said the cheerful woman, and she set to, threading the long, narrow, well-packed stretcher under and around obstacles until it reached Kate.

Who now had a dilemma.

No way could she keep up the pressure on the woman's uterus *and* load her on the stretcher.

She lifted her top hand and fished in her bag for a tightly folded cloth that could be fashioned into a sling, or if necessary used as a towel for messy hands.

Carefully she removed her other hand, wiped it swiftly on the bandage and began to unpack the stretcher, sliding one side in under the woman's body, then rolling her slightly to click the other side into place.

The bleeding continued, so as quickly as she could she wrapped the stretcher's wings around the woman's upper body and tightened straps to keep her securely in place. Pulled on a clean glove and once again invaded the poor woman's body to apply pressure on the bleeder.

'Now, if you can pull the stretcher towards you, I'll do what I can to push with my knees, but once we get her out to where you are, you'll have to go up the shaft to give the two of us room to be pulled up.'

'I could take over from you,' the soldier, now introducing herself as Laura, said.

And I could look for the baby.

The thought sneaked into Kate's mind but she pushed it away. What point in finding the baby if the mother died through blood loss that she, Kate, might be able to prevent.

Laura somehow got them back to the bottom of the shaft, then, aided by her harness and rope, made her way up to the top.

'Call when you're ready to come up,' a voice yelled from above.

'Anytime now,' Kate answered, 'but pull us slowly as we're coming up in tandem.'

And slowly but surely they made their way to the top, where waiting hands unhooked both the stretcher and Kate, and carried the patient, Kate still bent over her, still applying pressure, into the tent.

'We've got one of our gynaes up on the screen in a live feed from the hospital,' Blake told her as the woman, now free of Kate, was lifted onto an operating table. 'We'll take it from here.'

Kate nodded, anxious to get away and get cleaned up—even more anxious to get back down that shaft.

Would they let her?

The thought made tears prick at the corners of her eyes.

Of course they would, she told herself as she stripped off and stepped under the shower.

Where tears really didn't matter as it was all water running down her cheeks.

She had no clean underwear or a clean overall, and she was running short of gloves, but she'd noticed piles of clothes just inside the door of the facilities tent.

Khaki but who cared! Wrapped in a towel, she already had underwear sorted—a singlet would do instead of a bra—and was checking out a thick sweater that would keep her warm under her overalls when Angus appeared.

'Stealing army clothes, are you?' he teased, and, startled, she turned towards him, not having felt his presence as she usually did.

'It's okay, that's what they're there for, but I wouldn't bother putting overalls back on, you need a proper break. A new response team has arrived, so it's time to sleep—perhaps eat something and then sleep.'

But Kate clutched the overalls to her, backing towards the privacy of the shower stall, so anxious to get back down that shaft and start looking for the baby she didn't stop to argue.

'Kate?'

He sounded puzzled—perhaps anxious.

'Not just now, Angus. I really do have to get back down there.'

She shut the screen between them and pulled on her purloined clothes—including the overalls and, oh, the bliss of clean socks!

Angus stared at the screen. Okay, she'd closed it in case someone else came in and saw him staring at her getting dressed, except it wasn't modesty or possible embarrassment at all, it was to shut him out—or maybe off! To stop him arguing with her, which he fully intended doing. She must be exhausted and he knew only too well that that's when accidents happened.

Yet when she reappeared, everything clean but her boots, it was to hurry past him, hurrying not to the tent to see how the woman she'd rescued was but back to the shaft, jogging now for all she'd said she didn't jog.

He wanted to follow her, to try to stop her, to speak to whoever was in command over there and order she be stopped.

He gave a huff of despairing laughter.

Like she'd thank him for that!

He headed for the tent instead. Surely there he'd find a clue to her impetuous flight.

Blake's face was bleak, although the woman on the table in front of him looked relatively uninjured.

'She'll be okay,' Blake said. 'We've stopped the bleeding and they'll fly her straight out.'

'And the problem?'

Blake hesitated, shook his head and finally explained.

'She's just given birth,' he said quietly. 'There's a baby down there somewhere.'

A picture of Kate as she held the little girl, Libby, in her arms, flashed through Angus's head. Kate holding her tightly, tears on Kate's face...

A baby?

Had there been a baby somewhere in her life?

Or did she just long for one?

He knew she was estranged from her parents, who hadn't understood—or bothered to understand—why she'd cancelled her wedding. Would a baby be someone for her to love—someone to love her?

He had no idea but he did know, for certain, that it was the baby that had taken her back down that shaft.

He shook his head as he realised just how little he knew about the woman he loved.

Loved?

Hadn't he recoiled from that thought once before?

But that must be it, love, and now she was in danger.

Might be in danger.

Turmoil he'd rarely if ever felt was gripping his body, while his thoughts ran riot in his head.

He left the tent, intending to go down to the head of the shaft, but paused. He'd only be in the way, and if Kate *was* down there he certainly didn't want to distract any of the people up top who'd be responsible for her safety.

So?

First things first—start thinking clearly.

He'd eat and maybe rest—no, no way he could rest.

He'd eat and…

His mind went blank again.

He needed a distraction—any distraction—something to focus on…

Mail, there was mail!

He clutched at the idea, something positive he could do. Anything to take his mind off Kate down some deep tunnel…

He'd eat then check that great wad of mail he'd picked up on his way through the base, whenever that had been. Probably mostly rubbish but maybe something from family—cousins who kept in touch in a spasmodic fashion, all posted on from base to base as he was transferred or out on missions.

And there was usually something from someone—in India, or Angola, anywhere, in fact—wanting details of the tent.

Tent!

Damn those Bondi Bayside people—he couldn't think of it by any other name, even to himself!

Kate inched her way forward, tugging at the rope she dragged behind her to keep it free from snags. The only way she'd been allowed back down the shaft had been by promising not to detach it, no matter how awkward it might become.

The passage through to where the woman had been was easier to negotiate now, much of the rubble knocked away as the stretcher had gone in and out. But once there, Kate knew she had to be careful. The trail of blood she'd seen when she'd first arrived suggested that the woman had crawled to the space in search of a way out or help of some kind. What Kate had to do was find that trail and follow it, being careful that she didn't obliterate it with a less than cautious step.

First she listened, listened for a cry. Surely a newborn would be crying?

Hypothermia. Even if the woman had managed to wrap the baby it would still be suffering from the cold, and in that case unable to cry.

Carefully threading her way through the crushed building, on hands and knees most of the time, slithering on her stomach at others, she followed the trail of blood.

It ended abruptly, and Kate peered around in the gloom, shining her torch into every crack and crevice, sure the baby must be here somewhere.

There *had* to be a baby!

Over there!

About three feet further in—

A bundle of what could be rags, motionless and silent. Dead?

Kate refused to believe it. From somewhere a random bit of information flashed through her head— something about a newborn being able to live for up to three days untended.

But probably not in these cold conditions; probably not suffering from hypothermia. Although wasn't hypothermia good for injured people at times?

One part of her mind was thinking these things while the other part worked out how she could get to where the bundle was—so near and yet so far at the moment.

If she moved that blue board a bit to one side she could reach through…

First, see what else might move with the blue board. She didn't want to bring half a ski lodge down on the baby.

She moved the blue board, very slowly and cautiously, checking all the time whether anything else was moving with it.

So far, so good!

A little more and she could prop her end of it on that timber over there and—

Another ominous creak sounded above her and she stopped, but it was soon followed by a crash somewhere out of sight, so she knew she hadn't caused it.

She propped the blue board on the timber she'd chosen and reached through the gap she'd made to retrieve the bundle.

What if it wasn't the baby?

* * *

The thought made her pause, but only for an instant. She grabbed the bundle and lifted it, backing with it out to the relative safety of the space where the woman had been.

Now she could check it, see…

The baby was still, so still Kate feared the worst.

Lips tinged with blue.

She lifted it—him—and cleared his mouth, blew warm air into his mouth and nose. Then, with him still wrapped, she pressed her fingers to his carotid pulse. Nothing, then the faintest flicker. Keeping him wrapped as best she could, she used two fingers to compress his chest, counting as she went. The faint pulse was still there. She had to warm him. She tugged him out of the old black parka in which he had been wrapped and, ripping open her overalls, she hauled up her singlet and the sweater, and tucked the baby inside, against her skin, manoeuvring him up so his head was near the top and she could feel for breath and warm his lungs with her breath.

She put her hands on his back, warming him with her body heat, willing him to stay alive.

'You'll be okay,' she whispered against the little head. 'You'll be okay.'

Remembering tales of people suffering from hypothermia getting up off tables in the morgue—definitely exaggerated as most morgue stories were.

But hypothermia shut the body down to maybe one breath a minute and a negligible pulse.

'All okay?'

The voice in her ear startled her. She'd been supposed to keep talking to the people up the top, or at least make positive noises occasionally.

'All okay,' she said, although she wasn't at all sure it was.

But she held the baby close and breathed warm air into him until she knew she had to move—knew more and better help awaited this child up at the top.

'So let's get up there,' she whispered to him, and she began to worm her way back to the bottom of the shaft, where she signalled she was ready to be hauled up.

The crowd at the top startled her even before the great roar went up. Charlie had come over to help her out of the harness, now fitted only around her waist.

'Someone heard you talking to the baby and the word spread like wildfire. I think everyone needed a good news story as they've found a few more bodies.'

'But I don't know if he *is* alive,' Kate whispered to Charlie as he wrapped a thermal blanket around the two of them.

'Well, let them think he is,' Charlie cautioned. 'It's what everyone needs right now.'

An army vehicle arrived and she was bundled into it, the baby still tucked against her skin.

She'd have to give him up soon and examine him properly, or let someone else do it, someone not so terribly, terribly tired.

Someone she didn't know took him gently from her, and someone else she didn't know guided her towards the mess.

'A hot drink, food?' the kind stranger asked, and Kate shook her head.

'Just a bed," she said. 'Nothing more.'

CHAPTER EIGHT

How LONG SHE'D slept she didn't have a clue, but she awoke to noise and bustle all around the makeshift camp, voices yelling instructions, motors revving.

She sat up, slowly and experimentally, small movements while still prone suggesting she might be stiff and sore.

Two words that hardly covered it, she realised as she bent over to unlace her boots.

Every muscle in her body ached.

A shower—that would help.

Somehow she managed to make it that far, pausing only to grab clean army-issue clothing as she passed their neat supply.

The shower helped—even to the extent she now realised she was hungry. From the noise and yelling outside she presumed they were packing up. She hoped they hadn't shut the mess tent yet.

She also hoped, shocked by her original selfish thought, that the movement meant everyone had been accounted for. Hoped the death toll hadn't been too great.

The mess was still where it should be but the big tent—Angus's tent—lay like a deflated balloon on the ground, a soldier Kate didn't recognise barking instructions about how it should be folded.

The tent!

It had brought Angus back into her life, if only briefly—and had brought a very special time with him as well. But this latest reunion—meeting again here—had been pure chance. And now he'd tested his tent in a disaster response situation, he'd be off far and wide—he and his tent. Taking it to wherever it was needed, like drought-stricken or war-torn villages in Africa or disease-riddled refugee camps in South East Asia.

She closed her eyes briefly, shutting out images of him in danger in some foreign land, and bumped straight into a broad chest.

'I was coming to check you weren't dead,' he said, steadying her with firm hands on her shoulders, sending messages she shouldn't feel right through her body.

'I'm fine, just starving,' she said. 'I was pleased to see the mess tent still standing.'

He smiled at her, although for some reason the smile, while kind, didn't quite reach his eyes, didn't crinkle the skin at the corners of them.

Because this was goodbye all over again?

Because their meeting up like this had been chance, nothing more, and the now was definitely over.

But he was speaking to her and she had to listen. Something about the mess tent always being the first one up and the last one down.

'Haven't you heard the term that an army marches on its stomach?'

She probably had, but it was *her* stomach troubling her.

Her stomach and something in Angus's manner.

Forget that, she muttered inwardly as she made her way towards the servery. His manner has nothing whatsoever to do with you!

'Did you hear how the baby is? Did he live?' she asked, when she realised he was walking beside her.

What she couldn't ask was had the baby been alive. She really, really didn't want to think she'd failed to get there in time—failed to save him.

'The baby's fine,' he said, and to Kate's dismay tears began to leak from her eyes, sliding silently down her cheeks. Tears of relief, she knew—but unstoppable.

She felt a soft touch on the small of her back and a handkerchief pressed into her hand with an extra squeeze of her fingers. Angus's way of comforting her in the busy and no doubt gossip-rife mess.

She wiped her eyes but couldn't stop the tremors of relief that threatened to make a fool of her again.

'Find a seat, I'll bring food. And coffee?'

She nodded, and hurried to a seat beside one of the plastic windows, seeing, yet not seeing, all the activity outside.

'Bit late for breakfast, but I thought bacon and eggs were probably appropriate.'

Angus set down a tray on the corner of the table as he spoke and proceeded to lay out the table—knife and fork, coffee cup and pot, salt and pepper, and finally a covered plate, the cover lifted to reveal not only bacon and eggs but a small sausage and two pieces of grilled tomato.

Kate smiled up at him, still hovering by the table.

'That looks fantastic,' she said, and, although disconcerted by the now silent presence by her side, she began to eat, savouring each mouthful as the hot comfort food brought her slowly back to life—conscious life, real life.

Even if he wasn't sitting with her, this was probably the last meal she'd eat with Angus, so images of other meals they'd shared rose unbidden in her mind.

Tender salt and pepper squid in a little café in Manly, the fairy floss—hardly a meal—at Luna Park. They'd only had time for a coffee and tiny muffin at the art gallery—now bacon and eggs before he went away again.

She set down her cutlery, aware the lump in her throat would prevent her swallowing.

She looked up at the cause of all her problems— although, in truth, her loving him wasn't really *his* fault, especially when he'd warned her from the start that his career and marriage didn't mix.

'Aren't you even having coffee?' she asked.

'I should be outside, supervising things, but I wanted…'

He sounded hesitant, so unlike Angus she gestured to the chair opposite.

'Sit down, Angus. Sit down and tell me, although if it's anything to do with this meeting up again—about it not meaning anything, not being part of that "now" we had—then I already realise that.'

He sat so she could look at him—at this man she loved but couldn't have—and wondered if her own face looked as gaunt and troubled as his did.

She hoped not.

'So?' she prompted.

He spread his hands.

'It's hard to explain—the way the army works, that is—to someone not in it. It seems all ordered and regimented, which it has to be to move so many people around the place, continually training them, testing them, sending a group here, a group there. It would be chaotic if there weren't strict procedures and protocols and everyone in the army understands and obeys them.'

So, is this part of telling me why he can't see me again, which I already know? Kate wondered, pushing her half-eaten breakfast aside, no longer the least bit hungry, the lump in her throat replaced by a knot in her stomach.

'But the thing the army does really well—really commits to—is making sure mail gets through. It's not so important now with email and texts and such but parents still write to their sons and daughters, lovers write to each other, and the army prides itself on getting the letters to the right person, no matter how long it takes. A kind of "the mail must get through" sentiment it's always had.'

Angus knew he was making a total mess of this, and the perplexed look on Kate's face reinforced this knowledge. But he'd been awake all night thinking about it, wondering, coming up with a dozen different scenarios, none of which were very satisfying or even plausible.

Then her tears earlier when she'd heard the baby was alive and she should have been happy—there were things going on that didn't add up. Did she regret not marrying the solicitor who'd cheated on her, regret not having a baby—a family—of her own? Or was it something to do with the deep inner sadness he'd sensed in Kate since meeting her again—a sadness he was sure hadn't been there on the island, for all she'd just cancelled her wedding?

And was he puzzling over this to delay bringing up the letter?

Because he wasn't sure how to approach her about it?

In the end, here at the table, he pulled the crumpled, much-redirected letter from his pocket and set it in front of them.

'I collected mail before I left the base, and only had time to go through it yesterday. Mostly rubbish and then this!'

He used one finger to push it across the table towards Kate, who had grown so pale he thought she might faint.

But she'd picked it up and looked at all the places it had gone to before it had finally reached him, touching each address.

'It partly took so long because letters are usually addressed to us by our ranks. Back then I was a captain so Dr Caruth probably didn't mean much to whoever sorted it. But the army, as you can see, is persistent.'

'Did you open it, read it?' she asked, in a voice so hesitant he barely heard the words.

'Of course,' he said, and waited.

And waited.

Until, perhaps realising she wasn't going to offer any explanation for the brief note he'd found inside the much-abused envelope, he said, 'You wanted me to phone you.'

If anything, she grew paler and her fingers on the envelope shook so much she put it down, steadying herself by flattening it against the table.

More silence, then she raised her head and looked directly at him.

'Not wanted so much, more just a suggestion.' Hesitated, then added, 'I really should be going—should find Blake and the rest of the team. If everyone's pulling out, I need a lift.'

She stood up, staggered a little, then straightened, and offered one of the most pathetic smiles he'd ever seen.

'It was good to see you again. I'm glad the tent worked.'

And on that note she marched steadily out of the mess.

Out of his life?

Again!

Not a request, a suggestion?

He pulled the straightened paper towards him and although he knew the words, he read them again.

Would you like to give me a call some time? My number is 0623 348 876.

It still sounded like a request to him.

And why had it upset her so much that she'd virtually fled from his presence?

Embarrassment?

Confronted with it after so long?

Upset, even after all this time, over sending a note to someone who had been, as far as she'd known, about to be married?

He had no idea!

He shook his head, realising as he did it that women were largely foreign territory to him.

He'd known Michelle, or had thought he'd known her, yet hadn't realised just how much he'd hurt her by telling her about Kate. Kate had called him insensitive for telling, yet to him it had seemed the right thing to do—the honest thing to do. Yet looking back he wondered just how well he had known her, or understood the pain and fear she must have felt when he'd disappeared to who knew where.

And other women he'd dated, during times when Michelle had taken a break of her own, well, he'd never really been interested enough to try to work out what made them tick.

Pathetic!

That's what he was!

A great, big, pathetic lump of material, moulded by his training and the army into something very useful—someone who knew exactly what to do in any given situation in which he was involved.

But that was useful to the army, not a woman…

There was something he was missing here. He needed Gran with the common sense she'd tried to instil in him as a child, but she was long gone and no matter how hard he tried to figure out what advice she might give, he came up with a big fat zero.

Except Kate *had* sent the note.

He'd start from there…

Kate found the SDR helicopter as it was about to leave. Paul hauled her on board, whistling at her get-up, Blake saying he'd been about to send out a search party for her.

'I fell asleep,' she told them.

'Well, you deserved it. You were really amazing,' another team member said.

But the words of praise washed over Kate. The knowledge that Angus had her letter had shaken her so much she couldn't even begin to work out *how* to think about it, let alone what to think.

Surely it shouldn't matter why she'd written it. Not now—not after three years.

So why had he been so persistent?

Or had it been her own shock at seeing it that had made her think he'd been persistent?

Maybe he'd just been mildly interested.

Ha! That was about as likely as the moon being made of cheese.

She might not have known Angus long if you counted the time in hours and days, but she knew enough of him to know that he'd be like a terrier with a rat, refusing to let the matter go until he'd got to the bottom of it, however inconsequential it might be.

And she'd made it worse by not giving him an answer. She could have said something, anything. Said it had just been a spur-of-the-moment thing. She'd forgotten all about it.

But she'd not only been too shocked to think of anything to say, her reaction must have been obvious to him from the glower he'd given her before she'd departed.

She tried to put it out of her mind—wasn't she already adept at that—but today little things like the almost-not-there touch of his hand on her waist as he'd guided her into the mess, the strength of his fingers as he'd pressed a handkerchief into them had got to her.

Handkerchief!

She fished in her pocket and pulled it out. A per-

fectly ordinary white square—fine linen, she thought.
Or good cotton, soft to touch but firm at the same time.

She shook her head and jammed the offending scrap
of material back where it belonged. Was she losing it
that she could sit here mooning over a square of white
linen?

Or cotton?

Pull yourself together, right now!

It was over, whatever it had been, and she had exams
looming so would need all her wits about her when she
got back to work.

Work had been her solace once before and it could
be again—*would* be again.

Kate pulled the note out of her pigeonhole at the hospital a couple of days later. Saw the SDR initials in the
corner of the envelope and wondered why the formality.
Usually when anything was happening, Mabel phoned.

She opened and read it, realising as she did so that it
wasn't a time and date for a regular SDR meeting but
for a debrief for all those who'd been in the mountains.

Counsellors—that's what they'd be offering, she decided. That's why it's not a general meeting. Everyone
was edgy about counselling—some certain they would
never need it while others hated to admit they might.

Kate wondered if perhaps she might, whether it
might help her sleep better, get through the night without dreams of Angus—Angus in danger, Angus touching her, Angus asking about the letter.

But it would be trauma counselling on offer rather
than—

Well, *love* counselling!

She groaned, startling someone else checking for

mail or notices. But this 'love' idea that kept popping into her head was really getting to her.

And what if it *was* love she felt for him? It wasn't as if she could do anything about it. He'd explained all that—explained any form of permanent relationship with him was out of the question.

So?

She checked the note. The meeting was an afternoon one, and as it was in the middle of her days off she'd certainly be able to make it. No doubt Blake, or more probably Mabel, had arranged the time for when most of the team who'd gone south *would* be available.

Kate knew the mother and baby were doing well, as the newspapers seemed to be carrying regular reports on their health status.

Apart from that…

Angus returned to Western Australia to finish his business there, and with that sorted, he only needed the debrief with the USAR and SDR teams who'd attended the recent operation before giving the go-ahead for production. He was reasonably sure there'd be some new ideas to improve it.

He'd received a text from Mabel alerting him to the date and time of the meeting, and later a note advising him that three of the USAR team would also be there.

But would Kate?

Or would she find some excuse not to come, not wanting to meet up with him in case he asked more questions?

Perhaps the note she'd sent had meant nothing more than it had said—*give me a call some time.*

Had the fact that he hadn't called disappointed her?

Hurt her in some way that even now she didn't want to talk about it?

He didn't think so—their time together had been short, but he was absolutely certain she wouldn't hold a grudge, not about something as trivial as a missed phone call anyway.

Which left him ready for this debrief with more than usual excitement. True, he'd be hearing the first reports on his tent from people who had actually used it in an emergency situation but, even better, he'd see Kate again.

See her when she wasn't exhausted and overwhelmed by all she'd been through in the mountains.

But would she talk to him?

He'd made such a huge production of their relationship not being a relationship in the usual sense because he could be called away any time and be gone for weeks or months—maybe even for ever if it was a war zone.

And the last thing he'd wanted to do was hurt her—to hurt Kate as he'd hurt Michelle—coming and going without a thought for how she must feel about it.

He'd pushed the 'just for now' idea hard with Kate, and he was sure she'd been happy to go along with it.

Because it had suited her as well?

He stopped thinking about it all at that point, mainly because he didn't want to consider she hadn't cared enough to want more than 'now'.

Not when, after a few short days, he'd known for certain that he did.

Had known that he loved her—for all the good that would do him.

He groaned, then looked quickly around in case someone might have heard him.

* * *

Kate was shocked that she hadn't figured out Angus would be at the meeting. She'd been so certain it would be about counselling that she hadn't considered the obvious.

His tent had been on trial, its first actual deployment on a rescue mission. Of course he had to be there!

She'd just have to avoid him, that was all.

But if he asked again about the note she'd sent…

Perhaps she could lie.

Lie to Angus?

No way!

She couldn't lie to anyone—was a hopeless liar at the best of times—but with something so personal…

'You with us, Kate?'

Blake's voice brought her out of the futile arguments going on inside her head. He was doing a roll call—he always did a roll call so Mabel could make a note of who was present.

She waved her hand to let him know she *was* present, and proceeded to focus on the meeting.

All thoughts of the note were shoved aside as she concentrated on Blake's summary of what they'd done.

The main representative of the USAR summarised their work before beginning a long discussion with Angus.

'It was the inflatability of your tent,' he said, and Kate smothered a smile. 'It had me wondering if we aren't underutilising air power, say, to provide safe tunnels through debris.'

And as Kate listened to the pair of them, others present adding suggestions or asking questions, she realised just how important sessions such as these really were because, with everyone sharing their expertise, new and safer ways of providing services would come into being.

Blake eventually diverted the meeting back to the suitability of the tent as a triage and emergency centre. Sam made a suggestion about the placement of surgical instruments, and it was Blake who answered, looking to Angus as he finished for a confirming nod.

And after thank yous had been said, and the reminder for counselling, the meeting broke up, Kate saying goodbye to Charlie from the USAR team and nodding to most of the others as she headed for the door.

Where Angus had been caught by the USAR man, wanting more information about the tunnels he was hoping might work.

So it was the USAR man, not Angus, who touched her on the shoulder, asking her to wait a minute.

'Kate,' he said, 'you were down there having to get through to the injured woman, and later to the baby. Do you understand what I mean about some kind of protection around a rescuer in that kind of situation?'

Kate nodded, kind of including Angus in the nod.

'I don't understand enough about aerodynamics if that's what it is that keeps things inflated. And, yes, I think we'd all like more protection in hairy situations, but you have to look at it against cost. I don't know about USAR but the SDR is always looking for extra funds. And even more important is time. How long would it take to get something like that operational twenty or thirty feet below ground level? We needed to get that woman out fast.'

The USAR man nodded, but she could see he wanted

more information from Angus, so she said goodbye to
the two men and walked away, every nerve in her body
conscious of Angus behind her.

CHAPTER NINE

THE MEETING HAD been held on the ground floor of the sprawling six-storey building, which meant Kate hadn't realised it was raining until she stepped outside.

And not just raining but pelting down, thunder rolling ominously somewhere to the west, lightning flashing across the grey sky.

She'd be soaked on the way home in this downpour!

Was there an umbrella in her locker? One she'd left there accidentally some time ago?

Her old parka—that would help.

Or maybe she could just get wet.

'Walk you home?'

She turned to see Angus just outside the foyer of the staff entrance, a huge umbrella held above his head, his face unreadable in its shadow.

Probably unreadable anyway, was her instant thought, knowing exactly why he was here and what he wanted to know. Although that knowledge didn't stop a huge skip in her heartbeat.

But nearly a week of sleepless nights and long discussions with herself during her runs hadn't resolved the dilemma in which she found herself.

Although it wasn't really a dilemma, was it?

He wanted to know and she would have to tell him.

She would tell him as concisely and unemotionally as she could.

The concise bit was okay. It was the next part that might be difficult.

Would be difficult.

Thanks,' she said, wondering if she'd taken an age to reply or if it had only seemed that way to her.

She stepped under the shelter of his umbrella and the simple act of sharing it with him, pressing close against him to avoid the rain, made her forget all the rational reasoning that had, only seconds earlier, gone on in her head.

Right now, she wanted nothing more than to be close to him.

Like this!

For whatever reason!

And for ever?

Did he feel the same that he didn't speak, simply putting his hand in the small of her back and guiding her towards the apartment block?

Except he didn't *do* for ever—he'd told her that...

But remembering the question he wanted answered banished the little dart of pain that thought brought in its wake.

But Alice would surely be home, so she, Kate, might be saved the question.

For now.

They reached the entrance and it was only polite that she ask him in.

'That'd be great,' he said, as if they hadn't ever been more than casual acquaintances—had never spent hot, steamy, and yet sometimes languorous, hours in bed.

Never talked until their throats were dry, on ferries, and out walking, in restaurants, and on the Ferris wheel at Luna Park.

'Coffee?' she asked when they were safely inside, his umbrella dripping water on the balcony.

The word came out as a squeak, her nerves so tense it was a wonder she could breathe.

'Lovely,' he said, settling himself into an armchair for all the world as if he belonged in the apartment, not her.

But making coffee gave her time to calm down, to settle her unruly nerves, and calm the inner longings being close to him had generated.

It was only as she set some shortbread on a small plate and carried the tray out of the kitchen that she realised finally that Alice wasn't there. Closed her eyes briefly when she remembered it was Alice's charity shop day.

She waited until he'd picked up his coffee, surreptitiously studying him when she could.

Got nothing!

Not a hint of what he might be thinking or feeling.

Nothing.

Which meant she'd have to bring it up, because there was no other reason he could be here. Their 'now' time was over, she'd understood that was all it could be right from the start.

And the fact that it had been cut so short had reinforced the impermanence of their...

Relationship?

Hardly.

More a fling.

'I was pregnant!'

Suddenly the words were out there, not that difficult to say after all, but from the disbelieving look on Angus's face—or maybe it was shock—it wasn't what he'd expected to hear.

He set his coffee cup unsteadily down on the table and stared at her.

'When I wrote the note,' she added, because now she'd started she just wanted to get it over with. 'It was a shock. I'd been on the Pill, then with the cyclone and all the huts getting flattened, I had missed a few, and then I was back home and that's when I realised.'

She should stop now, let him speak, but there was more she had to say—to explain—for all she felt like curling into a ball and crying herself to sleep.

She swallowed hard.

'At first I couldn't decide what I'd do, but then I knew I wanted to keep it and I thought if I was doing that you had a right to know.'

You can do this, she told herself, just tell it as it was, the practical stuff.

'Just to know, not to help me or to put pressure on you. I knew I'd be okay financially and I could afford to take some time off, and then there'd be childcare but I could work part time so I could be with him as much as possible.'

Deep breath—nearly there—only now the memory of telling her parents and their immediate reaction— get an abortion—had returned to throw shadows over her words, so her voice, as she continued, wavered just a little.

'I had it all worked out but thought I should probably tell you, so that's why I wrote the note.'

Kate sat back, biting her lip, tense—with fear—

when she should have been pleased with herself for getting it all out into the open without the hint of a tear or a shading of self-pity.

'And when I didn't phone?'

The words sounded as if he'd strangled them on the way out, but he was probably shocked.

It hurt! Kate thought but didn't say.

She closed her eyes, back in that time, but after a moment found the strength to answer.

'I felt you'd drawn a line under what had happened, and I honestly believed that was for the best. I didn't want it mucking up your and Michelle's marriage, either with guilt if you didn't tell her, or an extra child somewhere on the outer edges of your lives if you did.'

He sat in silence, staring at her as if he didn't know her, disbelief written clearly on his face.

Kate sipped her coffee, holding her cup in two hands in the hope he wouldn't notice she was shaking. She'd done her part and answered his question. Now she hoped like hell he wouldn't take it further.

She didn't handle the further very well.

Except he would—he'd have to really. Even now he was looking around the apartment as if to find a child she'd hidden somewhere. Or even a toy, a hint of a child…

'You miscarried?' he asked at last.

Kate shook her head.

'If only it had been that straightforward,' she said, standing up and walking to the long glass door that led onto the balcony, looking out over the streets awash with rain.

Angus tried to figure out that statement. If only it had been that easy? What the hell did she mean!

Damn it all, he'd run the whole gamut of emotions in the last few minutes and his brain wasn't working all that well, but surely he should be able to figure out...

Something hot was stirring inside him. He'd felt a jolt of it when she'd told him she'd been pregnant—she'd been pregnant with his child and he hadn't known. Yes, that had started the fire.

But this!

What he was thinking now!

He stared at her—at her straight back turned away from him, no doubt concerned about his reaction.

And so she should be!

'You had my child adopted?'

The heat propelled the words out far more sharply than he'd intended, and he saw her swing to face him.

'He was *my* child, and he was stillborn!' She flung the words at him, matching his anger with some of her own.

The enormity of what she'd said—the realisation of what she must have gone through—doused his anger faster than a cold shower. He stood up, walked across to where she was once again facing the window.

Put his arm tentatively around her waist, and very slowly drew her to him, turning her so she stood in the shelter of his arms, holding her loosely until she all but fell against him and he could wrap his arms more tightly now and feel the shudder as she let go of the tension she had to have been feeling.

The pain she must have suffered was unimaginable and all he could do was hold her, rocking her slightly, hoping his body might tell her things his mind couldn't put into words.

She pushed away—not immediately—and returned to where she'd been sitting on the sofa.

Could he sit beside her?

Should he?

Realising there were so many more questions he wanted to ask, he went back to where he'd been sitting and finished his coffee, which wasn't cold but close.

'Can you talk about it? Do you want to?' he asked, and she frowned at him, confused.

'The baby,' he prompted. 'Did you find out what had happened? Did anyone give you a reason?'

'No, and no,' she said at last. 'It wasn't an obvious umbilical cord related death and although there have been numerous studies done through examination of the placenta, they rarely tell us anything constructive. The experts talked about placental insufficiency and foetal death syndrome but they were just words and what it all boils down to is that, apparently, it just happens.'

It was Angus's turn to get to his feet, needing to move, to pace the room, trying desperately to get a grasp on Kate's situation at the time. For all those months she'd been expecting this child, looking forward to its—his, she'd said—arrival, then suddenly there had been nothing. The pain, the tragedy of it was hard, almost impossible to comprehend. No wonder she'd changed, shut herself away from people, become, as someone had said, a loner.

He paced some more, still trying to get his head around it, more questions bubbling in his mind.

Would she answer them?

She was sitting there, so he knew she was still reliving it and he'd brought it all back to her—brought back her pain.

He sat beside her, put his arm around her shoulders and drew her close.

'Kate, I am so, so sorry, not only for not being there for you at the time but for bringing it all back up now. I can only imagine how much it must hurt to have to talk about it. How it must take you back.'

She rested her head on his shoulder. 'It's not the first time I've been back there,' she said quietly, 'and every time I imagine a different outcome.'

He hugged her closer.

'Do you want to talk about it?' he asked. 'I'll stop now if you don't.'

He felt her head shake and heard a quiet, 'Of course you want to know. I don't mind.'

He moved so he could look at her, see her face, though his hand still rested on her shoulder.

'Did you know? Before the birth, I mean.'

She nodded.

'Only at the end.'

'And they did a Caesar?'

Headshake and a wry smile.

'Believe it or not, many obstetricians, including mine, believe a natural childbirth is better in such instances. They believe you get over it more quickly— no scar to heal then keep reminding you, or some such twaddle. I was too numb to argue so just went ahead.'

'On your own?'

She smiled—a better smile this time.

'I was in Brisbane, and not totally friendless. I had good support, although my parents wanted nothing to do with any of it. They were so against my keeping it, cut me off completely. But in one way the obstetrician was right—I was back at work within a week and that was the very best part of all. It gave me time to think of other things and that's when I began to apply to join a surgery programme. I joined the Brisbane SDR as well, and life went on.'

Angus closed his eyes, imagining not just the death of a child but the death of someone you'd spent nine months getting to know, a little bit of yourself you'd probably talked to every day, bought supplies for, longing for his arrival. He could feel Kate's pain in his heart.

Then the knowledge that it had been his child struck him once more, and he felt the loss as though he'd been there, felt the pain in his own heart, had to do something—comfort her, feel her comfort himself...

Had to do something to make things right between them.

Something.

Anything!

He tightened his arms around her body, moving so they rocked together.

'Marry me,' he said, shocking himself when the words burst out yet suddenly knowing they were right—that it was what he wanted. To marry this woman he loved and had probably loved for the last three years.

And *that* knowledge added further shock!

But he wasn't as shocked as Kate, who sprang away from his sheltering arms.

'Marry you? Now, there's a bolt from the blue! Why ever would you want to marry me?'

'We had a child,' he said, still numb from all the revelations. His head was still trying to deal with his totally bizarre—not to mention inexplicable—suggestion. 'Shouldn't that count?'

'A child who died,' Kate reminded him bluntly. 'There *is* no child and no reason whatsoever to get married. Didn't you spend considerable time and energy telling me all the reasons you couldn't or wouldn't get married, all the stuff about never being here for a family, for your wife and children? I didn't tell you about the baby so you'd feel sorry for me, but because you asked me—kept asking me. And now you know, and nothing's really changed in either of our lives, and we can go our separate ways.'

He got to his feet and resumed pacing, something she'd seen him do before, and seeing the disbelief on his face, reading his consternation in the way he paced, her heart went out to him. She wanted to stand up, hold him in her arms, tell him everything would be all right.

But would it be?

The news she'd just given him had brought on the pain she'd lived with for the past two years—more now. Wouldn't he be feeling at least a little of that pain?

'I need to think. I'll go now,' he said suddenly, as if the room had become too small to hold his need to move.

So now she did hold him, putting her arms around him and saying gently, 'I know you have to take it in, but once you have, put it behind you, don't let it affect your life the way I've let it affect mine. I've got beyond that now, thanks to meeting you again, having that time together, short though it was. I'm moving forward, and you will too.'

A quick kiss, then she opened the door for him, trying hard to avoid the dark eyes that held shadows she recognised from the eyes she'd seen in her mirror for two long years.

He had a child—he'd *had* a child. This thought was caught up in a mix of battling emotions—anger that he hadn't known, resentment that Kate hadn't told him, pain for what she'd been through.

And loss.

That emotion overwhelmed them all, although it was stupid, pointless, if not downright nuts to feel a loss for a child he'd never had—never known he was going to have.

But loss was definitely there.

A child.

A son…

Had she given him a name?

What had he looked like?

About to turn, to go back to the apartment, Angus stopped himself in time. He'd already put Kate under tremendous strain, forcing this story out of her, and he couldn't make it worse.

So, back to the base where he should have gone an hour ago—straight from the debriefing—so he could type up the notes he'd made and think about the suggestions he'd heard.

On the whole, the tent had been a spectacular success, and although this should bring him joy, or at least pleasure, all he felt was flat—empty—bereft…

CHAPTER TEN

KATE GOT BACK to work—normal work—busy in Theatre, studying and surprising herself and her supervisor, Nick Warren, when she topped the state in the second-year surgical exams.

'Are you sure you don't want to specialise in a narrower field than general surgery?' he asked her. 'Orthopaedics offers the widest range, because you can choose just about any part of the body you want—hand, knees, backs, necks.'

She smiled at him.

'You don't need to keep naming skeletal parts I could study because, honestly, general surgery suits me just fine. I enjoy that I can work in the ED because there I do a little bit of everything. An open break in an arm doesn't always need a consultant orthopod called in—in fact, a nurse could probably do it—but I might be doing that one day, then some stitching of a wound another day, and sometimes cutting down to remove infection from a penetrating wound. It's the variety that keeps me going, Nick.'

'Well, it's how surgery started and there'll always be a need for general surgeons so you'll always have a job.'

He hesitated for a moment, then said, 'You *are*

happy here? You're not thinking of leaving? You could get a job anywhere, I'm sure you get offers.'

Only one totally absurd one of marriage, prompted by shock, and that for all the wrong reasons, Kate thought as she assured Nick she had no intention of leaving.

'I just wondered,' he said. 'One of the big bosses, Justin Alexander—have you met him?'

Kate shook her head.

'It's just that he was asking about you and I thought you might have put in for a transfer or something, that he was interested. But it was probably just that you'd done so well in your exams.'

'I've never heard of him,' Kate said, although the name did ring vague bells.

'You probably wouldn't have. He's come across from North Shore. He's one of the pen-pushers these days, an administrator, although he was a top O and G man in his day.'

An administrator?

Angus's uncle?

Had Angus spoken of her to his uncle—to any of his family?

Surely not!

Kate turned the conversation to other things, the upcoming operations they had scheduled, in which ones she'd be the lead surgeon, anything special she'd need to know.

But as she walked home, she thought about the interest of a man called Justin Alexander and felt a little uneasy that people she didn't know might be discussing her.

Not about the baby—she was sure Angus wouldn't have passed that on.

But the conversation had left her head feeling muddled. She'd almost succeeded in clearing most of Angus out of it, packing him tidily away in yet another box, and now this! One of the powers-that-be discussing her with her supervisor.

It made her feel uncomfortable, to say the least.

She'd go home, change her clothes and go for a run. A little sit in the cemetery, a chat to Joshua, and life would right itself.

Except it didn't.

Joshua had nothing to offer her so she rested a while, looking out to sea, watching a tanker move at what, from the distance, seemed like a snail's pace towards Botany Bay.

Harriet's arrival at what Kate considered 'her' place surprised her, especially as she'd heard the camera clicking and guessed she'd been photographed.

But Harry?

Here?

'You're out and about?' she said, unable to hide the surprise in her voice.

'Thanks largely to you and the photography suggestion,' Harry said with a smile. She held up the camera. 'You've made a monster of me, I'm completely hooked, and looking for new places to photograph has strengthened my leg no end.'

'That's great,' Kate told her, the shine in Harry's eyes telling her as much as the words.

'Of course, I'm still limping along like a three-legged dog, but you got me out and I've been meaning to thank you, but you're either rescuing babies in the

Snowy or working all hours in Theatre so I haven't had a chance.'

She lifted the camera and snapped another shot.

'This place is magical—so much history here. You talked about the ocean in all its many moods, and this place is the same. I came here one day in the rain and I reckon got some of my best shots.'

Kate had to smile. Alice had pushed her into seeing Harry, and inadvertently she'd done some good.

But Harry had had another visitor that night and, remembering, Kate had to look away lest Harry saw her pain.

'I've got to get back,' she said, standing up and stretching. 'Great to see you out and about.'

Then she fled, running from her memories, afraid she'd never be fast enough to really escape them.

Without consciously realising it, Kate curled herself back into the protective shell she'd grown over the last couple of years. Missing drinks with the SDR team after meetings, saying no to Charlie when he phoned to ask her out, making her work and study her whole life.

But now she was more aware of the emptiness of it and the hollowness inside her. Aware she should do something about it but unable to try.

So she almost welcomed the phone call from Mabel, although she knew it meant people were in danger of some kind. But it brought a jolt of adrenalin that stirred her back to life.

Hostage situation in the nearest shopping centre—armed gunman, reports of shooting, specialist police units in charge and the SDR tasked with helping the injured, stabilising those who needed it before passing them on to the ambos, hospitals all over Sydney already on alert for victims.

The gunman was on the second-floor balcony that ran around the centre and shooting down towards people in the main food court below. The police and the building security men and women were trying desperately to evacuate the centre, but panicking people didn't take orders well.

To Kate and the SDR team, it looked about as easy as herding chickens, although most of their attention was on the wounded, lying on the floor, several of the injured slumped on the escalator, which had either jammed or was now turned off.

'We have to get out there,' she said to Sam, who was standing beside her in the little shelter offered by a pillar. 'Those people need attention.'

'The police are bringing in a negotiator,' Sam told her. 'Maybe they'll ask him to stop shooting so we can get to the injured.'

It was then Kate saw the child, obviously separated from her mother, now wandering past the shops on the first floor, crying quietly.

'He wouldn't shoot a child!' Sam said, catching sight of the little girl at the same time.

'But we don't know that,' Kate argued. 'You stay here, I'll go back to the food court and see if I can get to the child from there before she wanders into his line of fire.'

'Blake said remain under cover,' Sam reminded her.

'The far end of the food court is under cover—he can't see it from where he is. Besides, his attention is on the escalators in case someone tries to come up.'

She sidled, careful step by careful step, back into the

shadows, keeping the pillar between her and the gunman. If she could reach the food court without being seen she knew there was an elevator towards the rear of it, and with any luck could get to the little girl before she moved into sight on the floor below him. But the gunman was wary and his peripheral vision would catch the slightest movement.

The plan fell to pieces when the elevator pinged on reaching the first floor, and although she couldn't see the gunman on the floor above she could tell from the cries of the people trapped below her that he'd moved, while a shrill scream suggested he'd taken a hostage.

But Kate's attention was focussed on the child. Slipping from shadowed doorway to doorway, she realised that part of the centre's plan must have been to close all the shops and dim the lights. The child's mother was probably behind one of those closed doors.

She reached the child and lifted her, but was uncertain what to do next.

Which way had the gunman moved—to the left or right? Choosing the wrong direction could bring Kate and the child into his sights.

So she stayed where she was, sitting down in a darkened doorway, talking quietly to the little girl. And tried to think what had been decided after an enquiry into another hostage crisis in the city some years earlier.

Were specialist army personnel coming in to handle things, or had the police devised a new protocol for dealing with these situations?

Either way, Kate was content to stay where she was, certain all the businesses would have rear exits and as many people as possible would have been evacuated when the shooting had begun.

She couldn't see the negotiator but heard him introducing himself through a bullhorn. Talking to the gunman, quietly and calmly.

The gunman's response was a new barrage of bullets, and now Kate held her hands over the little girl's ears, although she doubted that would help.

So she talked, quietly, about birds and animals, about family and friends, rocking the child in her arms as she rattled on.

'And just what do you think you're doing here?' a far-too-familiar voice whispered angrily in her ear.

'Where did you come from,' she demanded, as quietly as her shock would allow.

'I was at the hospital to talk to Blake about joining the SDR team,' he said. 'Sam told me where you were.'

'The child was wandering around this balcony looking for her mother, she'd have come into his line of sight within minutes,' she explained, while the 'I'm at the hospital to talk to Blake about the SDR' comment he'd made snagged somewhere in her head but was making no sense at all.

'We're quite safe,' she told him, adding, 'or at least we were until a great hulking man appeared and we had to share our shelter.'

Angus ignored her protest, instead settling himself on the floor beside her and the child, his back against the door of the closed shop.

'Who's handling it?' Kate asked, assuming the army given that Angus was here.

'Specially trained police squad. They're moving

men in through the rear doors and will come through the shops and get him.'

'Not kill him?' Kate asked, feeling there'd been enough bloodshed.

'Only if they have to,' Angus told her, adding, 'Did you miss the bit about me talking to Blake about joining the SDR team?'

She turned to peer at him in the gloom.

'You're what?'

'Quiet,' he whispered, holding a finger to her lips and sending such a jolt through her body it was a wonder she still held the now sleeping child.

'What do you mean about joining the SDR team? *Our* SDR team?' she whispered back at him, tension adding anger to her words.

'Just that!' he said. 'Mind you, I'm exaggerating slightly. It takes a while to get out of the army but, looking ahead, I was at the hospital talking to Blake today when the call went out, and I thought I might as well come along. Though not in time to stop you putting yourself in danger.'

Kate shook her head. Nothing he'd said made any sense to her, but she doubted this was the time to be considering it. Right now they needed to stay safe—to keep the child safe.

She could hear the negotiator still talking, although Angus's whispered words had all but blotted the negotiations out.

Now it was her thoughts making it difficult to understand him.

But something must have happened because black-clad men—and possibly some women—heavy with bullet-proof gear—were carrying the injured swiftly into the shadows on the ground floor, while muted sounds from above suggested another group was approaching the man.

The negotiator kept talking, and Kate realised he was distracting the man's attention and possibly using the noise of the bullhorn to cover the slight movements on the second floor.

It was only later that evening that Kate saw what had happened on the news channel, five men converging on the gunman and putting him on the ground, relieving him of his weapon, searching and then handcuffing him, finally leading him away to a waiting police van.

In the shopping centre, someone had yelled the all-clear and chaos had erupted as people who'd been separated during the evacuation searched for their friends or relations, oblivious to police commands to remain calm and seek police help in their search.

Angus had disappeared as silently as he'd approached and Kate wondered if he'd been a dream, although his whispered words still jangled in her head. Had he really said something about getting out of the army?

But why?

She found a frantic mother and reunited her with her child, both of them in tears, and went looking for whatever members of the SDR team who might still be around.

Sam and Paul were by the van that they used in the city and she returned to the hospital with them.

'Blake went to the hospital with a critically injured man,' Sam explained. 'He'd lost a lot of blood because of the stand-off. If we could have got to all those injured faster than we did, there'd have been less chance of anyone dying, but as it is this man and a younger woman are both listed as critical. Kate, you've been in SDR longer than I have, is there any training for this kind of thing? Can we as a response team do more?'

Kate thought about it, then said, 'I don't think so. We all have our roles in these crises, although that's the first hostage situation I've been in. But generally speaking the police have jurisdiction, especially in the city, and they have an elite squad that responds. A special squad from the army is the next lot called in, along with the fire and ambulance services—or maybe they come before the army. But we're there to treat the injured and in things like mass shootings there could be plenty of those.'

'Too many to be worrying about other aspects of the situation?' Sam said, and Kate nodded.

But once back at the hospital it was hard to settle into work, with images of Angus, and whispers of the strange things he'd said, foremost in her mind.

The page requesting her presence in the ED came as a relief. She really didn't want to be operating on anyone without her mind one hundred per cent on the job.

Down there, it soon became clear that most of the damage was collateral. People cut by broken glass when a shot had shattered a shop window, others injured by flying masonry chipped from a wall near them by a bullet.

Several people had been hurt in the panic to get to safety, and all in all the place was chaotic.

The nurse at the triage desk saw Kate walk in.

'Cubicle twelve,' she said. 'Cuts from flying glass.'

Kate moved towards the cubicle—the curtained room providing some privacy but certainly not soundproof, which was how she couldn't avoid hearing a deep, familiar voice from the cubicle next door.

Undoubtedly Angus, which made as little sense as his earlier SDR conversation.

But she had a patient, the clothes the woman had been wearing already replaced with a gown, and on a drip to replace blood loss, provide pain relief and mild sedation, but the woman's wounds were from more than flying glass.

'Someone pushed me through a window,' she said weakly, and, lifting protective cotton pads on her arms and legs to see the damage, Kate knew it would be a long job.

She looked at the nurse assisting her.

'We'll need to flush every wound very carefully to see there's no glass embedded in it. Some we can close with strips but others will need stitches. Could you start that while I check that none of them are bleeding badly enough to be treated immediately? If not, we'll start at the top and work down.'

Kate checked all the wounds, irrigating them as she worked, pleased that they were mostly shallow.

But the face was important. She didn't want to leave the woman scarred for life—a permanent reminder of a terrifying time.

Together, they washed and stitched and dressed the woman's wounds, Kate especially careful to minimise any scarring.

'So this is what general surgery is all about,' a voice said quietly, and Kate froze for a moment, before turning to see Angus, dressed as she was in bloodied scrubs.

A thousand questions rattled in her head, not one

of which she could ask right now. Instead she had to concentrate on her patient, giving her all her attention, so distractions like her body's reaction to Angus had to be hastily slapped down,

'I might see you later,' he said.

'What's he doing here?' she asked the nurse when she'd tied off the last stitch in her patient's cheek.

'Something about joining the ED in the near future—checking the place out,' the nurse replied. 'Gorgeous, isn't he?'

Too gorgeous for his own good, Kate thought, but as the nurse's explanation left her more bamboozled than ever, she ignored it too.

Somehow she got through the day, although an eight-hour shift had turned into fourteen hours, with brief stops for coffee and food to keep her going. She had admitted the woman with the myriad glass cuts, wanting her kept on IV antibiotics for a few days in case there was any infection.

The woman's husband was with her when Kate came to check on her patient before leaving the hospital, profuse in his thanks for all she'd done.

'Visiting hours are over so I'll walk out with you,' he said, and she stepped outside while he said goodbye to his wife, waiting because she sensed he wanted to talk to her.

'Will the wounds heal?'

The question burst from his lips when they were only yards from the ward.

'They will,' Kate assured him.

'But completely? No scars?'

Kate shook her head, suddenly exhausted, but the man was concerned so she had to explain.

'Can we grab a coffee? It's only machine stuff and any resemblance to coffee is purely accidental but I need a hot drink and we can sit in the visitors' chairs and drink it while we talk.'

He hurried to get them both a cup of weak, warm liquid, carrying both to a small seating area by the elevators.

She took a sip, grimaced, but forced a little more down.

'She's had multiple injuries, but it's mostly shock we're worried about now. Some of the deeper cuts may leave scars but I'm reasonably certain her face will be okay. Some scars will leave faint white lines for a while, but nothing that can't be covered by a fine film of make-up.'

The man gave a sigh of relief.

'It's not that she's vain or anything, but she always looks after herself. She goes to the gym, only eats the right foods and looks after her skin. She'd be devastated if she was badly scarred.'

It was Kate's turn to sigh.

'You have to remember that they will look bad at first—red and even puckered—but give it time, use the creams she'll be given when she leaves the hospital, and they should all end up minimal at the most.'

'Oh, thank you,' the man said, abandoning the coffee and getting to his feet, bending to give Kate a hug of gratitude before heading for the lift.

'Do all the men you meet give you thank-you kisses?'

Kate looked up to see Angus looming over her.

'Why are you here?' she asked, far too tired to explain what had just happened, and far too confused to work out what was happening with Angus.

'They told me in the ED you'd come up with your patient.'

She knew she was frowning.

'So?' she asked.

'I came to find you. I want to talk to you.'

'Oh, Angus, I am so tired I've been wondering if I'll make it home or if I can find a spare bed somewhere here to sleep, if only for a few hours.'

She studied him, trying to read the expression on his face.

Nothing there.

So she added, 'I'm really far too tired to talk about anything.'

'Then I'll walk you home.'

And talk even if I don't want to listen, Kate thought.

She shook her head.

'I'm going to find an on-call bed—there's sure to be a vacant one somewhere in the hospital. I just need to crash for a few hours. Can we talk later?'

Although did she really want to talk to him?

This thing about getting out of the army, maybe joining the SDR, stuff she'd heard in snatches today was making her feel very unsettled. Was it something to do with the Snowy situation? Did he feel his tent had failed?

Could he be doing it for her?

Surely not!

Just thinking about it made her feel worse.

'Tomorrow morning, breakfast. I'll meet you at Lu-igi's at seven.'

Kate bit back a groan and nodded, but as she got

rather shakily to her feet, Angus was there, holding her elbow, steadying her, so close that, even exhausted, her body responded to his with all the usual fervour.

'Come on,' he said. 'I'll get a cab, see you home. You'll sleep better there.'

He took her home, asking the cabbie to wait while he went up to the apartment with her.

'You don't have to come in and undress me,' she said, as he took the key and unlocked the door for her. 'I'll go straight to bed.'

'You'd better,' he told her, then dropped a kiss on her lips and disappeared back along the corridor to the elevator.

Once inside, she showered and fell into bed, her mind wanting to go over the strange things that had happened that day—mainly the strange Angus things—but sleep claimed her immediately, a deep, dreamless sleep…

CHAPTER ELEVEN

KATE WOKE AT SIX. It was habit from as far back as school. And now if she was on duty at seven she had plenty of time to get ready, and if she wasn't on until nine she could go for a run first.

She was contemplating the run when something echoed in her brain—words—a meeting. Angus!

He wanted to talk and she was wary about the talk.

Slowly, the events of the day and the stray snippets of Angus stuff filtered back into her conscious mind.

It took a while to get out of the army—talking to Blake about the SDR—checking out the ED. Oh, hell! That explained her wariness, although surely he wouldn't be doing this because of her.

Please let it not be about her…

She loved him desperately but if he was doing it for a wife and family—well, that made her stomach ache.

And the alternative that it might be about some other woman only made her feel worse.

She forced herself out of bed and dressed hurriedly.

Seven at Luigi's!

At least she'd find out.

Angus couldn't recall ever feeling this nervous, not even when mortar shells were exploding around him.

Nervous, *and* excited!

Everything was falling so neatly into place. Only this morning he'd had a text from Blake about an apartment in the building where Kate lived with Alice. Three bedrooms, up for sale—once owned by another Bayside doctor. He could move in and rent until the sale went through...

So why the nerves?

Because Kate had seemed a little strained last night?

But he could put that down to the long and traumatic day she'd had.

Kate!

He smiled to himself, pleased with all he'd managed to organise in such a short time.

He reached the café before her and found a quiet table on the pavement, looking out over the beach. Then there she was, walking towards him, not smiling—well maybe a small pretend smile—but she'd still be tired.

He stood up to greet her, took her in his arms to kiss her, felt her stiffen, turn a little so his kiss hit her cheek.

Tired?

She sat down, ordered coffee from the hovering waiter, then turned to him.

'So, talk!' she said, and Angus felt his throat tighten and his mouth go dry.

This wasn't how he'd planned it.

'We should get our breakfast order in before it gets too busy,' he said. 'We should tell the waiter when he brings the coffee.'

'One slice of banana bread toasted,' she said, and although he wanted to tell her she should eat more than that for breakfast, he had finally caught on that this was not the joyous reunion he'd somehow imagined.

He gave the orders, watched as she stirred sugar into her coffee and took a sip, looking at him over the rim of the cup, eyes making the same demand.

Talk!

'I don't know how much you took in of what I was saying yesterday. It was all so chaotic, and nothing definite's been organised yet, but—'

She put down her coffee, tilted her head to one side, and looked at him—really looked.

'Angus, start at the beginning. Start with the army.'

His hands seemed to be shaking so he put down his coffee cup. He'd have liked to reach out and take her hands in his but hers were still firmly wrapped around her cup.

'I'm getting out,' he said. 'I've done enough.'

'But your tent?' she protested. 'You wanted to go wherever it went. It was your dream from the very beginning.'

She sounded perplexed, which was understandable, although he had hoped for a little excitement...

'I've got others who know as much about it as I do. Now we know it works and with a few modifications after the Snowy experience I'll go to China where they'll manufacture them, but after that I'm free.'

'Free?'

Still perplexed!

'Free to take a job here at Bondi Bayside. Apparently, they've had locums working in the ED since someone called Luc Braxton left and the job's mine if I want it.'

Still no sign of excitement. He was starting to feel jittery. This wasn't going at all the way he'd planned.

Long silence, Kate studying him, expressionless now.

Then—

'Why are you doing this, Angus?'

She didn't know!

Couldn't guess?

Had he been mistaken about how she felt?

Had the love he'd been slow to recognise but was now strong enough to move mountains—and get out of the army—been one-sided?

That thought made him feel very hollow, so hollow he knew that answering, 'For you, for us,' would be a big mistake.

He took a deep breath.

'Finding out about the baby, it spun me off course. For days I felt…not lost but completely disoriented. For the first time in my life I didn't have a compass in my head telling me exactly what lay ahead. Yet I *did* know what lay ahead—things I'd spent what seemed like for ever planning, going with the tent wherever it was needed. Suddenly it wasn't enough.'

He paused, looking at her across the table, wondering if any of his words were making sense to her.

'I thought maybe it was because the tent had been successful and I needed a new project, or maybe the deaths down in the Snowy had affected me more than I'd thought. I haven't been much fun—a bear with a sore head had nothing on me as I mooched around the place, snapping at people who'd done nothing to deserve it, and generally making everyone around me miserable too. I was seriously considering counselling when I began to realise it wasn't me at all, it was the army.'

'The army?'

'Don't get me wrong, I love the army. It's been my

life—my dream since I was a child—given me so much, but suddenly I knew I didn't belong there any more. It was time to leave,' he said firmly.

And that was true. He'd had enough of army life, and wanted something more, something settled, normal. And if he didn't find it with Kate—

He wouldn't go there.

Their breakfast arrived, just in time to ease the tension that had suddenly built like a thick cloud between them, but as he watched her butter her toast and cut it into neat squares his heart knew he wanted to see her do that again—and again—if possible every morning for the rest of their lives.

Kate picked up a small square of toast, not really wanting to eat it, sure it would taste like sawdust, she felt so uptight.

Angus hadn't said it, but she was reasonably certain that this whole idea of leaving the army and coming to work at Bayside was something he'd done for her.

And her heart ached inside her, that he would make such a sacrifice. No one who'd spent any time with Angus could help but know how much the army, and particularly his tent, meant to him.

He'd asked her to marry him, and she'd reminded him that he'd learned from past experience that the uncertainty of army life, particularly his army life, was too hard on relationships—too hard on a wife and children...

And if that was why he was getting out of the army then she, for all she loved him—because she loved him—wasn't the one for him.

But what could she say?

I love you but I won't marry you?

Too hurtful.

Make light of it?

Could she?

She ate another square of toast—sawdust.

Looked at a point just beyond his left shoulder and—well, gabbled really.

'Well, it seems as if you've got it all sorted. And if you come to Bayside it will be great to have you in the SDR! You can bring such a lot of different experience to it. I bet Blake was thrilled at the idea. And if you're replacing Luc in the ED his—'

Apartment was for sale at the moment.

That's what she'd been about to say when she'd realised that while working in the same hospital as Angus would be a permanent source of pain to her, having him living in the same apartment block would be sheer torture.

Especially when he found the wife and children...

But she, Kate, could get out of the SDR—her surgical work would be getting more extensive this year, less time in the ED. She could do this.

She risked a glance at him, but his head was bent over the enormous breakfast he had ordered.

His hair was a little longer, showing the curls that probably made him keep it short, and her fingers twitched with the urge to touch it, feel its softness, run her fingers through it. She watched his hands, cutting a sausage neatly and precisely, and remembered them sliding across her body, bringing it alive at the slightest touch.

And her body ached for him, ached to hold him, feel

his warmth, his heat, to kiss him and be lost in his kiss, to lose herself in him—in love…

Angus ate with grim determination. Somehow, somewhere along the line, his careful planning had gone disastrously wrong. He'd heard Kate's words—had felt them like knife wounds, in fact—but they were…

False?

He ate another slice of sausage.

No, they hadn't rung false, yet *some* emotion had been there behind them.

And as if he'd take the offered job at Bayside, knowing she was working in the same hospital, being so close to her yet not hers—she not his…

He needed to get away, out of the café, go for a long walk, anything to clear his head, but he was damned if he'd leave his breakfast—damned if he'd let her see how upset he was by her casual brush-off.

Because that's what it was!

Or was it?

Something niggled at him.

Something whispering that there was more…

'I've got to go—on duty.'

She was on her feet, beside him, and he caught her hand.

'Kate?' he said, and looked up in time to see her squeeze her eyes shut, but not before he'd seen the sheen of tears.

'I'll see you around,' she said, oh, so casually, after which she retrieved her hand and walked away.

CHAPTER TWELVE

IT TOOK ANGUS five weeks to finalise his 'return to civvy street' plan, then suddenly he was there—in the ED, at SDR meetings and, worst of all, living in the same apartment block.

So how could she not walk home from work with him if they happened to leave the hospital at the same time?

For Kate, it was agony. All the memories she'd tried so hard to pack away had escaped, so her body hummed with inner excitement, her skin tightened at the slightest accidental touch, while his voice—though often she barely registered a word he said—filled her body with an aching longing she hadn't known existed.

Not that Angus felt any of these manifestations—not even awkwardness—prattling on as he would to any colleague about the new challenges he was finding in the job.

It was only after she'd changed shifts three times that she began to suspect these meetings, the walks home together weren't entirely accidental. Was he doing it to torture her?

Prove something?

She had no idea, but it was affecting her to the point

that it was only by maintaining the strictest self-discipline that she could concentrate on work.

But once home, inside, she was a mess, distracted, picky, even short with Alice at times, wanting nothing more than to shut herself away in a dark hole and wait for the storm of emotions to go away.

Had Alice spoken to Harry that she came knocking on the apartment door on Kate's day off, finding Kate still in her pyjamas at ten o'clock?

'Not running today?' Harry asked, raising her eyebrows at Kate's attire, knowing that Kate ran every day she could—especially on days off.

'No!'

Simple answer, not exactly rude but fairly blunt.

'Because of Angus?' Harry, undeterred, continued.

'What the hell's it got to do with Angus?' Kate growled, and Harry smiled at her.

'You can't honestly believe that the entire staff of the hospital hasn't seen that something's up between you and Angus. I'm working in Geriatrics before I get back to ICU and it's even whispered about up there. Gorgeous new doc who'd tempted Kate Mitchell out of her shell, now working at the hospital and being ignored by said Kate while the sexual tension between the two of you could cause spontaneous combustion!'

'That's ridiculous,' Kate snapped, while her stomach clenched and unclenched.

'Is it?' Harry said gently. 'Kate, you gave me a prod when I was feeling too sorry for myself to be bothered with life. Now it's my turn. Even the most self-focussed member of the staff—and you know we get plenty of those—can see the sparks that fly between you and

Angus. And anyone being caught between the two of you can feel the force field of whatever it is you share.'

She paused, obviously waiting for some input from Kate, but she was too flabbergasted by Harry's words to say anything at all.

'All I'm saying,' Harry carried on, 'is to at least explore the situation. Talk to the man, throw yourself into his arms, do something, anything, even if it's a risk, but don't let something as powerful as whatever's between you go to waste without at least giving it a go.'

Throw yourself into his arms?

Oh, how she longed to do that! One last time because surely it would lead to them making love. And in the languorous bliss after that she could explain— even tell him she loved him and then explain—and maybe after that she'd go back to Brisbane. He'd find someone else—

That thought was like a knife wound in her chest.

'Well?' Harry said, and Kate found a smile for her. Not a very good one, she was sure, but Harry had spoken out of kindness and friendship.

'Thank you,' Kate said, and she leaned forward and gave Harry a hug, walked her to the door and let her out.

But thinking Throw yourself into his arms was far easier than working out how to do it.

Except that Alice had gone back up to the island for an old staff reunion and she was alone in the flat.

Entice him in?

No, she had to be proactive.

Would he be at home?

His—Luc's—apartment was at the front of the

building with the ocean view, so she couldn't see if lights were on or not.

So she'd visit!

But in her daggy pyjamas?

She smiled to herself, remembering the day he'd left her at the art gallery, suddenly called away. She'd gone to the Queen Victoria Building and as well as some fancy underwear she had bought a gorgeous nightdress, soft cream silk with a low V-neckline trimmed with lace and tiny rosebuds.

She'd meet someone in the corridor for sure if she paraded down to Angus's apartment in that, but if she wore her terry towelling dressing gown over it she could be popping down to borrow a cup of sugar from a neighbour.

More or less!

Her excitement was growing. She might be planning to say goodbye to Angus, but let it be a glorious goodbye.

She showered, used moisturiser and perfume, not too much, pulled on the slinky gown and shook her head.

What on earth was she thinking?

What if someone was there?

What if someone *from the hospital* was there?

She was about to take it off when the knowledge that this might be her last chance to lie in Angus's arms hit her with the force of a tidal wave.

Damn it all, she'd do it.

But she'd ring him first.

She dialled his number—fingers shaking on the keys—heard his deep 'Angus Caruth' and her courage faltered.

'Kate, is that you?'

Of course, her name had come up on his screen.

She drew a deep breath and then, oh, so casually, said, 'I just wondered if you were home. I could pop in. That's if you haven't any visitors.'

Long silence.

'No, no visitors,' he said, which wasn't exactly welcoming but she was too uptight to dither any more.

'I'll see you soon.'

She went swiftly down the corridor—it would have been too easy to turn back if she'd dawdled—and knocked on his door.

Given that Kate had barely spoken to him since he'd arrived at Bayside, Angus was already puzzled by the phone call, but opening the door to Kate, clutching a towelling dressing gown around her slim figure, he was completely thrown.

'Are you going to ask me in? Just for now?'

There was a quiver in Kate's voice that pierced the armour he'd begun to build around his heart, and he put his hands on her shoulders and pulled her gently towards him, shutting the door behind her.

And for a moment, it was enough just to have her in his arms again.

He had no idea what had gone wrong between them, let alone why his change of career had obviously upset her, but for now she was here.

So he kissed her, gently at first, then, as a tiny moan escaped her lips, his kiss drew harder, hotter, more demanding.

The thick towelling robe had fallen open and underneath was fabric as smooth and soft as her silky skin.

'I should say wow but I doubt it will be on you long enough for me to truly appreciate it,' he said thickly, and heard her chuckle, felt it in her throat as he pressed kisses to the slim column of her neck and downwards, teasing at the deep V of the gown to find her breast, her nipple.

She wove her fingers in his hair and gave a gasp as he licked and nipped the thickened nub, then she was in his arms, the slinky material torturing him as he carried her to his bed, set her down on it and took in her beauty.

'Love me,' she whispered, and he needed no second bidding, stripping off his clothes to join her on the bed.

He kissed her. Teasing kisses at first, while his hand slid the soft fabric up her leg, his kisses more insistent as his fingers found her warmth. Then brushing tiny roses aside, he teased her nipple again, her fingers holding his head to her, wanting more yet squirming at his touch.

And when his lips claimed hers again, she took him in her hand and guided him into her, moving slowly at first as they adjusted to each other, before it became a race, a battle to be one, their bodies demanding more and more until finally they lay, depleted, joined and close, slick sweat warm on both their bodies…

Together.

And with her arms tight around him, his head resting on her breast, she began to talk, so softly and slowly he knew every word held tears.

'I love you, Angus. Love you more than I could ever imagine I could love anyone. But leaving the army, coming to Bayside. You should have said, we should have talked. I would have told you it was only ever going to be for the "now". Not this now but the "now" we had back then. That's what we'd agreed, and even when I knew I loved you, I felt at least I'd have that memory for ever.'

Angus heard the words, even understood them for they were simple English, but the meaning was eluding him, so he kept silent, waited, aware now that this was why Kate had come.

Oh, going to bed with him had obviously been a big part of it, but he saw now it had been her way to break down the walls that had risen between them.

Break them down so she could talk.

'You told me once you wouldn't marry because being married to an army officer in the job you did was no life for a wife and family. Some people obviously do it and do it well, but you felt with the tent and calls to dangerous or just disease-ridden places it was unfair to have someone waiting and worrying at home.'

She paused, held him closer, ran her fingers lightly over the planes of his face, kissed the top of his head.

'Then suddenly you're out of the army, working here, talking about a wife and children.'

Her voice cracked and he guessed they'd reached the heart of the conversation.

'What I hadn't said, hadn't told you,' she whispered, snuggling closer to him now, 'was that after the baby was stillborn, the specialist was doubtful I'd carry a live child to term. He had some garbled explanation but I wasn't listening because I didn't ever want to go through what had happened again, determined I wouldn't—couldn't. Not all that waiting and the caring and excitement and then nothing but a huge hole in my heart and aching, empty arms…'

He eased away, seeing clearly now. This woman he loved and who definitely loved him backing off because he'd been foolish enough to talk about a wife and children—a family—the children part being the barrier that had grown between them.

He propped himself on his elbow and looked down at her, traced her lips with his thumb.

'Did you honestly believe I'd turn my back on you— find someone else to marry—because you might not be able to give me children? Did you think I was so shallow that some vague idea of family would make me reject you?'

He heard his voice, knew it was harsh, but would have continued had he not seen the tears on her cheeks. And with aching heart he gathered her into his arms and held her tight, rocking her as he would a crying child, the love he felt for her enveloping them both.

'My darling Kate. It's you I love, just you. Yes, should we happen to have a child I'd love it too, but, no matter what, I love you. And anyway I don't believe the pundits who told you such rotten news, probably when you were very vulnerable. I've read up on stillbirths, mainly to gain an idea of even a fraction of the pain you must have gone through, and for pregnancies where there might be problems, there are now foetal monitors the mother can wear in the last trimester, and with any hint of the foetal heartbeat faltering, it's straight into hospital.'

He kissed her then, gentle kisses, before adding, 'Not that children are important—not as long as I have you.'

And Kate relaxed in his arms—right where she belonged.

CHAPTER THIRTEEN

THEY MARRIED QUIETLY, asking a celebrant to perform the ceremony on the balcony of Angus's unit, Alice beside Kate and Angus's uncle supporting him.

'Your mother will be furious,' Alice told Kate, as she slipped on the long, linen shift she'd chosen for her wedding, flowers scattered on a cream background, including cornflowers that she loved and often took to wee Joshua's grave.

'I'll make peace with Mum,' Kate promised her aunt. 'We're already talking and when Angus has been at Bayside long enough to take some time off, we'll fly north to see them. He's already won some brownie points by being Scottish!'

Alice laughed and kissed Kate's cheek.

'Just be happy, both of you. I know it's trite and clichéd but make the most of every day and never be afraid to show your love.'

Too overcome for words, Kate kissed this woman who'd taken her in and probably saved her sanity.

Then they walked together out onto the balcony, looking out over the deep blue of the ocean and the white foam on the breakers closer to the shore.

Angus's smile and the pride in his eyes told Kate

all she needed to know. She stood beside him, took his hand and said the words that would bind them together for ever.

'So, how do you like being Mrs Dr Caruth?' he asked as he bent his head and kissed her lips, gently yet firmly, promising so much more than words could ever convey.

Promising her love…

* * * * *

RESCUED BY
HER MR RIGHT

ALISON ROBERTS

MILLS & BOON

For Linda and Meredith, with much love.

CHAPTER ONE

SHE HAD BEEN aware of the sound for longer than she'd realised.

It wasn't until Harriet Collins had finally reached the flat part of this cliff walk that her focus relaxed enough to acknowledge the sound.

A dog barking.

It had just been part of the background for what felt like a long time. A background that included the warmth of a late Australian spring day and the sound of waves rolling onto the rocky shore far below where she was now. Her concentration had been on more important things. Like the occasional uneven steps and rough stony patches on this clifftop walkway.

Like the pain in her leg that had reached an intolerable level a while back but hadn't been allowed to do more than slow her down because Harriet needed to find out how far she could push it before it let her down completely and refused to keep her upright—as it had so many times over the long, long months of her rehabilitation so far.

Someone else must be walking this track, she decided, as she paused long enough to fish her water bottle from the mesh side pouch of her small backpack.

She could feel other lumpy shapes inside the pack as she slotted the bottle back into place.

Exciting lumps. She had chosen this walk to try out her new camera for the first time. And that expensive zoom lens. When she found the right spot, she could wait until the sun was starting to set and hopefully capture some amazing shots of the waves crashing on those fearsome rocks at shore level. She had a head-lamp tucked inside as well, which should make it safe enough for her to get back down the track to where she'd parked her car when daylight was fading.

It did seem odd, though, that this dog was being so vocal. And the sound wasn't getting any fainter, which you would expect if an overexcited pet was running ahead of its person on a long walk. If anything, it was getting louder, as Harriet started walking again.

Her limp was more pronounced than it had been for some time but that was only to be expected after that long uphill stretch. The paracetamol she had swallowed along with that drink of water should kick in soon and, by the time she'd had a good rest while she took her photographs, she should be ready to tackle the return trip.

The barking got louder and Harriet stopped in her tracks when she saw the dark shape rushing towards her.

A beat of fear stopped her inward breath.

A dog attack? *Really?* After so many months of fighting to get her life approaching anything like normal, was she about to get sent back to square one by being mauled by a big dog? To be even more disfigured than she was already?

No way...

The sound that Harriet let out was a half-scream merged with an angry growl that expressed quite a lot about the struggle she'd been through and her desperation to not allow any new setbacks.

It seemed to work. The dog stopped in its tracks, too. And it stopped barking. It stared at Harriet.

Harriet stared back.

It was a black Labrador but not nearly as fat as most Labs she'd met. Maybe it got a lot of exercise running along these clifftop tracks with its owner.

Where was its owner? When he or she appeared, Harriet might have something to say about letting their dog run loose and frighten people. What if she'd had children with her?

The dog started barking again. It turned, ran a few steps and then stopped to look back at her. This time the barking felt like an attempt to communicate something.

'Oh, for heaven's sake,' Harriet muttered aloud. 'You've seen too many Lassie movies.'

But it felt right to follow the dog. Cautiously, because it was taking her off this well-marked and relatively flat pathway. Through long grass and big boulders towards the edge of the cliff. The dog didn't stop until it seemed to be standing on the very edge. It peered down the cliff and then turned back to Harriet. Its barking sounded more urgent now.

One step and then another brought Harriet nearer the dog.

'What is it?' she asked. 'What's wrong?'

A tail wagged encouragement and the dog sat down

as Harriet got within touching distance. It nudged her hand and licked her.

'At least you're friendly,' she said. 'What's your name?'

There was a collar with a disc on it. 'Harry? Are you kidding me? That's *my* name.'

Harry the dog nudged her again and then stood up to peer over the edge again.

'Okay…' Harriet lay down, just to be safe, and inched forward.

It wasn't a straight drop but it was steep enough to be dangerous with areas of loose scree amongst boulders and weathered shrubs that were clinging to life. At the point where the intermittent vegetation gave up, there was a drop onto a ledge. She couldn't see the whole ledge but what she could see made a shiver run down her spine.

Legs.

And one of them was twisted at a very unnatural angle.

'Hey…' she yelled. 'Can you hear me? Are you conscious?'

There was no answering call. No flicker of movement from the legs.

'It's okay,' Harriet yelled again. 'I'm going to call for help.'

She hauled her mobile phone out of the pocket of her cargo pants and then punched in the emergency three-digit number, giving a curt response of 'Ambulance' when she was asked what service she required.

'I'm at the top of the Kookaburra walkway,' she told the call taker in the communications centre. 'There's someone who's fallen from the cliff. He's on a ledge about a hundred metres from the top and…and he's not responding to calls. I can see from here that he's probably got a badly fractured leg.'

'No…' she said a minute later. 'There's no access from the top unless it's by abseiling. I think we're going to need a helicopter.' She listened for a few seconds and then interrupted the young woman she was speaking to.

'Look…my name is Harriet Collins. I'm an intensive care nurse at Bondi Bayside Hospital but I'm also a member of the Specialist Disaster Response team based there.'

It wasn't exactly true. Not now… But they hadn't yet officially removed her from the membership list, had they?

'I know what I'm talking about, okay? We need a helicopter. This is a winch job. Anything else is going to take too long.'

And that was that. Help was on its way and there was nothing more that Harriet could do other than sit and wait and maybe signal the helicopter crew when they got close.

Harry the dog didn't think so. He nudged her elbow and his whine was an easily interpreted plea.

Harriet peered over the edge of the cliff again.

The dog walker had trainers on his feet. And socks. And…yes…the foot on the leg that looked normal was moving.

'Hey…' Harriet could hear the alarm bell going off in her head. She yelled even louder this time. 'Don't move, okay? You're safe where you are and help's coming. But…just don't *move*…'

If he'd been unconscious, he might have a head injury and not be thinking clearly. What if he managed to

drag himself right off that ledge? There'd be no chance
of survival if he finished the drop to where the surf was
roiling around those black, jagged rocks.

Had she been wrong in saying that ledge was a
hundred metres from the top of the cliff? It looked
more like fifty at second guess. And maybe it wouldn't
have needed abseilers to get down. There were enough
protruding rocks to provide good footholds and those
scrappy little trees would give handholds for balance
if you didn't trust them with your whole body weight.

It didn't need another nudge from Harry the dog to
trigger Harriet's decision. It didn't seem to need any
conscious thought at all. If she had stopped to think,
she would have known how crazy this was. That her
bad leg couldn't possibly cope with this challenge.

But Harriet didn't think. She just sat on her bottom,
holding a branch of the nearest shrunken tree and let
herself slide, very slowly, until her feet reached the first
rock below her. The foot of her bad leg touched it first
and a spear of pain lanced upwards to reach her thigh
but her leg didn't crumple and, as soon as she transferred to her weight to her good foot, the pain receded.
When she did it again, she made sure it was her strong
leg that found a solid object first. Now she was several
metres below where Harry had started running back
and forth on the flat area, barking encouragement, and
the enormity of what she'd started was enough to make
her head spin for a moment or two.

At least this incarnation of Lassie was someone to
talk to.

'I'm not sure that this was such a good idea,' she told
him. 'I'm going to have to crawl sideways to reach that
next tree. Do you reckon it's got strong roots?'

Harry the dog seemed to think so.

She had to cling to the next rock for a minute, to get over the fright of her foot slipping a little in the scree. She didn't look down. Instead, she looked up at the black head that was getting smaller every time she looked.

'What you don't know,' she said casually, 'is that until very recently I was wearing a pretty hard-core brace on my leg. Because I had a rock that landed on it a while back and it was so squashed they almost had to chop it off. Yeah… I know dogs can manage quite well without one of their legs but it's a bit more of a problem for a person.'

The sound of the waves was getting louder and Harriet knew perfectly well that the dog couldn't hear what she was saying and wouldn't understand if he could but it seemed to be helping her.

'But look at me right now… It almost feels like I'm back in the SDR team and I don't mind telling you that that's the thing I miss the most about my old life.'

Except that if this was a team callout, she'd be appropriately dressed in heavy-duty overalls and with a hard hat and gloves for more protection. And she'd be on the end of a rope with people who knew what they were doing holding the other end to prevent a fall that would have meant two victims instead of only one.

If she'd done anything this irresponsible as a team member, their leader, Blake Cooper, would have probably sacked her, and Kate and Sam would have been watching her with horror. But she wasn't a team member any more and she never could be, with the disability that was highly likely to be permanent now. A weak leg. Pain levels that could be hard to manage. A mindset that was very different from the passionate and adventurous person she'd been all those months ago.

Maybe she was going to get stuck herself and the rescue crew would have to winch two people off this cliff and she'd cop an awful lot of flak. But...

But the fact that she was even trying to do this—that she *wanted* to do this so much—made her feel like the real Harriet Collins had finally stepped out from the black mist she'd been shrouded in for so long.

And she was more than halfway down now. That ledge was starting to look bigger and hiding the terrifying drop below it. Another controlled slide on her bottom, a careful climb over a tumble of rocks without trusting her weight to her bad leg and then a downward, sideways crawl and she could almost stand up to push her way past rough bunches of tussock and through the stunted trees onto the ledge.

Harry's owner was probably in his sixties, his grey hair matted with a stain of blood and a badly bruised and grazed arm. And he was groaning.

'Hey...' Harriet crouched beside him, picking up his hand and then feeling for his pulse. 'My name's Harry. Same as your dog...'

The man's eyes opened. 'Harry...'

'He's fine. He's up on top of the cliff. He came to find me and get help for you. Just like Lassie.'

The man's eyes closed but his lips twisted into a smile. 'Not so much. It was Harry who went over the edge. Got...stuck on a rock and I went down to help. I lost my footing and...argh...that *really* hurts...'

'Your leg? Or is it something else?'

'My leg...and...and my head doesn't feel great.'

'What's your name?'

'Eddie. Eddie Denton.'

'Okay, Eddie. Take a deep breath for me. Does that hurt?'

'No. Feels okay…'

'That's great. We don't need to worry about your breathing then. And you've got a good pulse so that means your blood pressure's still okay.'

'You a doctor, Harry?'

'No, I'm a nurse. I worked in the Intensive Care Unit at Bondi Bayside, although I'm somewhere else at the moment. But I'm also a member of a specialist rescue team there.'

She was checking Eddie out as she kept talking. 'I'm just going to have a feel of your tummy, okay? Does that hurt?'

'No. It's just my leg.'

The pain from an obvious femoral fracture could well be masking something happening internally but there was nothing Harriet could do other than keep Eddie company and make sure he didn't move and fall further. There was no time to do anything else, anyway. She could see the dot of the approaching helicopter now and only seconds later the sound of the rotors drowned out the faint barking she could still hear from the top of the cliff.

This was one of the bright red and yellow helicopters of the ambulance service here in Sydney and the crew member she could see leaning out from the skid and preparing to be winched down would be one of the elite, intensive care paramedics that dealt with calls like this. It was a relief to see the big pack of gear being attached to the winch line along with a stretcher but she expected nothing less from a team who were well used to dealing with emergencies on the shorelines of this huge coastal city.

What she would never have expected was to be addressed as if this paramedic knew her.

'Harry? How did you end up on this ledge?' He pushed up the visor of his helmet as he unhooked the gear and then held the winch line clear, giving the winch operator the 'thumbs up' sign to retrieve the hook. 'I thought the job had been called in from up at the track.'

'Oh, my God...' Harriet's jaw dropped. 'When did you start working on the choppers, Jack?'

'Months ago.' His tone was clipped. Cold, even? 'Fill me in, Harry.'

'This is Eddie Denton. He's sixty-three. He slipped and fell after trying to get his dog out of trouble.'

There was a nagging voice at the back of her head telling her that she deserved the brush-off. How many times had she done that to Jack after the accident, when he'd tried to visit her?

But not being part of the team any more had made it too painful to be reminded of how devastating the loss of this part of her life had been. And he'd given up eventually, just the way everybody else had stopped talking about it. Harriet couldn't actually remember the last time she'd heard Jack's name mentioned.

'Hiya, Eddie. I'm Jack Evans. I've come to get you out of here, mate. How are you feeling?'

'Gotta sore leg.'

'Fractured mid-shaft femur,' Harriet put in. 'Limb baselines are intact.'

'Anything else I should know about?'

'Head injury. I'm pretty sure he was unconscious

when I arrived on scene and he's been complaining about a headache.'

'And that arm?'

'I don't think it's fractured but it's badly bruised and there's a fair bit of skin missing. Blood loss was minimal as far as I can tell.'

It could have been worse. If Eddie had been bleeding badly, she could have stopped that. Did that justify her putting herself in so much danger and giving the rescue crew another person to manage? She hadn't really thought about the consequences when she'd started that climb down, had she?

Instinct had overridden sense.

Or maybe it was because she hadn't been able to resist the pull of being that person again. The one that did the dangerous stuff because she could potentially save a life.

'Can you find some dressings in that pack? I'd like to get an IV in and some pain relief on board before we get a traction splint on that leg.'

It wasn't just Eddie who had a sore leg. The jolt of pain as Harriet moved to open Jack's pack was almost enough to make her stumble. Maybe it was a good thing that they were on a relatively narrow ledge above a dangerous drop so it was a perfectly normal thing to do to crawl carefully from one point to another.

Jack wouldn't have even noticed.

'You okay, Harry?'

The swift glance from those dark eyes and the furrow between them told Harriet that he'd noticed her wincing, all right. She broke the eye contact abruptly. She didn't want anybody's pity but to be pitied by Jack was worse, somehow. He was one of the younger members of the SDR team and one of the best. He was going places, young Jack Evans, but he wasn't cocky about it. He was, in fact, one of the nicest people Harriet had ever known.

In her old life…

'Be careful,' was all Jack added. 'We're a long way up. Hand me that IV roll, would you?'

She handed over the roll that contained everything Jack needed to insert an IV. The wipes, cannulas, Luer plugs, flushes and adhesive covers. She didn't need reminding of how far above sea level they were. Every few seconds, even given the sound of the helicopter hovering nearby, she could hear the rolling crash of a huge wave below.

'Sharp scratch, Eddie. There you go… Are you allergic to anything that you know of?'

'Nah…not that I know of.'

Harriet had all the sterile dressings and a bandage in her hands so that she could cover the raw wounds on Eddie's arm but she stayed by the pack for a moment longer. Jack was going to need a giving set and a bag of saline to set up fluids that would keep Eddie's vein open in case he needed more intravenous drugs. The morphine would definitely be helping his pain level within the next few minutes.

'What score would you give your pain now, Eddie? Out of ten, like before?'

'I reckon it's only a five now. Maybe even a four.'

'Good man. We're going to get that splint on your leg in a tick. And then I'm going to get you up into our nice comfy chopper.'

'But what about Harry?'

'We'll take her, too, don't you worry. I'm not about

to let her try climbing up this cliff by herself. God knows how she managed to get down to you in the first place.' Jack was waiting for Harriet to look up as she snagged the bandage she'd wound around Eddie's arm with a crocodile clip to keep it secure. 'Good job,' he added as he finally caught her gaze.

He sounded impressed. And not the least bit cold. Quite the opposite, in fact.

'No.' Eddie shook his head. 'I meant Harry—my dog…'

'Oh…right…'

'He's a hero,' Harriet said. 'I wouldn't have found Eddie if it hadn't been for Harry. He came and got me and made me follow him.'

Jack grinned. 'Like Lassie, huh?'

Harriet found herself smiling back. 'Just like Lassie.'

The shared smile broke whatever odd tension she had been aware of ever since Jack had touched down on this ledge. It was a link back to the very real friendship they'd shared during their time together with the SDR team. A friendship that Harriet couldn't deny she'd shunned since her accident because it was such an integral aspect of the part of the life she'd lost for ever.

But maybe there was a way back? To a small part of what she'd lost, anyway.

And that felt good.

'In that case, I'll call the crew.' Jack nodded, reaching for his radio. 'We'll get someone to head up the track and find him. Don't you worry, Eddie. He'll be well looked after until we can get him home for you.'

Whether it was the relief of knowing his pet would be rescued, or the effects of the narcotic pain relief, Eddie seemed to relax into the care they were giving him. It was painful to get the traction splint locked into place and doing its job but, for this kind of fracture, it was essential to get control of any internal bleeding and added pain of the movement that would be happening very soon.

'I'll take Eddie up on the stretcher and then I'll come back down for you and the pack.' Jack raised his arm to signal the crew in the hovering helicopter that he was ready for the winch line to be lowered again. 'Okay?'

Harriet nodded.

For several long minutes, she was alone on the ledge, watching Jack control the swinging of the stretcher Eddie was strapped onto as it was lifted skywards. And then she saw it being tipped and dragged into the cabin of the helicopter. It seemed to take a long time until Jack was standing on the skid again, ready for his second descent, but she watched him coming down with an increasing sense of relief.

There was no way she could have climbed back up that cliff.

It was no wonder that Jack had been impressed that she'd managed it at all. The last time he'd seen her, her leg had been skewered with long pins and encased in the rods of external fixation for a fracture that had been bad enough for her to have had to give consent to amputation if that had been deemed the best option during her surgery.

He'd been so determinedly cheerful, she remembered. He'd brought a brand of chocolate she'd once announced was her all-time favourite and some magazines, but the choice had been unfortunate, including the latest edition of an emergency medicine journal. And, okay, maybe that publication had also previously been favourite reading material but it had been the last thing she'd wanted to see then.

The visit had been awkward. What did they have in common other than the team callouts, training sessions and rare social occasions? Jack was a good six years younger than Harriet. Just a mate.

At least he hadn't been around to see her limping return to work at Bondi Bayside. If he was with the helicopter crew he wouldn't even be spending time in the emergency department, although he might still make an occasional visit to the intensive care unit if he wanted to follow up on a patient. Not that Harriet was working there any more—not when that environment needed people who could be quick on their feet when needed and in no danger from being distracted by pain or fatigue.

An echo of the awkwardness that had only increased between them until Jack didn't come to visit her any more reared its head as he arrived back on the ledge and helped Harriet into the 'nappy' harness that would hold her close to his body as they were winched back into the helicopter. Maybe it was a good thing that it was noisy and scary and there was no need to say anything other than to confirm she understood all the instructions.

The scariest part was when her feet lost contact with the relative safety of that ledge and she was dangling in mid-air, with the rocks of the cliff looking alarmingly close and the roiling surf a terrifying drop below.

Oddly, she felt safe at the same time.

Jack was big. Tall and muscly. Not with the kind of muscles that her ex-boyfriend Pete had nurtured in his gym sessions, though. Just like his looks were a

complete contrast to the sun-streaked, surfer vibe that
had attracted her to Pete in the first place. It felt like
Jack had just been born that way, and maybe he had.
The young paramedic had island heritage—Maori or
Samoan—with the dark eyes and black hair that went
with his olive skin. He had the gentleness that could
come as such a pleasant surprise in a big man but he
also had strength and that was what Harriet could feel
surrounding her now as they rose slowly in this vast
sky.

How long had it been since she'd felt a man's arms
around her like this? Making her feeling safe. Cherished, almost.

Maybe that foolhardy challenge of climbing down
that cliff had been worth it.

Just for this…

CHAPTER TWO

FUNNY HOW MANY thoughts could flash through your brain when you were dangling in mid-air. Even when most of your concentration was so focused on keeping both yourself and the person you were holding safe.

But the thoughts were there. Drifting past like fragments of a half-forgotten dream.

Because he *had* dreamed of this. Once upon a time.

Holding Harriet Collins in his arms…

Part of his soul had recognised her as the perfect woman the first time he'd met her, back when they had both been new and on their very first training session for the SDR team. Everything about her had been fascinating. Those shiny, auburn curls that bounced when she moved her head. The cute freckles that dusted her milky skin. Hazel eyes with the sparkle of sheer *joie de vivre*. That easy smile and the contagious gurgle of her laughter. How *nice* she was. Warm and open and friendly.

It had taken a long time to screw up the courage to ask her out on a date. He'd had to fight the doubts about how unlikely it was that she could be as interested in *him*. She was years older than he was. Older and wiser and with a circle of friends that were part of a very different world but the attraction was so strong, he'd had to try.

The sheer delight that she seemed to think it was a great idea had been short-lived. She'd seen it as no more than a mate suggesting a team outing, in fact, because she'd shared the invitation with those around them, including the new guy who'd just joined the team— a good-looking firie by the name of Pete Thompson.

And it had been that very night—that had been supposed to be his first date with Harriet—that the spark had been ignited between her and Pete. Jack had felt every jolt of electricity that had passed between them and every one of them had been tipped with the flame of rejection. Of not being good enough. Of not having the kind of charisma that blokes like Pete Thompson had. He knew that that charisma often came with a price. That they were often shallow, egotistical people.

But there'd been nothing that he could do, other than watch it happen. And accelerate. And he'd got over it. So Harriet wasn't for him? It didn't matter. They were still friends and he'd find someone else who made him feel this way—without those doubts that he'd made the mistake of ignoring. One of these days, he *would* experience that 'falling in love' business. Preferably with someone that he knew he would want to spend the rest of his life with.

Someone like Harriet Collins maybe, but with some island blood so that she could embrace being part of an extended family that could sometimes smother you with the responsibilities of belonging but would never tolerate being shut out of any dark times in your life.

The way Harriet had shut *him* out.

It still hurt, Jack realised, as they got close enough to

where his crewmate, Matt, was leaning out of the chopper door, ready to pull Harriet to safety and unclip the nappy harness. It was almost a relief when he couldn't feel the shape of her body against his any longer.

He'd wanted to hold her in his arms so much, that day, when he'd gone to see her after the accident, still reeling from the shock of witnessing that rockfall on their team day out in the Blue Mountains with a day of abseiling training underway. He'd seen that rock hit Harriet and the fear that she'd been killed had made it seem like the ground had been opening up beneath him. A world without Harriet Collins could never be quite the same. He'd had to swipe tears of relief from his face when he'd heard that she'd come through the surgery and still had her leg but he'd known the moment he'd walked into her room for that first visit that even getting close enough to touch her wasn't going to be welcomed.

She'd put up a barrier that might have been transparent but it was impenetrable. And, from what Jack had heard over the last months, he hadn't been the only person who'd been relegated to the other side of that barrier. Harriet's life had fallen apart after the accident but it had been deemed none of his business, however much he might have wanted to try and help.

But she had needed his help today.

Welcomed it, in fact.

And it almost felt like that barrier had somehow evaporated—on her side, anyway. Perhaps he'd put up one of his own, to protect himself from having his friendship rejected again. From the reminders of that even more painful rejection of something that he'd believed could have been a whole lot more than simply friendship.

She was watching him now, as he and Matt made sure that Eddie was as comfortable as possible, monitored his vital signs and tried to check him out for any significant injuries that might have been missed. It was only a short flight to the nearest hospital so it was a busy time but Jack's glance caught Harriet's on more than one occasion—like when he'd tightened the loop anchoring the nasal cannula for oxygen and moved to attach the end of the tubing to the on-board supply. And when he reached up to change the flow rate on the IV fluids they were administering to stabilise Eddie's blood pressure.

What was so different about her?

She was a bit thinner, which was hardly surprising given the physical ordeal she'd been through. Her skin was paler. Because she wasn't outside every free moment she could find—doing fun runs or surfing or something? Her freckles had faded too but the change he was trying to identify wasn't anything negative. Quite the contrary. It was…a bit of a spark, that's what it was. As if a glimmer of the woman he'd admired so much had returned. A woman who'd all but vanished within weeks of that terrible accident.

The last time Jack had gone to visit her in hospital, she'd been fighting an infection that had again raised the awful possibility that her lower leg might have to be amputated. She had been feeling very unwell, lying there with intravenous antibiotics dripping into her arm, and the visit had been more than awkward. Jack had felt helpless and hated it.

Harriet had looked…hopeless, which had been even worse.

She hadn't wanted to see him. She certainly hadn't wanted to talk about the SDR, which was pretty much the only thing they had in common. And when she'd looked directly at him—just before she'd said it might be better if he left—her eyes had been like nothing he would have ever associated with Harriet. So dark. So flat you wouldn't know there were little golden flecks in that hazel warmth.

That was it in a nutshell. The sparkle was back. Not the way it had been but it was there in the interest she was showing in the information being recorded on the ECG monitor and the new set of limb baselines Matt was doing to check on the blood supply to Eddie's leg below the level of the fracture.

It had been there, as part of that smile, when he'd made that lame joke about Lassie.

As they came in to land at one of Sydney's larger hospitals, a long way from Bondi Bayside, Jack leaned close and raised his voice.

'Stay on board when we land. I'm off duty once we get back to base and I can take you home.'

'I left my car,' Harriet told him. 'Back at the cliffs.'

'No worries. We'll sort it. We can check that Lassie's been rescued, too.'

Her eyes widened as if she was surprised he was worried about his patient's pet but then her face softened as if she was remembering that it wasn't out of character at all. It was the kind of person he'd always been.

Her smile—and her nod—told him that she liked that.

'Sounds great.' Harriet leaned close to Eddie as they

were unhooking the stretcher ready to wheel him towards the waiting staff members on the far side of the
helipad. 'I'll come and see you as soon as I can. Don't
worry. I'll make sure Harry's okay.'

She would, too, Jack thought as he bent to move
under the still moving rotors of the helicopter that
would take them back to base very soon. She was that
kind of person as well.

And he'd always loved that about her.

It felt like the old days.

The time when life had been full of excitement and
promise. Before it had all come crashing down around
her in such spectacular fashion.

The climb down that cliff face. Treating someone
with traumatic injuries. Being winched into a helicopter and then flying over the city she loved so much.
Somehow, in recent months she'd forgotten how gorgeous it was.

Being with Jack was another link to her past life
and, oddly, she didn't have a compelling urge to push
it away in order not to add weight to the miserable
shroud of what she'd lost. Today, it didn't feel quite so
lost and the reminder of what it had been like was poignant but also precious.

Jack's car was parked at the back of the air rescue
base, far enough away from where they'd landed to
make Harriet very aware of how far she'd pushed her
new boundaries today.

'You okay?' Jack's sideways glance was casual.
'You could wait here while I get the car.'

Harriet didn't meet his gaze. 'I'm good. This is what
I do now, Jack. I limp.'

The silence made her realise that she'd slipped back into that defensive mode that made her tone too sharp and pushed people away.

'Sorry,' she muttered. 'But I think I can make it. I need to try.'

'I'm sure you can make it. You climbed down a cliff today, didn't you? And you don't need to apologise. I understand...'

People said that a lot, with the best intentions, but it was never true, was it? You couldn't really understand unless it had happened to *you*.

But it felt like maybe Jack did understand. More than others, anyway.

'It will get better,' she told him. 'It's just that I've only been out of my brace for a week or so. And I probably did more today than I should have, even before I climbed down the cliff.'

'What *were* you doing up there? Testing yourself? Might be a good idea not to do stuff like that by yourself, you know.' His smile was crooked. 'Just sayin'...'

'Yeah, yeah... It was a bit of a test, I guess, but the real reason was to try out my new zoom lens. I wanted some shots of surf crashing on rocks, preferably as it got close to sunset when the light gets awesome.'

'You've really got into photography, haven't you? I saw you taking all the photos at Kate and Angus's wedding.'

She'd noticed him there as well. Not that she'd made any attempt to go and talk to him. She'd stayed behind that camera the whole time and had left as early as she could without being rude. It had been hard, being there but not being one of the team any longer.

'I really have.' It was a relief to reach the car and

take the weight off her leg. A quick glance at her watch told Harriet that she could take some more painkillers soon. As soon as Jack wasn't around to notice because those sharp of eyes of his didn't miss much. Had he been aware that she'd avoided talking to him at the wedding?

'It started because I was taking photos of my leg, actually,' she found herself saying quietly as the car pulled out onto the road. 'I wanted a record so that, on bad days, I could remind myself that things were improving. And then I started taking photos of other stuff and I got hooked. Not only did I have a topic of conversation that had nothing to do with my leg but I could kind of hide behind the camera when I was out with other people. Win-win.'

She'd never admitted that to anyone. She'd kept people at a distance by being distant herself with a forced cheerfulness or, shamefully more often, a bad-tempered snappiness. Jack hadn't seen the worst of it but she knew she'd hurt him by rejecting his support early on. Opening up, just a little, was a kind of peace offering and, judging by the intensity of the swift glance he gave her, he realised that it was a big thing.

'I'm sorry,' he said softly. 'I can only imagine how rough it's been for you.'

'Actually, I think it's me that should be apologising.'

'What on earth for?'

'I was horrible to you. When you came to visit. You didn't deserve that.'

Jack shrugged. He seemed to be concentrating on the road ahead. 'It was no big deal. You had your friends around.'

'You're one of my friends,' Harriet said. Then her voice trailed away. 'Or...you were...'

This time Jack turned his head. 'I still am, Harry.' But his tone held a note of wariness. 'If you want me to be, that is.'

For a long minute, Harriet stared, unseeing, at the industrial buildings they were passing. She could hear echoes of the laughter of shared jokes and the teasing that Jack had been such a master of. She could feel the warmth of the kindness that was so much a part of him. Like the way he would always make sure that others were being cared for during any breaks on an exhausting disaster response and getting some rest and food and water.

And it hadn't been just his teammates or other people he cared about.

'Do you remember that last callout we were on together?'

'The bush fire?' Jack blew out a breath. 'Sure do. That was a tough one, wasn't it? A whole town lost. So many people killed or injured.'

'And the animals. You found that dog with burnt paws and you carried him all the way back to base.'

'If I'd known what was going to happen, I would have made you carry him.'

Harriet grinned. 'You mean that photograph of you that went viral?'

Jack shook his head. 'The attention was ridiculous. I started getting emails from all over the country. Girls who'd never met me but wanted to marry me, for God's sake.'

Harriet was still smiling. 'Of course they did. You

were a hero. Young, gorgeous and single. And you love dogs. What more could a woman want?'

Jack was concentrating on changing lanes on the motorway that was leading them out of the city. He made a sound that could have been embarrassment at her singing his praises. Or it could have been dis-agreement.

'You mean you don't like dogs? Or you're not still single?'

'I like dogs,' Jack muttered. 'And, yeah…if you must know, I'm still single.'

Weird, Harriet thought. There must be an unlimited number of gorgeous young women who would love to catch his attention.

Then she sighed into the silence. 'Me, too…'

Jack didn't say anything for quite a while and Har-riet could feel a tension that made her wish she'd kept her mouth shut. A lot of it was probably being inter-nally generated, mind you. The rejection of having Pete walk out on their relationship had been soul destroying. She was damaged now. Unattractive. Unlovable, even?

Yeah…she was single and that wasn't about to change. Maybe it never would.

'I heard that Pete transferred to a Melbourne sta-tion,' Jack finally said. His tone was laced with dis-approval.

Was that what some of the tension was about? Jack had been friends with Pete. Everybody had been.

'Mmm…' Harriet tried to keep her tone casual. 'I think he wanted a fresh start. With Sharleen.'

Jack shook his head. 'Yeah, I heard about that too. I can't believe he walked out on you. What a moron.'

'It's okay,' Harriet said. Though the aftermath of

that breakup had been agonising, she'd refused to let it drag her down further. 'Everything we'd had in common was gone and he just couldn't handle it. And then there was Sharleen. With two good legs. A top surfer. A gym bunny. That was where they met—at the gym.'

Jack took the exit that was signposted for the Kookaburra park and walkway. 'You've still got two legs,' he said, matter-of-factly. 'And, from what I heard, that was a pretty big deal.'

'Yeah…' Suddenly the fierce ache in her leg seemed much more bearable. 'I know. I was lucky.'

'And they must be pretty good legs if you got yourself down that cliff today. I would have thought twice about attempting that.'

'You don't know how dodgy it was. And I'll probably be reminded of it for a few days now, I expect. I might have to admit defeat and use my brace again at work for a while.'

'You didn't even have a rope.' Jack's glance was one of admiration. 'Weren't you scared?'

'I didn't give myself time to think about it. I just looked one step ahead for a foothold or for the next branch that might give me a safe handhold. And then I was past the halfway point and it would have been just as hard to go back as it was to keep going.'

'But you chose to keep going.'

'I was worried that Eddie might start moving and roll off the ledge.'

'So you gave yourself the biggest physical challenge you've had in a long time and put yourself in danger to save someone else.'

Harriet tried to smile but she could feel her lips

wobble. 'It made me feel like…like I was still part of the team.'

Jack was slowing the car now to pull into the parking area at the park, which was the entry point to the cliffside walkway. He stopped, turned off the engine and then turned to give Harriet a very direct look.

'You *are* still part of the team.'

'Don't be daft.' The fact that his words opened an emotional wound that had barely begun to close up made her tone sharp again. 'That's never going to happen and you know it.'

She could hear the edge of bitterness souring a moment that should have been a reconnection. A step back into a friendship that could be an important bridge between her old life and this new, difficult one.

'Sorry.' The apology came out as a sigh. 'There I go again, being not nice to be around.'

Jack shrugged. 'You're allowed to be angry. I get it.'

'I'm dealing with it. I hope… And I've got my next goals. Two of them, in fact.'

He nodded. 'Like going down the cliff, huh? Just look as far as the next step or a safe handhold?'

'Something like that.'

'So what are they—these goals of yours?'

'Well, you know that Blake and Sam are getting married, right?'

'Yeah…' Jack grinned. 'So much for Blake's rules about team members not hooking up. He's changed, hasn't he?'

'He's in love. They both are. Sam's my best friend and I'm thrilled for her. I offered to take photos at their wedding but it turns out that I'm going to be her bridesmaid. So that's my first goal. I don't want to be taking any attention away from her by limping down the aisle.'

'The aisle?' Jack's eyes widened. 'They're getting married in a church?' His grin widened. 'I don't believe it. Our maverick ED consultant who wears cowboy boots and a ponytail to work is going to do something as conventional as getting married in a church?'

'They haven't decided where yet. It was a figure of speech. It might happen on a beach and sand is even harder to walk on.'

'How long have you got to train for it?'

'I don't know that either.' The parking area around them was dark now but Harriet could see some people moving off to one side. 'You'll be coming to the wedding, won't you?'

'If I get an invitation, sure.' Jack had turned to look in the same direction as Harriet. 'So what's your other goal? You said you had two.'

'I want to get back to my old job. In intensive care.'

'Where are you now?'

'Geriatrics.' Harriet screwed up her nose. 'I mean, I love the oldies. I hear the most amazing stories every day but I really miss the ICU.'

'Why can't you work there again now?'

'My leg's not strong enough. Imagine if there was an emergency and I turned to grab a defibrillator or something and I ended up falling over.'

'Hmm…' But Jack seemed distracted. 'There are cops over there. With a dog…'

'Oh…' Harriet wrenched at her door handle. 'It must be Harry the dog. Let's go and check that he's okay.'

The two police officers were about to load Harry the dog into their car but were happy enough to stop and chat when they learned of Jack and Harry's connection to the unusual job they'd been dispatched to.

'You never know what's going to happen on a shift,' the young officer said. 'We get a good hike up a hill in a glorious sunset and we're getting paid for it. How great is that?'

'Was he hard to find?'

'No. He was just lying there, with his nose on his paws, right on the edge of the cliff.'

'Oh…poor Harry.' Harriet crouched down to hug the dog. 'It'll be okay,' she told him. 'Someone's going to look after you.'

'He's going to the pound,' the older officer told them. 'We've tried to find a family member to take him but there doesn't seem to be anybody.'

Harriet felt the nudge of a cold, damp nose against her hand. He was good at communicating, this dog.

'I'll take him,' she heard herself saying. 'I don't want him to go to the pound. How scary would that be? He'd think he was being totally abandoned.'

'If you want to.' The police officers exchanged a glance. 'Can't see a problem with that as long as we get all your details.'

'Are you sure?' Jack sounded concerned. 'He's a big dog. He'll need a lot of exercise.'

Harriet straightened. 'A lot of exercise is exactly what I need, too, if I'm going to get to where I want to be.'

'Are you allowed dogs in your apartment?'

She shrugged. 'Sometimes it's better to apologise later than ask for permission first. I think this is one of those times.'

Jack's gaze was thoughtful. 'I could help, maybe. With the exercising?'

'Sure.' This time, Harriet wasn't going to brush off Jack's offer to help. It was like another peace offering. 'That'd be great.'

A few minutes later, Harry the dog was installed on the back seat of Harriet's car and she was ready to drive home as soon as Jack let go of her door so that she could close it.

'I'll be in touch,' he said. 'We can make up a roster and I can give him a good run on the beach or something.'

'Okay. I'd better get going, though. I need to get to the supermarket and stock up on some dog food and stuff.'

Jack closed her door but he was still standing there so Harriet rolled the window down.

'What?'

He shrugged. 'Nothing. Just that I reckon you could add a third goal to that list.'

'Oh?'

'Yeah…' He threw a smile over his shoulder as he walked away. 'Getting back on the team for real. Reckon you could do it if you really wanted to.'

CHAPTER THREE

'SAM...WHAT ARE you doing here?'

'I had to come and find you. They told me on the ward that you'd brought someone to X-Ray.'

'Yes.' Harriet glanced sideways to where the patient she was accompanying was already snoring gently. 'Poor old May fell out of bed during the night. She's not complaining but it looks like she's fractured her neck of femur. We've got a bit of a wait, though.' She raised her eyebrows at her friend. 'Why did you have to come and find me? Have you set a date for the wedding or something?'

Sam shook her head, flopping into the seat beside Harriet. 'No...it was too late to ring you by the time I got home last night. There was an SDR meeting and I heard all about your cliff rescue. Oh, my God, Harry... what did you think you were *doing*?'

There was only one person who could have been spreading that news but Harriet wasn't entirely sure whether she was disappointed in Jack for talking about her behind her back or quietly pleased that the team now knew all about it.

'Jack said it would have been an astonishing thing for anyone to do but for *you* to do it was just mind-blowing.' Sam was looking down at Harriet's leg. 'Are you okay? You're wearing your brace again.'

'Just a precaution.'

'Maybe you should have an X-ray after May.' Sam glanced at the elderly woman and then caught Harriet's gaze. There was amusement at the snoring but also sympathy. To sit and wait without even conversation was so very different from the challenges of nursing in the intensive care unit.

'I'm fine. Honestly.'

'Better than fine, from what I heard. Jack reckons you should be back on the team.'

Harriet shook her head sharply. 'Not going to happen.'

'Why not?'

'Because I couldn't do it, that's why. You know the kind of things that go with a callout. Tramping miles into the scene of something like a flood or a landslide. And remember the Urban Search and Rescue course that you did? I still have enough trouble walking on a flat surface. I couldn't climb over a pile of rubble after an earthquake if my life depended on it.'

'You just climbed down a cliff and it was only someone else's life that was depending on it.'

'But *I* couldn't be depended on and that's like the number one requirement of an SDR team member.' Harriet wanted to change the subject. 'So, *have* you set a date for the wedding yet?'

Sam groaned. 'We mentioned that we might prefer a beach wedding and now my dad wants to fly everybody off to a tropical island up north. Hamilton or Fraser Island, maybe.'

'Wow… How cool would that be?'

'It would be outrageous.'

'I'll bet Blake hated the idea.'

'My dad's not stupid.' Sam shook her head. 'He offered to donate the same amount of money he would spend on the wedding to *Médecins Sans Frontières* because he knows how passionate Blake is about helping to provide medical care in developing countries. Did I tell you that we're thinking of getting a posting next year? Just for three months or so. Maybe in Africa.'

But Harriet was distracted by the idea of a luxurious island holiday that would be a part of her bridesmaid's duties.

'So it might happen, then? An island wedding?'

'Well, Blake did have a funny look on his face when he said that his mum had never had a tropical island holiday in her life.'

'What's his mum like?'

'Lovely. Tough. She's still struggling to come to terms with her limitations after the stroke.'

'We'd have a lot in common then.'

Sam's face creased into serious lines. 'You're doing amazingly well, Harry. Better than anyone expected. Better than you expected, I would think. Could you have imagined yourself scrambling down a cliff a few months ago?'

'No way…'

'You should have heard Jack singing your praises. He really does think that you could come back on board. If you want to, that is…'

Harriet shrugged, turning to check on her patient. She smoothed white, fluffy hair back from May's face and the old woman stirred and groaned softly.

Being part of the team wasn't an option, she knew that. But, oh…the pull was there, wasn't it? The longing…

'Maybe one day,' she murmured. 'When I'm capable of doing everything that I could do before the accident.'

Which would be never.

'Perfection is overrated,' Sam said. 'We're a team and everyone brings something a bit different to the overall performance. You could still contribute a lot more than you're giving yourself credit for.' She was chewing her lip now. 'And…and you wouldn't have to worry about seeing Pete there any more.'

'I'm not worried. I don't hate him, Sam. I understand that it would never have worked out.' Harriet managed a smile. 'Turns out that broken hearts heal faster than broken legs. Who knew?'

'Mmm… Still, I couldn't believe it when I heard what you'd done. You must be so proud of yourself.'

'You know what? I think I am.' The warmth of the internal glow she was still aware of wasn't just due to hearing that Jack had been singing her praises. Harriet *was* proud of herself. Proud of her leg standing up to the challenge and of overcoming her fears enough to challenge herself that much.

'I just wish someone had got a photo of that.'

Harriet laughed. 'Maybe I should have fished my new camera out and taken a selfie halfway down the cliff.'

'Oh, my God…' Sam's jaw dropped.

'What?'

'I've just had the most brilliant idea.'

'What's that?'

'That could be your contribution to the team—until

you're ready for the whole deal. You could be our official photographer.'

'No...' The suggestion made Harriet cringe more than a little. 'That would be like going on a ride-along in an ambulance. Being a thrill seeker who just gets in the way.'

'Didn't sound like you got in the way on that ledge. Jack said you were right back in the swing of things, helping with the gear and the splint and everything.' She was looking thoughtful now. 'Bet he would have loved a photo of winching that guy up to the chopper.'

A distressed sound made Harriet's head turn swiftly. May's pale blue eyes were wide open. And frightened.

'Oh, where am I?' Her words were trembling. 'What's happened?'

'It's okay, May.' Harriet took hold of her hand and stroked it with her thumb. 'We're in X-Ray. You've hurt your leg and we need to find out if something's broken. I'm here with you. You're safe.'

'I hurt my leg? How did that happen?'

Sam was looking at her watch. 'I've got to run. My lunch break's over in two minutes.'

Harriet could see an X-ray technician heading towards them. 'And it looks like it might be our turn. I'll call you later.'

'Yes...do that. I haven't even asked about the dog yet. Is it true that you've sneaked him into your apartment?'

'Shh...it's a secret.'

'Don't think it'll stay that way. Kate already knew.'

'That's because her great-aunt Alice is letting him out for me when I'm at work. And she and Angus took him out yesterday because they had a day off.'

Sam was on her feet and already heading for the doors of the X-Ray waiting area. 'Just yell if there's anything I can do to help. Like taking him for a run.'

'Thanks, but Jack's coming to give him a good run on the beach tonight. It's all good.'

'We're going to the beach?' May sounded thoroughly confused now. 'I don't mean to be rude, dear, but I don't like sand.'

Harriet smiled, standing on the pedal to release the lock on May's bed. 'Don't worry, May. Not you. It's Harry the dog who's going to the beach.'

She could see that she'd confused her elderly patient even more now but fortunately she didn't have to explain the odd coincidence of having the same name as the dog. The X-ray technician was holding May's hand to check her ID bracelet.

'Just the person we've been waiting for.' His smile was cheeky. 'Are you ready for your photoshoot, Mrs Greene? You look like you're ready to start your modelling career.'

May perked up and seemed to become far more aware of her surroundings. Was she actually batting her eyelashes?

'I like that young man,' she whispered to Harriet as he went ahead to open the doors to the X-ray room.

Harriet grinned. 'I think he's a bit young for you, May.'

May tutted. 'When you're as old as me, dear, you'll realise that it doesn't matter. Age is just a number.'

Harriet was still smiling as she pulled on a lead apron so that she could stay close to May and make sure she didn't move. She might be determined to get back to her more exciting position in the ICU but moments like these—when you got a glimpse of the personalities within these frail old bodies—were a joy.

Harry the dog clearly adored the beach.

As soon as he was let off his leash, he ran straight into the surf, barking in excitement. Jack had a moment of alarm when the black head vanished beneath the foam of a breaking wave but then he reappeared to bound out of the water, pausing only to shake himself vigorously before heading back in.

'I'm tempted to have a swim myself.'

'Go on, then.'

'Will you come in, too?'

'Are you kidding? I'm not in my bathers.'

'You're in shorts, same as me. I reckon they'd be pretty much dry by the time we walk back to your apartment.'

'I only came to watch. And to see how hard it is to walk on the sand. This is the first time I've been on a beach since the accident.'

They'd already come through some soft sand after the grassy area with its picnic tables and barbecue areas that separated this small beach from the road that led back to her apartment block.

'How hard is it?'

Harriet didn't meet his gaze. 'The jury's still out. If you go and have a swim, maybe I'll take my brace off and see how I go.' She flashed him a wry smile. 'That way, you won't see if I fall flat on my face.'

There was something more than trepidation in that smile. It was more like…embarrassment? About being seen to try something and fail, or was it more than that? Whatever it was, Jack could read the signal.

'You're on.' He kicked off his jandals and stripped off his T-shirt, leaving them beside where Harriet was sitting. Then he strode towards the water, pausing only to pick up a stick of driftwood that looked like something a dog like Harry would love to chase.

He'd been astonished to hear that admission that this was the first time Harriet had been on the beach since her accident. Even during the period that she'd relied on crutches, the distance between here and her apartment would have been manageable.

Everybody knew how much she loved the beach. She hadn't been a competitive surfer, like Pete, but he'd seen the way her face used to light up when she talked about the thrill of riding waves. And she'd been part of the surfing community. Competition days had been exciting events on her social calendar and she'd been very supportive of Pete's ambitions.

Maybe that was it. Maybe she'd been avoiding the beach all this time because it reminded her of the man she'd obviously been head over heels in love with. Why hadn't he thought of that? How insensitive had he been to suggest that she come with him and Harry the dog this evening? Everybody had known how much she'd adored Pete. She'd made light of the breakup of that relationship the other evening but he wasn't convinced that she was over it that well.

How could she be? She'd been living with the guy, for heaven's sake. Committed. He'd been crushed enough when she'd rejected his offer of a date. How much more devastating would it be to have the offer of a lifetime commitment thrown back at you? Did you ever really get over that kind of a blow? Enough to trust anyone with your whole heart again?

Damage like that left scars. And scars could be enough to conceal a very real disability.

The shower of cold water that came as the dog raced to greet him and then shook himself again was enough to break the exercise of berating himself over any insensitivity of suggesting that Harriet come with them to the beach. She had seemed perfectly happy to accept the invitation.

'I'll take some photos,' she'd said. 'That way I can show Eddie how well we're looking after Harry when I go and visit him tomorrow.'

'Great idea,' he'd agreed. 'And I've got a day off tomorrow, too. I'd love to come with you and see how he's doing.'

A glance behind him now showed Harriet with her camera held up to her face and an impressive-looking zoom lens pointing straight towards him. He grinned, holding up the stick of driftwood and pausing for a moment with Harry the dog poised to start chasing it into the surf. That would make a good shot.

There was something a little voyeuristic about staring at people through a camera lens but Harriet didn't feel the least bit guilty.

Jack just happened to be in the same screen as Harry because he was poised to throw a stick for the dog.

But there he was, in nothing but his shorts, with that glorious physique glowing bronze in the low evening sun and the dark swirls of an ethnic tattoo on one shoulder, flowing down to accentuate the muscles of his upper arm.

And that smile! She'd captured that on one shot and knew that it would be an image she'd want to see again.

Jack had the kind of smile that could just light up a room. A whole beach, even. It radiated happiness and good humour. Nobody could have a smile like that and not be a really nice person.

She watched them bound into the surf together and then saw the way Harry stayed right beside Jack swimming in water that was way out of his depth. She saw the way Jack kept turning his head to make sure the dog was safe.

He'd be like that when he had kids, one day, she thought. Encouraging them to do things that might be a little dangerous, but he would always be there, right beside them, making sure they were safe. He wouldn't be walking away from his girlfriend or wife if things got a bit tough, either. There was something so solid about Jack Evans and you just knew that your trust wouldn't be misplaced. And friendship *was* something that she could still trust, wasn't it? The real risks only came when you went further than that and she'd never find that kind of trust again. She suspected that it was broken for ever.

Right now, though, that didn't matter. She knew that anything more than friendship wasn't even a blip on any radar that Jack Evans had regarding her. He was just being the lovely person he was.

He was encouraging her as well. Probably more than he realised. It had actually been a huge thing for her to come to the beach this evening and it felt like she'd crossed a barrier she hadn't even been conscious of erecting. The one that enclosed the old life she had shared with Pete and included the heartbreak of that relationship ending. But here she was and…and it was so nice to be here with the warmth of the sun on her skin and the feeling of sand between her toes and the company of a gorgeous young man who still seemed to want to be her friend even after she'd pretty much dismissed him from her life—as well as a dog who had to be missing his owner terribly but was a shining example of how to live in the moment and make the most of any joy that life had to offer.

So why was she stopping here, just sitting on the sand like a human blob?

Harriet put the cap back on the lens of her camera and slung the strap around her neck. Then she reached down and pulled open the Velcro straps that held her leg brace in place. She pushed herself slowly to her feet and then took a tentative step forward. And then another.

It wasn't easy. But it hadn't been easy getting down that cliff and look how proud she was of that achievement now.

Another step. Harriet knew she was limping badly and could feel a shaft of pain every time she put her weight on her bad leg but she was almost at the water's edge and the temptation to feel the swirl of sea water over her feet was irresistible. Maybe the massaging effect of the dying waves might ease the aches and pains as well.

The first rush of water was cooler than she'd expected and she gasped with the surprise of it. The second wave was bigger and the foam reached her knees and she could feel the sand shifting beneath her feet as the water receded. By the time the third wave had come and gone, it felt like warm silk against her skin and the desire to go further out and swim was as surprising as that first chill of the sea had been.

She wasn't about to go swimming in her clothes, however, and Jack was coming out now, with Harry the dog close on his heels. His face lit up when he saw where Harriet was.

'Feels good, yes?'

Harriet simply nodded but it felt like the smile on her face was wider than it had been for a very long time. She bent to pat Harry.

'It's such fun. I've always envied people who had a dog with them on the beach.'

'You didn't have a dog when you were a kid?'

'No. My parents were older when they adopted me. I think the mess of having a kid around was enough of a shock. I begged for a puppy every birthday but the closest I got was a stuffed toy.' She threw a smile over her shoulder. 'Much cleaner.'

Jack had to slow his pace to let her walk beside him.

'Is the jury back in yet?'

He glanced down at her leg and, for a moment, Harriet had no idea what he was referring to because she suddenly realised just how much he could see.

She'd had jeans on when they'd been on that ledge together. And she'd had the solid brace on for the walk to the beach. This was the first time he was seeing the horrible scarring she'd been left with—not just the angry red marks on her skin but the misshapen muscle from where the initial damage and the complication of infection had destroyed so much of her normal tissue. In fact, it was the first time anyone had seen these scars, other than her doctors and physical therapists. She hadn't even let her best friend see how bad it was.

Her leg was ugly, there were no two ways about that. She'd looked at it so often herself and cringed at the thought of any man seeing it and still being attracted to her. Not after Pete had almost thrown up when he'd seen it for the first time after the accident. He'd actually dry retched, although he'd tried to cover it up with a cough and he'd avoided ever looking at it directly again. But this was Jack, not someone who could be sizing her up as a potential partner. He was her friend and his query was only concerned with the function of her leg, not its appearance. He was talking about how hard it was to walk on the sand. And, if he could ignore her scarring, then she should at least make a good attempt to follow his example.

'It's definitely harder, but not impossible.'

'That's great.' Jack stooped to pick up the stick that Harry had dropped by his feet. A flick of his arm sent it flying with the dog in hot pursuit. 'We should do it more often, then, and it might get easier.'

'Mmm...' The idea of having company and more visits to the beach was...well, it was really nice. That it had been Jack's suggestion made it even better. He had missed the worst of her struggle to get back on her feet and, after conquering the challenge of that cliff climbing, this felt like a new stage in her recovery. A fresh start.

'The water felt great, too,' she added shyly. 'I might even try a swim next time.'

'Have you been doing any swimming as part of your rehab?'

'No. It took so long for the wounds to heal properly I think it got forgotten. It would have been an infection risk not so long ago.'

'They have those lovely heated pools in the physiotherapy department.'

'I'm an outdoor, cold water sort of person.'

'Yeah… Me, too. But…' A furrow of concern appeared between his eyes.

'But what? You think I couldn't cope in the surf?'

'It's not that. I just think…well, you know what you said about climbing down the cliff? That you just looked ahead one step at a time?'

'What's that got to do with swimming?'

'Before you throw yourself into surf that might be a bit much, why not try one of the salt water pools around here? Some of them have waves that break over the top at high tide.'

Harriet was silent as they arrived back to where Jack's T-shirt and jandals were lying on the sand. He was right. Getting dumped by a big wave could be disastrous and might set back her recovery or even break a bone again. She had to remember her limitations and the possible consequences of pushing too hard but the reminder was less than pleasant.

'I'll come with you, if you like.' Jack's head popped through the neck of his T-shirt as he put it back on and that heart-stopping smile was as bright as ever. 'I love the pools.'

'Harry wouldn't be allowed to swim there.'

'He'll probably be able to go home soon. Let's see how Eddie is tomorrow.'

'Okay.' Harriet shook the sand from her brace and eased her leg into it. It was a relief to hide the scars again but not as much as she might have expected. They'd both ignored it, as if it was no big deal, and maybe next time it *wouldn't* be such a big deal. Jack was just a mate. He wasn't her best friend and he wasn't a boyfriend so it really didn't matter to him what she looked like, did it? He didn't work with her so what she was, or wasn't, capable of doing as well as she once had wasn't important to him, either. He wasn't judging her.

Perhaps that was what was making his company so easy. It seemed perfectly natural to be meeting up to take a dog for a walk like this or to be making arrangements to go somewhere together tomorrow.

No big deal.

Just…nice…

'Oh…that's such a great photo.' Eddie's eyes looked suspiciously bright as he unwrapped the framed image of Harry in the surf, poised to chase the stick that Jack was holding.

'He loves the beach.' Jack's grin was exactly the same as the one Harriet had captured in the photo.

'It's a real treat for him. Hey… I can't thank you guys enough for taking care of him.'

'He's a great dog,' Harriet said. 'I'm loving having the company. I've been living on my own for a while now so it's been a treat for me, too.'

The swift glance from Jack made her realise how easily he picked up on what wasn't being said. That he knew that Pete had moved in with her before the accident and that the toughest part of her recovery had been made that much harder by being left alone to deal with it.

'I always wanted a dog when I was young,' she added hurriedly. 'And everybody else loves him, too. I have a friend, Kate, who's a surgeon at Bondi Bayside, and her great-aunt, Alice, lives on the same floor in my apartment building. She's been taking Harry out during the day when I'm at work.' She eyed the heavy cast on Eddie's leg. 'Will you have someone to help after you get discharged tomorrow? I could keep him a while longer, if it would help.'

'It's all good,' Eddie told her. 'I have a big back yard that's all fenced and I can just leave the doors open all day. It'll only be a few weeks until I can get mobile again. And my neighbours will help. There's a lad down the road who would love to take him for a run.'

'Stay away from the cliffs for a while,' Jack said.

'Oh, I will.' Eddie was still looking at the photograph. 'This is really good,' he said. 'You could be a professional photographer, Harriet.'

'It's become a splinter skill,' she told him. 'And I love action shots.' Her glance slid sideways towards Jack. 'I didn't tell you, but Sam came up with the idea of me going out with the team on the next callout—in the capacity of official photographer.'

'What's the team?' Eddie asked.

'Specialist Disaster Relief,' Jack supplied. 'It's a team of medics from Bondi Bayside plus some extras, like me from the ambulance service and some guys from the fire service. If there's a callout to something big, like a bush fire or a flood or something, we get dispatched as first responders. They fly us in and we've got all the supplies we need to stay for a few days and do whatever we can.'

'Sounds exciting.'

'It is.' But Jack was staring at Harriet with an expression that was almost sombre. 'I think that's a fantastic idea,' he told her quietly. 'Let's make it happen.'

Harriet shrugged, trying to quell the beat of excitement that would make it disappointing if it didn't happen.

'I'll think about it,' she said. 'It'll probably be ages before the team gets deployed again. It's not as if we get disasters every week, thank goodness.'

She hadn't been entirely successful, Harriet realised as they ended their visit to Eddie and drove back to the other side of Sydney.

The excitement was still there.

Growing, even…

CHAPTER FOUR

DESPITE QUITE A few misgivings, this was turning out to be fun.

The SDR team's rare access to the HUET training facility had been the perfect opportunity for Harriet to tag along in the capacity of a photographer. She wasn't taking up extra space in a helicopter or chartered plane and everybody was keen to get a record of one of the more thrilling training sessions that was occasionally available.

HUET stood for Helicopter Underwater Escape Training. After a classroom training session, everybody moved to a deep, purpose-built diving pool dominated by a crane at one side. Attached to the crane was a metal cage designed to replicate the structure and seating of a helicopter. Participants wore float suits that kept them warmer than their normal overalls because they would be submerged more than once. They could take on a vertical escape and one where the 'helicopter' was submerged and then tipped on one side. For the more advanced or bravest amongst the team, they could get tipped completely upside down and even wear blackout goggles.

Harriet was recording everything from the beginning of the session, with people donning life jackets and getting strapped into the harnesses in their seats—even the expressions of trepidation that were obvious despite the dive masks covering half their faces.

She loved the shots she was getting as the cage was swung out and lowered into the pool, with the rush of bubbles exploding around the vanishing figures. She found she was holding her breath as she snapped murky images of the shapes at the bottom of the pool, waiting for people to unclip their harnesses, for someone to open the door and then to see the 'survivors' kick their way to the surface. The grins on faces and thumbs-up signals at that point were a joy to capture.

Harriet hadn't been able to do this training the last time it had been available because she hadn't been able to get time off work but Pete had gone on for weeks about what a thrill it had been and she'd been gutted to have missed out.

She was still missing out, being on the sidelines like this, but it was better than nothing.

Much better.

She could sense the excitement of the others. The fear. The pride in pushing oneself to do something scary and the sheer exhilaration of success. She would have been even more nervous than Kate if she was doing it herself but it certainly wasn't something she could have attempted now. What if she kicked against the metal structure and her leg didn't have the strength to give her the impetus needed to get the door and escape? Someone would have had to help her and that could have put them in danger by making it too long a time to be able to hold their breath.

She snapped a quick series of pictures as Blake climbed out of the pool after the sideways escape and then extended his hand to reach for Sam and help her out. The looks they gave each other were priceless but it might not be one they wanted to share. It was a shared moment of triumph. Total pride in each other and a very deep love.

For a moment Harriet lowered her camera, focusing instead on taking a few deep breaths to counter the sense of loss that swamped her.

Would she and Pete have ever looked at each other like that? It was an irrelevant thought because Pete was long gone but the longing was still very real. Not for Pete but for *someone* who would look at her as if nothing else in the world could ever be that important. That cherished.

And the sense of loss wasn't just due to the empty aftermath of a failed relationship. She shouldn't be standing here, dry and safe, while her teammates were literally immersed in this training session. She still felt like a part of this team and the longing to be properly involved was just as powerful as the need to be loved.

At an even deeper level, it brought back feelings of not being cherished as a child. Not the way that the parents of her friends seemed to love their children. In later years she'd wondered if she'd been added simply to complete a picture of a family. That maybe she'd been a disappointment of some kind. Too messy—the way a dog would have been? Or a sibling?

Maybe being here hadn't been such a great idea after all.

'That was terrifying,' Sam told her, as she came closer.

'You did it, though. Well done. I've got some great photos.'

'Ooh…let me see…'

'Later. I don't want to miss any of the next one. It's the biggie, isn't it? Upside down?'

Sam shuddered. 'Not for me. I've had enough. I'm freezing.'

'Are you heading for the showers?'

Sam shook her head. 'I can't go yet. Not until I know that Blake's out of the pool.'

'He's going to do it?'

'Yeah. And Jack. One of the firies said they wanted to but I think he's changed his mind after the sideways one. I think he swallowed a bit of water.'

Harriet's gaze shifted to where the two men were climbing back into the cage. Lifting her camera was an automatic shield as much as a desire to capture every moment of this experience. It had been Jack, with Sam's backup, who had made this possible and, even if there were painful moments of loss to deal with, Harriet knew she was a whole lot closer to being the person she used to be and that had to be a good thing. Eventually, anyway…

Was Jack nervous? She zoomed in on his face and it felt like he was aware of her watching him because he turned his head, lifted a fist with his thumb up like a flag of confidence and grinned at her.

He had the most amazing smile. Harriet put her

camera into video mode. She wanted to give Jack a record of every second of this.

The cage lurched as it was lifted and swung over the water. Harriet's heart lurched right along with it. This was dangerous. No wonder Sam was standing there, hugging herself and looking distinctly pale. Jack was only a mate, not the person she was planning to spend the rest of her life with and she was feeling nervous now herself.

In all honesty, she had been missing Jack's company since Harry the dog had gone home to Eddie. When Jack had called to see if she wanted to come and take photographs today, knowing that he was going to be there had tipped the balance in favour of coming.

The cage swung for a moment and then started to tilt. The two men were lying sideways like the last exercise but then the movement continued until they were both hanging in their harnesses upside down. Harriet knew that her video would capture Sam's distressed sound as their heads touched the top of the pool and then vanished.

She was holding her own breath now as the cage slipped into the effervescence of the escaping air bubbles. Did being upside down make it harder to follow the rules they'd learned in the classroom, to wait until all those bubbles had cleared before they released their harnesses and opened the door?

Surely it was taking too long? Harriet was already starting to fight the urge to suck in some more oxygen but there was no sign of any movement from the bottom of the pool. Sam had her hand pressed against her mouth and the rest of the team looked frozen as they waited. And stared at the surface of the water. Had the men had difficulty with unclipping their harnesses or opening the door? Or had they become disoriented and couldn't kick towards the surface? One of the instructors dropped to a crouch on the edge of the pool. Was he wondering whether he needed to dive in and help?

The tension escalated until Harriet's hands were starting to tremble as they held the camera. Was she about to record a rescue attempt? Or worse…had she snapped the last smile the world would ever see from Jack Evans?

No…suddenly she could see blurry shapes that were moving underwater and almost instantly a head appeared. And then another. It had been a good decision to take a video, after all, because it captured the cheer that came from the whole team and the handshakes and congratulatory hugs that came from every direction as Blake and Jack hauled themselves out of the pool. It was possible it had also recorded the sound she'd made herself. A sigh that expressed the most profound relief that she'd ever felt in her life.

The session broke up a short time later with everyone heading for the showers and changing rooms. Except for Jack, who came over to where Harriet was sitting in the first row of the tiered seats.

'How was that?'

'Awesome. Were you scared, doing that upside down bit?'

'Of course.' But Jack was smiling. He was also dripping wet and had to be cold and exhausted but he sat down on the plastic seat beside Harriet. 'You'd be a bit stupid not to be scared doing that but I figured it was a good thing to try. If it ever happens for real, maybe I'll be a bit less scared and I'll remember what to do.'

'I took a video.'

'Great… I'll look forward to seeing it.' His smile faded. 'How was it, really? Did it make you feel like you were missing out?'

Harriet looked away in case he could see too much in her eyes.

'A bit,' she admitted.

'So how would you feel about giving it a go?'

Her gaze flew back to meet his. *'What?'*

'I had a chat to our instructor, Chris. He knows your story. He—and the guy operating the crane—are both happy to stay a bit longer. Just for a vertical dip. Just you and me. Nobody else has to know about it.'

'But…' Harriet was dumbfounded. 'But…*why*?'

'Because this type of training doesn't come around too often and you might find yourself back on the team before then and feel like you missed out on something important.'

Harriet found herself shaking her head slowly. 'I don't think I could, Jack…'

'Hey…' His tone was firm enough to still the negative movement she was making. He leaned closer and held her gaze. 'I believe in you, Harriet Collins. I think it's time for *you* to start believing in yourself again.'

He reached out and took hold of her hand.

'I know how hard it can be to take that first step,' he said quietly. 'But you're not alone. I'm here. I can be here for every step it takes to get you back to where you want to be. If you want that,' he added, his lips curving into a smile. 'Kind of like a personal trainer.' He gave her hand a quick squeeze and then let it go. 'Or maybe just a good friend.'

The wave of emotion was threatening to drown Harriet. She didn't recognise what it was that was so huge, however. Was this what real friendship had at its core? She could sense that closeness that came with special friends, like Sam, for instance, where you could always count on loyalty and support. But this was different.

Bigger.

Was this what real family was about? The bond of unconditional love that could be there from parents and siblings? From the kind of family she'd never been lucky enough to have herself?

That had to be what was so big it felt it could explode in her chest. What was threatening to bring tears to her eyes. Yes…if she could have had a brother, she would hope he would have been exactly like Jack.

She swallowed hard. 'You really think I should do it?'

'I know you should.' He stood up. 'Come on, let's not keep these guys away from their well-deserved beer for too much longer. There's a float suit waiting for you. You can put it on in the life jacket cupboard and that way nobody else will know what's happening and hang around to watch.'

Had he pushed Harriet too far?

She looked suddenly small, strapped into the seat in the cage beside him. Small and frightened and so, so vulnerable.

This was a much bigger deal for her than for any other members of the team but he'd talked her into giving it a go and here she was.

Trusting him.

As the cage lurched and slipped into the water, he reached out and took hold of her hand.

'Deep breath. Hold it until we're out. Don't worry. I'm not going to let anything happen to you.'

Trust was a precious gift and he wasn't going to let her down.

Good grief…had he really believed that he could keep himself safe from offering anything to Harriet that could put him at risk of being rejected again? He'd done it again, hadn't he, by offering to be a personal trainer and to spend as much time as it took for her to start believing in herself again?

But it still felt like something he was prepared to do. Wanted to do, very much, in fact. He might be shifting the barrier that had been there as far as a real friend-ship was concerned but he could still protect himself by making sure he didn't let himself hope for anything more than that. Friends were important, too.

Right now, as the cage sank below the surface and kept going down, he wanted nothing more than to pro-tect this woman and the feeling was so strong it felt like it could last a lifetime.

But friendships could last that long, couldn't they? From what he'd seen happening around him, they often lasted far longer than relationships or even marriages. And trust was a two-way street. If she was prepared to trust him *this* much, he had to let himself trust her as well—at least as far as being true friends.

More importantly, Harriet needed to learn to trust herself and not depend on him and he had to trust himself to know where that balance was. She needed a push, as long as she had protection nearby. So he let her hand go when the cage finally stopped its de-scent. Let her find the buckle on her own harness and

release it and then pull herself clear of the cage to kick
for the surface.

He couldn't resist touching her again when they
reached the edge of the pool, however. Putting his arm
around her shoulders and pulling her close for a hug.

'See? Wasn't that bad, was it? Want to try a sideways one?'

Shooting a few hoops on the basketball court was supposed to be a fun way to end an intense workout session at the gym but when you were playing with Blake
Cooper, it was an extra workout.

Jack grabbed his towel to mop the sweat from his
face and neck and then picked up his water bottle.

'You're killing me, mate…'

Blake grinned. 'Keeping you in shape, more like.
You can thank me later.' He took a long pull of his
water and then wiped his mouth with the back of his
hand. 'While you're in a weakened state, though, I've
got something I wanted to ask.'

'Oh?' Jack had something he wanted to ask Blake,
too. 'Shoot.'

'We've set a date for the wedding. Two months from
today. On Hamilton Island.'

'Wow…' But Jack's jaw dropped. Blake Cooper getting married in an exclusive island playground for the
rich and famous? It didn't fit, somehow.

Blake's face acknowledged the reaction. 'Yeah,
yeah… I know. But it's for Sam, you know? Or rather
her family. She's the only kid they've got left and
money's no object.'

Jack put his water bottle down and picked up the
ball. 'Guess you'll have to grin and bear it, then. Tough

job, but you know...' He bounced the ball and grinned at the SDR teammate and leader who'd become a good friend over the last few years. 'Someone's gotta do it.'

'Glad you understand.' Blake dropped his bottle onto his towel. 'Because I want you to be my best man.'

Jack's hand slipped on the ball and it rolled across the court. *'What?'*

'I need a best man. Harriet's going to be Sam's bridesmaid and...' Blake shrugged. 'I don't have that many good mates. You've got the short straw. D'ya reckon you could put up with a free trip for a weekend? A few hours on a beach, possibly dressed in a penguin suit?'

Someone had caught the escaping ball and sent it rolling back. Jack stopped its track with his foot but didn't stoop to pick it up.

'I'd be honoured, mate. Let me know the details and I'll juggle my shifts if I need to.'

'Hey...' Blake's face was serious as he gave Jack a friendly punch on his arm. 'Appreciate that. Wanna shoot a few more hoops?'

'Sure...' Jack swooped on the ball and bounced it again, this time moving further onto the court. This was the best opportunity he was ever going to get for what he wanted to ask Blake.

'So... Harriet's going to be bridesmaid, huh?' He kept bouncing the ball, ducking away from Blake's attempt to intercept.

'Yep. She's Sam's best mate.'

'She's doing well with her recovery, isn't she?'

'Amazingly well.' Blake grimaced as he missed another attempt.

'She did well at the HUET training last week, too.'

'Sure did. Some of those photos were awesome.'

'No… I meant she did well when she got in the pool for an escape.' Jack took advantage of Blake's distraction to stop, aim, and send the ball through the hoop after a good smack against the backboard.

'What are you talking about?' This time Blake reached the ball first and was already moving out of Jack's reach.

'After we'd finished, I stayed behind with the crew and we took her through a vertical escape. And then a sideways one.'

'Why?'

'Because she thinks her days of being on the team for real are over.' Jack had his arms up to try and deflect Blake's attempt at a goal. 'It was my idea. Because I don't think they have to be.'

Blake took aim and scored. 'Come on, Jack… You know what it's like out there. There's no way she's going to get up to speed again.'

They both dived for the ball but it was Jack who got there first. He didn't try and run with it, though. He stopped still and tried to catch his breath.

'What would it take?' he asked. 'To prove you wrong?'

Blake shook his head. 'You had enough? Shall we hit the showers?'

Jack wasn't about to let the subject drop. 'How 'bout a five-kilometre hike?' he suggested as they picked up their towels and bottles. 'A hundred-metre sprint or an open-sea swim?' His gaze travelled as they turned towards the exit. 'How 'bout the orange track on the climbing wall?'

Blake was frowning. 'What's this about, Jack?

You know as well as I do that she couldn't do any of those things.'

'I reckon she could get there. She's determined enough. Maybe all she needs is the right training programme and a good coach.'

'PTs are expensive. And who knows how long it would take—even if she's actually physically capable of getting there, which I have my doubts about. You saw that injury, man. She's lucky to have kept her leg.'

'As you said yourself, she's doing better than anyone expected already. And PTs don't have to be pricey. I'd do it for free.'

Blake was about to open his locker. Instead, he turned and stared at Jack.

'You'd do it?'

'Sure.'

'How much spare time have you got, mate? Have you any idea what you'd be taking on?'

'I think so.'

Blake kept staring. 'This is important to you, isn't it?'

Jack turned away from the scrutiny and opened his locker. 'Yep.'

'Why?'

'She's part of the team. We're like family.'

'Haven't you got a real family?'

'Are you kidding?' Jack pulled a clean towel and soap from his locker. 'I've got family coming out of my ears. Aunties and cousins and nieces and nephews. Whole tribe, like any good Island family.'

'But you want to help Harry.'

Jack paused as he was turning away. 'Yeah...'

She hadn't had that kind of family, had she? He

hadn't known that she'd been adopted but it had been more shocking to learn that she hadn't been allowed to have a dog. It was heartbreaking to wonder just how lonely she might have been as a child and that only made him more determined to help her now, if she'd let him.

Blake followed him to the showers. 'You've got a big heart, mate. But…'

'But what?'

'Don't go getting her hopes up too much, okay? Keeping her off the team if she's not up to it is for her safety as much as anything else.'

Jack nodded. 'But…you'll keep an open mind? If she *can* prove herself, you'd consider putting her back on the roster?'

Blake shrugged. 'Sure. I'd be stupid not to. She used to be one of our best.'

Jack put his face under the spray of water, letting it sluice the sweat away. He was unaware of the smile on his face. What he was aware of was confidence that this could happen. With his help, and a hell of a lot of work from Harriet, she could get there.

And, maybe, he wanted that to happen almost as much as she did.

'So…are you up for it?'

Harriet needed to suck in a slow, deep breath. Slow, because it needed to get past a rather large lump in her throat. Deep, because she needed the time to get her head around the enormity of this.

How much time and effort had Jack put into this plan?

He'd set the goals, in order of her own priority. To

walk without a limp in time for Blake and Sam's wedding and to be fit enough to go back to her position as
an ICU nurse. He'd also added a goal that she'd considered out of reach.

To be an active member of the SDR team again.

He'd also come up with a list of physical achievements that would be enough to convince Blake and the
other team committee members that she was capable
of meeting any challenges the team was likely to face.
Things like long walks, climbing, abseiling and swimming but he'd gone a lot further than that, by making
a step-by-step plan of how to achieve an acceptable
level of performance without risking injury to her leg.

Spreadsheets. Actual spreadsheets were on the table
in front of her in this corner of this trendy beachside
wine bar that was close to Bondi Bayside Hospital, and
where he'd suggested they meet for a drink after work.

'I can't believe you've done this,' she said, finally.
'It's…mind-blowing…'

'We can get too much downtime when it's a quiet
day on the choppers.' Jack reached for his tall glass of
lager with a shrug that suggested it wasn't a big deal.
'I'm not studying for anything at the moment so it's
been kind of nice to have a project.'

A project? She was a *project*—like a high school
assignment?

She could choose to be offended, Harriet realised
as her gaze flicked up to catch Jack's.

Or…she could choose to feel…honoured?

There was nothing patronising about the way he
was looking at her.

Jack cared. It was as simple as that.

And he *believed* in her.

That statement alone had been enough to get her underwater in that diving pool, strapped into a harness in a metal cage that she knew would soon have several metres of water above it. A place where it was quite possible that her disability could put both her, and Jack, in danger.

But this was bigger than that.

She'd been head over heels in love with her fireman, Pete Thompson, and had been well on the way to happily committing to spending the rest of her life with him until the accident that had marked the beginning of the end of their relationship.

He would never have seen her as any kind of 'project'. In fact, in a blinding moment of clarity, Harriet could see exactly why their relationship had faded into oblivion. Because she had no longer been able to fulfil her role in making his achievements the focus of their life together. She was no longer capable, or even interested, in being his support crew for surfing competitions. Appreciating the dedication he put into keeping his body in perfect shape had gone out the window as well, because it only rubbed salt into the wound of her own imperfections. Without the shared bond of the physical aspects of their relationship, like surfing and sex and the SDR team, there had been nothing left.

That wasn't love, was it?

When you loved someone, it had to go deeper than that. You had to care about someone enough to help them to be the best person they could be, even if it meant sacrificing something yourself.

She would have sacrificed whatever it took to help Pete if he'd been in her position. But he'd just walked away in the end.

And here was Jack. Just a friend. Not a lover or even someone who'd been an integral part of her life. A friend that she hadn't treated well at all, in fact, but he'd put all this time and effort into a plan to help her regain what she'd lost. To help her become the person she wanted to be again.

Yeah… Harriet caught her bottom lip between her teeth. Blinked a few times to make sure she wasn't going to embarrass herself by shedding tears over the fact that someone cared this much about her.

'Thank you,' she said quietly. 'This is…quite possibly the most amazing thing anyone's ever done for me.'

'So…you're up for it, then?' Jack's smile lit up his face.

'I'll start tomorrow,' she promised. 'With the walking. Increased hill work and then uneven surfaces and soft sand. Ten minutes for the first week and then twenty for the second.' She was tracing the boxes on the spread sheet. 'Good grief…you've even suggested the places to go to for some rocky surfaces or the soft sand.'

'I've used a few of them myself.'

'And I'll re-join the gym.' Harriet nodded. 'And factor in some swimming time.' It wouldn't be hard to find the time. Her life had become rather empty in the hours she wasn't at work.

'I've got my roster here, too.' Jack fished a folded piece of paper from his pocket. 'Let's find at least two or three slots a week that I can work with you.'

Harriet shook her head. 'God, Jack… I wouldn't ask you to do that. You've done enough already. I've got a plan now. My goals are broken down into steps that I can aim for.' She smiled at him. 'I can do this.'

'But I'm your personal trainer, remember?'

'You've got your own life. I wouldn't expect anyone to put that much time into my rehabilitation.' Even if they had chosen to be her life partner. Like Pete. 'Unless I was paying them, of course…'

Jack looked offended. 'I'm not asking to be paid, Harry. I *want* to do this.'

'But…*why*?'

'You're part of my team. Feels like you're part of my family, you know? And we're friends, aren't we? We enjoy each other's company?'

'Yes, of course. But…'

'Stop with the "buts". I like keeping fit myself. We can combine the sessions. Like when you're walking, I can be running. When you're on the sand, I can get a swim in.'

'But what about your social life? I don't want to interfere with that.'

'My social life? You mean my family?' Jack grinned. 'We could make that work, too. Look…' He pointed to a slot on his roster. 'This Saturday here? That's my grandma's birthday and there's a whanau party at a beach that would be perfect for you to swim at because the surf's usually really gentle. We could go early and get a training session in. See?' His grin was triumphant. 'There's always a way to make things work.'

'So I'd be crashing your family party?'

'You haven't met my whanau. Everybody's welcome. Anyway…that's weeks away. We need to get your sand walking skills up to speed before then, what with our weekend away at Hamilton Island on the agenda.'

'*Our* weekend? You've been invited to the wedding?'

'Better than that. Blake asked me to be his best man.'

'Oh…that's brilliant.'

'I know. You and me as the support crew. Team wedding, huh?'

'I've been looking at pictures of the island with Sam to help her choose the wedding venue.'

'There's a choice?'

'Huge choice. There's a yacht club with different decks and a chapel or grassy spots on hilltops. One beach needs a helicopter to get there but I reckon they're going to choose another beach, which looks perfect. White sand, blue ocean and a backdrop of all the other islands.' Harriet's smile was dreamy. 'It just looks incredible and I can't wait to go.'

'That's that, then.'

'What is?'

'Sand training starts tomorrow. I'll meet you straight after work, okay?'

'You don't have to do this, Jack.'

'I know that. I told you that I want to. Did that rock damage your hearing as well as your leg?'

'Just as long as you know that it's not an obligation. You can stop if it gets to be any kind of a nuisance.'

'Done.' Jack held his drink up in a toast. 'Just as long as you know that the same rules don't apply to you.' He clinked his glass against hers. 'You *don't* get to stop if it's any kind of a nuisance. I may be new at this personal trainer business but I have my standards. If you're in, you're in for the long haul.'

It was that sacrifice thing again. Jack had already done so much by making this detailed plan but here he was offering to give up a significant portion of his free time in the near future to help her try and become the person she used to be—maybe even a better version?

Harriet had to blink again and it was a challenge to find a smile that wasn't stupidly wobbly.

'I'm in.'

CHAPTER FIVE

SHE WAS IN PAIN.

Jack could recognise the signs now, despite how well Harriet managed to conceal it. He could see the crinkles appear at the corners of her eyes or the tiny frown line deepening between her eyebrows. He could hear it by the note of extra cheerfulness that was in her voice.

Most of all, though, he could sense it. As if he was feeling the pain himself and it made it hard to push her that little bit further when what he really wanted to do was…

Was to take her in his arms and hold her for a moment.

To tell her how much he admired her courage. How proud he was of the way she was continuing to face this struggle.

What he *would* do was exactly what he'd been doing for weeks now. He would push her until he knew that she was on the point of admitting defeat and then he would stop the session and let her know that she'd done a great job. Before she uttered anything negative about her current abilities. That point was close now so he was watching her carefully and he saw the briefest hesitation as she gathered her resources to tackle the last, steep part of this hillside track.

He held out his hand.

'Last bit,' he told her. 'We don't want to overdo it.'

Her fingers grasped his and he could feel her letting him take most of her weight as she took the oversized steps these rocks provided.

'We'll stop and rest,' he said. 'And then take the easy route down, nice and slowly.'

Harriet merely nodded, lowering herself carefully to sit on the edge of a boulder.

Jack slipped off his backpack and opened it to produce two bottles of water and a bag of snacks.

'My sister made this track mix for me,' he said. 'Might have a bit much chocolate in it but there's lots of seeds and nuts and dried fruit as well.'

Harriet picked out a large chunk of chocolate. 'I think I like your sister.' She didn't put it into her mouth straight away. Instead, she closed her eyes and blew out a long breath. 'That was a tough one,' she admitted.

'You couldn't have done it a few weeks ago.'

'I didn't think I was going to be able to do it today.' Her words were slightly muffled by chocolate. 'I almost gave up back there.'

'I know…' Jack caught her gaze as another surge of that pride squeezed his heart. 'But you didn't. Go, you.'

'I would have if I'd been on my own.'

'There you go, then. Having a personal trainer is good for you.'

'Mmm…but is it good for you?' Harriet was reaching for the snack bag.

'Are you kidding? I probably wouldn't have come out at all this morning. It was a bit of a big night last night.'

'Oh?' Harriet grinned at him, another piece of chocolate poised in her fingers. 'Who was she?'

Jack focused on getting a handful of nuts and fruit from the bag. The question was…what…annoying?

'Nothing like that,' he muttered. 'It was a birthday party for one of the firies on the team. Dan?'

'Oh…' Harriet's tone had changed. It sounded almost wistful. 'He was Pete's best mate on the station.'

Was she disappointed that she hadn't been invited?

'It was just a barbecue at the station. Mostly the guys. Too much beer.' Jack's gaze slid sideways but Harriet wasn't looking at him. She was licking some melted chocolate off her fingers.

It was just as well she wasn't looking at him because he suddenly found he couldn't look away. He hadn't bothered really trying to nail how her question about a female companion had made him feel. He certainly wasn't going to even start analysing what watching her lick her fingers was doing to him.

Man…this woman wasn't just courageous. She was…*hot*…

He needed to shore up that barrier between this friendship and anything else. Anything like the kind of thing he'd once dreamed of. It wasn't going to happen. He wasn't even going to think about the possibility of it happening.

'Did they say anything about Pete?' Harriet asked. 'Has anyone heard from him?'

Okay…this turn in the conversation was disturbing. Was Harriet still in love with the guy?

'Do you really want to know?'

She shrugged, making it no big deal. 'Just curious, I guess.'

'So he hasn't been in touch with you since he left?'
Harriet shook her head.

'Not even to see how you're doing? Or to apologise?'
The burn of anger was uncomfortable. Jack got to his
feet to shift it. 'And, no, I didn't hear anything about
him last night. I don't think anyone thinks much of the
way he treated you.'

Harriet didn't say anything and again he wondered
how she felt about her ex. The thought of her even talking to Pete again make him feel sick. But it was none
of his business, was it? He'd never been in a relationship serious enough to move in with someone so what
did he know? Harriet was older and presumably wiser.

She was trusting him with her friendship and he
wasn't about to wreck that by telling her what he
thought of her ex-boyfriend.

Or, worse, admitting the way he still felt about her
sometimes. Like in that moment when he'd watched
her licking chocolate off her fingers.

She needed a rock in her life. A good friend. If she
knew how often he wanted to take her hand or hold
her in his arms to comfort her, she'd think twice about
spending time with him at all. If she knew how it made
him feel to see her play with her hair when she tied it
back in a ponytail or the intense desire provoked by
watching her lick her fingers, she'd run a mile and
never look back.

It wasn't going to happen.

He stuffed the bag and his bottle into his backpack
and then held his hand out for Harriet's bottle. 'You
ready to head back?'

She nodded. 'Feels like we've done enough for
today, that's for sure.'

'Yeah...' Jack found a smile. 'More than enough. I hope you won't be too sore tomorrow.'

The day room for the geriatric ward at Bondi Bayside was a lovely place for patients to spend time with their visitors with its comfortable chairs and a view of the beach.

'Fancy a cuppa, Nurse?' The woman pushing the tea trolley through the doors of the day room had a badge that advertised her position as a hospital volunteer. 'We've got cheese scones today and, although I don't want to blow my own trumpet, they're pretty darn good.'

'That's very kind of you.' Harriet smiled. 'I'm just coming in to check on one of my patients but I just might sit for a few minutes after that and a cup of tea would be lovely.'

She could use the hot drink to wash down a couple of her anti-inflammatory tablets and maybe they would kick in a bit faster. Her leg was sore today after that hill climb yesterday but she'd been determined not to go back to using her brace at work.

The patient she was going to see was in a wheelchair at the far side of the large room. Poor old May, who'd broken her hip when she'd fallen out of bed, was still an inpatient and it looked as if she was never going to recover enough to be discharged back to her nursing home. Her son, Bruce, a man in his late sixties, had been an increasingly frequent visitor and he'd thought his mum would enjoy a change of scene today. He'd asked Harriet if he could take her outside to smell some sea air but she'd suggested the day room and a view of the sea instead. May had refused to go anywhere with the nasal prongs that were providing some extra oxygen so Harriet needed to check that she was managing without it.

'There's a cup of tea on its way,' she told May. 'And I hear there's some cheese scones as well.'

'Ooh… I do like a good cheese scone.' May reached out to pat her son's arm. 'You do too, don't you, Bruce?'

'Mmm… I'm not very hungry at the moment, though, Mum.' Bruce pulled a large handkerchief from his pocket and mopped his brow. 'It's very hot in here, isn't it?'

Harriet's gaze shifted instantly. 'Are you okay?'

'To be honest, I feel a bit sick.'

He was sweating profusely and his skin was looking grey. Harriet took hold of his wrist to feel for his pulse but she knew he was in trouble before she realised it wasn't palpable. His blood pressure had clearly dropped dramatically.

'Let's lie you down on the floor,' she said calmly. 'I'm going to get one of the doctors to come and see you.'

Bruce nodded. His hand went to the centre of his chest as he started to move and he gave a low moan.

Harriet was holding onto his other arm to help him down so she felt the exact moment that he lost consciousness and crumpled the rest of the way. All she could do was to stop his head hitting the floor too hard.

'Oh, my goodness,' May said. 'Whatever's happened?'

Harriet rolled Bruce onto his back and tilted his head to make sure his airway was open. She tried to find a pulse again, this time in his neck, putting her

cheek close to his mouth and her other hand on his abdomen to feel for any signs that he was still breathing.

He wasn't.

Harriet looked up briefly, to catch the horrified gaze
of the tea lady. 'Call for help, please,' she told her.
'Tell them we've got a cardiac arrest here. We need
the crash trolley.'

Without pausing, Harriet positioned herself on her
knees and began chest compressions. She hadn't done
CPR for a very long time now but it felt as familiar as
if she'd done it only yesterday. Bruce was a big man
and it took real effort to make her compressions deep
and fast enough to be effective. She only looked up
when she heard the rattle of trolley wheels behind her.
It was one of the younger nurses on the ward who was
pushing it and she looked terrified.

'Is the crash team on its way?'

'Yes. I pushed the cardiac arrest button.'

'Can I do something to help?' The tea lady was
wringing her hands.

'Yes,' Harriet said. 'Take May back to the ward.
And ask everybody else here to leave.' She still didn't
pause her compressions as she looked back at the nurse.
'Open the defibrillator pack and get the patches out.
I'll tell you where to stick them. You'll have to work
around me.'

One patch went below the collarbone on the right
and the other on the left side of the chest. Harriet kept
up the compressions, giving directions to her assistant,
and she was well out of breath by the time the machine
was switched on and she could pause long enough for
any heart rhythm to be detected. Not everybody had

left the room, she noticed. And there was no sign of the crash team yet.

'Shock advised.' The voice on the defibrillator's automatic program was clear and calm. 'Push "Charge".'

Harriet pushed the button and listened to the whine that changed to an alarm when the charge had been reached.

'Stand clear,' she said, looking up to make sure no one was within touching range of Bruce, including herself. She pushed the shock button and Bruce's arms jerked, then she positioned herself to start chest compressions again.

'Do you know how to use a bag mask?' she asked her junior colleague.

'I think so. I've practised on mannequins.'

Harriet's heart sank but they were still within the window of time when compressions alone were sufficient. If necessary, she could change her position and do CPR from over Bruce's head, which would mean she could ensure that she could deliver respirations as well, but her arms were tiring and, ideally, there should be a change of personnel to deliver the compressions.

Two minutes and then it was time to try and shock Bruce's heart back into action.

'Stand clear…' she called. This time, when she looked up to check safety, she could see the crash team arrive. A bigger trolley, two doctors and another nurse. 'Shocking now.' She pushed the button and closed her eyes for a moment as she let out a relieved breath.

'Well…look at that.' One of the doctors on the crash team was crouching beside her as she opened her eyes again. 'Looks like we've missed all the excitement. Good save, mate.'

And there it was, on the screen. A little erratic but it was close enough to a normal rhythm.

'I've got a pulse.' The other doctor had his hand on Bruce's neck. 'I'll get some oxygen on.'

It wasn't until much later, when Harriet finally went back to the ward, that she noticed her leg was still aching.

She'd never got round to taking those tablets.

And she hadn't given her abilities, or any lack of them, any thought at all during that emergency.

'May?'

'Oh…no…' Pale blue eyes looked more frightened than she had ever seen them look.

'It's okay, May.' Harriet took hold of her hand. 'Bruce is going to be all right. He's having a procedure called an angioplasty now and that's going to fix the artery in his heart that's blocked.'

'His heart?' May's voice trembled. 'He's had a heart attack?'

Harriet nodded. 'It was enough to stop his heart for a little while, and that's why he collapsed. But we got it going again.' She was smiling now. 'He woke up again and he told me to tell you that he's going to be fine. And that he loves you.'

'Oh…' There were tears pouring down May's face. 'You did that? You saved my son?'

'We did. It was a team effort.' Harriet wasn't about to take all the credit, even though the crash team had made sure she knew exactly what a good job she'd done. The conversation she'd had with one of the doctors as they'd got ready to transfer Bruce on a stretcher had made her feel even better.

'You used to work in ICU, didn't you?' he'd said.

'Yes. I got sent here to recover from an injury. It was supposed to be a bit quieter.'

'Well, you look like you could cope with anything again now. Let me know if you need a reference for getting your old job back.'

Harriet sat with May for a while, until her frail patient finally slipped into a peaceful sleep.

And then she sat there for a bit longer because she was actually officially off duty now and she wanted a moment to get her head around what seemed like turning a new corner in her life.

She *had* coped. And coped well. She was ready to ask if she could be considered for her old position again.

She couldn't have done that a couple of months ago and there was someone she needed to thank for her new level of physical ability.

Jack.

The rush of gratitude was a warmth that enveloped Harriet as she sat in this quiet corner of May's room. It held notes of pride and excitement and a hope for the future that was so strong and positive it was the best feeling ever.

And then it seemed to coalesce into something a little bit different.

A feeling that was all about Jack Evans. She couldn't wait to talk to him and tell him about what had happened today. She wanted nothing more than to bask in the gaze she knew she would be under from those warm, brown eyes.

Told you so, that gaze would say. *I've always believed in you...*

They didn't have another session planned until Saturday and that was days away. Harriet found herself actually reaching for her phone. If Jack wasn't working or busy, maybe they could meet up for a drink or something. Her fingers closed around the phone in her pocket but then she froze.

She remembered this feeling of wanting to tell her news to just one person. Of wanting to be with them so much.

The last time she'd felt like this had been…when she'd fallen in love with Pete.

Which was ridiculous.

She wasn't in love with Jack. This was gratitude, that was all.

But a prickle of awareness was trying to contradict that assertion. Flashes of memories that could be interpreted with a very different slant. Like that evening at the beach with Harry the dog, when she'd noticed how gorgeous his skin looked, glowing bronze in the last sun of the day. The way the tattoo highlighted the muscles on his arm. The way his smile made the world a brighter place.

Another flash reminded her of how it had made her feel when he'd told her that he believed in her and how it had persuaded her to do the HUET exercise. That she'd felt like she finally understood what a real family was all about.

And what about yesterday, when he'd taken hold of her hand to help her up those steps when she'd already pushed herself to the limit? She had welcomed the strength in that hand. The touch of his skin against hers…

Oh…*help*…

It was there, wasn't it? If she wasn't already in love

with Jack—and she *wasn't*—the possibility that she could be, in the near future, couldn't be denied. She'd believed that that kind of trust was broken for ever for her, but had he somehow slipped behind her defences?

It had to be stopped. Good grief…imagine how Jack would react? Any girl he would choose for a partner would probably be ten years younger than Harriet. He'd probably have a laugh about it with his mates if he knew and they'd make jokes about toy boys or cradle snatching. Call her a cougar, even?

Harriet could feel colour heating up her cheeks. The phone slid from her fingers and she pushed herself up out of the chair.

Not that she believed Jack would be cracking jokes with his mates, he was far too kind to do that. But he would be disturbed, that was for sure. He would find a way to ease off spending time with her and their training sessions would rapidly become just another memory.

She couldn't let that happen. Not when at least one but possibly both of her goals were within touching distance.

Waiting till Saturday to mention today's triumph was no big deal. If she needed to tell somebody else about it before then, she could ring one of her friends. Like Sam. Or Kate. Or even Luc, now living in Namborra with his wife Beth and stepson Toby. Anybody, as long as it wasn't Jack.

'Sleep tight, May,' she murmured aloud. 'See you tomorrow.'

It wasn't the first time that Harriet had used her camera as a buffer between herself and other people but she hadn't needed it this much since her early days of trying to get herself past that dark time when she'd been sure her life would never be the same again.

This was different. It was a buffer between herself and Jack more than anything. A barrier that she had no intention of stepping past.

He looked so happy in the midst of this family gathering. Right now, he was playing a noisy game of barefoot soccer with participants who ranged in age from his grandfather, who was a goalkeeper, to some small boys who couldn't have been more than about five years old. A couple of dogs were determined to join in the fun and looked like they were presenting quite a hazard but nobody seemed to mind.

There were other men who were in charge of the barbecues, including a spit roast. There were gales of laughter coming from a group of women who were setting out platters of food on one of the big picnic tables and shrieks of glee from toddlers who were being supervised in the shallows by some teenaged girls. A couple of young mothers were breastfeeding their babies under the shade of a tree.

A few members of Jack's extended family had already been here when they'd arrived at the beach.

'This is my friend, Harry,' Jack had introduced her, as they'd gone past. 'We're going for a swim. Look after her bag, will you? It's got her camera in it and she's going to take some photos of the party later.'

And, as easily as that, she had been accepted and welcomed into the rapidly expanding group. They had no idea that this was a big step for Harriet. She'd been doing a lot of swimming in pools recently but this was the first time to tackle real surf since the time before her accident and she was nervous.

She was nervous of being in Jack's company as well. What if he guessed any of the crazy thoughts that had been going through her head since she'd had that disturbing realisation that she had inappropriate feelings for her personal trainer?

At least he seemed blissfully unaware at the moment. He'd stood beside her as ankle-deep water had rushed over her feet and she'd hesitated before walking further into the waves and his smile had offered nothing but empathy and encouragement.

'It's a nice, gentle surf,' he'd said. 'And I'm going to be right beside you. We'll swim out, catch a wave and body surf in, okay?'

Harriet's voice had deserted her. She'd done this a thousand times before and loved the sensation of the water's power rushing her back to shore but she also knew what it was like to get the timing wrong and to be pushed down and held underwater. How much strength you needed in your legs to get you back to safety.

And then Jack had reached out and taken her hand, as if it was the most natural thing in the world.

'You can escape from a helicopter underwater,' he'd called, as he tugged her forward. 'You've got this.'

They'd waded out further, jumping up to avoid being knocked over by waves breaking at chest height. Jack had let go of her hand as they'd had to start swimming, being lifted up and then sliding down the roll of waves that weren't ready to break. Jack had dived through some of them, popping up beside her like a dolphin, his brown skin glistening and a huge grin on his face.

'This one,' he'd shouted, and Harriet had turned

her head to see a wall of water coming relentlessly towards them.

There had been no time to panic. She'd needed to turn and point her body towards the shore. To kick her feet to keep at the front of the wave and then hold her breath as it began to break and cover her in foam as she'd shot forward. Within seconds, she'd been in water that was shallow enough to stand up, salt water streaming down her body.

Jack hadn't paused for any longer than it took to give her a thumbs-up before he'd turned back.

'Good, huh?' he'd called. 'Let's do it again.'

They'd stayed in the water for nearly an hour, catching wave after wave, and it had been the most exhilarating therapy Harriet had experienced since her accident. It was not only good for her body…it was doing something wonderful for her soul. She loved the sea and being in the surf.

And…there was no avoiding the truth now, she loved Jack as well.

So, here she was, hiding behind her camera as she stayed to share in the family celebration of Jack's grandmother's birthday. Having dried herself off after the swim, she was also hiding in her favourite maxi dress with its strappy top and swirly skirt that had a ragged hemline reaching her ankles. Her hair had gone super curly after being soaked in salt water, she had no make-up on and bare feet but it didn't matter. Harriet hadn't felt this happy in a very, very long time.

She was tired and her leg was aching but it was actually a joy to be wandering around capturing candid shots of this huge, loving family. She caught an auntie stooping to kiss and comfort a toddler who'd fallen over. A father laughing up at the baby he was holding above his head. The grandmother who was sitting regally on a beach chair that had been draped with flowers and, of course, the action shots of the fierce but friendly soccer game.

She'd never known what it was like to have a close family and this was completely at the other end of the spectrum. They would just absorb whoever Jack chose as his partner in life, wouldn't they? The wedding would be a huge celebration and someone would always be there to help if they needed a babysitter or something. Their children would have an endless supply of cousins to play with.

A stab of envy dimmed the happy shine of the afternoon for Harriet.

She wanted to be that girl.

And she knew she never could be.

A little later, she had to abandon her camera to sit on the grass with a plate of delicious food. She was amongst a laughing group that included Jack, two of his sisters and several of their children. A sea breeze had picked up but, focused on eating, Harriet didn't notice that she'd lost the safety barrier of more than her role of photographer.

'What's wrong with your leg?' a small boy asked.

'Um…' A glance down showed that her skirt had folded back and her bad leg was completely exposed in all its misshapen glory. Hurriedly, she tugged the fabric free and covered her scars.

'I…um…'

'Harry had an accident.' Jack spoke up from the other side of the group. 'She had climbed down a mountain and then a big rock came down and landed on her leg.'

'Wow…' The boy's eyes grew as round as saucers. 'You can climb mountains? That's *cool*…' And then he turned to his mother. 'Can I have some ice cream now?'

'Go on, then…' His mother ruffled his curls. 'Bring some back for your sister, too.' She smiled at Harriet. 'That must have hurt so much,' she said. 'But it looks like you're recovering well.'

'That's because she's got the best personal trainer around these parts,' Jack put in.

'Says you.' His sister grinned. 'Hope you're not paying him too much, Harry. I think he just wants an excuse to keep fit and have someone to play with.'

Harriet just smiled. They thought she was paying Jack? That she didn't qualify as being a real friend? Any fragments of longing to be part of a family like this evaporated. She really didn't belong here…

Her appetite had vanished. The conversation moved on swiftly but Harriet wasn't contributing. The return of the little boy, holding two enormous ice-cream cones, gave her the excuse she needed. She scrambled to her feet, ignoring the shaft of pain that trying to look normal doing so provoked.

'That looks really good,' she murmured. 'I might go and find one, too.'

Not that she wanted an ice cream. What Harriet wanted right now was to escape. She had come with Jack, though, so she'd have to wait until he was ready to leave. The best she could do for the moment was to find a rubbish bin for her picnic plate and then wander off down the beach to find a quiet spot to sit for a while.

Minutes ticked past as she watched the waves gather

momentum and then break up to roll onto the sand. She heard the sound of many voices singing 'Happy Birthday' and then bursts of clapping as speeches were probably being made. She needed to go back but if she waited a bit longer, maybe the cleaning-up process would be underway and Jack would be ready to drive her back into the city. Had he noticed her absence? Would he be angry at how rude she'd been?

'Hey…' The smile on Jack's face as he walked towards her didn't suggest anything like anger. 'My tribe got a bit much for you?' He flopped down onto the sand beside her. 'Sorry about that.'

'Don't apologise. Your family is lovely. I just…'

'Needed some space. I get it.'

The breeze was tugging at the hemline of her dress again so Harriet held it down. She caught her breath in a gasp as Jack put his hand over hers and pulled it away.

'You don't need to do that,' he said quietly. 'Don't let your scars embarrass you.'

'They're ugly,' Harriet muttered. 'I hate them.'

For a moment they sat there in silence that was broken only by the soothing sound of the waves. Harriet closed her eyes. She didn't want to see that empathy in Jack's face. But she didn't try and hide her leg again either. He'd seen it before.

The touch of his fingers on her leg was so shocking that Harriet froze. She couldn't even open her eyes.

'I don't think they're ugly,' he said softly. 'I think they add to your beauty.'

Now it was even hard to breathe. Nobody had touched her leg when it wasn't medically required for the longest time. Nobody had touched any part of her body like this for even longer.

As if it was…something special. Something to be honoured.

'It's evidence of the kind of strength you have, Harry,' Jack continued. 'You should be proud of what you've achieved. *I'm* proud of you…'

It was embarrassing to feel so close to tears. It was worse to open her eyes, see the way Jack was looking at her, and have to fight the urge to lean in and…*kiss* him?

But, dear Lord, he looked as if he was thinking the same thing. As if the only thing he wanted was to kiss *her*.

She couldn't let it happen. No matter how much she longed to be touched the way he had touched her leg, she couldn't do that to Jack. She would be taking advantage of their friendship. Risking losing it even. She was misinterpreting that look, that was all. Making it something she *wanted* to see? He was proud of her and he was invested in her success because he'd put so much time into it himself.

Such a short time ago, she'd thought about the girl who might be lucky enough to become part of his family. Someone a lot younger than herself. Someone who would be introduced as more than simply a 'friend'. Someone who might be used to being part of a real family and wouldn't feel awkward or like they didn't really belong. Whatever the reason, she'd known that it wouldn't be her.

Harriet pushed back at that desire so hard it was enough to get her to her feet.

'Thanks,' she said lightly, pasting a smile onto her

face. 'It's just as well your family doesn't know how bad your rate of pay as a personal trainer is.'

She knew Jack was following her. She could also sense that he had been bewildered by her comment and didn't know what to say in response. The silence felt awkward, even when he broke it.

'Do you know, you're walking on sand almost without a limp?'

'Just as well, with the wedding coming up in a couple of weeks.' This was better. A line of conversation that would take them well away from anything too personal and cover up that weird moment when a kiss had hung in the air between them, just waiting for one of them to make the first move. 'Have you been measured up for your suit yet?'

'Not yet. I think that's happening this week.'

'It's going to get busy.' Harriet nodded. 'My bridesmaid duties are hotting up.' They were nearly back to where the party was finally winding down. 'I don't think I'm going to get much time for any training before then.'

She couldn't miss the flare of surprise in Jack's eyes. Or the tiny frown that followed, as if he was drawing a more significant meaning from her words. Then he nodded and turned away.

'No problem. You ready to head back yet?'

'Sure. Let me just go and find my bag.'

They walked in opposite directions. Harriet to gather her things and Jack to say his farewells to his grandmother and other family members.

Harriet could feel the distance between them growing more than physically.

It felt as if they'd been at some sort of crossroads

back there. As if there'd been an offer of something hanging in the air but it hadn't formed enough to be accepted. Or, more likely, rejected. She had chosen to walk away and Jack was respecting that.

It had been the right thing to do.

So why did it feel so very wrong?

CHAPTER SIX

'YOU LOOK *PERFECT*.'

'You think?' Sam glanced over her shoulder at the full-length mirror and just the movement of her head gave the impression that the shimmering fall of her dress was floating in a sea breeze.

Harriet did a quick twirl to make her own skirt float a little, too. 'I would never have thought to wear something yellow but I really love it.'

'It's my frangipani theme.' Sam touched one of the tiny white and gold flowers dotted amongst the soft braids that was an elegant style, just messy enough to be perfect for a beach wedding. 'We chose the fabric of your dress to match the centre of the flowers.'

Harriet dipped her head to sniff the bouquet she was holding. 'They're gorgeous. And so tropical. Perfect choice.'

'I was going to go for gardenias because they smell so wonderful and they look all white and bridal but then I got into researching the meanings of the flowers and…' A poignant smile touched Sam's lips. 'I couldn't go past frangipanis.'

'Oh?' Harriet moved towards the silver tray with the

flutes of champagne they hadn't touched yet. 'What do they mean?'

'They symbolise intense love and a lasting bond between two people and the strength to withstand tough challenges. The boys have got them in a buttonhole, too. With a little spray of ferns behind them.'

'Nice. I love that.'

Harriet handed Sam a glass of champagne, noting the immaculate French polish they both had, on their toenails as well as their fingernails. They had pretty sandals to wear so she had submitted to the pedicure in the salon this morning and tried to ignore that her scarred leg was on display. Now she was pleased that she had. Not just because her hands and feet looked so good but because it had been a lovely time, with both Sam and Blake's mothers sharing the pampering. It had felt like family. Not like the exuberant and welcoming gathering of Jack's family on the beach the other week but still close and warm and special.

'Oh... I've got something for you.' Sam pulled a tiny package from her bag. 'It's just tiny but I wanted you to have something to remember today by. I got one for both of us.'

'I'm not likely to forget it. I can't believe I'm even here. Hamilton Island is stunning.'

The gift was a pretty ankle bracelet, a silver chain with tiny ceramic flowers. Frangipanis.

'It's gorgeous. Does it matter which ankle you put it on? Am I going to be advertising my single status or anything?'

Sam laughed. 'I'm sorry it's not a huge wedding with some surprise guest who's going to sweep you off your feet.'

Harriet was looking down at her ankles. In this long dress, it looked like both her legs were perfectly normal so it didn't matter which one she chose.

What did matter was that she couldn't even think about her ankles or legs without her brain taking her instantly back to that moment when Jack had touched her scars so gently.

When he had pretty much told her that he thought she was beautiful.

When that kiss that hadn't happened had seared itself into her brain. And her heart...

She put the bracelet onto her scarred side. Because she liked the symbolism of withstanding tough challenges.

And the lasting bond between two people. A sharp pang of loss made her catch her breath. She hadn't had either of those things with the man she'd thought she'd been going to marry. But she was over Pete now, she reminded herself firmly. Completely over him. And, in a different way, she had both of those attributes with Jack. A tough challenge that he'd been with her on, every step of the way. And friendship was a loving bond, wasn't it?

If she still had that with him?

She took a long sip of her champagne, unable to answer that question. She hadn't seen him in the last couple of weeks. Ever since that family party at the beach. He'd told her to text him if she found she had any free time and wanted a training session.

She hadn't made any contact at all. They hadn't been on the same flight to Hamilton Island from Sydney and the wedding preparations had meant, of course, that she and Sam were separated from the groom and his best man. She wouldn't see him until she accompanied Sam down the strip of white carpet on the beach to the spot between the palm trees where Blake would be waiting for her, Jack by his side.

Would she even be able to make eye contact with Jack, given the kinds of things she'd been thinking in the lonely hours of the nights since that almost kiss?

A knock at the door interrupted her anxiety. It was Sam's mother.

'I have to go and find my seat in a minute but the photographer wants a few more of the "getting ready" shots. Can he come in again?'

'Sure.' Sam smiled at Harriet. 'Let's get one of our matching ankles.'

'Hey... I'm the one who's supposed to be nervous, not you.'

Jack's smile was wry. 'Guess I'm not used to being in the spotlight. Or in a suit, for that matter.'

'You and me both, mate. But today's for Sam and I wanted it to be perfect for her. I did draw the line at a tie, though.'

'Good thing, too, in this heat.' The open-necked white shirt beneath the cream linen suit was ideal for a beach wedding and Jack felt right at home with sand between his toes and the mottled shade of palm trees overhead. If he ever got married, he'd want a setting like this. His family would all be keen for a trip home to Samoa, wouldn't they? And island parties were the best...

It was unfortunate that any thought of having a wedding of his own or finding a bride inevitably took his thoughts straight to Harriet Collins because that made him fidget again.

He *was* nervous but it had nothing to do with the small crowd of people now settled into the rows of white chairs on the beach. Or that he still had best man duties to perform, like making a speech later.

It had everything to do with the fact that he was going to see Harriet very soon and he hadn't seen or heard from her since that moment on the beach when he'd stupidly given in to the urge to touch her skin in a way that no personal trainer ever should. When he'd had to fight an even more overwhelming urge to kiss her because, for a crazy blip of time, he'd thought she wanted him to.

And now she'd run away. As he'd known she would if he ever took that step closer.

Sure, she'd been busy helping Sam. There must have been all sorts of last-minute details that had to be organised and women had a lot more to do in the run-up to a wedding than the men did. When one of his sisters had got married a while back, there'd been endless discussions about hairstyles and manicures and goodness knew what else.

But how long did it take to send a text message, even if it was just to say that she didn't have time for a training session? He'd deleted more than one message on his own phone before hitting 'send' because instinct told him that if she was avoiding him or running away, chasing her would only make it worse.

'You've lost the rings, haven't you?' Blake had noticed his restless movement again.

'No way. Toby's got them, remember?' He turned his head to smile at the small boy wearing a miniature version of their suits. He was sitting on his mum's lap in the front row on the groom's side of the gathering. His new stepdad gave Jack a thumbs-up signal and grinned.

'I miss having Luc in the team,' he murmured. 'We were a bit remiss in not giving you a stag night, too.'

'Not into that kind of thing,' Blake said.

'No kidding…' Jack's smile was more relaxed now. Blake's hair might be tied back the way he kept it at work in the emergency department but he'd already pushed up the sleeves of his jacket enough to make a personal, casual style statement. It was just as well that casual beach shoes had been deemed appropriate or the groom would probably be wearing his beloved cowboy boots as well.

'And Luc's a family man now,' Blake added. 'Namborra's a bit far to have come to Sydney for a night out. We'll make up for it later. Oh…' His voice cracked as soft music began and every head turned. *'Wow…'*

Jack caught his breath at the first sight of Sam, looking so radiant and beautiful, but it felt like his heart had stopped in sympathy the moment he saw Harriet. She looked like a ray of sunshine in that pale yellow dress and he'd never seen her hair lifted up from her neck like that. With the tiny flowers amongst her curls, she looked almost like a bride herself. He knew that Sam was the star of this show but, for him, Harriet Collins was outshining the bride. Without the slightest doubt, she was the most beautiful woman he'd ever seen in his life.

And…and she wasn't limping. Not even a little bit…

He felt incredibly proud of her at that moment. So

proud he had to blink hard to get rid of the extra moisture in his eyes.

Maybe it was just as well she wasn't looking at him. Even when they'd stepped aside so that only the celebrant was framed between the palm trees in front of Sam and Blake, Harriet kept her gaze firmly on what they were here for—the exchange of vows between two people who were making a public declaration of a love they both believed would last for the rest of their lives.

Jack tried to keep his own gaze focussed on Sam and Blake as well and it wasn't hard. The vows they had written were personal and beautiful and little Toby was very cute as he played his part in delivering the rings. But then it came, finally. That moment when they had their first kiss as a married couple and there was nothing Jack could do to stop his gaze sliding towards Harriet.

Had she already been looking at him or had she just felt the same pull at exactly the same moment?

It didn't matter.

The kiss between Blake and Sam had made her remember and, in that long moment of connection when neither of them could look away, Jack knew he hadn't been wrong.

Harriet *had* wanted that kiss on the beach that day.

As much as he had.

They both broke eye contact as the applause from the guests began. They had duties to perform now, like the signing of the register and then the official photo session. He still had his speech to make later, too, but Jack wasn't feeling remotely nervous any more.

He wasn't quite sure what this enormous sensation in his chest was. Relief? Excitement? Pure joy?

Whatever it was, this wasn't the time to think about it. Or to try and talk to Harriet about it.

It was enough that it was there.

And, suddenly, Jack thought he recognised what this huge feeling was.

Hope...

Oh, man...

The way Jack had been looking at her.

Maybe it was a result of the most romantic setting ever, on this gorgeous beach with the background of a turquoise sea interrupted only by the lush green shapes of outer islands and the blue of the sky by some harmless, cotton-wool puffs of cloud.

Or maybe it was a reflection of the palpable love between the two people who had just joined their lives together in the most beautiful exchange of vows Harriet had ever heard.

Weddings were notorious for sparking romance amongst the witnesses and guests, weren't they?

Except that she'd seen a paler version of that look in Jack's eyes before. When he'd touched her leg, as if her scars were a part of her that was as acceptable and important as any other part of her body. She could have drowned in that gaze and it had been a shock when the guests had begun clapping because, for a heartbeat, she'd totally forgotten that anyone else was here. Even Blake and Sam.

She didn't dare catch his gaze again. She busied herself, making sure that Sam's dress was in perfect folds and that the breeze hadn't messed up her hair for the photos as they signed the register and then moved to a more formal photo shoot further down the beach.

It was easy to smile at the camera as group shots were taken but it became harder as the photographer suggested some more casual ideas.

Towards the end, both Blake and Jack had discarded their jackets and shoes and rolled up the legs of their trousers so they could stand in the gentle wash of waves.

'Grab your girls.' He grinned, then. 'Hold them up high enough so their dresses won't get wet.'

Blake had no hesitation in scooping Sam into his arms and walking back into the water. She had her arms around his neck and was laughing up at him and then he dipped his head to kiss his bride and Harriet knew it would be the best photo. She was so caught up, watching them, she barely noticed that Jack was right beside her.

'Yes,' the photographer called. 'Awesome. Now we need the whole bridal party in the sea.'

Harriet caught her bottom lip between her teeth. She had to look up at Jack now, to see whether he was feeling anything like she was—as if she was about to take a flying leap off a cliff.

But he was smiling, his eyebrows raised in a query. He liked this idea.

With a tiny sigh, Harriet gave in to the moment, reaching up to put her arms around his neck. She felt strong arms take hold of her and then lift her as he turned and walked into the water.

She hadn't been in a man's arms like this for longer than she could remember. Once, Pete had picked her up on the beach and run into the surf, but only to dump her in deeper water. It had been a game. Fun.

Nothing like how this felt.

Jack wasn't about to drop her and it wasn't just because it would ruin her dress. The feeling of having his arms around her like this suggested a safety that went far beyond any clothing.

She trusted this man. And he was the sweetest, most generous person that she knew. She couldn't do anything that would cause him harm—physical or emotional. He might think he wanted to be with her as more than a friend but she couldn't allow that to happen if it had the potential to hurt him. She might think she was capable of trusting someone again but what if she was wrong? Was she really ready to risk having her heart broken again?

It was a huge thing to contemplate. Terrifying, even.

Not that she could give that fear any headspace right now and spoil this fun. They were all laughing, even when Blake's trouser leg unrolled and got soaked. Their feet were caked with sand as they made their way back to the reception in the yacht club and neither of the men put their jackets back on but nobody seemed to mind. The venue was gorgeous, on an open deck with the fabulous views that were getting more and more stunning as the sun sank. Tables were sheltered by umbrellas that had hanging lanterns that would look like small moons as it got darker. The food was amazing, the speeches all went well and the dance floor was ready for them to party on into the night.

Harriet knew that she would have to dance with Jack, at least once, as they joined the bridal couple after their first dance. She wanted to dance with him so much that it was ringing alarm bells. If he looked at her the way he had during Blake and Sam's kiss, while he was holding her in his arms and moving to soft, romantic music, she would be totally lost. It might be impossible to even remember the reasons why anything more than friendship with Jack wasn't a good idea. That one—or both—of them would only end up getting badly hurt.

That was why she took a moment to have a private word with Sam. To whisper that her leg had reached its limits for the day and that she was scared she might fall on her face if she tried dancing. She saw Sam whispering to Blake a short time later and then Blake got up, resting a hand on Jack's shoulder as he bent to say something to his best man before taking his bride's hand and leading her to the dance floor.

A part of her heart was breaking at the smile that Jack gave her as he leaned closer.

'No worries,' he murmured. 'You've done so well today, Harry. Not even a limp. We won't push it.'

'Thanks.' She couldn't quite meet his gaze. 'I did it, didn't I? Met my first goal of being the bridesmaid that didn't limp. Thanks to you.'

'I reckon you would have got there without any help from me. I'm just glad I got to go along on the ride.' Jack cleared his throat, reaching for his glass of water. 'How 'bout that other goal, of getting your old job back?'

'I'm getting a trial next week, thanks to that cardiac arrest I told you about. I know I can do it.' But the shine of this new step forward in her life had dimmed. Jack sounded as if their training sessions together were a thing of the past. A 'ride' that was now over. It would make things easier not to spend so much time together but there was a hollow feeling in her stomach that felt a lot like loss.

'I know you can, too.' Jack was smiling again. 'Reckon it's time to talk to Blake about getting back on the team.'

They both turned to watch Blake and Sam as they were dancing. It was clearly something they both loved to do and their dancing was a pleasure to watch. The joy that emanated from the couple made Harriet catch her breath.

'One step at a time,' she said. 'I doubt very much that Blake wants to think about the team while he's on his honeymoon.'

If she joined the team again, it would mean regular team meetings and training sessions on top of any actual callouts. More time in Jack's company, even if the personal training was done. She needed to get her head around that and make sure she could handle it and stay strong. For Jack's sake as much as her own.

The silence felt a little awkward until Jack broke it. 'They're staying on here, aren't they?'

'Yes, for a week. They've got a private bungalow on one of the smaller islands and a line-up of amazing things to do like snorkelling and swimming with turtles. I'll have to come back here one day myself, I think.'

The first dance was ending and Sam and Blake went in opposite directions to find new partners to bring to the floor. Sam came towards the bridal party's table.

'Jack… Blake says I have to dance with our best man.' But her smile faded a little as she looked at Harriet. 'You don't mind, do you, Harry?'

'Go for it,' she said. 'Blake's got your mum up on the floor and look…your dad is asking Blake's mum.'

'He knows about her disability. He'll be gentle.'

They all knew that Blake's mother was limited in her physical abilities after her stroke but here she was on the dance floor, in the arms of a man who would be taking care of her. Beth was there as well and she had problems with her vision but Luc was there to protect her and they had little Toby holding each of their hands and bouncing enthusiastically to the music.

Harriet could feel Jack's gaze on her. Telling her that he would have been gentle as well. That he could protect her. That she could cope if she wanted to.

It was just as well that Sam was dragging him away to join the increasing number of people who were getting up and into the fun. Harriet was left alone at the table. She watched for a few minutes but then stood up and walked towards the end of the deck. Nobody was going to miss her if she took a few minutes to herself and went out to enjoy the shine of the moon on the sea.

'Where's Harry?'

'I have no idea.' Jack had noticed the empty space at the table a while ago but he'd assumed that Harriet was mingling to talk to other guests.

'I thought she'd gone to the loo but I've just been and she's not there.' Sam was looking worried. 'Do you think she's okay?'

'She seemed fine. Apart from not wanting to dance.'

'Maybe her leg's worse than she was letting on.' Blake appeared beside Sam and slid his arm around his new wife. 'Could you go and look for her, Jack?'

'Sure.' Except that he might not be welcome if he found her. This would be chasing her in a far less subtle manner than sending a text message or something. But now he was worried, too.

'Tell her it's no problem if she's tired and needs to go back to her bungalow. We'll see her at the breakfast tomorrow.'

'Will do.'

'And thanks, Jack. For everything. It's been the best day.' Sam stood on tiptoe to plant a kiss on his cheek. 'And now I need to go and dance with my husband again.'

'Call us if there's a problem,' Blake added, but he was smiling down at Sam. 'Husband, huh? How soon can we slip away, do you think?'

Jack paused at the bar at the end of the deck. 'Have you seen a gorgeous redhead in a yellow dress recently?'

'Couldn't miss her,' the barman said with a wink. 'Looked like she was heading to the beach for a bit of fresh air.'

The sand still felt warm beneath his feet as Jack walked along the beach. The sounds of the party faded behind him until all he could hear was the soft wash of tiny waves. The beach looked completely deserted and he was walking away from the main part of the resort where he could have made enquiries about which bungalow she was in for the night.

Instinct told him that there was a problem. Not with her leg necessarily but...with *him*.

That same instinct told him that Harriet wouldn't have shut herself away in a room. That she probably wasn't far away and that she was finding peace in this soft symphony of sea music and moonlight.

And...there she was, her skirt bunched up in one hand, her sandals dangling from the other, walking close enough to the sea to have her feet covered by foam at the end of every wave.

'Harry?'

She turned. And stopped.

'Sam was worried about you. She sent me to see if you're okay.'

'I'm fine.' Harriet bit her lip. 'I just came out for a minute but…it's so beautiful I guess I lost track of time.' She came away from the water and let the skirts of her dress fall. 'I'd better go back, hadn't I?'

'There's no rush.' Without thinking, Jack put out his hands to touch Harriet's shoulders and stop her moving forward. 'I… I think we need to talk…'

He could feel the softness and warmth of her skin beneath his hands. Her eyes looked huge in this soft light and her gaze was holding his as if she couldn't look away. As if she didn't want to…

A puff of breeze caught a curl of her hair that dangled in front of her eyes. Jack moved his hand to brush it back and then his fingers cupped the back of her head. He could feel the way her head tilted into his hand and his gaze dropped to where her lips had parted. There was no way on earth he could have resisted the force of what felt like a reflection of his own longing. He bent his head and touched her lips with his own.

This was every bit as astonishing as any fantasy kiss that had haunted her nights recently.

Only so much better, because it was real.

That first touch of Jack's lips had been so gentle. So slow and thoughtful, as if he was soaking up something way more than physical contact. Building into an inevitable rush of sensation that she knew had taken them both by surprise because of that brief moment in time where they both froze. A tiny part of her brain registered her sandals falling from her hand before she reached up to put her arms around Jack's neck. And then it was an avalanche of a kiss on a very different level that was sweeping her into a place that felt totally new.

Huge.

Scary, definitely... But it didn't feel wrong. Quite the opposite, in fact.

It was hard to catch her breath when they finally broke apart.

For a long, long moment, Jack held her gaze. And then one corner of his mouth lifted.

'Sorry.'

Her eyes widened. How could anyone be sorry about a kiss like that?

'I didn't ask for permission, did I?'

And then she remembered what she'd said when Jack had asked whether she was allowed to keep Harry the dog in her apartment. That sometimes it was better to apologise later than ask for permission first.

She felt her own lips curve into a smile that just kept growing and any awkwardness between them seemed to vanish. Their friendship was still intact, and it had just stepped onto a completely new level.

A miraculous, totally unexpected level.

'I'm not wrong, am I?' Jack asked softly. 'You're feeling this, too?'

'You're not wrong.' The words were a whisper. Harriet had to close her eyes for a heartbeat. Feeling it didn't quite cover this overwhelming surge of emotion. Amazement and joy. A warmth that only came from love and an excitement that was pure sexual desire. But there was also trepidation mixed in there. Guilt even…

She opened her eyes to find Jack's steady gaze locked onto hers.

'But…?'

'But…it couldn't work, could it?'

'Why not?'

'I'm older than you, Jack. Maybe enough that your mates would laugh at you. People would look at me like I'm a cradle snatcher or something.'

Jack's breath came out in a huff of laughter. 'You're kidding, right? You know how hard it is to find somebody that you feel like this about? What the hell do a few years' difference in age make? Age is just a number. And who cares what anybody else thinks, anyway?'

Harriet couldn't look away from those dark eyes. He really believed this. Other people probably did, too. She could almost hear the echo of May's voice at the back of her head saying exactly what Jack had just said. That age was just a number…

'Hey…when you're eighty-something and I'm only seventy-five, do you really think it's going to matter a damn?'

Now she couldn't breathe again. This was more than just sexual attraction Jack was talking about, wasn't it? Could he see them still being together when they were that old? Did he really see this as the start of…*for ever*?

Oh…*wow*… Yep. This was terrifying. But irresistible…

'But…but what about your family?'

'What about my family?' A frown creased Jack's brow. 'You didn't like them?'

'I loved them. They're the kind of family I would have dreamed of having as a kid. But…you introduced me as just a friend. They thought I was paying you for being my personal trainer.'

Jack laughed. 'If I'd introduced you in any way that made you more significant than a friend, they would have been planning our wedding before the birthday cake got cut. They've been waiting for me to find a proper girlfriend for so long that I think they believe it's never going to happen.'

A proper girlfriend? A significant relationship?

'Oh… *Jack*…' A part of Harriet's brain was making a final search to find another way to stop this roller-coaster and keep them both safe from any kind of heartbreak. But he hadn't said that he was in love with her and she hadn't said anything like that either. Surely any relationship had to start somewhere so that you could find out where it might lead? She could actually feel the moment when her brain simply gave up and shut some internal door in her head.

This was happening. Whether this was the real thing or simply physical attraction or gratitude or whatever, she couldn't stop it. She didn't *want* to stop it.

Apparently Jack could feel that door closing as well. Because he was smiling again. Drawing Harriet back into the circle of his arms. Kissing her forehead and then the tip of her nose before his lips settled once again onto hers. And this time there was no soft conversation of questions and answers. They had both willingly climbed instantly onto a new kind of roller-coaster that was purely physical for the moment. A steep climb as increasing desire made this so urgent and a wild descent into bliss as skin was exposed and touched in ways that made intimacy feel completely new.

'Not here…' Jack's voice was raw as he finally held Harriet away from his body.

'I know…' Harriet dragged in a ragged breath. 'They'll be expecting us back at the party.'

But Jack was smiling. 'I didn't mean that… I'm thinking about sand. You know…getting into uncomfortable places. And…protection. It didn't occur to me to put anything in my pocket for the ceremony.'

Harriet actually blushed. And she was supposed to be the older, wiser one here?

'Nobody's expecting to see us before the big breakfast tomorrow. They think you got tired because of your leg.' Jack brushed her cheek with his fingers. 'You're not, are you? Too tired?'

Harriet took a slow breath. 'I've never been less tired in my life.'

Jack took hold of her hand. 'See that path over there? Through the gardens?'

'Mmm?'

'That leads straight to my bungalow.'

Harriet started taking a step forward but Jack's hold on her hand stopped her. A beat of fear that he might be having second thoughts vanished as she caught the mischievous gleam in his eyes.

'You forgot your sandals.'

CHAPTER SEVEN

'So, HOW WAS IT? Your first day back in ICU?'

'Long…'

Harriet settled back in her armchair, still smiling. She hadn't expected a call from Jack while he was on shift and just the sound of his voice gave her a delicious tingle deep in her belly.

They'd been on the same flight back from Hamilton Island yesterday and Jack had insisted on sharing her taxi to make sure she got home safely. He hadn't left her apartment until many hours later.

Harriet would have sworn that nothing could have been better than the first time she and Jack had made love but, unbelievably, this second time had been so much better. Any shyness or residual doubts about the wisdom of starting this relationship were almost forgotten already. This was an unexpected gift in her life and it would be crazy not to accept it. And maybe it wouldn't last because one of them would come to their senses or hit the wall as far as trust was concerned but, while it was happening, she had no choice but to revel in the joy it was bringing. She was almost drowning in it, to be honest.

'I hope they didn't have you running around too much.'

The note of concern in Jack's voice changed that tingle into a squeezing sensation that seemed to involve her heart. Did men realise how incredibly sexy it was to say something that suggested they really cared about you? Not that she was going to tell him how it made her feel. Or that the happiness she was basking in, thanks to their lovemaking, had definitely done wonders for her energy levels today.

'I think I was given the easiest patient there. A sixty-four-year-old woman with diabetic ketoacidosis. She just needed intensive monitoring while we got her blood sugar levels under control.'

'What caused the DKA?'

'She thinks she got food poisoning. She lives alone and was too sick to even think about taking her insulin. She could have died if her neighbour hadn't got worried about her.'

'Was she conscious?'

'Yes, but I had to do a neurological assessment every hour. Along with measuring her blood glucose level and hydration and keeping a close watch on her ECG. She was getting some atrial arrhythmias.'

'So you were on your feet all day?'

'Pretty much. I'm tired now but it was so good to be back. I'm so happy…'

'I'm happy for you.' She could hear the smile in his voice.

'So, what are you up to?'

'Not much right now and we're due to clock off in twenty minutes or so. We've only had a couple of call-outs. Car crash up north a bit and a kid in respiratory arrest from an asthma attack who was more than an hour's drive from the nearest hospital. He'll be in the paediatric ICU now.'

'You got him back? From a respiratory arrest?'

'He didn't arrest until we were en route. It was touch and go. You have to be so careful ventilating someone like that so you don't cause lung damage.'

'Sounds like a tough job.'

'I thought the worst part was that his mum didn't get to the school in time to come with us, but it was probably better that she didn't see how close a call it was. He was properly ventilated mechanically by the time she got to the hospital.'

'Is he going to be okay?'

'They think so.'

'Go you.' Harriet's breath came out in a small sigh. 'You're a hero.'

The chuckle of laughter was soft. 'Hardly. Just doing my job. But it's nice that you think so. What are you up to this evening?'

'Hot bath,' she told him. 'And an early night. My shift starts at six a.m. tomorrow.'

'When's your next day off?'

'Friday. How 'bout you?'

'Also Friday. How good is that?'

'It's very good.'

But the fact that it seemed a rather long time to have to wait to see Jack again was a bit worrying. Was she throwing herself in too deep and too fast to whatever this was? Being a little needy?

'We should plan something.' She kept her tone light. Casual, even. 'If you're not busy, that is.'

'I'll make sure I'm not busy.'

The promise in his voice made her smile again but

then she heard the strident beeping over the line that could only be Jack's pager sounding.

'Uh-oh... Have to go.'

For a long minute Harriet simply held her phone in her hand after the abrupt termination of the call. She could imagine Jack and the rest of the crew running out to the helicopter, putting their helmets on and buckling into their harnesses, the way he would have done that day he'd arrived to get her and Eddie off that ledge.

They only got called to serious cases so it was highly likely he was on the way to save another life.

He was a hero all right...

The sun was low enough to make the distant Blue Mountains look even more rugged and beautiful. It was a favourite destination for Jack because it often involved a winching job but this time it sounded as if there was a clear space to land near the mountain bike track where a young man had had a serious tumble. That the job might not be as much of a challenge wasn't what was dimming any adrenaline rush right now, though.

Normally, a late job that meant their shift could run on for even a couple of extra hours wouldn't bother Jack at all. It might mean he'd miss a session at the gym or be late for a family dinner but everybody knew how passionate he was about his job so it didn't matter.

It felt different now. Even though Harriet was tired after her first day back at her old job and he wouldn't have suggested a visit or a date or anything, his time away from work had suddenly become a whole lot more important.

His job wasn't the only thing he was passionate about now.

He couldn't stop thinking about Harriet. This destination of the Blue Mountains was taking him back to that dreadful day when she'd had the accident. He would never forget how it had made him feel to see her lying there with her leg all but crushed by that rock. He almost felt responsible, because he'd seen that she'd been standing too close to the path of that rockfall. He'd shouted a warning, even gone closer to grab her hand and encourage her to run to safety, but she'd tripped on the uneven ground and her hand had pulled away as she'd fallen and his momentum had carried him forward for too many steps. If only he'd been a few seconds earlier. Or had held onto her hand more tightly...

But if he had, life would be very different now, wouldn't it? It could well have been Harriet and Pete's wedding he'd been attending the other day, instead of Blake and Sam's.

And that would have been so wrong. Another memory of the day of that accident was how frustrated he'd felt. Harriet's distress had felt like physical pain for him, too, but there'd been nothing he could do to help, other than offer to take Blake's motorbike back to the city. Pete had been the one who should have been trying to comfort her but all he'd done was sit there and pat her shoulder occasionally and he'd actually looked relieved when she'd asked Sam to go with her in the chopper. What had that been about? It certainly wasn't the kind of concern and care you would want from the person you were planning to spend the rest of your life with.

But she'd been in love with him. She would have

stayed in that relationship if he hadn't walked out on her, wouldn't she? Even now, she believed that she was the one who needed to apologise. What the heck was that all about?

'ETA ten minutes.' The pilot's voice cut into his memories and Jack forced himself to focus.

'Can you find out if the patient's still conscious?' The information they had so far was that the bike rider had come off at speed, landed on rocks and was having trouble breathing.

The pilot radioed through for the link to people on the ground.

'He's drowsy,' he reported back to the crew a short time later. 'And confused. Doesn't know where he is or what day it is.'

'Sounds like head as well as chest injuries,' Matt said. 'Let's hope we do have a spot to land and don't need to set up for winching.'

Jack nodded but, as he turned to look out of the window again, his brain was already straying back to Harriet. To winching her off that ledge—the first time he'd ever been that close to her body.

He'd been a hell of lot closer in the last couple of days.

That first kiss had been everything—and more— that he'd ever dreamed it could be. All it had taken was that first touch of her lips beneath his own to make him realise that he'd been kidding himself that he'd got over that crush long ago. That he'd accepted that Harriet Collins was completely out of his league and, even if she hadn't been older and part of a cooler social set, she was so much in love with someone else he would never have stood a chance.

He'd actually been in love with her for the best part of the last two years, hadn't he? That was why he could never find a connection with any other woman that interested him for more than a date or two.

Not that he could tell her any of that. It was way too soon.

She'd had her own doubts about them being together like this and he understood. The age thing, anyway. He knew his family would accept her with open arms and who could resist an invitation to be a part of a huge and supportive family, even if they might drive you crazy sometimes? Especially someone who had never had that as a child. That was a gift he could provide that meant she would never have to feel lonely again.

No...what really held him back was that part of him still wondered if he was going to be enough for Harriet. If, somewhere in the unforeseeable future, another rejection might be waiting for him? One that would be infinitely worse than a request for a date being dismissed as nothing more than a gesture of friendship.

It wouldn't be the first time either. There'd been a girl he'd been close to, back at university but she'd broken off their relationship when someone more exciting had come along.

'You're such a lovely guy, Jack. I love you to bits... as a friend...'

How could he compete with even the memory of someone who'd been the poster boy for the fire service? The first one to be picked for their famous yearly calendars? He'd seen one of those shots of Pete, with his uniform pants unbuttoned, held up only by suspenders over a bronzed, bodybuilder's bare chest. He'd been holding a kitten or puppy or something and that sun-streaked blond hair had oozed a beachy surfer vibe. He could imagine how many women had envied Harriet.

'Target sighted, four o'clock,' Matt said.

The helicopter dipped and turned and, this time, Jack managed to push any thoughts of Harriet firmly into the background. Only time would tell if this miraculous new connection would become solid enough to trust that he was enough for her. And he could take it as slowly as he needed to. He'd waited this long so it would be a huge mistake to rush things.

At least he knew he had everything needed to do this job well. And someone was waiting for them who needed their help. And there it was, finally. The adrenaline rush of potentially being about to save a life.

'So he had a flail chest and a haemopneumothorax that was starting to tension and we had to get a chest drain in as soon as possible but his head injury was bad enough to be making him really combative.'

'Did you sedate him?' Harriet had stopped eating her lunch, a forkful of salad poised halfway to her mouth.

'He would have been another respiratory arrest to cope with if we hadn't. It was a full-on job, that's for sure. I went for a run when I finally got home, just to unwind.'

'A soak in the bath works wonders for me.' Harriet was eating again. Enjoying this lunch in one of her favourite beachside cafes. Enjoying being with Jack again after the pressures of their work had separated them for days. 'I've needed a few of those this week.'

'But you've done it. You've managed your first full week back in ICU. How's the leg holding up?'

'Better than I expected.' But Harriet made a face. 'Don't think I'll be running any time soon, though.'

'Never say never.'

'You're right. Six months ago I would never have believed I could walk down the aisle with Sam without a brace, let alone without even limping. Oh…she's sent me through some of the first photos.' She pushed her plate to one side and reached for her phone. 'Some of them are gorgeous. Look…'

That wonderful day on Hamilton Island had been special enough because it had been the wedding of two of their closest friends, but because it now also marked the beginning of what they had between them, it was so much more significant.

Jack stared at one of the images for the longest time. The one that had been taken with the men holding the women in their arms, a breaking wave rolling over their feet. It was *such* a happy photo. Sam had her arms wound around Blake's neck and she was laughing up at him, clearly so much in love. But Harriet also had her arms around Jack's neck, looking up at him, and she must have been laughing as well. None of them were looking at the camera. Blake was smiling down at Sam. And Jack…oh, wow…the way he was looking at her. How could she not have known that what had happened late that night had been inevitable?

'This one,' Jack said, his voice a little hoarse. 'I'm going to keep this one beside my bed.' He winked at Harriet. 'After I crop out the bride and groom.'

He held her gaze a moment longer. Opened his mouth as if he was about to say something else but then paused as if he was changing his mind.

'It was the best day,' he finally said, quietly. 'I'll never forget it.'

Harriet took her phone back to cover a beat of disappointment. Instinct told her that Jack had been about to say something very different. A lot more significant but he'd decided against it.

Because it was too soon? Because neither of them could know if this astonishing feeling of connection was going to last or whether it was just a friendship that had slipped into something more?

'They're due back from their honeymoon tomorrow.' Harriet kept her tone light. 'I hope they've had an amazing time.'

'I'm sure they have. Maybe I'll see Blake at the gym this week and we can shoot a few hoops.' He raised an eyebrow. 'He'll be ready to think about the team again by then. When he knows that you're back on deck in the ICU, I reckon he'll agree it's time you came back on the team properly.'

Harriet caught her breath. 'Do you think? Do you really think I could do it—without risking being a problem for everybody else?'

'I know you can.' Jack reached out and put his hand over hers and squeezed it. 'Look how far you've come already.'

'I know I can walk well. And swim. But I don't think I can run. And I haven't even tried climbing properly.'

'Then let's work on that together. Some walks with a little bit of jogging to start with. Some easy work on the climbing wall at the gym.'

He was back in his very personal trainer mode. Was this the real bond between them? The only bond apart from the intense physical attraction? It wasn't disappointment that ambushed Harriet this time. It was more like…fear.

She swallowed whatever it was. 'Let's do that,' she said. 'Let's start this afternoon. And then…maybe we can go back to my place and…um…have dinner?'

'Oh, we'll have something all right.' Jack's smile told her that food was a very unimportant item on the agenda. He gave her hand another squeeze and then let go, tilting his head to peer under the table. 'You're wearing your trainers. Let's head somewhere nice and see what your leg thinks about a very gentle re-introduction to jogging.'

'I'm up for it.' Harriet slipped her phone—and those photos—back into her bag. 'But don't say anything to Blake yet, okay? Not until I'm sure I'm ready.'

It was nearly a month before Harriet felt she was nearly ready to put her hand up to be on the team again.

A month where she and Jack had been spending more and more of any free time they had together. Time when they were learning that, despite any difference in their ages or backgrounds, they had more in common than they might have believed.

'You like rom coms? No way… I would have guessed action movies for sure. Testosterone and guns.'

'I like them, too. But I grew up with a bunch of sisters, don't forget. I got outvoted every time it was movie night at home.'

Their beach walk that day, with some jogging on firm sand, had become a competition to identify the best romantic movie they had ever seen and the arguments, punctuated by a lot of laughter, had made it so much easier to cope with any pain from pushing herself physically.

Eating together became a real pleasure as they discovered they loved the same kind of food, especially the less healthy treats. Hot, crusty bread with butter and raspberry jam. Fish and chips. Chocolate fudge brownie ice cream.

'We'll have to do twice as much jogging this week, babe...'

And as for the sex...

It took only a look to ignite a desire that seemed to be growing instead of being slaked. Just a touch or maybe a lick to change the pace from a deliciously slow exploration to an urgent need to reach that point of absolute bliss as soon as possible. The time after that was even better, in a very different way, when they could lie together, skin to skin, with their limbs tangled, and they could just breathe and feel the beat of each other's hearts.

That had become the time that Harriet loved the most. The place she would choose above anything else if she needed to feel protected.

Loved.

But while Jack told her in a dozen different ways, through his touch or his thoughtfulness or even simply his smile, how much he cared about her, he'd never actually said the words. Neither had Harriet but it didn't seem to matter. They were together and their bond was getting stronger every day. They hadn't advertised their relationship in any way but it was only a matter of time before others were aware that this was a great deal more than friendship. And maybe it was something that needed to happen slowly so that people got used to it and nobody would say anything that had the potential to dislodge the foundations of what they were building around them.

'What's going on with you two?'

'Huh?' Jack didn't take his eyes off Harriet. She was several metres off the ground and the next hold on the wall was one she needed to access with her left foot. It was a good-sized boulder but this was still going to be a real test of whether she could trust the damaged muscles in her leg to take enough of her weight. She was safe enough, of course. As a certified climbing wall instructor, Jack had tied her into her harness himself, with a figure-eight follow-through knot. He was clipped to a floor anchor and he had control of her ropes as her belayer.

'We're just doing a bit of training,' he added. 'Harry's giving the orange route a go tonight.' He was giving her a little rope with his guide hand as he spoke, his other hand ready to act as the brake in an instant, to limit the distance she could fall if she missed her footing. Or her leg wasn't up to this new challenge.

'I'm not talking about the climbing,' Blake murmured. 'I was watching you when you were getting ready and... I dunno... I got the feeling there's something going on.'

Jack said nothing. He was too focused on what Harriet was doing to respond anyway.

'Keep your arm straight,' he called. 'Find your centre of gravity and keep it close to the wall. Step with your toes and push off with your leg, don't pull with your arms.' He held his breath for a moment as her foot landed on the boulder and Harriet twisted a little to stay balanced. He could feel his own muscles tightening as he willed her leg to be strong enough to push her upwards and he let out a huff of breath as she succeeded.

He adjusted the ropes he was holding once again. 'Keep going, babe. You're doing great...'

'*Babe*...?' He could hear Blake's grin around the word. 'I *knew* it... You and Harry, huh?'

'Yeah...' Jack slid a quick sideways glance at his friend. 'Me and Harry.' His tone was almost a challenge but their relationship couldn't be used as an excuse not to let Harriet back on the team, could it? Not when Blake and Sam had hooked up to the ultimate degree and were both still team members.

Blake shook his head. 'Should've seen that coming, I guess. What with all the time you two have been spending together lately.' He was still grinning. 'Puts a whole new spin on personal training...'

'That's all it was to start with.' Jack was watching Harriet again as he handled the ropes. She was almost at the top and had to be tired but she was smashing this challenge. The way she had with pretty much every challenge he'd ever seen her take on.

And he was so proud of her he could burst.

'How 'bout that?' he said, as Harriet let out a whoop of triumph on reaching the last set of holds. 'Is she awesome, or what?'

'Amazing,' Blake agreed. He waved at Harriet as she relaxed into her harness, enjoying her success before starting her descent. 'I can't believe how well she's managed to rehabilitate herself.'

'Hey, Jack?' Harriet called. 'I'm ready to come down now.'

He gave her the rope she needed slowly and steadily.

'She's ready for more than this,' he told Blake. 'She's ready to come back on board for the team.'

Harriet landed on the floor and began to unclip herself from the ropes.

'It's lucky you're here to see this,' Jack added as he moved towards her to help. 'Maybe you can invite her back yourself and save her having to ask.'

Blake made a grunting sound but he stayed where he was, watching as Jack helped pack up the gear they'd been using. Then he walked towards them.

'Looking good, Harry,' he said. 'Well done.'

'I know, right?' Harriet was beaming. 'I can't believe I just did that.' Her gaze swerved to Jack and he knew he was smiling just as hard. 'You were right... I *can* do it.'

Jack turned his head and raised an eyebrow at Blake to go with his pointed look.

Blake cleared his throat. 'Reckon it's time we had you back on board for the team,' he said. 'If you want to be.'

Harriet's grin faded until her face was as serious as Jack had ever seen it. Her eyes were still shining but he suspected it could be from an unshed tear or two. He could feel a bit of lump in his own throat. How amazing was this, to see the person you loved this much achieving a huge milestone towards being the person they most wanted to be?

Harriet didn't say anything, she simply nodded.

'There's a team meeting next Wednesday, then,' he added. 'And make sure you've got your pager with you from now on.' Blake made it sound as if a callout could happen at any moment. Which, of course, it could. 'Jack? You fancy shooting a few hoops before you go?'

'Next time, mate.' Jack looped his arm around Harriet's shoulders. 'We've got a spot of celebrating to do right now.'

It was Blake's turn to raise an eyebrow. 'Sam thinks you guys are just good friends,' he muttered. 'How come she doesn't know about the benefits bit?'

Harriet was smiling again. 'I haven't seen her for a while. She's too wrapped up in being a new wife, I think. Tell her I'll call her soon.'

Jack picked up the coils of rope and the harnesses and led the way to the equipment room. Was that all this was as far as Harriet was concerned? A friendship... with *benefits*?

Maybe it was time to tell her how he really felt. But what if it was too soon? The seed of doubt was disturbing but undeniable. Harriet hadn't even told her best friend what was going on yet and Jack knew that girls spent an awful lot of time discussing important emotional stuff. Had she not told Sam because it wasn't important enough yet? Because she wasn't sure that what he could offer was as much as Pete had given her?

It was getting harder to close down the urge to push things forward but Jack knew he had to try. This was too important to risk damaging.

CHAPTER EIGHT

LIFE WAS ALMOST back to normal.

But everything felt so very different.

The ache in her leg was so familiar now that it was just a part of day-to-day reality. Soaking it in a fragrant, hot bath at the end of a long day had become one of life's new pleasures.

With a deep sigh, Harriet rested her head against the back of the bathtub and closed her eyes. She needed to make the most of tonight's soak because she wouldn't get one tomorrow with the team meeting being the focus of the evening.

Yes…everything was the same, but different. A year ago she'd thought she'd had everything she wanted in her life. A job she loved, the added excitement of being part of the SDR team, great friends and a relationship that seemed to be heading for forever. But life could change in a heartbeat, couldn't it?

Even now, she could relive that instant in time when her life had been shattered so convincingly. Standing at the bottom of that cliff on a team training day, having completed her abseil some time ago, she was watching Sam take on the challenge. Holding her breath, because she really wanted her friend to ace this and get to achieve her dream of being accepted into the team. She'd actually seen the moment that rockfall had started and she'd been terrified that one of those boulders was going to hit Sam as it bounced down the cliff. And then she'd heard the warning shout and Jack had grabbed her arm and then her hand and he had tried to pull her to safety. She'd tried to run but… she'd tripped, ripping her hand from Jack's grip, and she'd fallen and…

Harriet's eyes snapped open. The jolt of pain that had just flashed from her ankle right up to her back had to be imaginary. Just a nightmarish flashback. She hadn't thought about the day of the accident with a clarity like this in months. She'd almost forgotten that it had been Jack who'd tried to save her.

She'd never thanked him for that, had she? The time between the rock hitting her and waking up after her surgery was a bit of a blur but she knew she'd been looking for the people that mattered most to be with her. Pete. And Sam. That Jack had now become the most important person in her life was a twist of fate that would have been unimaginable that day.

But it was also one of life's new pleasures.

No…it was way more than that.

The pieces of her life had been put back together. She was coping with her beloved job in the ICU and now had the excitement of knowing that she would be part of the next callout for the SDR team, but her relationship wasn't simply a bonus. It had been Jack's support—his belief in her—that had made it all possible.

She wouldn't be the person she was right now if she didn't have Jack in her life. And she couldn't imagine life without him in it.

He was working on the road tonight but maybe he would call her later, if his crew got a quiet spell between calls. Maybe she would tell him that she'd remembered how he'd tried to save her that day and thank him. Tell him that, while she hadn't had a clue at the time, it was one of the things she loved about him.

Or maybe not...

He had to be the one to say it first, didn't he?

Why? Because that would give her the confidence to take that final leap of faith? To let her get rid of the fear that giving someone that kind of trust was too much of a risk?

Jack would be taking a risk as well. Blake had certainly seemed surprised the other night at the gym when he'd realised that there was more than friendship going on between her and Jack. Did that have something to do with the age difference? He didn't believe it was serious either, or why would he have made that comment about it being a 'friendship with benefits'? Jack hadn't said anything to dismiss that idea and it seemed like they'd both simply pushed it out of sight and out of mind for the rest of the evening, as they'd celebrated her renewed status as a member of Bondi Bayside's SDR team.

It was coming back to haunt her now, though. As much as any memories of the accident did. Was that how Jack saw their relationship? Had he just been a bit carried away by the moment, after that first kiss, when he'd said that the gap in their ages wouldn't matter a damn when they were old and grey?

No. He'd also said that his family would be thrilled to know he had a 'proper' girlfriend, and he'd been right. Only last night they'd been to have dinner with his older sister, Talia, her husband Mark and their three gorgeous small children, who'd cuddled up to their Uncle Jack and accepted their new 'Aunty Harry' without a beat of hesitation.

There'd been a moment when Talia had been busy with something in the kitchen and Mark had gone to get some beers from the fridge in the garage, having handed the youngest of his offspring, Minny—the cutest six-month-old ever—to Jack. Harriet had had to shuffle over to make room for the baby's siblings, who'd crowded onto the small couch to join them and share in the cuddles.

They'd all been laughing as Talia had poked her head through the door to see what the commotion was all about. She'd laughed as well.

'Suits you,' she'd said. And then she'd disappeared into the kitchen again. 'You may as well get used to it, I guess.'

Jack had caught her gaze and he'd wiggled his eyebrows and she had grinned back even though she'd been trying to gently extract some small sticky fingers from her hair.

Of course they both saw kids in their future. It was a question of 'when', not 'if'. And how beautiful would those babies be, with Jack as their father?

But he was only twenty-eight. It could be years before he felt ready for that role. And Harriet was thirty-four, nearly thirty-five. Was that hollow feeling in the pit of her stomach, as she remembered the moment, her biological clock starting to tick? It was probably true that this kind of age gap meant nothing when you were older but they were at a stage of their lives when it could create an issue and put pressure on a relationship.

Harriet sat up and pulled the plug from her bath. The water was getting cool but she had no desire to top it up. To do so would invite tapping even deeper into those insecurities she'd never quite squashed about the wisdom of allowing this relationship to develop. The bottom line was that she would trust Jack with her life.

Maybe she just needed to start trusting him with her heart as well.

'So…you and Jack…' Sam had waited only until Blake and Jack headed to the bar to get their drinks and some snacks before grinning at Harriet. 'When were you going to tell me?'

'We haven't spent any time together since you got back from your honeymoon.'

'I know… I'm sorry. I'm a bad friend. But not as bad as you, keeping a secret like this. I do still have a phone, you know.'

'I know. And I'm sorry. I guess I was waiting to see if it was really going to last.'

'Why wouldn't it? He's obviously crazy about you.' Sam lowered her voice. 'And he's gorgeous.' She cast a glance over her shoulder to check that the men were still in the queue. 'So when did it start?'

'Um…' Harriet almost blushed. 'At your wedding…'

Sam gasped. 'No way…you mean when you disappeared and were worried about your leg and I sent Jack to try and find you?'

'Mmm…' Harriet couldn't help smiling. 'He found me.'

'And I didn't suspect a thing at breakfast the next day. I can't believe you didn't tell me.'

'It felt a bit weird for a while,' Harriet confessed. 'You know…with the age difference.'

'Oh, *pfft*…' Sam made a dismissive movement with her hand. 'If the age gap was the other way around, nobody would blink an eye, would they?'

'I guess not.' Harriet tilted her head to warn Sam that their drinks were on the way.

'Anyway. I'm thrilled. Couldn't happen to two nicer people. I'm so happy for you.'

'Happy about what?' Blake put a glass of wine in front of Sam. Jack was carrying one for Harriet.

'That Harry's back on the team, of course.' She caught her husband's look and her lips twitched. 'Okay… I'm also happy to have it confirmed that Harry and Jack are an item.' She raised her glass in a toast and then grinned at Blake. 'Are you making an announcement under "new business" at the meeting tonight?'

He laughed. 'Only if Jack and Harry really want me to.'

Jack's gaze caught Harriet's. There was laughter in his eyes but a question as well. About whether she was ready for the whole world to know how they felt about each other. The warmth in this look suggested that he was more than ready and Harriet felt suddenly completely confident. In him. In *them*. In their future.

'Why not?' she said, holding his gaze.

'Ah…because we have actual team business to deal with?' Blake shook his head. 'And I don't want word to get around that the SDR is really a secret dating agency.'

The sound of laughter faded as Harriet dropped her gaze, cringing just a little. Had Blake forgotten about her and Pete? They'd been an item within a week of him joining the team.

Fortunately, the arrival of their bar snacks diverted everybody.

'We don't have much time,' Blake warned, passing a basket of tiny spring rolls and samosas, along with their dipping sauces. 'I need to be back in twenty minutes to set up for the meeting.'

As usual, it was Blake who was chairing the Specialist Disaster Response team meeting.

The room, not far from the theatre suite at Bondi Bayside, was often used for staff meetings or visiting speakers and it had the benefit of tiered seating and a screen for data projection. It was an easy venue for all the medics involved with the team who were available on any given evening but it was also open to interested people from the emergency services they worked closely with, like the fire service and ambulance.

Harriet and Jack chose seats together quite high in the room and Sam sat beside Harriet.

'First order of new business,' Blake said after welcoming the group, 'is that we have a potential new member. I'd like to welcome Tim Schofield to the meeting.'

A man in the front row raised his hand and there was a polite round of handclapping.

'Many of you know Tim as one of our best anaesthetists,' Blake continued, 'and he's keen to come to our next training session to see if he's up for the challenge of joining us. Please give him any encouragement because it would be a major asset to have him on board. It would give us a valuable resource for the kind of pre-hospital surgical trauma management that's usually beyond our current scope, especially in an isolated environment.'

Blake was scanning the upper rows now and he smiled as he caught sight of Harriet.

'Next bit of news concerns someone we all know and love,' he said. 'Welcome back, Harry. I know I'm not the only person here who's delighted that you're back up to speed.'

Harriet ducked her head, not having expected the attention. She felt Jack's hand cover hers and give it a squeeze and, for an uncomfortable moment, she wondered if Blake was going to say something about her and Jack once this new round of applause died down.

The clapping was more enthusiastic this time, accompanied by a cheer or two, and every head turned to look up at Harriet.

Which was probably why nobody noticed the door at the front opening. Or that a latecomer was approaching Blake.

'Sorry I'm late, mate,' he said. 'I'm still getting the team emails so I figured I'd still be welcome.'

Blake's mouth opened and then shut.

Sam turned to look at Harriet, her eyes wide with what looked like shock, and, in the same instant, Harriet felt Jack's hand go rigid over hers and then slide free.

'Did you *know*?' Sam whispered. 'That Pete was back?'

'Of course not,' Harriet muttered.

Heads were turning again but the expressions on people's faces were very different from those of a moment ago.

Her ex had just walked back into her life and everybody was curious about what her reaction might be.

Shock. That's what it was.

She sat there, unable to move even her line of sight, which was unfortunate because that was filled by Pete, as he walked towards an empty seat in the front row.

He looked exactly the same as ever. Tall, blond, confident...

What was he doing back in Sydney?

Back at a team meeting?

The joy of having just been welcomed back herself had been hijacked. Had it only been less than an hour ago that she'd felt such a blast of confidence about her relationship with Jack? She could feel how tense he was now. As frozen as she was herself. What was he thinking—that she was comparing him to her previous partner and that he was coming up short?

Tilting her body slightly, she pressed her arm against Jack's and, a heartbeat later, she felt him relax a little. Pete was sitting down now and all that she could see was the back of his head with its spiky, blond streaks. Blake had turned to pick up the remote control for the data projector.

'Knowing that we were going to have Tim here, and that there are some of us who've been absent for a while, I thought that a good topic for our professional development this month was a bit of a revision of the purpose of this team.'

Harriet tried to focus. Blake had known that she was coming back but had he had any idea of Pete's intention to return? Surely not, or he wouldn't have joked about making a public announcement about her and Jack. He would have warned her. They all knew how devastating it had been when Pete had backed away from their relationship in the wake of her accident. When he'd moved out of her apartment. When he'd hooked up with someone new and finally left town.

She might be completely over Pete but echoes of the old feelings were still there. Anxiety. Fear. Rejection. Loneliness. Anger…

Baggage, that's what it was. And she wasn't the only person who was going to have to deal with it. Jack would have his own feelings about it all. Maybe he was thinking about the way his offer of support had been rejected back in those early days after the accident, when all she'd wanted had been for Pete to demonstrate that he'd really cared.

A slide had appeared on the big screen at the front of the room as the lights had dimmed a little. Blake's voice was calm.

'The World Health Organization defines a disaster as an event when "normal conditions of existence are disrupted and the level of suffering exceeds the capacity of the hazard-affected community to respond to it".' Blake clicked his laser pointer. 'An MCI, or Multiple Casualty Incident, is more common and is defined as a situation that places a significant demand on medical resources and personnel.'

He glanced at Tim the anaesthetist. 'Our Specialist Disaster Response team can—and does—respond to both disasters and MCIs, a recent example being the callout to that landslide that buried the ski village. There's a fine line between disasters and MCIs and our objective is always the same. To get the best possible patient outcomes for the greatest number of victims.'

Harriet had heard all about that disaster callout to

the landslide from both Sam and Kate, who'd still been her neighbour at the time. More than she'd wanted to hear, in fact, because she'd still been in the mindset of having lost the most important things in her life. Her job, her place on the team. Pete…

The days before she'd reconnected with Jack. Before he'd helped her regain everything that she'd lost. She leaned into him again, and this time his hand slid back to catch hers and her breath escaped in a small, relieved sigh. It was going to be all right. Wasn't it? Every relationship got tested at some point and this situation looked like it was setting itself up to be their test.

She just had to convince Jack that Pete was part of the past. He was unimportant and he couldn't threaten what they had.

'Are you sure you're okay?'

'Of course.' Harriet was kneeling in front of the coffee table in her living room. She'd spread out the handouts Blake had provided at the end of the meeting, along with sample triage tags. She seemed to be comparing the algorithms for two of the major international triage protocols. 'START is easier to remember,' she said. 'Simple Triage and Rapid Treatment. SALT is a bit more complicated, isn't it? Sort and Assess, Life-saving interventions and Treatment-slash-Transport.'

'They reckon it helps the problem of over-triaging.' Jack sank onto the couch behind Harriet. 'And giving people a higher priority than they should get.' He didn't want to discuss triaging patients. There was a far more important aspect of tonight's meeting that they needed to talk about as far as he was concerned.

'I had a word with Pete when the meeting broke up,'

he said carefully. 'He's moved back to Sydney, to his old job with the fire service. He wants to be put back on the active roster for the SDR.'

He saw the way Harriet's shoulders moved as she shrugged. 'I guess it's up to Blake whether that happens.'

'Blake asked me how I thought you'd feel about it. He's not the most popular person in these parts, you know. After the way he treated you.'

'It's history, Jack. I don't care what he does.' Harriet scooped up the coloured tags and turned to hand them to Jack. 'Can you test me on these? I want to make sure I remember this stuff.'

How could she simply dismiss the fact that Pete Thompson had come back as if it meant nothing? Did she not want to talk about it because she knew he wouldn't like what she had to say?

He stared at the tags in his hand as he tried to collect his thoughts and then chose the red one.

'Priority One.' Harriet nodded. 'Immediate attention needed. In the global sorting on arrival at a scene, they're the ones who don't walk or wave when asked to move. They don't move at all.'

She wasn't looking at the handout. Harriet knew this stuff.

'Individual assessment?'

'They're breathing, after any lifesaving interventions that are needed, like opening the airway, controlling major haemorrhage and chest decompression.'

'And what else?'

'Level of consciousness—do they obey commands or make purposeful movements?' Harriet was checking off points on her fingers. 'Do they have a peripheral pulse? Major haemorrhage is controlled and they're not in severe respiratory distress.'

'And if any of those things are negative?'

Harriet's face was grim. 'You have to decide whether they're likely to survive given the current resources. If they are, they keep the red tag. If not, they get a black tag which is "expectant" or no priority.'

Jack nodded. The black tag meant a person was either dead or expected to be dead soon.

Harriet was looking expectant right now, waiting for him to test her knowledge on the yellow tags for delayed treatment or the green ones for people with minor injuries that only needed eventual treatment, but Jack didn't want to play this game any more. The knot in his gut was getting tighter.

He dropped the cards. 'You don't need to do this, Harry. You know it. Talk to me instead.'

'What about?'

'You know what we need to talk about. Pete.'

Her face looked pale, making those gorgeous hazel eyes look huge. 'You don't have to worry about Pete,' she said quietly. 'Yes, it was a shock to see him again like that but it's over, Jack. It was over a long time ago.' She offered him a tentative smile. 'That relationship gets a black tag.'

Harriet was on her knees now, close enough to raise her face for a kiss, and Jack didn't hesitate to lower his head and oblige.

But it felt different somehow. This wasn't a kiss that was about to ignite the kind of passion they had both become accustomed to. He could actually feel a tiny tremble in her lips that told him she was a lot more emotional than she was prepared to admit. She wasn't being entirely honest with him, was she?

He wasn't convinced about the black tag idea for Harriet's relationship with Pete either. She had avoided talking to her ex tonight, other than giving him a cool nod. She hadn't seen the way his gaze had followed her around the room as she'd caught up with other team members and introduced herself to Tim. Maybe she didn't know yet that Pete had decided to come back to Sydney because his relationship with Sharleen had ended. What if lifesaving interventions were attempted, on his part, and the item that had been Harriet and Pete was given a red tag instead? The possibility of survival?

Old insecurities weren't that deeply buried yet. He'd always known he couldn't compete with what Pete had to offer. Not when it came to something like charisma. And Harriet had never told him that she loved him. Not with words, anyway.

Harriet was still looking up at him as their kiss ended. 'You going to stay tonight?'

He wanted to. But what if their lovemaking was tainted by bottled-up insecurities or emotions, like that kiss had just been, and it only made things worse? Jack needed to get his head around this. And he needed for Harriet not to look as if the shock waves hadn't worn off yet. Not to be trembling under his lips. And, more than anything else, he needed honesty from her.

'Are you sure?' he asked softly. 'That Pete's not a problem for you? For us?'

'I'm sure.' Her response was immediate. Too quick? 'Believe me—if I had a choice, I wouldn't even want to *see* him again.'

* * *

He was there.

Standing outside the main doors of Bondi Bayside. Clearly waiting for her.

'Go away, Pete,' Harriet snapped. 'I don't want to see you. I certainly don't want to talk to you.'

'I know. I get that.' But he fell into step with her as she headed for the main gates. 'I just want to say I'm sorry.'

Harriet ignored him and increased her pace. The sooner she got out of the hospital grounds the better. She didn't want to be here. Didn't want to be hearing his voice. Especially not with that note of sincerity in it.

Pete broke the silence as they reached the gates. 'I can't believe how well you're walking, Harry. How great you're *looking*. I was blown away to see that you were back on the team again. You'd never know that you almost lost your leg.'

That did it. She had become attractive to him again because she looked like she had nothing wrong with her any more? Because the trauma of the last, long months could simply be forgotten? Harriet stopped abruptly and rounded on him.

'Yeah…well, I *did* almost lose my leg.' Her voice was low and fierce. 'I almost lost everything that mattered to me.' Her breath came out in an angry huff. 'And I'm talking about my job and the SDR team, here. Not *you*. You couldn't even hang around long enough to find out if I *was* going to be okay.'

Pete took a step back, his face creased as if her words were painful.

'I know. I was a complete bastard. And I'm sorry. That's all I wanted to say. I freaked out, Harry. I couldn't handle it. You know what I'm like with medical stuff. That's why I became a firie and not a paramedic.'

Harriet blinked. Was he trying to compare himself to Jack? Had he heard already that she and Jack were together?

'I do care about you, Harry,' he added, his voice cracking. 'I know I didn't show it enough when we were together and I just want to make it up to you...' Harriet shook her head sharply. She didn't want to think about any of it. Didn't want to hear the emotion in Pete's voice that made him sound so genuine.

She turned away. 'I don't want to talk to you,' she said. 'Go home, Pete. Talk to Sharleen.'

She'd started walking but Pete's voice followed her.

'It's over with Sharleen,' he said, speaking fast. 'That's why I'm back. It was a terrible mistake and... and I was hoping that we could be friends, at least?'

Then he was right beside her again and this time he caught her arm and trying to shake it off didn't work.

'Please...?' He had his hands on both her arms now and his voice had slowed. 'I miss you, hon...'

He was smiling. Looking right into her eyes. Leaning down towards her in a way she remembered all too well. She knew he was going to try and kiss her and, to her horror, she almost let it happen. Because, for a heartbeat, it felt like she'd stepped back in time. That nothing had happened to change everything.

She jerked her head back, out of reach, just in time. 'Let go of me,' she snapped. 'I've moved on, Pete. I'm with someone else.'

'Who?'

He'd find out soon enough, wouldn't he? 'Not that it's any of your business but it's Jack.'

'Jack?' Pete looked bewildered. 'Jack *Evans*?'

'Yes.'

'But…but he's just a kid. One of the lads…' Pete's breath came out in a huff of laughter. 'You're having me on, aren't you?'

Harriet wrenched herself out of his grip.

'Leave me alone. It's over, Pete. It was over a very long time ago.'

'No…' He was shaking his head. 'It's not over… It'll never last—you and him… He'll find someone his own age…'

Harriet was already moving. Walking away from him so fast she was almost jogging. Trying to escape the kaleidoscope of emotions washing over her. That sincerity in Pete's voice. That moment when he'd almost kissed her. The way he'd tapped into one of her own fears about her relationship with Jack.

She was moving so fast that by the time she crossed the intersection near her apartment block her leg was dragging enough to make her limp.

Her spirits were, too.

She was over Pete Thompson. So why did she feel so churned up now?

Did it mean she did still have feelings for him, even if she didn't want to? She *had* been in love with him, once. He'd been the first person that she'd been willing to commit to spending the rest of her life with.

Did feelings like that ever go away completely? And if they did, did that mean she couldn't trust the way she felt about Jack?

She was very close to tears by the time she fitted

her key into her door. All she wanted right now was to hear Jack's voice but he was working. Probably in the sky somewhere in the middle of saving someone's life. Doing the medical stuff that freaked Pete out so much.

And how could she tell him what had just happened or how she was feeling, anyway? It wasn't just that he was seeing Pete as some kind of threat.

Was it because she wasn't yet really sure herself?

Not about whether she wanted to be with Pete or not. She was sure about that.

What she wasn't completely sure about was how Jack felt about her. Whether it was strong enough to crush any potential obstacles—one of which Pete had just reminded her of in no uncertain terms.

'It'll never last...

'He'll find someone his own age...'

CHAPTER NINE

HE COULDN'T JUST stand there, holding his car keys as if he'd forgotten what they were for.

Jack had a job to do. There was an overnight bag on the back seat that his sister, Talia, had hurriedly filled, in case his grandmother was going to be kept in overnight. She'd been the one to call the ambulance when Gran had collapsed. And then she'd called him and his boss had stepped in to cover the rest of his shift so that he could go to his family. He'd collected the bag on his way to the hospital. His mother and another sister were in Emergency with Gran but he hadn't had any update on her condition and he had been doing his best to get there as soon as possible.

But, right now, he was watching Harriet almost running down the street, leaving Pete Thompson standing almost as still as he was himself.

He'd seen them walking towards the gates as soon as he'd stepped out of his car. Had they planned to meet when Harriet had finished work?

It didn't look like it. If anything, it looked like they were having a row. Not that he was close enough to hear anything but Harriet had looked angry when she'd stopped and turned to speak to him.

The keys had dug into his palm as he'd curled his fist. Did she need help? The only thing that stopped him moving towards them was that Harriet was moving again herself. And then Pete caught up with her. He was holding her. Bending his head as if he was about to kiss her.

He couldn't move a muscle then. There was a bottomless pit where his stomach was supposed to be and it felt like he was falling into it.

Then he saw her jerk back and hope rushed in to fill the pit. She was almost running away from Pete. She hadn't wanted him to kiss her.

Except she had, hadn't she? As he watched Harriet rapidly disappearing along the street, his brain rewound that little scene in his head and, this time, he could see that moment of hesitation. Or feel it. And it felt like history was repeating itself, only with a lot more kick to it. He wasn't just asking her out on a date, he was in a relationship with her. And now Pete Thompson was back in the picture again.

Pete was watching her disappear as well. He had his fingers in his hair, making it even spikier than usual, but then he turned back and started walking towards the gates again. Casually, as if he wasn't at all bothered by the rejection he'd just been subjected to. He had a half-smile on his face as well. As if he was actually pleased about something. Confident, anyway.

A flash of anger broke whatever spell had been holding Jack hostage. He wrenched the car door open, snatched up the bag and then slammed it shut. He heard the locks engage behind him as he pressed the remote, already striding back towards the emergency department. He wasn't about to get caught by any encounter in the car park. He wasn't even going to give Pete—or even Harriet—any more headspace right now.

His family needed him.

The first person he saw when he went into the department was Blake.

'Hey…' Despite the cowboy boots and the ponytail, Blake looked every inch an emergency department specialist. 'I've just found out that it's your grandmother that was brought in earlier. Can I do anything to help?'

'Do you know what's going on?'

'Yeah… I checked. Supraventricular tachycardia. Must have been rapid enough to cut blood flow and make her faint. It's settled now but we're going to keep her in and monitor her. She's been started on some medication and I don't think it's anything to worry about.'

Jack had to swallow the sudden lump in his throat. 'I thought I was going to hear that she'd had an infarct. Or a stroke or something.'

'Go and see her.' Blake smiled. 'And you can stay with her as long as you like. Come and find me when you need a coffee or anything.'

Family members kept arriving, although most of them had to stay in the waiting room because only two people at a time could be with a patient in the observation area, and his mother wasn't about to leave *her* mother's side.

Jack was more than ready for a coffee after a couple of hours of what felt like traffic management. He'd send everybody other than his mother home soon. His grandmother was going to need follow-up to ensure that the new medication was doing its job but this was no longer a crisis.

Blake was due to go off shift but he stayed to have a coffee with Jack and they chose a quiet corner in the cafeteria rather than the department's staffroom.

'You look wrecked.' Blake's smile was sympathetic. 'It's under control, you know. Your gran's not in any danger.'

'I know.' Jack couldn't find a smile, though. He fiddled with the little paper tube of sugar, shaking it into his drink. 'I've got other things on my mind as well.'

'Oh?'

Jack picked up the spoon to stir his coffee. 'I saw Pete Thompson outside when I was coming in.'

'Yeah…' Blake's gaze was cautious. 'He'd been in to see me and pick up a team pager. I couldn't really say no when he's been a member before. And a good one.'

'Wouldn't expect you to.'

'Is it going to be a problem?'

Jack shrugged. 'I don't know. Maybe.'

Blake looked serious now. 'We can't have problems on the team like that. You know how I feel about distractions.'

'Maybe I should stand down for a bit.'

'Wait…*what*? No…if anyone's not going to be on the team, it'll be Pete. Or possibly Harry, if she finds out that it's too much for her.' He was watching Jack's face. 'It's a lot more than a friendship with benefits between you two, isn't it?'

'For me?' Jack had finally stopped stirring his coffee. 'Yeah…'

'What about Harry?'

'I think it is for her, too.'

'You *think*?'

'We've never really talked about it. I've kept stuff

light, you know? She was worried about our age difference and I didn't want to push it. And I wasn't sure that she was completely over Pete. She'd been living with the guy. Probably planning to marry him.'

Maybe he should have pushed things. He should have stayed the night after that meeting. He could have simply held Harriet in his arms. So that she would understand that he would always be there for her.

If she wanted him to be.

Had he made a huge mistake in not telling her how much he loved her? That he couldn't imagine wanting anyone else to share the rest of his life? Waiting for a sign that she would welcome that kind of commitment?

Blake's quiet voice broke the rush of unanswerable questions. 'You don't really think she'd want to go back to *Pete*, do you?' His face twisted with distaste. 'After the way he treated her?'

Jack swallowed a mouthful of his coffee. 'You see it often enough. Women who go back to relationships that everyone else can see are abusive. Or wrong for them, anyway. There are some guys that have that edge, you know? That "bad boy" vibe that women can't seem to resist.' He let his breath out in a sigh. 'D'you know, I actually asked her out on a date once? She thought it was just a friend thing and she spread the word. Invited Pete along, in fact—and that was the night it all started between them.'

Blake's huff of sound was sympathetic. But then he frowned. 'You need to tell her how you feel, mate. Took me a long time to tell Sam how I felt and that was when I found out that she felt the same way about me. The rest, as they say…is history. And if she does feel the same way about you, you won't have to worry about Pete Thompson. Or anyone else.' He raised an eyebrow. 'I don't claim to be an expert on women or anything, but if she's bothered by the age difference, I reckon she's the one who needs the reassurance. To be told that it's not an issue. Call her.'

As if to emphasise his advice, Blake's pager sounded, despite his being off duty now.

Except that Jack's pager sounded at exactly the same time.

Three buzzes. A short silence and then three more.

Blake reached for his phone and his call was answered instantly. 'Mabel? What's happening? Is this a Code One callout?'

He was nodding briskly as he listened. And then he cut the call. His chair scraped on the floor as he leapt to his feet.

'Train versus truck down south,' he told Jack. 'Code One. Let's *go*…'

The scene on the rooftop of Bondi Bayside Hospital was one of controlled chaos. The big doors of the shipping container, well away from the helipad, were hanging open and a group of people were focused on shifting gear and making personal preparations.

Harriet was getting into her red overalls with their reflective strips. She hadn't taken the time to change at her apartment, she'd just grabbed her team backpack and got here as fast as she could. She was to one side of the group, near the perimeter fence, which proved useful because it was difficult to try and balance on her left leg when it came to putting on her steel-capped boots and she could hang onto the fence.

The reminder that her physical abilities were still

less than they had been was making her nervous.
Was she up to this challenge? The flood of adrenaline she'd experienced when her pager had gone off
was still there. She could feel her heart thumping
and her senses seemed to be heightened. Against the
background noise of a helicopter warming up and instructions being called, she could hear snatches of information being exchanged between team members.

'Sounds big… Semi-trailer truck that failed to stop
in time at a level crossing…'

'I heard that the passenger train was pretty full.
Could be up to a hundred people involved.'

'Who's going in the first chopper, do you know?'

'Listen up.' That was Blake's voice, carrying clearly
in the hubbub. 'We're going to run out of daylight soon
after we're on scene. Check the batteries in your headlamps. Put some spare ones in your pocket.'

'Harry?' Sam was hurrying towards her. 'You good
to go?'

Harriet straightened from zipping up her second
boot. 'Just need a hard hat.'

'Come on, then. You're with me, on the first flight.'
Sam led the way to the equipment storage in the container but turned to glance at her friend. 'You okay?'

'Bit nervous. It's been a long time.'

'You'll be fine. Even if you stay in the treatment
area, you'll be an asset. You don't have to go climbing over wreckage or anything, just to prove yourself.
Grab a hat.'

Harriet stepped into the container. Someone was
sorting through the bigger packs of gear at the back but
she didn't need to go that far. She reached up to take

a helmet from the shelf beside her and then turned to find Pete right in front of her.

For some reason, this was the last thing she'd expected to have to deal with. Again? So soon? She could feel herself glaring at him.

'Hey…thanks, hon.' He reached for the helmet in her hands and she let it drop before his fingers could touch hers. 'Just what I was looking for.'

He was grinning at her, clearly excited to be here.

Harriet didn't return the smile. Something else had just been added to the uncomfortable mix of adrenaline and nerves. Something that felt totally inappropriate to this situation, like…anger? Resentment, anyway. This was so important to her and the last thing she needed was something that had the potential to make it a whole lot harder. She turned back to pick up another helmet. She heard Blake shouting again outside.

'Who's got the airway packs?'

'They're right here.' Sam stooped to pick something up and then vanished. 'I've got them.'

'Just like old times, huh?' Pete seemed to be waiting for Harriet. 'Some things never change.'

Harriet ignored him, turning back. She had forgotten to get some extra batteries for her headlamp. From the corner of her eye she saw Pete vanish through the door and felt a beat of relief.

Another figure appeared at the door. Blake. 'We seem to be missing the extra IV gear.'

'I've got it.' The person at the back of the container turned.

Jack…

The relief Harriet had felt when Pete had gone evaporated as her nervousness kicked up a notch. Jack had to have heard the way Pete had just spoken to her and it wouldn't be doing anything to dispel the tension that had been there ever since the night of the team meeting.

'Thanks, mate.' Blake took the pack and ducked out of the door. 'You're on the first run,' he called back. 'It's time to go.'

Harriet caught his gaze. 'I am, too,' she told him.

His smile gave her an anchor in the swirl of nerves. 'Come on, then.'

She took a deep breath but held his gaze for a moment longer because it was giving her something else to hang onto. Determination. She wasn't going to let Pete's presence distract her in any way from this mission. If anything, she was going to use it as even more motivation to do the best job she possibly could. She wanted Jack to be proud of her. Proud of all that he'd helped her achieve.

He must have sensed the tiny hesitation.

'You worried?'

She nodded. 'A bit. I just hope I can do this. And do it well.'

The expression in Jack's eyes was so intense it made her catch her breath.

'I think you can do whatever you want, Harriet Collins,' he said. 'You just have to decide what it is you really *do* want.'

She followed him to the helicopter, crouching as she went under the spinning rotors.

Sam was on board, she noted. And Blake. A few others but not Pete. He must be going with the next group that the chopper would return for. She buckled herself in and resolved not to even think about him again.

But it was difficult because Jack's words of encouragement were echoing in her head as they took off.

He hadn't been talking about her dream of being back on the team, had he?

Had he been warning her that she had a choice to make—between him and Pete?

That he would even think she might want to go back to Pete was a problem that threatened to be more of a distraction than the presence of her ex-boyfriend. It meant that Jack had no idea how she really felt about him, didn't it?

And why would he?

She'd never actually told him. Because she'd been waiting for him to say something first. Harriet closed her eyes for a moment. Maybe now he never would...

Circling overhead as they waited for an air rescue helicopter to land first gave everybody on board the big picture of what had happened.

And it *was* big.

They had already seen traffic backed up for miles in both directions on a rural highway that was now closed.

Now they could see the massive truck and equally big trailer that had caused the accident by failing to stop at a level crossing. It was lying on its side, the driver's cab crushed beyond recognition towards where the last carriages of the train had derailed and were also twisted and overturned. The engine of the train and the first carriage looked intact further down the line but in the middle there were at least two carriages that had taken the brunt of the impact, with the sides closest to the truck ripped out completely or mangled into metal shards.

There were already at least a dozen emergency vehicles on the ground. Police cars, ambulances and fire trucks, all with their beacons flashing. From the air, the red, blue and white lights almost looked festive. Every member of the SDR team, however, knew that the reality was going to be grim.

They carried their gear and headed straight for the scene command truck. Behind them, their helicopter was already taking off to go and fetch the rest of the team. Another helicopter, from a major television channel, was hovering overhead, preparing to land.

'We've got a treatment area set up,' the scene commander told them. 'The ambos will be glad to see you guys. We've also got people trapped in the carriages and haven't been able to get close enough to assess their condition yet. Head count so far suggests that there's at least six people unaccounted for.'

'Fatalities?' Blake was looking at an area under police supervision that had blanket-covered bodies on the ground.

'Seven.' The scene commander's tone was grim. 'So far.'

'Where do you need us first?'

'In the treatment area. But maybe a couple of you could join the teams working in the wreckage, for when we get access to the people who are trapped?'

Blake nodded. 'Jack? Come with me. The rest of you, see what you can do to help in the treatment area.'

Ambulance service personnel were overwhelmed by the number of people already needing treatment. One team was fully occupied, intubating someone, and others were amongst a small crowd, many of whom were crying out for help. A man walked towards them, holding a bloodied dressing to his head.

'Please, can someone come? It's my wife. I don't think she's breathing properly. She says it hurts too much…'

'Show me…' Sam followed him instantly.

There was a baby, Harriet noted, lying quietly in the arms of a young woman who was sitting on the ground, just staring into space. Was it too quiet?

They had two doctors, other than Blake, who'd come in this first wave. One headed straight to where the intubation was happening. The other caught Harriet's gaze.

'Let's get some triage happening. We need to clear this area of anyone who doesn't need immediate treatment.'

Harriet paused beside the woman with the baby.

'How old is he?' She crouched beside them, putting her hand inside the baby's blanket, both to feel what his breathing efforts were like and to see if it provoked any kind of response.

'Eight months.'

'Is he normally this quiet?'

The woman shook her head. 'I saw the truck coming,' she told Harriet, her voice breaking. 'I saw it coming but there was nothing I could other than to hold my baby as tight as I could.'

'Where were you?'

'In the first carriage. We didn't get hit. We just got thrown around a bit and then the train stopped with a horrible jerk.'

The baby was moving irritably under Harriet's hand

and then it started crying. She was pleased to hear the sound but it wasn't enough.

'He'll need to be checked out, because of his age if nothing else. Stay here for now, okay?' She took a yellow tag from her pocket and slipped the elastic around the baby's arm.

She moved on swiftly. Several people had cuts and bruises but nothing major. A very young-looking ambulance officer was putting a dressing on a laceration. They all needed green tags.

'Take these people to the next tent,' Harriet told her. 'And anyone else who's walking and can talk to you.' She could see someone sitting slumped behind the ambo so she moved on again, dropping to a crouch beside a middle-aged woman.

'Hello, can you hear me? What's your name?'

There was no response. She shook the woman's shoulder gently and felt her tip sideways to crumple to the ground. Immediately, she tilted the woman's head back to make sure her airway was open and checked for breathing.

It was shallow. And rapid.

'I need some help here,' Harriet called.

It was Sam who came and a paramedic. 'Let's get her on a stretcher.' The paramedic nodded. 'Red tag?'

Harriet nodded. And moved on.

How much time was passing was difficult to assess. She knew they'd been here for a while because it was getting dark enough to need her headlamp on. Even after the less seriously injured victims had all been moved to another area, there still seemed to be something urgent to be done every time she turned around. Bleeding that had to be controlled. Broken limbs that needed splinting. Head injuries that had to be carefully and repeatedly assessed to watch for any signs of deterioration.

More of their team was here now, including Angus and Kate. The patient she'd seen being intubated on arrival had been taken away by a flight rescue team for transport to the nearest trauma centre but another seriously injured person had been brought in. Jack was beside the head of the stretcher, using a bag mask to assist breathing.

'Head injury,' he said. 'And there's a tourniquet on his upper right arm.' He turned to head outside again as soon as the doctors took over but he spotted Harriet as she hung a bag of IV fluids on a hook beside the patient she was monitoring.

For a split second their gazes held and there was a question in Jack's eyes. Was she coping? Was she okay?

It only took a nod and the hint of a smile and he was gone again but Harriet was left with the impression that he would have stopped to talk to her if she hadn't given him that reassurance.

That moment was enough to give her a new burst of energy. She had no idea how long she'd been on her feet now with so much swift moving, crouching and getting up again, helping to lift heavy people and racing to find equipment or medication needed, but she *was* okay.

Stable patients, including the baby, were being taken by ambulance crews to the nearest hospitals. A bus had arrived to take people with minor injuries to get a thorough assessment from nearby medical centres. The most seriously injured people were being taken by the air rescue medics to major hospitals that could provide emergency surgery if needed.

Gradually, the treatment area was getting empty. Rescue personnel were being sent to take a break in a tent that had been set up to provide hot drinks and food.

Blake came back, his face pale and weary. Jack was beside him and Harriet had to fight the urge to go to him and put her arms around him. He looked more than a bit shattered. Instead, she filled a polystyrene cup with coffee and added the sugar she knew he liked and took it to him. Sam was doing the same for Blake.

'Two more fatalities,' Blake told them. 'One was still alive when they cut through enough wreckage for us to get to him but...'

He didn't have to say any more. Whoever it was hadn't made it out.

'There's still two people unaccounted for,' Jack added. 'So we're staying on. If some of the team want to get back to town, there's a flight leaving soon. There's no real need for us all to stay now.'

'I'll stay,' Harriet said.

'Me, too.' Sam nodded. She glanced over her shoulder as someone pushed their way to the table with the urns of hot water and supplies for drinks.

'I'm not going anywhere. This is great.'

Harriet was watching Jack's face, concerned about just how bad it had been in that carriage, with the person they hadn't been able to save, so she saw the way his eyes narrowed.

'Having fun, are you, Pete?' His tone was cold.

'Best job I've been on ever, kid,' Pete agreed. 'How 'bout you?'

Jack said nothing, which was hardly surprising. Had Pete really just demeaned him by calling him 'kid'?

'I've been with the firies who are trying to get access to the back of the worst carriage,' Pete added cheerfully. 'We reckon that's where the last of them are.'

Of *them*? Harriet just stared at Pete. Did he actually see the victims of this disaster as real people? With families and friends who were probably frantic with worry right now and who could be about to be devastated by news of their deaths? Right now, it felt like they were extras, somehow, in the movie that was starring Pete Thompson as a hero. Had he always been this shallow? Had he walked out on her when she'd been scarred and broken because she hadn't matched up to what his leading lady was supposed to look like?

She turned away. Walked away, until she was outside the tent. Sam was following her.

'Unbelievable, isn't he? What did you ever see in him?' She shook her head. 'I'm going to find the toilets. You want to come with me?'

'Don't need to, thanks. I went not long ago.'

What Harriet did need was just a moment to herself. To take a breath and try and figure out how to stop her buttons getting pushed so easily by someone who was no longer part of her life but had left enough damage to be a problem. He was the reason she'd never had the courage to say those words to Jack first, wasn't he? She'd been abandoned once. Rejected because of something that wasn't anything to do with who she was as a person but it had made her feel smaller. Less loveable.

And she wasn't. Jack had loved her.

She gulped in a breath. Was it really in the past?

This wasn't the time to even go there. She wasn't as alone as she needed to be to follow that line of thought. There were still a lot of people moving around out here. A lot of lights flashing and the noise of hydraulic cutting equipment in the background. A photographer who was snapping images of the scene, probably for a newspaper. She hadn't even thought to bring her camera, Harriet realised. Because she was a real part of the team again, not just there with a newly invented role because people felt sorry for her.

She felt, rather than saw, the figure who arrived beside her. The person who'd helped her get back to this point in her life. Who'd believed in her.

'They're going to call us as soon as they get near anybody else in the wreckage, if they're still alive,' Jack said quietly. 'We're supposed to take a break until then.'

'Was it awful?' Harriet whispered. 'The last one?'

'Yep…'

Someone else came out of the tent and Harriet couldn't help her head turning swiftly. The last thing she wanted was for it to be Pete. She let her breath out in a sigh of relief as she saw that it was Angus, heading back to the treatment area. She should probably go there herself and help tidy up and make sure they were ready if any of the missing people arrived needing help but something kept her still. She could feel the way Jack was looking at her.

'He wants you back, doesn't he?'

'What Pete wants doesn't make any difference.' Of course it didn't. He hadn't been there when it counted, had he? *Jack* had. He'd been there for her right from the start of the hardest part of her life, even though she'd pushed him away. And when she'd let him closer, he'd been there a hundred per cent. A thousand per cent. As invested in her achieving success as she had been.

So loyal. So trustworthy.

'I saw you... Earlier today. Outside the hospital gates.'

Oh, help... Harriet had an instantaneous flashback to that moment when Pete had tried to kiss her. This was way worse than anything Jack had overheard in the equipment container.

'He wanted to apologise, that's all,' she said. 'He knows how badly he treated me.'

Jack snorted. 'And that makes it okay or something?'

Something in his tone gave the impression of an anger that Harriet had never associated with Jack. It scared her.

'I know you've had your doubts about us,' Jack said. 'And I get that this is probably making things a whole lot worse.' He drained the rest of his coffee from the cup. 'It's up to you whether you believe in me,' he added quietly, 'but, for God's sake, Harry. Believe in *yourself*. You deserve better than Pete bloody Thompson.'

Harriet opened her mouth to tell him that she knew that. To confess that she had been confused by Pete's reappearance in her life because it had been so sudden and it had stirred up old feelings. That she knew it bothered Jack and that the tension between them had frightened her because it felt like there was a new obstacle they both had to deal with and it felt a lot bigger than any difference in their ages and how Jack might feel about starting a family and...the fact that he'd never told her that he loved her.

At the same moment that she drew breath to speak,

however, the shrill sound of a whistle cut through all the other sounds outside. And the radio Jack had clipped to his belt crackled into life.

'We've found the last victim. Medics needed, urgently.'

Jack crumpled the polystyrene cup in his hand and dropped it.

And then he walked swiftly away without even a backward glance.

Harriet could only watch him, her chest too tight to allow her to even take a breath.

It felt like she was watching him walk right out of her life.

CHAPTER TEN

BLAKE EMERGED FROM the tent only seconds after Jack had walked away.

He had an extra pack in his hands and he was scanning the scene in front of him.

'Have you seen Sam?'

'She's gone to the toilets.'

He hesitated for just a beat. 'Take this,' he said, then, handing her the pack. 'And come with me. We might need an extra set of hands.'

Harriet shoved her arms through the straps of the pack and jogged a couple of steps to catch up with Blake. Her heart was thumping. She wasn't going to be in the safety of the treatment area now. They were heading into the heart of the mangled wreckage of the train and, sharply illuminated by several powerful floodlights, it looked as intimidating as anything she had ever faced. It was one of the overturned carriages and there was a ladder secured between wheels that led up to the side of the carriage that was now a roof.

Jack was already disappearing into a hole where access had been gained through broken windows. A fire officer reached out with a gloved hand to help Harriet climb the ladder.

'Keep clear of any edges,' he warned. 'Some of them are still sharp.'

Another fire officer was on the top. Another ladder had to be climbed, this time down into the carriage.

There were no floodlights in here. Just the beams of their headlamps.

'Over here,' someone shouted. 'Hurry... I can't stop the bleeding.'

Jack was there first. Harriet saw him crouch and then reach under what looked like the buckled framework of a seat half covering the shape of a body. She let Blake get past her and then the fire officer who'd been in the space moved back, climbing over the seat to where his colleagues were waiting.

'Looks like a femoral bleed,' Jack said. 'I've got as much pressure on as I can.'

Blake was bent over the back of the person. 'Can you hear me?'

Harriet could hear the response. A low groan that became words.

'Yeah...can you get me out of here, mate?'

'That's what we're here for. Are you having any trouble breathing?'

'It hurts...'

'It hurts to breathe?'

'Nah...it's just my leg...where he's pushing on it.'

'Sorry, mate...' Jack's tone was gentle. 'But I have to stop you losing the red stuff.'

'He's caught,' one of the fire officers told them. 'We were cutting the frame of the seat but then he tried to move and that's when the bleeding started. His name's Frank,' he added.

'Foot's still trapped.' Jack had angled his head so

that the light was further down than where he had his hands pressed to Frank's thigh.

It looked more than trapped from the glimpse that Harriet caught. His lower leg had been impaled by a thick metal rod and the foot was crushed beyond recognition.

Blake's head turned. 'Hand me the oxygen cylinder and a mask, Harry. And get the IV rollout. I want to get a line in and some pain relief on board for Frank.'

The oxygen and mask were in a side pocket of the pack but then Harriet had to find enough space to open the pack properly and find everything that Blake needed. The wipes and a cannula, a Luer plug and tape. A giving set and bag of fluids and then the ampoules of drugs. She was crouched in a position that was beyond uncomfortable but she still had to move as quickly as possible and make sure she didn't make a single mistake.

Jack asked her to find a tourniquet and dressing pads. The awful groans of their patient subsided as the drugs took effect but Blake wasn't happy.

'Blood pressure's dropping. Harry, come and squeeze this bag, would you? Let's get some fluids in a bit faster. And we need to get him out of here, stat.' He straightened up and moved towards the fire officer in charge of this group who'd been searching the carriage. He kept his voice too low to be overheard by Frank.

'Can you cut him free?'

'It'll take time. We'll have to cut through both ends of that pipe in his leg. Even to get the gear in there safely, we'll have to get rid of the seat on top.'

Jack stood up swiftly and his gaze locked with

Blake's. 'Take a look,' he said quietly, 'but I reckon that foot's beyond rescue.'

Harriet sucked in her breath with what sounded like a gasp. They were considering an amputation? *Here?*

Working in a medical field, there were always patients that you could identify with in some way. Maybe they were the same age or they reminded you of a friend or family member. And sometimes they were going through something that you had experienced.

Harriet had never felt quite this connected to a patient before. This could have been her, she realised. If that rock had been bigger. If her lower leg had been trapped and there'd been no way to free her quickly to deal with any other injuries.

Had Jack heard her shocked breath? His gaze caught hers as Blake crouched to peer under the seat and she could read the message as easily as if he'd spoken aloud.

The choice might well be between losing his leg or losing his life...

Blake, as the senior medical officer present, clearly agreed.

'We'll use ketamine anaesthesia,' he told Jack and Harriet. 'And go below the knee as distally as possible.' He turned to the fireman. 'Get a Stokes basket down here so we can get him out. And get a chopper on the way for immediate evacuation.'

'Roger that.'

It was the most dramatic medical intervention Harriet had even been a part of but it was remarkably quick and very smooth, thanks to the calm and confident actions of the two men she was assisting. Harriet's job was to monitor Frank's breathing after he had received the anaesthetic drugs and to assist with a bag mask if necessary. Blake did the surgery with Jack's assistance.

'That's the medial muscles out of the way. Look, the tibia's already broken above where that pipe went through. All we need to do now is cut through the lateral muscles and use the Gigli saw, if we need to, for the fibula.'

Harriet had to close her eyes in the moment the final cut was made.

This could have been her fate so easily. It had been touch and go in the aftermath of her accident and, for a while, she'd had to imagine what life would be like if she'd lost her leg.

But she hadn't.

Not only that, she'd fought her way back to reclaim her life.

Jack had been right, hadn't he? She shouldn't ever be ashamed of her scars. They were something to be proud of. A symbol of courage and stamina. For the rest of her life, they would be there to remind her of that struggle. And to remind her of the person who'd been by her side every step of the way. She had been very lucky to keep her leg.

But she'd been even luckier that Jack Evans had come into her life.

It was Jack's turn to take the lead now as they got Frank out from the tangle of metal and upholstery and strapped him safely into the Stokes basket so that the team of fire officers could lift him clear of the carriage. Blake was staying as close as possible to their patient, the bag mask in his hand, but Jack wasn't far behind.

Harriet was well behind by the time she got up the ladder and out of the entry access. Her leg had been squashed into awkward positions and now it was threatening to give way on her each time she put her whole weight onto it.

She saw that the stretcher was already reaching ground level, where a team of people was waiting to rush it to the treatment area. A television crew was nearby, clearly filming the drama. Jack was already on the second ladder but his head was still over the top and he saw Harriet stumble as she stepped towards him.

'You okay?'

Harriet nodded. She couldn't fall at the last hurdle, could she? It would be too disappointing. For Jack as well as herself.

Gritting her teeth, she reached the ladder, knowing that her limp had to be visible. Jack moved down as she turned but she felt his hand reaching for her. Supporting her.

He had his arm right around her as she stepped off the final rung.

'I'm okay,' she told him. 'Honestly... I just need to rest for a moment. You go ahead.'

'I'm not going anywhere without you.'

'But...' Harriet turned to where Frank's stretcher was already at the entrance to the treatment area tent. The television crew was in hot pursuit and others were heading in that direction as well.

'Every doctor on scene will be in there,' Jack said. 'They just need to make sure he's stable for transport and then the air rescue crew will take over. I've done my job.' He was smiling at Harriet. 'And you did yours. You were brilliant. Frank's going to make it, I'm sure of it. And, yeah, I know he's got a hard road ahead of him but we both know it's possible to get there.'

He had both his arms around her now and his head bent so that only she could hear his words.

'I'm *so* proud of you,' he said. She heard him suck in a ragged breath. 'I love you, Harry. I could have told you how much a million times by now but I didn't and I'm sorry I didn't.'

Something fizzed within Harriet and burst into what felt like the emotional version of a fireworks show. Relief? Joy? Or was it just love being unleashed, free of any restraints that doubt could create?

She threw her arms around his neck.

'I love you, too, Jack. I just couldn't tell you until you told me…' Her breath escaped in what sounded like a cross between laughter and a sob. 'How stupid is that? I've stopped myself saying it…oh, about a million times.'

Their helmets knocked together as Jack tried to kiss her. Impatiently he pulled his off and tried again. His mouth was pressed hard against her own and his arms were around her so tightly it was impossible to breathe but Harriet couldn't have cared less. It wasn't, in fact, hard enough or tight enough right now.

She had to gasp for breath when he let her go, though.

And then she was smiling and smiling and couldn't stop. Jack looped his arm over her shoulders and they both started walking towards the treatment area.

'We need to finish this mission,' he said. 'So we can go home.'

'Yes.' Harriet tightened her arm around Jack's waist. 'That's the place I want to be. As long as you're coming with me.'

'Try and stop me, babe.'

Harriet was still smiling. 'No. I'm not going to.'

Jack pulled her to a halt. 'How long will it take, do you think?'

'I don't know. I guess there'll be a debrief and then we'll have to wait for space on the chopper.'

'No...' Jack was grinning as he looked down at her. 'That's not what I meant.'

Oh...the love in that look. The promise...

'What *did* you mean?'

'How long will it take to make up for all those missed opportunities? To say a million times how much we love each other?'

'Oh...' Harriet was drowning in that gaze. 'I think it might take the rest of our lives. Until we're old and grey, anyway...'

Jack nodded slowly. 'That's what I was thinking.' His mouth quirked. 'May as well get on with it, then. I love you, Harriet Collins. I love you, I love you, I love you...'

'I love you, too, Jack.' Laughing, Harriet pulled him forward. The sooner they could get home, the better.

'I think I'm winning.'

'You could be right... Maybe I need a personal trainer to get me up to speed.'

'I think you do... Hope you can find one.'

Harriet's smile hadn't faded. She had found one, all right. The only 'one' she would ever need. Or want.

EPILOGUE

IT WASN'T HAMILTON ISLAND but it *was* a beach wedding.

This was much closer to home and there had been no limit on the number of guests because there were plenty of barbecue stations available and everybody had brought something to share, picnic tables and rugs and chairs and games to keep the children happy. And who knew that so many members of Jack's family had guitars? The music was live and loud and too tempting not to dance to as the party really got going.

Hand in hand, Harriet and Jack were simply wandering, stopping to talk to all their guests, unable to resist a slow dance whenever a romantic enough song started, sometimes just taking a moment to stand together and watch others.

'I hope someone's getting lots of photos. I should have brought my camera.'

'The bride isn't allowed to be the photographer. It would get in the way of this...' Jack bent his head to bestow a lingering kiss on his new wife.

'But look...' Harriet's gaze was misty as she turned back to the group on the grass. 'That's your gran up dancing. With Minny. That's the cutest thing I've ever seen. Minny's only just learned to walk and she's dancing...'

'It's in the blood.' Jack was looking pretty misty-eyed himself. 'You'll see…oh, in about six months, isn't it?'

'You still think we should keep it a secret?'

'Well…it is after the wedding, I guess. It has been just about us so far. But let's not make a big announcement. If it comes up in conversation, we can just slip it in and the news will spread like wildfire.'

Harriet was nodding, but her attention had been caught by something else. A dog had come running out of the waves, a stick triumphantly clamped between his jaws. Behind him, she could see surfers catching the larger waves and, for a split second, she thought of Pete Thompson.

And it didn't push a single button, other than gratitude maybe.

He'd disappeared from her life almost as suddenly as he'd come back into it—just a few weeks after that call-out to the train accident. The surf was so much better in Hawaii, apparently. Good enough to tempt Sharleen to join him even. She spared another fleeting thought to wish them well. Sometimes it took something big to make it obvious that perceived problems weren't really problems at all. To shine a spotlight on what was truly important. She squeezed Jack's hand tightly.

He returned the squeeze, looking down with one eyebrow raised. 'What?'

'I love you,' she whispered. 'That's all.'

'I love you, too.' His smile was mischievous. 'Love you, love you, love you.'

'This isn't a competition, Jack.' But Harriet was laughing.

The dog had reached the first picnic rugs now and

that was the moment he chose to shake off the copious amount of sea water still clinging to his thick fur. People ducked for cover amidst shrieks of laughter.

'I'm so sorry.' The dog's owner was apologising profusely to the group on one of the rugs as Jack and Harriet moved closer.

'Don't apologise, Eddie,' Harriet told him. 'Harry's a star. He's allowed to have fun now, along with everyone else.'

Sam was still wiping drops of water from her face. Luc was brushing sand off his trousers and Beth was giggling.

Sam shook her head as she looked up. 'I still can't believe you chose a dog to be your bridesmaid. I could be very offended, you know.'

'Harry was just the ringbearer. We decided to keep things simple.' Harriet stooped to pat the dog. 'Oh... he's lost the flowers from his collar.'

'I took them off,' Eddie said. 'I'm going to keep them in a special place. By that photograph you gave me. That was taken at this beach, wasn't it?'

'It was.' Had that been the day that her new, wonderful life had really begun? When she'd taken that photograph and been aware of the first stirring of an attraction that she now knew was going to last a lifetime?

'There's not many dogs that get to be an important part of a wedding ceremony.'

'We couldn't not invite him.' Harriet leaned closer to Jack. 'He was the one who started it all. If he hadn't done his Lassie act on the cliff that day, Jack and I might never have even seen each other again.'

'And I might have died on that ledge.' Eddie nodded.

'But I should probably take him home soon. Before he makes any more of your guests wet.'

'Too late…' Jack was grinning at the sight of Harry the dog now being cuddled by several small children, including Toby. 'I hope he likes sausages. Looks like he's getting some of the leftovers.'

'Oh, no… I know what happens when he eats too much.' Eddie moved away to rescue his pet.

'There's enough leftovers to feed a small army.' Blake put down the paper plate he was holding. 'I don't think I'm going to be able to move for quite a while.'

'Bit different to where you were posted in Africa, then.'

'You're not wrong, there, mate.' But Blake had caught Sam's gaze. 'It's good to be home again.'

'I thought you were planning to stay longer with MSF,' Harriet said. 'Not that I'm complaining you got back in time for our wedding, mind you. We've got the whole SDR crowd here.' She smiled at Kate and Angus, who were sitting close together, their hands entwined.

'Even Alice.' Kate waved towards her great-aunt, dancing away with a crowd, including Jack's grandma. 'Those ladies have got it going on, haven't they?'

'We had a good reason for cutting it a bit short,' Blake added, and there was something in his tone that instantly caught everyone's attention.

'Oh…' Beth's eyes widened, her hand moving to the impressive bump of her own belly. 'Are you suggesting…?'

'It was supposed to be a secret.' Sam frowned at Blake. 'We didn't want to steal any of Jack and Harry's thunder today.'

Harriet and Jack shared a glance. And a smile.

'It's okay,' Jack murmured. 'We've got a bit more of our own thunder, actually.'

Sam's jaw dropped as her gaze flew to Harriet's. 'No way…you're pregnant, too?'

'Oh, no…' Blake put his hand over his eyes. 'The SDR isn't just going to be known as a dating agency. Now people will reckon we're putting something in the water.'

Laughter followed Harriet and Jack as they moved on a few minutes later.

'I think we need to tell your mum,' she said. 'And your gran.'

'If she ever stops dancing.'

'And Talia, of course,' Harriet added. 'And the rest of your family.'

'*Our* family…'

That stopped Harriet. She had to look around at the happy crowd surrounding them. She'd felt the lack of any relatives she'd had to invite to this special day. The SDR team was the closest thing to a family of her own that she'd had in her life.

Until now…

'It really is, isn't it? I really belong.' She reached up to put her arms around Jack's neck. 'I love you,' she told him. '*So* much…'

'Love you, too.' His smile wasn't mischievous this time. It wobbled around the edges, even, but he wasn't going to let his emotions stop him. 'Love you, love—'

Harriet had her finger against his mouth. 'That was it. A million and one. You can stop now. You win…'

Except she didn't really want him to stop, did she? She lifted her finger, stroking his lip gently as she did so. It felt like *she* was the real winner, anyway.

Jack simply pulled her closer, his lips against hers as he spoke softly.

'Oh, babe… Get used to it. I'm just getting started.'

* * * * *

MILLS & BOON

Coming next month

REUNITED WITH
HER BROODING SURGEON
Emily Forbes

The gorgeous man with amazing bone structure stepped forwards and Grace's heart skipped a beat and her mouth dropped open.

Marcus Washington.

She could not believe it.

It had to be him. Even though he no longer resembled the twelve-year-old boy she once knew, it *had* to be him. There couldn't be two of him.

She hadn't thought about him for years but if she had she never would have imagined he would become a doctor. She knew that sounded harsh and judgemental but what she remembered of Marcus did not fit with her image of someone who had clearly ended up in a position of responsibility and service to others.

But what did she really know of him? She had only been seven years old. What had she known of anything?

Her father was a doctor and, at the age of seven, everything she knew or thought was influenced by what and who she saw around her. Particularly by her own family. And Marcus's family had been about as different from hers as a seven-year-old could have imagined. But she knew enough now to understand that it wasn't about where you came from or what opportunities you were handed in life, but about what you did with those opportunities, those chances. It was about the choices you made. The drive and the desire to be the best that you could be.

She would never have pictured Marcus as a doctor but now, here he was, standing in front of her looking polished, professional and perfect. It had to be him.

She knew a lot could change in twenty years and by the look of him, a lot had.

She was still staring at him, trying to make sense of what was happening when he looked in her direction and caught her eye. Grace blushed and, cursing her fair skin, the bane of a redhead, she looked away as his gaze continued on over her. She finally remembered to close her mouth.

Had he recognised her?

It didn't appear so, but then, why would he? She was nothing like the seven-year-old he had last seen.

Continue reading
REUNITED WITH
HER BROODING SURGEON
Emily Forbes

Available next month
www.millsandboon.co.uk

COMING SOON!

We really hope you enjoyed reading this book. If you're looking for more romance, be sure to head to the shops when new books are available on

Thursday
4th October

To see which titles are coming soon, please visit
millsandboon.co.uk

LET'S TALK
Romance

For exclusive extracts, competitions
and special offers, find us online:

f facebook.com/millsandboon

◎ @millsandboonuk

🐦 @millsandboon

Or get in touch on 0844 844 1351*

For all the latest titles coming soon, visit
millsandboon.co.uk/nextmonth